A vast amount of thanks goes out to my group of Survivors: Jacob Maynard, Callie Boyle, Matt Moore, Sandy Webb, Molly Maloney, Valerie Hammond, my mom Nancy Hoffman, my brother Josh Hill
and most of all my beautiful lass Jen.

I would never have even envisioned finishing this project without you, much less publishing it.

Keep those weapons clean, those blades sharp, and keep Surviving

Generation Z

A novel by

Caleb Hill

Chapter 1

Gunshots are a lot louder at night. I don't know if it's because your eyes are being used less, and your body compensates by heightening the other senses. I don't rightly know. I recall reading something about the subject, written by some scientist, back before ...

In the dark, though ... Constant darkness. The power grid went down pretty quick. So here you (or anyone, I guess) are, stumbling blindly through the dark. Your eyes would get better, later on. Suck up what little moonlight made it through the haze. But I'm talking about early on. The first few months. You'd be walking carefully, slowly, trying not to trip over all the shit scattered in the street. And when you did, you'd try not to think about what it was. But the imagination will do wild things. Especially when the whole world you thought you knew broke all of its own rules and went completely mad.

A suitcase, contents spilled and trampled on the ground?

A shoebox, with letters from long-dead loved ones?

A child's doll, soaked in blood?

You couldn't think about those things. Not then. Not now. It would make you crazy, if you let it. I saw plenty of people let it. Some would get angry and begin lashing out at the other people. Some would become quiet and shrink into themselves, trying to remember the world that was. And some ...

Some just fell asleep and didn't wake up. I later heard them referred to as "the lucky ones". I didn't know what to think of that label. I still don't.

But at night, surrounded by the darkness, with the stars removed by the constant cloud of smoky haze that seemed to take over the sky as soon as America went dark. All you could do was listen. Try not to trip on the imagined carnage at your feet and listen. Usually, if you were quiet enough, it would be fine, and you could slip into a town and back out without ever running into trouble.

But, sometimes ...

A low moan. Like air being forced through a drafty house. It was almost melancholy in a way. It was sad just hearing it. Like they didn't understand why they were back up and walking around. *We* sure didn't. Not then, at least. I'll never forget that first night we left the house. Two of us: Dan and myself. Alli stayed at the house. He was my roommate. She was his ... girl, whatever. We should have left town when things got bad, but we ... We were just scared, I guess. Missoula, Montana. Not exactly a big city. We figured the government would roll in any day and take control. I think most people did. It couldn't really be as bad as all that.

But it was.

We knew our supplies were running out. We knew we'd have to go outside, soon. Must have been, I don't know, September? Early October? It was getting cooler. I remember that. A real slushy snow had dropped that day and our food stores were low. We had ramen, tuna fish ... We were goddamn college kids. Of course we did. But we were hunkered down in that house for well over 3 weeks. Maybe close to a month. I'd filled the bathtub with water, and it too was low. We'd discussed a foray across the river. There was a Safeway there. A couple of convenience stores.

I should have known something was wrong a few days earlier. Alli was sick. I'd get up in the mornings to find the bathroom occupied by a sick girl. It annoyed me to the point I didn't connect the dots. Not until dusk as we sat around the makeshift fireplace, cooking our last can of pork and beans.

"Uh ..." Dan broke the silence.

Yeah?

"We need to go downtown. To a store or something."

Why? Our food will easily last another ... Two weeks. We all knew that wasn't true. And it would have been stupid to wait until the supplies actually dwindled down. I was just ... Scared, I guess. We all were.

"It's more than that, Nick. Alli ... She's ... We're pregnant. At least we

2

think so."

The silence that ensued was broken only by my spoon dropping into my bowl.

What words just came out of your mouth?

" And she's been sick, in the mornings."

We haven't had proper sanitation in a few weeks. Are you sure?

"She's ... Late, man. You know?"

I put my face into my open palms, hands side by side.

Are you ... Fucking kidding me? We're *pregnant? You sound like the world outside is normal! Like we're sitting around goddamn sun tea in the backyard and you're off to build this wonderful life together!*

"Nick ... You don't need to get angry about it, man." Dan brushed his dreadlocks onto his shoulder. "We ... We're kind of excited."

Excited?! Tell me which part you missed! The news reports? The screams? The gunshots? The fires? Tell me how you're going to bring a baby into that! How will it survive?! How will she *survive?!*

I recall gesturing furiously at Alli.

"Man, I know how it sounds. But ... The government. The Army will be here any day and clean it all up. We talked about that! Remember?"

Three weeks, guys. I looked at Dan and Alli. In the eyes. *It's been almost three weeks since the last TV broadcast. Over two since the radio went to static and the power went out.*

White noise. All that's left.

"What are you saying?"

That they're not coming! I don't think there's a government left *to clean up!*

As if to emphasize what I was saying, a lone gunshot punctuated the night outside. Loud.

I was shaking now. I put my bowl down, in front of my crossed legs.

Alright.

"Alright?"

3

I stood and went into my room. I strapped my .357 to my belt, then picked up my crowbar and my rifle. A gift from my grandfather, when I was 13. An old bolt gun with open sights. .30-06. I'd had the rifle since high school, but hadn't ventured outside with it, yet. Not after what we'd seen on the bridge just blocks away. We were ... well, you know.

I came back out to the living room and put my coat on.

Grab that little pea-shooter of yours. Dan had a .22 pistol his father had given him the past year, at Christmas. The last Christmas.

"Really, dude?" Dan's eyes lit up.

How long has it been? I looked at Alli.

"About ... 5 weeks. Maybe."

So this was, what, right after Safeway? You know what the fuck you two need to do, after you've pulled your heads from each other's asses?

At that rebuke, Dan had looked at his feet. Alli's eyes narrowed.

We need to get supplies.

"And a test. A pregnancy test. And some vitamins. The pre-natal stuff."

It won't matter, you know. Do you know? You'd be better off ... Without it. So would the child ...

I'd never been assertive in my life. Always kind of out of touch and passive-aggressive. The pragmatic voice that issued forth from my lips sounded foreign. A stranger speaking out of my mouth. A mouth I'd owned for 23 years.

"Fuck you! You want me to abort my baby! My ... baby ...." Alli's explosion muted to tears.

"We'll ... Let's just see what there is." Dan clutched his little revolver like a child who doesn't know what to do with something unfamiliar. He turned lamely towards Alli.

Fine. Take care of her. Calm her. I'm going to have a look outside. I'm going to make sure Neighbor Frank isn't lurking.

I stormed through the mudroom and outside as quietly as the heat in my brain would allow. I didn't dare turn on my headlamp. Not yet. I cracked the door and did a quick sweep of the yard. In the almost pitch black, I couldn't see much. I didn't hear anything, either. It was a far cry from even a few weeks ago. Gunfire. Helicopters. Sirens, then. Now, nothing.

The porch was exactly as we'd left it when we'd still been in college. It seemed like so long ago then. It's like a story that happened to someone else, now. The bikes were still there, chained to the railing. The cigarette bucket, half-full of soggy butts and tobacco-colored, icy water. A yellowed newspaper, still wrapped in plastic. The headline visible.

Epidemic Reaches Rockies

Even at the death of civilization, some newswriter at the Independent saw fit to throw in one last bit of alliteration. One final line of poetry before the world ended

I walked down the concrete steps. My hiking boots sank into the slush. I'd thought then that my eyes were playing tricks on me, but the slush looked gray. Dreary. I realize now that it was all the smoke from all the fires in the air, falling back to Earth with the precipitation. The world on fire. Or what was left of it, I guess.

I didn't see Neighbor Frank. He was probably standing in his backyard, staring dumbly at the back of his house, swaying. The same backyard I'd waved to him in, years previous. Old Frank, must have been in his seventies, in his sun hat, tending to his garden. He'd given us a bag of potatoes that fall. All the potatoes were gone now. Before things had gotten bad ... Before the gunfire and the looting, we'd visited him and his wife, Edith. Really nice people. The kind you wished were your neighbors. She'd even made lemonade once. Hand-squeezed all of them. I'd just come back from a kayak trip, and Dan and Alli were in the backyard with Frank and Edith. Frank in his sun hat, telling stories of his days in the Navy. The lemonade. It was so good.

These days, I'm afraid I can't remember what lemonade tastes like, sometimes ...

When the trouble started, when the initial outbreak had reached the American West, people started going outside less and less. We'd shopped, right before the Collapse. Is that what they're still calling it? The Panic, the Collapse, I can't keep them straight. We'd stood in line at the Safeway across the river for 3 hours or more. People were going crazy. Getting violent. I saw two women fighting over the last box of shells and cheese. One woman pushed the other. She hit her head, on the metal shelf. There was a lot of blood. She wasn't moving. We left the store, and I remember thinking *I hope I have enough in my checking account to pay rent next month.* Right? That was my thought as I watched one woman kill another over a box of pasta and fake cheese. There were children there. Watching.

We left the store and loaded our groceries. I heard Alli gasp and Dan and I turned simultaneously. There was a man in a suit, two parking rows over. He looked He could have been drunk. He was just kind of stumbling, like he was in a daze. His coat, his tie, his collared shirt were soaked, just *soaked* in blood. Blood like you see in the movies. Maybe I thought he was hurt. I don't know what I thought. I'd only seen that much blood, once, when I watched my buddy gut an elk he'd shot. I'd never seen a human look like that before. I took a few tentative steps forward, around the front of Dan's Honda. I called out to the man. He didn't look, not at first. He squinted, like he was trying to figure out a math problem in his head. I called again.

Hey, dude! Are you okay? Do you need an ambulance or something? The hospital is just a few blocks ...

And that's when my blood froze. Forever, I think. I don't think it's thawed yet. That moment ... It stands out in my mind. Such clarity. The sun, dazzling off of car windshields and polished chrome bumpers. A slight breeze. Hot. Vapor ghosts drifting off the burning asphalt. It was still late summer. That bloody man, just squinting and swaying. Then he turned. Such clarity. Such dazzling clarity. The day my world changed.

His face, this man in the suit ... His left cheek was ... Gone. Just gone. Part of his nose, too. I could see his teeth. A bloody snarl, frozen in that bright

6

sunlight. His eyes ... No life there, but ... Just ... Shit, how can I even explain it? You've seen them. Feral. Like this jaguar that had stared at me through the bars at the zoo, when I was a kid. Then he ... It ... Moaned. I'll never forget that sound. A beautiful, blue 80 degree day turned glacial in an instant. The man in the suit lurched toward me, as if unsure of himself. *Him*self. See? I keep doing that. It stumbled, at first, but started to pick up speed. A lumbering gait, more. They can't run. You know that.

I couldn't move. What my eyes were showing me, my brain was telling me wasn't real. How could it be? We'd all seen them on the news. We knew they existed, on the TV. But here? In real life? In your face and your grocery store parking lots? It had to be a dream ... This man, in his bloody, tailor-cut suit ... He was dead. I don't know how I knew. I just knew. The TV told me that fact- that the scientists were working on it. But seeing him ... it, with my own eyes ... I knew. *There was a dead person walking towards me with half of his face ripped off and I couldn't fucking move.* My shoes might as well have weighed a thousand pounds each. I was stuck. It got closer, then put up an arm, like he was going to grab my shoulder and tell me what a good job I'd done on my final paper last semester. But it wasn't going to do that. His lips ... What was left, parted into a snarl, like a dog that just had food taken away from it. Somewhere, in the back of my mind I could hear Dan screaming my name. The man in the suit came around the side of the last car between me and him ... It. *It. Goddamn.*

I don't know what I expected to happen. I figured when the bloody man touched me, I'd wake up. I'd have to wake up, right? I heard a deep, booming voice yell something. I couldn't pick it out well among the blood rushing through my ears. I think it was something along the lines of ...

"You just gonna stand there, dipshit?!"

For whatever reason, perhaps by the grace of a God who can't possibly exist, I snapped from my reverie. I looked to my right in time to see a huge redneck with a bigger mustache aim a giant revolver at the man in the suit. He touched off a round and its head ... Just ... Exploded. A shower of

7

blood, bone and brain matter painting the van behind it. That's when I pissed myself. No, I'm not ashamed to admit it. I peed right down the front of my shorts, all over my sandals.

Let's get the fuck out of here! I heard the redneck scream. But, no .... It wasn't him. It was me.

I ran back to the car and as I jumped in the backseat. That's when the screams started. Coming from inside the store. Dan screaming "What the fuck, whatthefuck, wuthafuk!". Over and over and over. As he gunned his little car out of that parking lot, nearly sideswiping a pickup truck, I looked back. I've learned this lesson since then: *Never look back. Ever.*

You won't like what you'll see.

I looked out at the store, neatly framed in the Honda's back window. The world divided cleanly by the horizontal lines of the rear defroster. I watched as a crowd of people ran out of the store. No, a mob. I watched people disappear underneath trampling boots and shoes and sandals. I knew they weren't going to get back up. I felt sick; I was wet; I smelled like piss. I thought that maybe I should have let the man in the suit touch me. So I could wake up ... So I could have just woken up. There's no nightmare so deep you can't wake up.

My eyes stayed glued to the scene as we sped down the street, trying desperately to get to the bridge at Orange Street. Across the bridge, the world was okay. Across the bridge, everything made sense. Across the bridge, I wouldn't see an old lady get knocked down by another bloody corpse- a younger girl missing most of her scalp- and have the lower part of her face chewed off. I'd seen that shit in all the movies. American cinema. I hadn't thought of it, then, when it was on a movie screen. At that point, I would have given anything I'd owned ... Everything I could ever hope to own ... To make the back window of that Honda Civic a movie screen ...

The door opened behind me, shaking me from my thoughts. Idiot! How could I just space out like that? Standing in the front yard, swaying like a

8

goddamn zombie!

"You ready, Nick?" Dan looked scared. I was scared.

As ready as ... Yeah, I am.

"Any sign of Neighbor Frank?"

No. No, I haven't seen or heard anything.

"Good."

We hadn't seen Frank in a while. Not since the Collapse. His son had fled Seattle and came to stay. He'd worn a bandage on his arm. He looked sweaty and pale when he'd stepped out from behind the wheel of his car. Not well. Not at all. The last time I'd seen old Frank, besides waving through the window across the street ... He and his son were hunched over in the front yard, eating his wife. Eating Edith.

There's no nightmare so deep you can't wake up.

Chapter 2

Dan and I walked around the corner. We lived on a street corner back then. A nice yard butting up against a dismal alley. But all alleys are dismal. I guess they're even worse now. Just too many ... Shadows. Too many of them.

We had flowers once, too.

That night was cold, but there was no wind. The trees had already budded, but there were no leaves. No rustling to make us turn around and lose our minds. The autumn had been warmer than usual. Probably because of the ash, right? Trapped in the heat from the fires and the dying? It had to have been. It snowed inches at a time throughout the early fall. Wet, heavy snow.

Sometimes, it rained.

Tonight, though, was slush. And I didn't know yet, but slush was a good thing. We walked as silently as possible. I almost tripped over something in the road. The toe of my boot hit it with a wet thud. I didn't want to know what it was. I took a deep breath and moved forward. I had light gloves on, and my hands were freezing. Easier to push the button on my headlamp with. Easier to pull a trigger with. But I hadn't actually done that yet. So what was easy? Some amount of discomfort would do. Then, it would do. We moved forward, past a derelict lumber yard. The hulk of a truck sat in the yard, barely visible through the gloom. Both doors were open.

We took a right at the bend, by the bicycle place. The gates had since been torn open, and there were bike parts strewn all over the road.

A thump.

"Shit." Dan picked himself up off the pavement. "I think those were handlebars. Should we use our lights now?"

No. We should keep quiet, too. They could be around.

"It's too cold for them."

Not anymore. This fall, there was only that couple of nights. A quick

10

freeze, then it thawed. They started moving again. Faster than anyone thought. The bridge ...

"Yeah."

I shot Dan a sideways look, but he didn't see it. It was too dark. *Too cold? You alright, man?* I didn't say this. Just a thought.

Another rifle shot split the silence, filling the void. It reverberated up the valley. It was far off. Up in an outlying neighborhood. Maybe Bonner. We reached a roundabout. I'd always hated the goddamn things. When more than one car went through, everyone would freak out, not knowing whose turn it was.

Oh, the problems of the normal world. I would have given anything ... Those weeks ago ... For a movie screen.

There were cars here, in the roundabout. Two, both wet, covered in old leaves and dirt. One had the driver side door open. The other was shut completely. They faced each other, in the same lane, but were still a few yards apart. I walked tentatively to the open car. I ducked down, and flashed it with my light. A faded, bloody handprint on the driver's window. A human leg, half buried in trash, just below the door. A bloody, infant carseat in the back. There was a pack of cigarettes. Completely untouched, just sitting in the driver's seat. I hadn't had a smoke since the day at the bridge. I'd smoked an entire pack that day. Camel Lights. The bridge ... Goddamn, that was just ...

I heard Dan swear and fall to the slush. I swung my light onto the car, jogging over. Sitting in the driver seat, a zombie was buckled in. It must have been a man, as its hair was short. Beyond that, how could I tell? His... Its skin was so dehydrated, it was just a leather mask stretched over a skull. But it clawed at the window, trying to reach our lights. Its eyes were milky blue, but it could see us. It followed us with those dead eyes. This was my first real experience ... Up close. Sure, there was a pane of auto safety glass between us ... But there it was. I leaned in close. I was still wearing my headlamp. I heard a crack and jerked back, then saw what it was. The zombie had broken its front row of teeth on the glass. But it still tried to get at us.

11

"Should we kill him? I mean ... Re ... Kill ... Him?"

I looked over to see Dan raising the .22 to the window. A quiet click as the cylinder rotated. I jammed my thumb between the hammer and the frame.

No. It's useless. It'll just make noise. He's ... Trapped. Can't get to us.

"How do you know they can hear? This one is responding to the light!"

I leaned in close.

Every law of everything we've ever known was broken a few weeks ago. Who knows what senses they have left. Better safe ... You know?

Dan nodded, stepped back. He eased the hammer down. I cut off my light and we turned and walked into the darkness. We left the zombie behind, still seatbelted in the car, as if it was driving to the store on a sunny afternoon. Still clawing frantically at the window, as if sensing the food was getting away. A block further, another roundabout. Just one car here. I flicked on my headlamp, careful to cover most of the light with my hand. An old Jeep Cherokee. All four doors were open. The glass was rust-brown with dried blood. I turned my light off and we continued on. Trying not to trip. Listening.

We soon found ourselves at Orange Street. One of a handful of streets with a bridge. But not just a bridge. The bridge. Across the way, a small, abandoned gas station. In the dark, as our eyes began to adjust, we were able to make out the pumps. All of the hoses were lying on the ground, as if they had tried to escape the madness and found they were still attached. A car was at the pumps. An older sedan. The driver's side door was open. I couldn't tell, in the murky dark, but it looked like something was hanging down, out of the door. A pair of legs. Human legs. Wearing high heels, I think. Maybe. I didn't want to know.

We walked into the street, Dan and I. We stayed low, trying to be quiet. Trying not to trip on the shapes under our feet. I didn't want to be on the sides, close to houses and bushes. We took a few more steps. Stopped. Listened. The sound of the low river entered our ears.

The bridge.

12

"Yeah."

I want your opinion. Should we use our lights and just run for it? We can just get over it, fast.

"Fast, huh? Yeah, I think that can work. We can just run for the intersection ahead and see what's-"

A moan. From across the bridge. We crouched and held our breath. Well, I held mine. I tried listening, harder than I ever had. My heart was beating in my throat and my ears. We didn't hear anything. It must not have heard us.

Okay. No lights. Nice and slow.

"Over the bridge?"

Over the bridge.

"You don't think we could ... wade the river, do you? The bridge, man ..."

It's almost winter, Dan. The hypothermia would kill us quicker than those things. Do you want to try to walk across? It's low, but it's not that low ...

"No ... What if ...?"

We jump.

I shuddered at my own words.

"Dude, it's like, two feet deep."

I know. Dan?

"What?"

Stay low. We'll stop every so often and listen. And ... try not to look at what's under us. But ... pay attention. In case there's one on the ground or something ...

"Yeah ..."

The two of us, hunched over in the night, waddling to the bridge. Listening.

It had to have been ... a few weeks back. I'm not sure. About two weeks after the grocery store, maybe. The Collapse ... This was right around all that. But people were still going outside. Shit, some people were still going to *work*. Right? The little freeze had slowed the zombies, but it was warming up again. People had been killing them with shovels, crowbars. The police that were still around, they didn't want guns fired in city limits. Life as usual. Dan, Alli and I went out to clear our sidewalks, but it was just a thin layer of gray slush that day. We heard car horns and excited yelling. Coming from the bridge. There was a lumberyard next to our house. It had a huge, sheet-metal building running along the road. You could see the bridge from it. Someone had already put a ladder up, a few weeks before. It was still there.

We climbed.

From the shed roof, we saw a line of trucks and a pair of police cars parked sideways across the bridge. The cruisers had the lights going. Red and blue strobes. Like a barricade. Like you'd see in the news reports. There were people standing on the trucks. Some behind. People had turned out. Had to have been 20 or 30. There were children there. Watching.

Like it was a goddamn picnic or something.

These men, standing on trucks, wearing hunting camo. Holding hunting rifles, with scopes. Scopes are useless at close range. There were a few soldiers, too. National Guard, probably. Mostly cops and civilians that day. On the bridge. People in the trucks were laying on the horns. We didn't understand. Then we saw them. A few. At first. Shuffling along. Slowly, sadly. Some were dressed in winter coats and boots. There was one ... A woman. In her underwear. She was missing her right arm. Just a bloody stump. As soon as a few crossed onto the north end of the bridge, some of the men started taking shots. One zombie, a heavyset man in a jogging suit took a round straight to the chest. It spun him around and he dropped to the ground. A moment later, he slowly got back to his feet. Still coming.

"Aim for the head, dipshit!" The same man, from the grocery store. Big mustache. He was holding some kind of military rifle. The first wave of zombies was put down, and the horns started blaring again. Drawing them in. A lot of them had been almost completely frozen. It must have seemed like a good idea. The people- families behind the vehicles and guns- cheered. Here was a group, doing something! Taking the city back! They must have been so excited.

So excited.

A few more zombies came around the side of a building. Coming in from the downtown area. The downtown had been largely abandoned, but there had still been people there. From the roof of that lumberyard, that didn't seem to be the case. Not anymore. More zombies started shuffling into view. 20. Then 30. 40. Soon, there must've been ... Hell, lots. A hundred, maybe? More? All those dead eyes. Fixed on that bridge. Fixed on those people.

The people on the bridge opened fire again. Hunting rifles. Some military rifles. Shit, there was a kid out there with a little shotgun. Those ones that break open ... They just take one shell at a time. Must have been the kid's dad behind him, coaching him. Smiling and laughing. As soon as the main mass of this zombie ... swarm, I guess. This swarm reached the bridge, and some of the men had to stop to reload. They were all just firing at once. And groups would stop. To reload their guns. When they started shooting again, the zombies had closed in to 50 yards or so. This was the point where people started panicking. You could feel it. Like the air got heavy. The shots started going wild. They weren't even shooting for the head anymore. One zombie down there ... A little girl. She would have been 6, probably. I saw her get a leg taken off by a rifle shot. She ... It fell face first onto the pavement. Didn't even try to catch itself. Then it propped itself up on its hands. Its little face just smashed and dripping blood. Blonde pigtails caked in blood. She started crawling toward the people on the bridge.

The zombies just kept coming. Tripping and falling over the bodies of ones that had been put down. Getting back up. Just kept coming. Some of the men, those behind the cars, they started backing away. No one was smiling or laughing any more. One guy ... I don't know what the fuck he was thinking. Dumbass in a Carhartt coat and backwards cap. He ran right at the closest zombie. He had a framing hammer. The claw side. He swung it into the temple of that zombie. Just dropped it, instantly. I could see the terror on his face, even from blocks away. The hammer must have gotten stuck in the zombie's head. He put his foot on the thing's neck and ripped it free. A zombie, just feet away, lunged at him. Grabbed him. Bit him, right on the carotid. A lot of blood. A *lot* of blood. I know I couldn't hear it. Not from that distance. Not with the gunfire. Not through his screams of pain and utter horror. But ... I guess my mind must have heard it. Flesh and muscle ripping. Tendons snapping. Another zombie lunged and caught his leg. Bit a chunk right out of his thigh. The men on the trucks started jumping down and retreating toward the onlookers. A cop got into his cruiser, started it. He must have shifted wrong. He must have been scared. He mashed the accelerator and the car launched backwards. Ran right over that boy with the shotgun. Smashed him. The car didn't stop. It shot through the railing and plunged into the river. Shallow, that time of year. Folded that car in half when it hit the rocks. The sound of crunching metal and rushing water. And screams.

We'd been so engrossed in the fight, we'd failed to notice what the people on the bridge had also failed to notice. Behind them ... On our side of the river ... zombies, just pouring out of this neighborhood, down by the park. 60 of them. Easy. Shuffling right up the bridge. All those people in the center ...

Trapped.

One of the soldiers got grabbed around the hood of a truck. He almost got away. The troops, though. They were wearing their goddamn body armor. As if the zombies were going to shoot back. Shit. Probably some captain, going by the book. That armor ... It's heavy. The soldier got a little off-balance and fell. The zombie fell partway on top of him and it looked like he tried to push it off. It bit all the fingers off of his hand. Another soldier shot it, spattering him with blood and brain. He just sat there. Screaming.

The unarmed people, the ones watching, now realized they were surrounded. The men with guns must have been running low on ammo. There wasn't as much gunfire at that point. One guy, in a skier's one-piece, like from the '80s. He was swinging his rifle like a club. He knocked a zombie down and

16

proceeded to smash its head. Another one came up behind him and bit him on the side of the head. Took his ear off. He dropped to his knees, screaming as it struck again. The top of his head. Some people had moved over to the railing, looking down on the low river. The smashed cop car. A man in that mossy camo, he climbed onto the railing and helped a woman up. She was holding a baby. His wife, I guess. He slung his rifle, and they jumped. He hit the water first. It could have only been a foot deep. He broke both legs and lay there, in the icy water, shouting for the woman. She was a little ways downstream, crawling for a little rocky island. Her legs must have been broken, too. She was screaming.

"Callie! Where's my girl! Oh, God, where's my little girl! CALLIE!"

I didn't see the baby. She didn't have it.

The two swarms had almost met in the middle of the bridge. The shooting that was still going was sporadic and in every direction. A man in a green coat jumped onto the railing and his hip was blown up by a stray bullet. He landed right on top of two zombies. Screaming. At this point, people started jumping into the river in groups. They were all landing in shallow water. I saw one guy get knocked off the railing by another who had just escaped the reaching arms of a zombie. They both fell onto the exposed rocks below. There was no way. Not with the river that low. There just wasn't enough water.

The shooting had stopped. The last people on the bridge, those with guns, those who hadn't jumped. The zombies were like dogs, fighting over scraps. All over those guys. Tearing them apart. A few of the dead had noticed the people jumping into the river. They moved that way, and as more joined, the started pushing the dead in front over the railing. It wasn't deliberate. It was just the force of all those bodies pushing on one another. Trying to get to the food.

The zombies started falling down among the people. Humans with broken legs, crawling through shallow, gray water. Zombies crawling after them. Catching them. I saw one guy pull out a pistol, shoot his kid, his wife, then himself.

17

I felt sick, but couldn't look away. Behind me, I heard Dan puke. I finally pulled my eyes from the carnage a few blocks away. There was one zombie in sight, a block down. It was headed towards the screams. Its back was to us. I grabbed Alli and Dan, motioning with my head. We ran back to the house, locked the door, inventoried our supplies and didn't go back outside again.

Until that night.

Chapter 3

That night.

We crossed onto the main section of the bridge. Up ahead, in the icy gloom, we saw the trucks and the remaining cop car. They were still there. We could see a few dark shapes, scattered in the road, covered in slush and ice. Nothing was moving. We waddled along, Dan and I, stopping every 20 feet or so to listen. My thighs were already burning. Muscles that had only been used in a house for the past ... While. We steadily approached the cars and my foot caught on something, in the slush. I tripped, catching my short fall with the crowbar my hands gripped so tightly. I looked down. I had to.

Beneath my feet, an arm. The elbow to the hand. Even in the gloom, I could make out a wedding ring.

"You okay, man?"

Yeah, I just tripped.

"On what?"

Nothing that can bite. Watch where you step, though.

"Yeah."

We were approaching the abandoned vehicles now. The police strobes no longer flashing, the battery long dead. The horns silent. All the dark shapes on the road ... There weren't as many as I thought there should have been. A lot of them, the ones who hadn't jumped ... They probably got up and shuffled away. We neared the only truck without a door open. We stopped and listened again.

"Nick, there might be a gun in that truck."

There might be another ... Thing in there, too ...

"I'm gonna at least have a look."

Fine. Keep your light covered. Small beam.

I couldn't see Dan's sneer through the darkness, but I knew it was there.

"No shit, man." He exhaled sharply.

We slowly stood and he flicked on his light. There was a dead body in the truck. It was a man in a flannel shirt. He was wearing a black beanie, but the top of the hat and the top of his head were mostly gone. Blown up all over the inside of the cab. His dried, bony fingers still clutched an automatic pistol.

"Dude! Nick! We could use that!" Dan grabbed at the door handle.

Will you keep your voice-

From off to our right, we heard a slapping sound, followed by a dragging sound through the slush. Dan turned his lamp in the direction, dropping one hand to his pistol. His light flared across the bridge. Dragging itself through the bloody slush and scraps of human organs, the little blonde girl who'd had her leg blown off ... She ... It was dragging itself toward us. Her smashed little face wasn't bleeding anymore. She only had a few teeth. She looked so angry.

"Jesus!" Dan fumbled for his pistol.

Don't ...

It must have been the adrenaline. Maybe augmented by the cold. By her tiny struggle. Her childish helplessness. I walked over to her. She looked up, her milky eyes glared at me. A small arm reached up, grasping at the air. Grasping at me. Her ... Her little wrist still had a charm bracelet. A big silver heart that proclaimed "#1 Daughter!". I raised my crowbar and brought the hooked end down directly onto the top of her head. It was the first one I'd killed. I guess I expected more resistance. But, that little blonde head ... Those bloody pigtails. It just caved in.

I felt sick.

Cover your light, Dan.

He did, as I quickly swept mine beneath the roadblock, then extinguished it. I saw nothing. Just more scraps. Hints from the massacre we'd witnessed. Nothing down the immediate bridge, either. I quietly walked around the truck and crouched a little ways beyond it. I called out, barely a whisper.

20

Dan. Let's go, man. We still have a few blocks to go.

"Nick, we could really use that gun, dude. It's only been shot once, apparently. There's gotta be bullets in it."

Leave it. We flashed lights up the river. We need to go. Now.

"Fuck, Nick. It'll be like two seconds."

Dan.

I looked over my shoulder. He was still on the other side of the truck. My eyes were adjusting to the darkness again, and I could see his form moving back toward the door. The click of the door handle sounded loud in the night.

And the car alarm that went off right after ... That was louder.

The trucks taillights and parking lights started flashing as its horn cut the night.

Shit! Run!

I flicked on my lamp and made a dash for the end of the bridge. I leapt every dark shape in the slush, almost falling on numerous landings. I could hear the pounding of Dan's shoes behind me. Barely audible over the pounding of my heart. The truck wailed behind us. Amber and red flashes immortalized our forms in long shadows. Larger than life. Our shadows danced across the bridge, then would abruptly cut out. The cold air pierced my lungs, but I didn't stop. I didn't even know where I was going.

Ahead, lit through the gloom with waving headlamps and flashing truck lights, a tall building, off to the right. It was an old folk's home, in better days. Overlooking the river.

It must have been really nice.

On a balcony, about 5 or 6 stories up, an old woman stood in her nightgown. It was stained brown with old blood. The glass door behind her was shattered. She turned as we ran by. Her whole body. She looked as though she were reaching down to us. She staggered forward, her waist came into contact with the railing. Her torso doubled over, taking her legs, and she fell. Down to the parking lot below. I saw it out of the corner of my eye ... A broken heap, piled on pavement. Her head, snapping and snarling. Its shattered limbs still

21

trying to pull itself toward us.

I remembered thinking then, that zombies would probably be stronger than any of us would have thought. They were just walking corpses. But ... Their brains ... They wouldn't feel pain, telling their muscles when to stop. Telling them that their bodies were broken. I almost stopped running then. I almost stopped and pulled my revolver from its holster. I almost joined the guy in that truck. They were never going to quit, I realized with sickening clarity. That old lady ... That zombie ... it had just fallen off of a building and it was still trying to get at us. They would never give up. They were just going to keep coming and coming and coming. They were just going to keep eating. There would be more of them, less of us. How could they lose?

I almost stopped.

The bridge connected to the edge of downtown. Ahead, I heard moans. At the very edge of my light, I saw zombies. 7. Maybe 10.

This way!

I hooked left at the first intersection, a short street that cut in on the main drag at an angle. I ran, still, even as my legs and lungs were begging me to quit. I heard Dan sloshing behind me. On our right, a brick building. We were almost to the Safeway. Just a couple blocks down ... Past ... The hospital.

Shit.

I came to a sliding halt in the slush as we cleared the building and I cut my light. Dan almost slid into me.

Turn your light off!

I still don't know what the hell I was thinking. The most direct route, I guess. Still thinking like it was all normal. The path of least resistance? Hardly. Ahead, in the gloom, there were zombies.

Hundreds of them.

I turned, grabbed Dan's shoulder and raced toward a squat, one-story building that over-looked the river. There was a covered walkway running along one side of it. I jumped and grabbed the edge of it. I pulled myself up and swung a leg over. I reached down and pulled Dan up. From there, we scrambled onto the roof. We lay there for a while, just panting. Listening. Terrified. My rifle dug into my back, but I didn't move.

I finally mustered up the energy and the courage to look over the small lip of the roof. Below us, hundreds ... Really. I know it sounds like maybe my fear just exaggerated it, in my mind. But they were there. Passing through the streets below us. Lots of them wore hospital gowns. Some in doctor's coats. A few soldiers ... Still wearing body armor and gas masks.

The truck howled in the distance. Still flashing on the bridge.

The zombies ... They were all headed toward it. They didn't even know we were up there, huddled and shaking in the dark.

We spent the night on the small, cold roof.

Chapter 4

I jerked awake when something cold and wet landed on my eyelid. I must have dozed off. I didn't think, after seeing all those zombies, that I'd ever sleep again. I think the adrenaline must have faded and the exhaustion had set in. I sat up, shivering. I could barely feel my hands. A heavy sleet was falling, all around. The truck had finally shut up. The world was ... Silent. That dense kind of silence where you're surprised you can hear yourself. When you live around a river long enough, it fades into the background. I was sore. Dan was still asleep.

I crawled over to the north edge of the building and looked across at the hospital. There were a few zombies wandering aimlessly in the streets and on the lawn. Not nearly as many as last night.

I turned my head and found out why.

The bridge was covered with zombies. I could barely see the trucks. All the way up and down both sides of the bridge. Beyond the north end, in the downtown area ... zombies. Everywhere. There had to have been over a thousand. Just ... Everywhere. I could barely hear them, on account of the sleet. I thought again, of last night. That moment when I'd almost stopped running and stuck the cold barrel of my .357 in my mouth. Tried to wake myself up. I looked down at all those walking corpses and thought of it again. I shivered. Not from the cold.

I shook Dan's shoulder and when his eyes opened, I had a finger to my lips.

"I have to piss." He whispered.

You'll have to do it squatting.

He sat up and I pointed to the bridge. His eyes widened.

"We're fucked, Nick. We're so fucked. What the hell were we thinking?"

24

I put a finger to my lips again and pointed down towards the hospital. Towards the grocery store. There were only a handful of zombies in sight.

There's that walking bridge down there. The Russell Street bridge beyond that. We can still check out the store, and cross back over.

Dan nodded. He looked scared. I gave him a hard smile. I was one step away from being frozen in terror, but I was trying not to let it show. I couldn't give in to it, or we never would have left that rooftop. My hands were freezing.

We climbed down as quietly as we could, dropping into the slush. It continued to fall from the sky. Gray. The flat light made everything look like an Impressionist painting. Like we'd learned about in school. The world was silent.

As silent as death must be, I guess.

We headed west, keeping along the river. Staying low and ducking behind abandoned vehicles. Trying not to look inside. We hid behind a Subaru as a zombie wearing a hoodie and those skinny jeans shuffled along on the other side of the car. I held my breath, but my heart sounded so loud. It had to hear it. It didn't. It just kept dragging its feet through the slush. It was holding an arm with bites torn from the flesh. Like those turkey legs you'd get at the fair. Just carrying that arm along, like it would be hungry later ...

We neared a boarded up fast food place, by the river. A taco joint, in better days. There was still a car at the drive-through. Across the street, a parking lot. A flash of movement caught my eye. Not zombies. Something faster. I looked across at the parking lot. Two figures, dressed in black, ran out from behind a car. One was carrying a sack. The other ... Some kind of sword, I think. The one with the sword ran up behind a zombie and split its head in half. Then they disappeared behind a building. I looked at Dan. He'd seen them, too.

"Should we ... Follow them?"

No. They're trying to survive. Just like we are. They might not like living intruders any more than they like dead ones.

"Yeah."

25

I could see the back of the store ahead. Just one more block. My heart was still racing. What if it was already ransacked? What if it was full of zombies? We'd come this far. We couldn't stop now, couldn't go home empty-handed.

Ahead, a half a block from the store, a tractor-trailer was turned on its side. The truck was burnt up, but the trailer looked almost untouched. We reached it and were able to stand. There were no zombies in immediate sight.

Just around the side of this trailer, and we're there. We'll take it quiet and slow. I'm going to look. I'll motion if the coast is clear.

Dan nodded. I moved forward, my back facing the undercarriage of the trailer. Like I was James Bond or something. The slush fell, and my breath came out as fog. It climbed toward the gray sky and faded. I worked around the wheels and axles. I could see one of the doors lying open on the ground. A few canned goods were lying on the ground. *This could be it!* I remember thinking to myself. I heard Dan's footsteps in the slush, but I didn't turn. I rounded the corner of the wrecked trailer. I froze.

I hadn't heard Dan's footsteps at all. It was a zombie, hunched over. Eating another figure in a black hoodie. A bloody baseball bat still clutched limply in the kid's hand. What I'd heard was that zombie ripping chunks out of that kid's neck. He looked like he was 13. He'd be 13 forever, I guess.

The zombie hadn't heard me. It was a girl with brown hair. It was focused on the dead kid, just stuffing as much flesh as it could into its mouth. It wasn't even chewing most of it. I could see big lumps passing down her ... Its throat. I moved forward ... And kicked a broken padlock hidden under the slush. It skittered along the wet pavement. The zombies are pretty slow. But sometimes ... Sometimes they surprise you. That zombie ... Her head jerked around so fast. I suddenly felt like I'd eaten molten lead for breakfast.

Katie?

I don't know if I said it or thought it. Not then, not now. My knees started shaking, threatening to buckle.

Katie was a girl I'd met last year, in an American history class we'd both needed for our major. I'd had such a crush on her. We'd gone on a few dates. That brunette hair, golden-brown in the July sun. Winning a trivia contest at a local pub. That smile ... That gorgeous smile. Floating down the Blackfoot River. Inner tubes and beer ... She was so beautiful ...

She had been.

Half of her face was smashed in. One eye socket sat below the other. The eyeball hung out, dangling from the optic nerve. Her brown hair now missing clumps, knotted with blood. A smile that could melt a man's heart ... Her teeth were foul with blood and meat. That smile now a carnage-filled snarl. She ... Katie ... Half moaned, half hissed. She started to get up.

Oh, Katie ... I'm so sorry ...

I swung my crowbar into the side of her head. Her skull gave way to the hard steel. Her body fell to the pavement. Her blood, thick and brown ... Coagulated. It slowly leaked out into the slush. I raised the crowbar and struck her again. And again. Again. Again. Again.

Before I knew it, hot tears were streaming down my face. I was sobbing and growling in helpless fury and just hitting the crowbar onto brown, stained, wet pavement. Sobbing uncontrollably. It wasn't fair! None of this was fair! This wasn't how it was supposed to be ...

"Nick? Nick, stop man. It's dead." Dan. Behind me.

I stopped swinging.

I know she is, man ... I know she's dead ...

I turned and vomited. Yellow bile. Nothing in my stomach. My knees finally gave out. I caught myself and dry heaved a couple more times.

"You okay, dude?"

I'm fine. I'm okay. Let's go.

I stood. There were canned goods scattered everywhere.

We should grab a grocery cart, if there are any. There's a lot of food here.

I picked up the bat, handed it to Dan.

Quieter than a gun.

27

Dan took it. His hand was shaking. I wiped the sour bile from my lips. *We're almost there.*

We started walking again. There were a few zombies, but they were blocks away. Almost as an afterthought, I turned back and planted my crowbar right between the eyes of the kid with the black hoodie.

Better safe than sorry. I don't want another zombie waiting when we come back for the food.

We crossed the railroad tracks. There used to be a gate, blocking the bridge. It was gone now. There was a walkway, made from crude timber along one side of the tracks. It wouldn't be easy to get a grocery cart down it, but it could be done. Besides, what was easy? Another short jog, and we were at Safeway, where we'd all seen our first zombie.

There were cars spread out through the parking lot. The front windows of the store were all shattered, except one. It still proudly proclaimed "Boneless Chicken Breasts: Only $.50/lb! Sign up for your Club Card and save!". The bottom half was covered in blood. There were bodies spread out, too. Ones that hadn't gotten back up, or had already been put back down. There were bullet casings scattered everywhere, among the death. We walked around the front of the store. It was dark inside.

We're going to have to use our lights.

Dan didn't reply. He only nodded. I could see panic in his eyes, just behind his corneas.

You alright? We're gonna have to keep it together.

I was immediately embarrassed by my words. I'd just lost it a few minutes ago. Who was I to say something like that? I'd never considered myself as brave, really. As brave as anyone, I guess.

Dan just nodded. We walked forward and entered the store, clicking on our headlamps. The interior was trashed, like there had been a riot or something. Shelves tipped over, lights torn down and hanging from the ceiling.

Stalactites of a civilization long gone.

Cash registers, empty. An ATM smashed open, a few $20 bills

28

scattered about. Even a DVD rack, pilfered. People before us ... They'd looted everything. What the hell did they need DVDs for, nowadays? You could look out your window and see more horrific things than Hollywood could have ever thought up. I suddenly wondered if, someday, they would make a movie out of this, when the world was right again. I chuckled out loud.

"What's up, Nick?"

Nothing. Just a stupid thought. A thought for a different world.

We passed the bank of cash registers. There was trash everywhere. Empty chip bags, scraps of paper. Dropped items. A purse, its contents spilled onto the tile. A tube of lipstick. Half a pack of gum. A tampon, still in its wrapper. Underneath a bank receipt ... A small pistol. I picked it up. It was one of those little derringer-style guns. Just a tiny little thing. .22 Mag. Both chambers were loaded. I put it in my pocket.

"What's that?"

A tiny pistol.

A last resort.

"Can I have it?"

You won't need it. Come on.

Among the items on the floor, I found a small backpack. I was already wearing one that I'd brought, but I figured we could carry more food with it if we couldn't find a cart. There was a pin on it. One like I'd always seen at those novelty stores.

It said "I ♥ zombies".

We walked up an aisle that hadn't been knocked down. There were a few things left. Some dish soap on the shelves. Another aisle held a leaking bottle of Gatorade. A few cans down another. The labels were missing. I put them in the little back pack.

"What are those?"

I don't know. There are no labels.

"How do you know we can eat them?"

Because the cans are still sealed.

"What if they're dog food?"

I looked at Dan, careful not to shine my light in his eyes.

I think we'll be so hungry enough soon that it won't matter.

There wasn't much else. Even the small toy aisle had been ransacked. There was a brown stain of the floor by the pharmacy. It might have been spilled cola. I don't think it was.

The produce section stank of rot. Decayed and molded fruits and vegetables were all over the shelves and floor. At my feet, a baby's pacifier. We circled the store as best we could, with only a handful of canned food and a bottle of ibuprofen.

In the back, the pharmacy had been ransacked. Various bottles of pills and boxes of medicine were spilled all over the floor. I shined my light inside and saw only the movement of shadows as the beam played off blood-soaked shelves.

"Do you think … They have any … Baby vitamins?"

I said nothing. I just hopped the counter and shined my light around, quickly reading bottles. There, on a lower shelf. Levonorgestrel. I tossed four of the bottles in my pack and climbed back over the counter. Dried blood cracked off under my hands and knees.

"You got them?"

Yeah ... Let's go back to the truck. We can load up our packs. See if you can find any of those reusable grocery bags.

We walked back to the cash registers, and I saw it under a tipped over soda cooler.

A cart.

Dan. Come help me lift this. We need to do it quietly.

We gently pushed the soda cooler back upright. Inside was an unopened bottle of Dr. Pepper. I put it in the little backpack. I uprighted the cart. Its wheels were true, though one squeaked a little.

This will do just fine. Did you find any-?

A rack crashed over behind us. We both turned, shining our lights. A zombie ... A man in a stained t-shirt and boxers. It had fallen over the rack. It climbed back to its feet. We saw that most of the meat and muscle was chewed off one leg. It fell over again.

"It must have just been lying there, until it heard us. It can't even stand up! Nick?"

Yeah?

"Can I get this one?"

Do it fast and quiet. We need to go. You saw how many were downtown. What if they decide to come back this way?

"Sure. Watch and learn."

Dan. Hit it harder than you think you'll have to.

He walked over to it, twirling the bat in his hands. He raised the bat behind one shoulder, like he was waiting for a pitch. He swung and the wooden back connected with its skull. A sickening crack. The zombie sprawled sideways, but was back up on its hands almost instantly. Its arm shot out and clutched Dan's pant leg. He screamed, like a little girl. Really.

Dan fell over backwards, kicking at it. Its other hand grabbing at him. I ran over and sank the crowbar into the top of its head. Its body went limp. Its hand released Dan's leg. I looked down at him. He was almost hyperventilating. A dark, wet spot spread over his crotch.

"Ohshit ... Ohshit ... Ohshit ..."

I said hard, Dan. Harder than you think.

"I hit it fucking hard!" Dan's eyes, wild with fear, burned into mine.

You can't knock them out. They don't feel any pain. You have to smash them. Split the skull.

I glared back at him.

Hard.

I reached down. He took my hand and got up.

"Let's get the fuck out of here, okay?" He sounded like he was about to cry.

Yeah. Let's go.

31

I wheeled the cart out the broken door. Dan was right beside me. Back out into the street. Down, past the tipped truck, I could see a group of zombies. They didn't see us and they weren't moving toward us. But they were closer. The sleet had stopped falling and a breeze had started blowing. Everything was still quiet and all I could hear was the constant squeaking of the grocery cart wheel as we took it back to the truck.

When we reached it, I shined my light into the trailer. There were still quite a few cans. Probably enough to fill the cart, but I knew that would make it too heavy. Not with those tiny, little wheels. We grabbed cans as fast as we could load them. Creamed corn, green beans, pears and chili. It was a feast packed neatly into metal cylinders. The packs filled first, then we put enough into the cart that we could both lift it with ease. I surveyed the cache.

Good enough. It'll be slow going. You know we're going to have to go over the bridge again ... Right?

Dan swallowed hard.

"Yeah."

We pushed the cart around the corner of the truck, heading back to the bridge. We immediately stopped.

Just around the front of the truck, not 50 feet away ... zombies. A group of them. Probably 15 or so. It seemed like they all spotted us at once and they came, moaning and lurching forward as a mass.

Shit!

"Shit!"

We both yelled in unison. I grabbed the cart, but it was being pulled the other way. Towards the railroad bridge that spanned the river.

Dan! Stop!

I turned, unholstering the revolver on my hip, pulling it free. The cylinder rotated as I pulled back the hammer and I shot the three closest zombies. The gunshots echoed throughout the dead city. The bodies thumped to the ground and a few behind them stumbled on the new obstacles. I turned and caught up with Dan.

32

What the fuck are you doing?!

"We can make it this ..."

Dan suddenly realized why we hadn't come this way in the first place. A group of people had decided to take a train. Must have been trying to get away from the madness. I don't know if it was just too heavy, or if the bridge hadn't been maintained ...

The railroad bridge had broken, and the train was a jumbled mash of metal, sitting in the river. Dan stopped just short of the jagged edge, the cart nearly falling into the river. Behind us, the zombies were closing in around the rail crossing on the street. We were blocked in.

Shit.

I began grabbing cans from the cart, stuffing the backpack and every free pocket I had.

"Nick ... What do we do, man?"

We run.

"Where?"

Over the train.

I handed him cans.

Come on. We have to be fast. There are handholds on the top of the cars.

I leapt onto the locomotive. I hadn't thought about the weight in my pockets and on my back, and I almost tumbled off, into the river, but I grabbed out and found a metal bar.

It's slick. Be careful.

I looked back. Dan was frozen in place, looking back at the zombies, then down at me.

Dan! Come on!

He didn't move. A zombie was right behind him. It reached out, clutching at the air. I pulled my revolver with my good hand and shot it. I missed the head, but the bullet took it in the right shoulder, spinning and dropping it. That set Dan into motion. He jumped ... Too short. He hit the train

33

and began to slide. I was still holding the gun, so I thrust it towards him. He grabbed the barrel.

"It's hot!"

Don't let go.

We scrambled over the locomotive and jumped to the next car. As I grabbed at the next handhold, I heard something underneath me. A faint scratching. Then a bump against the metal side of the boxcar. Then another. Hands inside, slapping against the walls of the train cars. Muffled moans echoed off the metal. An eerie song in the dim light.

We stood atop the train of dead and ran. Car to car, we jumped, the moans and pounding following our every move. The zombies on the other side of the bridge were almost lined up, falling into the river, trying to get to us. The zombies inside the train hammered against the walls of their coffin. We climbed over the dam of cars. The other end of the bridge was splintered wood. We scaled it, trying not to stab ourselves. The wooden planks ended abruptly in a rock bed. Below us, the walking trail that traced the river's bank. Two zombies were down there, trying to scramble a chain-link fence that separated the railroad and a park. They could only beat at it, howling.

We ran, clumsily, our pockets weighed down. About two hundred yards further was another, intact bridge, crossing over a street. Another walkway, and we could get down to a street that would take us back home. With all the noise the zombies behind us were making, I knew we would have to be fast. By the time we reached the end of the second bridge, we were both panting. My legs burned. I was starving. We stopped and surveyed the street below us. Nothing moved.

We slid down a dirt slope, to a parking lot with a few dirty Suburbans. Everything looked devoid of carnage. A refuge of sanity surrounded by a world of utter madness. We ran as fast as we could, away from the river. Back towards the house. Towards safety. To our left, a few zombies loitered in a parking lot. They stumbled after us, but we were both running on pure adrenaline at this point. Well, I was. We outpaced them. Up a small hill, and

34

back to the first roundabout from the previous night.

That was just last night?

It seemed like so many lifetimes ago. The zombie with the broken teeth was still sitting in his Buick. Going nowhere. It scratched at the glass as we jogged by. Around the corner at the bike shop, and we were home. As our movement around the house revealed the front yard, I saw Neighbor Frank's matted, gray hair poking up over his backyard fence.

Get this shit in the house!

Behind me, I heard Dan struggle up to the porch. The door opened.

"Baby! I was so worried! Are you alright? Are your pants ripped?"

"I'm fine, just fine."

"He's been out there all day! Just ... Walking the fenceline!"

"It's okay. It's all okay. Nick is going to take care of him. We found food! Help me get it inside."

I approached the gate across the street. I swung it open. It creaked. Frank had been staring at his garden plot. He turned ...

Frank ... It's me. Nick.

He turned and looked at me. Those cloudy eyes fixed on me. He didn't move. Not at first.

Hey ... Thanks for the potatoes. And that lemonade. I still think about that. You and Edith ...

I felt my face flush. Tears blurred my vision.

You two were just ... Real good people, you know?

I had to be strong. I had to hold them back. My voice threatened to crack.

I just wanted to thank you for your kindness, and tell you ...

Neighbor Frank lurched forward. His passive face transformed into a feral snarl. He hissed.

...That I was really glad to know you. I hope ... I hope you and Edith found peace, wherever you ended up ...

I swung the crowbar into the side of Frank's head. Hard.

35

I turned, walked into the house and locked the door.

Out with the old world, and in with the new.

Inside, Alli was cradling Dan. He was crying. Shaking. I wanted to be held, too. I wanted someone to wipe away my tears and run their hands though my hair. I wanted someone to tell me it was all going to be alright. But there was no one there. And it wasn't going to be alright. I sat down on my bed and everything suddenly seemed heavy, as though the gravity had increased tenfold. I blacked out, with all my clothes still on.

I blacked out and slept.

And dreamed of the dead.

Chapter 5

My eyes snapped open.

My heart raced.

I jumped out of bed and ran out into the living room. The house was hot. The woodstove kept us warm through the winters.

The Christmas tree sparkled in the early morning light. Twinkling with all the colors. A yule feast for the eyes. Red, green, blue, yellow. Even purple was there. Glinting off glass orbs and splitting through crystal prisms. I could smell the pine sap. Pungent in the heat. Something else, too. Cooking meat ... Christmas dinner!

My mom and dad came into the room. My mom handed me a cup of cocoa.

"Merry Christmas, Nick!"

Merry Christmas, Mom! Merry Christmas, Dad!

"Come and open your presents! Dinner will be ready, soon."

I followed them over to the tree.

"Open this one first, Nick." My dad handed me a box. The wrapping paper was green with little snowmen all over it. I tore into it. It was a shoebox. Inside, a brand new pair of hiking boots.

"You're going to need them. It's a long walk ahead."

I didn't understand. I was 8 years old ... The boots were size 10.

I looked up, in confusion. My mom was handing me a present. That comforting, motherly smile.

"This one next, Nick."

It was a box of .357 shells.

"You're going to need them. It's a dangerous world out there."

I ... I don't ...

My mother just smiled and walked into the kitchen.

"Here, son. Here's the last one."

I opened the box. Inside, a few canned goods. Missing the labels.

Dad, what's in these?

"You'll find out, when you need them."

But we have so much food here today.

"You won't eat."

It smells so good ...

I looked over at my father. He was just a mummified corpse, lying down by the presents. A big, toothy smile of fear etched permanently on his face.

Mommy!

I ran into the kitchen.

"What is it, Nick? What is it, my baby?"

I wrapped my arms around my mom's waist and buried my face in her apron, eyes clinched shut.

It's dad. He's ... something's wrong with him ...

I turned my head. In the oven, a human head blistered and broiled in the heat. I looked up at my mom. Milky, blue eyes stared back. Her mouth and chest were covered in blood.

"Something's wrong with the whole world, baby ..."

The whole world.

Chapter 6

My eyes snapped open.

My heart raced.

I sat bolt upright in bed. I was covered in sweat and was still wearing the clothes from the grocery store. My hip hurt from where I'd slept on my revolver. I stank.

I stood and stretched. Early morning sunlight was filtered through the haze outside. It was dark. I was so sore. I took off my shoes and socks, then stood. I took off my coat and belt. I opened the door and listened. Dan and Alli were still asleep. I stripped, put on my bathrobe and went into the mudroom. We had a small gas burner set up underneath a metal washbasin, but the gas was running out fast, so we'd moved it to the kitchen. We no longer used it to heat water, only food. There was a thin skim of ice on the surface of the water in the tub. I didn't care. I just wanted to be clean. To forget about the past ... While. Especially that dream. Could I not even escape in my sleep, anymore?

I grabbed a rag off of the drying rack and swished the icy water around.

Dan and Alli got up an hour later. I was dressed and making pancakes from cornmeal. I gave our remaining gas about a week, if we used it sparingly. Something had to be done. A decision made.

I knew, when I woke up that morning, something had changed in me. I cried while washing myself, and a part of me knew this would be the last time I'd cry over the hopelessness that blanketed me. I put a part of myself down, and I realized I would never get it back.

Breakfast was quiet. No one spoke. There was nothing to talk about. Finally, I looked at Dan and Alli.

I'm going to Butte.

Just like that. As though I was headed there for Spring Break. As though it would be a 2 hour drive and that would be that. They looked up in alarm.

"Dude, you can't just leave us!" Dan, spitting pancake.

I didn't say I was going to leave you. But a decision has to be made.

"You mean a choice? Right?" Alli looked scared.

No. A decision. We can't stay here. Not anymore. We're almost out of supplies. I don't know if either Dan or I can handle another trip downtown. Definitely not in the dark. It's ... Not safe in Missoula anymore.

"And you think Butte will somehow be safer?"

Alli was from San Diego. I knew she had always looked at Montanans like hicks.

I don't know.

"Then why?" Dan put his arm around Alli's shoulders.

I know people there. More than here. They're ... Tough, there. I think it beats staying here, waiting for everyone but us to die and get back up ...

"What about my baby? I'm bringing a life into this world!"

My face heated. I glared at Dan.

Did you give her those ... Pills? Did he give you the pills?

"He did, and I threw them out the front fucking door! You're an asshole! I never liked you!" Alli screamed at me, red-faced, tears running down her cheeks.

They probably wouldn't have worked anyway.

"The vitamins? You threw them away, baby?" Dan looked confused.

"They weren't vitamins! They were fucking abortion pills!" Alli glared at me

I stood.

I'm going to Butte.

"What?! When?!" Dan looked up at me, fear in his eyes. Alli had buried her head in her hands.

Keep your voice down. Tomorrow.

"What if we don't come?"

40

I turned. I looked Dan in his eyes.

Then I'll leave you two here.

"Wha- She ... She can't."

She's only a few weeks along. Yes. She can.

I turned to go, but faced Dan and Alli one more time. I didn't want to force anything. I didn't want to make these decisions. But the world had changed, and we had to change with it.

Or we would die.

Alli.

She looked up, eyes puffy and wet. I placed the baby pacifier on the table. The one I'd found at the grocery store. There was a faint bloodstain on the handle.

This is no world for the living. Not anymore.

I walked in to my room to pack. I spent the rest of the day in there, thinking.

After that, I ate, then slept.

I dreamed of nothing.

By the next morning, I had my backpack set up. It was a frame pack I'd bought a few years ago, for trips to mountain lakes. It was a nice one. I'd only used it a few times.

In my closet, underneath my ski gear, I found a box. It was wrapped up. Green paper with little, multi-colored balloons. A present from my parents, from my last birthday. They'd gone to Belize, and I'd gone to Jackson. I hadn't even gotten to see them. I slowly tore the paper off. It was a shoebox.

Inside, new leather hiking boots. Size 10.

I took a deep breath, pushing it all back inside myself. I put them on, laced them up. I walked out into the living room. Dan was packing his own pack.

You guys are coming, then?

"I ... don't know, man. Alli just rolled over and wouldn't talk. You

41

really pissed her off."

I was just trying to help.

"Yeah? You've got a real fucked up way of helping, Nick. What happened to you, man? You used to be one of the most laid-back guys I'd ever met."

Dan, that's not a laid-back world outside that door. It was just a few months ago. Now ... It just isn't. We can't afford luxuries like that anymore. Expecting them will put us in danger. You're going to have to adapt to this new life. So will Alli.

"I ... Won't, man. If I give in, it means they won."

They? They! Who are you talking about. This isn't about the government or the banks or the corporations! It's not conforming, it's goddamn survival. Those ... Things out there! I don't think they know what they're doing! They're just ... Doing it! This isn't us versus them! It's us versus Death. He has an army of walking dead out there and so far, it looks like he's winning!

My blood was boiling. I'd raised my voice. I hated doing that. Is this what we were to become? Is this how humans all over the world were reacting? Because, if that was the case ... I turned and walked back into my room. I strapped on my revolver. I put on my coat, hat, gloves. I finally remembered my little pair of binoculars. I stepped back out into the living room.

"You're leaving *now*?"

No. I'm just going out to have a look.

I looked through the boarded up glass on the front door. I saw nothing but Frank's body under a light dusting of snow. I quietly slipped out. I gripped my crowbar tightly. Across the street, in Frank's backyard, I could see what had been his son. It didn't see me. I figured I'd have to take care of it when I came back. I ran across the way and climbed onto the shed roof. I looked out across the bridge. There were still a few zombies, but not like two days before. Even the downtown didn't look as infested, but I knew the buildings were hiding them. The walking trail on the south side of the river looked fairly clear. I could only see a few. Down, by the campus, we could reach the highway ...

That would be the ticket out.

I was interrupted from my thoughts by car horns, off to the west. I heard the distant roar of a diesel engine. My heart soared, momentarily. The Army! It had to be the Army! They'd finally ...

It wasn't the Army. I saw a bulldozer painted red, yellow and green. I pulled the binos from my pocket. As the focus came in, my heart crashed back to Earth. There were men with bandannas over their faces, like they were going to rob a bank or something. They all had rifles. Behind the dozer was a line of trucks, big ones, and even a school bus, painted the same idiotic color scheme. It looked to be mostly men. There were a few women, in one of the trucks. When one of them turned to talk to another, I could see she was chained up. They all were.

A flag flew from the bus. It featured a red stripe, a bear, and the words "California Republic". A red "anarchy" *A* was spray-painted over the bear.

Refugees. From down south.

The dozer was pushing cars out of the way, steadily working towards downtown. Whenever any zombies got close to this convoy, a group of men with clubs and machetes would leap from the trucks and butcher them. They whooped and hollered. Men still on the trucks would shoot zombies that were further out. They reached the turned over semi. A group of men dropped down and began ransacking the trailer while another group stood watch. They even took the wheels off of it. Some of the lookout group shouted and pointed. The two figures in black, from the other day, dashed out from behind a bush. The men gave chase. One of the black-clad people fell, the other turned as the men caught up. They ripped her mask off. It was a girl. A teenage girl. The other person lunged at one of the men. He caught the ... kid, I could see that now, he was small. Caught him right in the face with a crowbar. The kid tried to stagger up but one of the men pushed him back down and tore the hood from his head. It was a boy, around the same age as the girl. The men started yelling back to the trucks. The distance and the river drowned out most of the words, but one came across to me, carried on the wind. It was a word I'd wanted so badly not

43

to hear that I think my ears were actually listening for it.

The word was "eat".

One of the men pulled out a pistol and shot the boy in the head. He picked up the limp body and walked back toward the convoy. Another man grabbed the girl by her hair and pulled her along, screaming.

Shit.

I climbed down the ladder too quick and missed a rung near the bottom. I fell, cursing, onto my back. I stood, wiping slush from my shoulders. I turned and saw Frank's son. He ... It was standing just across the street. It moaned and came at me. I smashed its head, then ran back to the house. I didn't even bother being quiet this time.

We have to go! Now!

"Nick, what the hell? I was just talking with Alli. She said, okay. We'll go, too-"

Good! Grab your things! We have to go!

"What was all that shooting out there? Is it because of that?"

Yes. Refugees, from south of here. They have a convoy. There's a bunch of them.

"Great!" Alli's eyes lit up. "They can help us! We could probably tag along with them, and-"

They just killed a kid. I think they're going to eat him.

I didn't mention the girl.

Dan and Alli's eyes widened at the same rate.

Let's go.

I grabbed my backpack, did a quick mental checklist and did a quick sweep for anything I might have forgotten. I knew it would be the last time I'd ever look at that room. My home for 3 years. I looked at my bed once more. I didn't know when I'd see another bed. Or if I ever would. A quick flash of homesickness suddenly came over me, and I had to brush it off.

I carried my rifle. It was awkward to sling it over my pack. We jogged through our neighborhood, reaching the walking trail in a few minutes. Alli was already panting.

If we can beat them through the downtown, we can get ahead of them on the highway.

Across the river, shouts. Gunshots.

"What if they beat us to the highway?"

We may have to go up the mountain.

Mt. Sentinel, above the university. A huge, white, concrete "M" halfway up.

We headed east on the path as fast as we could. I would stop occasionally to drop a zombie that got too close for comfort. I think Dan was still afraid, after the grocery store. There were abandoned bikes laying all over the course of the path. At one point, I swore I saw a dog disappear behind some bushes.

Downtown, the convoy's progress mirrored ours, but louder. The crunch of steel echoing around the buildings as the dozer slowly cleared a path. They would be safe, high up on those trucks. We had to hurry.

By the time we reached the walking bridge at Madison Street, Alli and Dan were doubled over, gasping for breath. I could still hear the convoy. It seemed like they'd matched our pace. They were pushing debris and vehicles out of the way, we were on foot with backpacks. I turned to Dan and Alli.

Don't rest just yet. We're going to have to go up and over Sentinel. It's not that far to Deer Creek. We can drop back down in Bonner. It's only a few miles east. Maybe the highway will slow them down.

Alli looked at me like I was crazy.

"I can't ... I just can't ..."

You have to.

I started up the small hill, to the university. I'd planned on skirting the football stadium, on a road that circled the campus, but it was choked with derelict vehicles. I decided that a direct route would be better, now. The campus was open enough that it would be hard to run into trouble. Not only that, but it had been evacuated even before fall semester had started. I was

45

hoping it would be largely devoid of zombies. It was, but we were still cautious. I felt like I was in a World War II movie, running from tree to tree, motioning to the others when the coast was clear.

We saw only one zombie, far down by the library. It didn't see us. The university was so empty. Trash had blown everywhere. No one left to pick it up. We passed the smokestack of the heating plant and walked out into a parking lot. We could see the trailhead to go up Sentinel a little further on. I looked down, and something caught my eye. I bent down to pick it up ... I bullet cracked over my head and struck a car behind me. The report of a rifle followed.

Down!

We dropped. I peeked through our cover's window. I could see a man on the 4th floor of a tall dorm building. His head was turned away from us.

"I think I got him!" He yelled to someone.

Son of a bitch!

I chambered a round and flicked the safety off my rifle.

"Nick, what are you-"

I jumped to my feet and used the top of the car as a rest. I lined the sights up, like it was a zombie. I squeezed the trigger. The gun bucked against my shoulder, and as the explosion of sound echoed across the mountainside, I saw the man's head explode. Not like a zombie's. A reddish gray mist.

Run!

We made it to the trail and started up. Switchback after switchback, constantly dropping behind shrubs and listening. No one shot at us anymore. Just wails of distress coming from the dorm. We could see the steady progress of the refugee convoy as they drove through the downtown area, far below. They were completely surrounded, but just kept pushing through block after block of the ruined city. A large section of the center of town had burned. Smoke still fumed out of blackened piles of rubble.

We climbed and climbed and soon found ourselves at the concrete "M". We'd planned on stopping there for lunch, but when we reached it, we changed our minds. There was a line of fresh corpses, all sitting next to one another. They were entwined in Buddhist prayer flags. There were knives and razorblades all over the ground. Their arms had deep cuts running from wrist to elbow.

"Oh, God ..." Alli buried her face in Dan's chest.

I turned and started up the mountain again. We made it to the ridge before midday. I outpaced Dan and Alli and made it to the top first. I was out of breath and hungry, so the scene below wasn't immediately conveyed from my eyes to my brain. By the time the other two caught up with me, I was transfixed on it.

"What is it ... Oh ..."

Below us, both strips of asphalt ... 4 lanes of highway ... Completely filled with cars, trucks, buses, campers. Anything that could drive. All headed east, out of Missoula. The only movement I could pick out was a few zombies. Nothing else. All the way up the valley to where it disappeared around a bend. As far as the eye could see. An endless traffic jam. A long, metal and concrete graveyard.

Dan put his hands on his head and dropped to his knees.

"Oh, shit. Oh, shit. How did we miss this, Nick? How did we miss this?"

I don't know.

"It's worse than we thought."

Yeah ... It is.

Chapter 7

I know what I thought. Gazing down at that dead highway ... All those people who had tried to get away, tried to escape. Just like we were doing. Maybe ...

"Maybe they made it ... Maybe the Army came and picked them up. Took them someplace safe. There's still someplace safe, right?" Alli looked terrified.

I don't know. Maybe. The radio said there was a government aid station in Billings, before the power went.

I didn't believe it. Deep down, I knew ... All those people were still down there. Somewhere. Gone ... But not gone. I didn't tell Dan and Alli any of that. I just nodded and gave them the best smile I could muster. I don't think it was a good one. We walked in silence for a while. The cold highway snaked below us.

"Nick?" Dan stopped for a breather. We were walking at a quick pace, picking our way over snowy rocks and logs.

Yeah?

"Do you really think there's still a Butte? I mean ... Missoula is ... Was a bigger town. What if there's nothing there?"

Gunshots from down the valley. The refugees, clearing the road.

I don't know. It's just a chance we'll have to take. We can't wait for more people like that to show up.

Dan nodded absently and turned away. Thick clouds had rolled in, and the gray rain began to fall again. Alli pulled her hood tight and Dan put his arm around her. I walked away from them, alone with my thoughts. I really had no idea what I was doing, but I was too afraid to say it to Dan and Alli. Before the TV had gone out... It was everywhere. They were everywhere. The whole world was infested. If the government in the United States had collapsed, how

48

much better could everyone else have fared? We were supposed to be the best. Weren't we? How could the government just abandon a college town full of 70,000 people? How many others had been abandoned? I looked down at the highway. I shuddered.

We all heard something. I low rumble. More of a roar, I guess. The three of us perked our heads. The sound grew louder, until it turned into a deafening cacophony of thunder. It had to have been a military jet. It passed over the clouds, but low enough to make us cover our ears. As soon as it had arrived it vanished, echoing up the alley.

"That has to mean something, right?!" Dan's eyes were wide.

I shrugged.

It was definitely military. I suppose so.

We stopped for lunch. Cans of cold tuna, saltine crackers, some canned pears and filtered water. We ate quietly until Alli finally looked at me.

"You shot that guy. You killed him."

I know.

I felt the blood drain from my face. It threatened to put me down, to take me into the darkness. I saw lights behind my eyes. I didn't know what to think of it, still. I'd shot him. It hadn't been like a zombie. There was blood. He'd been alive. He ...

He shot at us. If I hadn't killed him, he would have killed us.

"You don't know that ..." Alli stared down at her feet.

Guys ... This isn't the world we lived in a few months ago. It's different now. Everything has changed. The old rules ... Don't apply. Not now. We either survive, or we don't. Does that make sense? I don't even know if it makes sense to me. But ... It has to. Alright?

"We have to kill other people to survive? Nick ... You know me. I don't think I can do that." Dan had been in the Peace Corps. Africa.

Then ... I will. I have once. If there is a God ...

I stopped and chuckled dryly.

Let's finish up. We can make Deer Creek before nightfall. I don't know

49

if those savages will stop for the night, but they will at some point. They have to push a lot of those cars aside. It'll be slow going for them. We're on foot. We'll be a lot faster.

"What about all the ... Zombies down there?"

Look at it. It's a maze. We can run, jump, climb ... Think. They can't.

We packed out our garbage. I don't know if it was habit, or something deeper. We walked east. The sleet turned to rain. The ridge dropped into a saddle and for a while, the highway was hidden from view. I looked at the gray, wet hills surrounding us. I wanted to pretend the world was normal again, even if just for a moment. Pretend that Alli, Dan and I were just on a quiet walk through the mountains. Pretend that the world was still vibrant and alive on the other side of that ridgeline.

Remember Professor Holden?

Dan let out a dry chuckle. Professor Holden was our first year algebra professor at the university. He'd been a somber man, always speaking in monotone. He always seemed to hate mirth and I'd never seen him smile. Dan and I had despised his class, and we both had ended up failing it.

"Yeah, man. That guy was a wack-job, wasn't he?"

I wonder where he is now.

"He was in that car accident, remember? He was at the hospital ..."

I could see Dan shiver out of the corner of my eye.

Oh. Yeah.

We walked east, in silence. There was nothing more to talk about.

Just below the peak, there sat the sheet-metal building of a power station. The lines no longer hummed. Parked by the chain-link fence was a silver SUV. A Cadillac Escalade. The doors were closed and even from a distance I could see the blood on the windows. I slowly approached it.

"Nick ..."

I just want to have a look.

I peered through the driver's side window. Inside, a family. Father, mother, little girl and two boys. All shot through the head. The small revolver

50

still hanging limply from the father's hand. One of the boys had a laptop on his lap. A Spongebob DVD case rested on the seat beside him.

"What is it? Is there anything worth taking?"

No. Let's just go. There's nothing ...

We walked on.

The terrain began to drop into the Deer Creek drainage, which would lead into Bonner, a small town just east of Missoula. We would be able to access the highway from there. We knew we would have to watch out for zombies at that point. The three of us found ourselves on an old logging road, the surface rutted and washed out by years of rain and snow. We headed down through the mud, watching each step so as not to slip and fall. The ground was soft, gray.

As the three of us made our way to the creek, we could see a line of smoke working its way up through the trees. I smelled campfire. Dan and Alli smelled it, too.

"People! There's people down there!" Alli's excited voice carried through the misty rain as she released Dan's hand and took a bounding step down the mountain. She stepped on a stump and slipped on the slush. She fell, catching herself before her face struck the ground.

"Baby! Are you alright?" Dan grabbed her around the waist and lifted her to her feet.

Her hand was bleeding. A rock had cut it. Deep.

"It hurts, Dan. It really hurts." Her blood dripped onto the wet ground. Dark crimson.

I swore under my breath and unslung my rifle, then took off my pack. I dug out the meager first-aid kit I'd compiled and pulled out an alcohol pad and a gauze bandage. There was a small chunk of rock in the top of the wound.

Alli, this is going to hurt. I want you to try and ignore the pain. It'll be quick.

She nodded, and I pulled the rock out with one side of the pad. She cried out. It echoed down the valley.

51

Goddamit, Alli! You have to be more quiet. It's only a flesh wound and there are people down there. Maybe zombies.

"Nick, she's hurt, man. She can't help it."

I finished bandaging the wound. It wasn't as deep as it had first looked. The bleeding was profuse, but superficial.

Alright. Let's circle around that smoke and try to get a look. Quietly.

Dan and Alli nodded and in the next breath, the three of us heard a wet footstep behind us. There was a man in a cowboy hat and raincoat, holding a shotgun. It was aimed at us.

"Who the hell are you? You-"

He gestured at me.

"-Don't even think about going for that rifle."

I swallowed hard. Nodded.

"Are you refugees?"

We're travelers. We're from Missoula, but it's not safe there anymore.

The man's features softened slightly. He didn't move the gun.

"That town is dead. How did you survive there for so long?"

"We had supplies stored up ... We just ..." Dan spoke up, then trailed off.

Hid.

The man nodded and lowered the shotgun barrel a little. He looked at Alli.

"She been bit?"

"No. She slipped and fell. Onto a rock." Dan pulled her in close.

"That true, ma'am?" Water poured down from the brim of the man's hat. He looked like something from a movie.

"Y-yeah. I fell. Nick just bandaged me up."

The man looked at me.

If she'd been bitten, I wouldn't be traveling with her.

Dan shot me a venomous glare. I held his gaze until he looked away. The man seemed satisfied and pointed the shotgun at the ground.

"Where are you headed?"

Butte.

"Well, we ... Haven't decided yet." Dan studied his shoes.

"That's quite a ways. I haven't heard anything from over that way. We- me and my family are from down Hamilton ways. My wife has relation in Great Falls. We figure with the Air Force base, well ... There's gotta be something. Anything."

He looked strained. It showed around his eyes.

I'm Nick. This is Dan and Alli.

I held out my hand. He shook it.

"Name's Douglas Henrich. Everyone calls me Doug." He turned and gave a short, crisp whistle.   There was a slight amount of movement in the woods, and a man around- must've been my age, wearing that mossy camo- emerged from the brush. He held a scoped rifle.

"This is my boy, William."

He gave us a short nod. Overhead, thunder boomed and the rain instantly increased its tempo.

"It's gonna get nasty out here, real quick. You three can join us at our camp tonight. Supper should be just about ready."

"Are you sure that's a good idea, dad?" William's voice, barely audible against the pounding rain and restless sky. Lightning darted overhead, spreading throughout the low clouds.

"The day it turns into a bad idea to give a hand to a neighbor in trouble is the day we join in with those goddamned things, son. Now run ahead and tell everyone we'll have three more for supper."

William nodded and disappeared into the rapidly growing darkness.

"Follow me. It'll be dark soon." Doug turned on a flashlight.

"Won't that attract the z- the dead people?" Alli clutched Dan's hand.

"We came up over the hills from Hamilton. Haven't seen a one up here. Me and the boys went to have a look at the highway a few days back. Only saw a few. That way's pretty well blocked, though."

53

Not if you have a bulldozer.

I told Douglas about the refugees headed east. He looked concerned.

"That's why we left the ranch. People started coming up, from the south. Troublemakers. Some were right-down violent. I think people are starting to lose it, these days. We figured we'd do better to find the military. They'll know what to do."

He didn't sound sure.

I simply nodded and clicked on my headlamp. We made our way down to Deer Creek.

By the time we reached the camp, the rain was coming down in sheets. My raincoat was sturdy, but I was cold. We walked by an assorted mix of cars, trucks and horse trailers. I heard horses stamp inside. Beyond that, a group of people were seated around a fire. There must have been 10 or so. A tarp had been made into a lean-to. A dutch oven hung just over the flames. After months of canned foods, the aroma was maddening. A woman got up and walked over to us.

"I'm Mary, Doug's wife. We're so glad to see there are still decent folks left. Seems harder to find nowadays ..." She visibly shook thoughts away. "William will take you to the tent. You can put your things there."

William reluctantly got to his feet. He didn't seem to relish going back out into the rain.

"This way." His voice was a mutter.

He led us to a wall tent. Inside, a trench had been dug to divert the rain. Cots and sleeping bags lay at every angle. A woodstove gave off heat on one side. We put our things down and took a moment to warm up by the stove.

"Is that your rifle?" William asked suddenly.

Yeah. .30-06. My grandpa gave it to me.

"My grandpa had one just like it ..." He didn't say anything else.

We went back to the fire. Introductions were made. I don't remember many of the names. There was Doug, Mary and William. They mentioned William's sister, but she wasn't there. I didn't ask about her. A few of their neighbors from Hamilton, and another couple with two little boys who had fled Boise.

Everyone bowed their heads to pray. I never really considered myself religious, but I bowed mine, too. Bowls of elk chili were handed out. It was delicious.

Behind me, someone turned on a small radio. A voice, from the airwaves ...

"This is K-Wow 104.3 FM Boise bringing you the best of the new and the greats of the old country! The 43rd Boise Roadster Show was a huge success! We want to thank all the fans who came out and gave their support for little Darren McMurray! After an alleged coyote attack behind his home on Torridon Drive, the son of Boise natives Amy and Chad say he's still unconscious but in stable condition at St. Luke-"

"Sorry." The guy from Idaho- Ted, I think his name was- smiled sheepishly and pushed the fast forward button. "It's just a tape. Something ..." His voice cracked a little and he took a deep breath. His wife put her hand on his shoulder and he drew his sons in tight. "Like the world is still okay out there ... So it can still be okay ..."

He hit play.

" ...ext up is a song we all love by the man himself, Mr. Willie Nelson!"

The chords of an acoustic guitar cried out against the storm. We all sat in silence for a while. When the group started talking again, they started asking us about our lives before ... The Collapse. Before everything. We gave the appropriate answers and I found myself talking about a journalism degree like it was something I could have. A life I could just go back to tomorrow. As if there would be anything to write about. Or anyone to write to.

As though we were camped out in the night, a group of perfect strangers, and in the morning we would all just wake up and go back to our lives.

Our old lives.

55

Alli and Dan soon got onto the subject of the pregnancy. The women at camp surrounded her and began smiling, laughing. Dan sat down by Doug. For advice. I don't know. My subconscious stirred at that point and anger flowed forth. How could they just sit there and pretend like everything was sane? It ... It wasn't healthy. I couldn't watch. I stood and pulled the pack of cigarettes from my pocket. I stepped into the rain and found a tree to stand under. The lighter flared and the end of the smoke flared in the night as I inhaled. I felt something come up beside me. My hand instinctively dropped to my revolver. It was William.

"Can I have one of those, man?"

I offered the pack. He lit one. We stood without talking, staring out into the rain. Finally, he spoke.

"Deb was pregnant, too."

Deb?

"Deborah ... My sister."

Yeah ...

I didn't know what to say.

"She was fixing to go to college. She and Mike really loved each other. They were gonna move to Spokane. She was gonna be a nurse ..."

I nodded, in the dark. I don't know if he could see it.

"When it all started ... When people started getting sick ... She volunteered at the medical center in town ..." I could hear him swallow. "One day, a few weeks back, she came home. One of the patients had ... Bit her ... We didn't know anything about that, not then."

He inhaled deeply on his cigarette.

"It didn't look bad, y'know? It was like ... When the dog got me as a kid. It was bloody. They cleaned it out real good. She was pale for the first day or so. Sweaty. That's when mom noticed she had a fever. A bad one. She fell asleep after that. Mike stayed by her bedside ... Wouldn't leave it. He took his food in her room. A few hours later ... Dad musta heard something in her room. He'd caught her and Mike once ... You know ..." A fleeting smile, on his

56

face. It vanished.

"It ... It wasn't that. Dad opened the door ... I peered in over his shoulder. Mike was ... On the floor and Deb was ... Was ..." His voice was rough. "She was eating him. Just tearing off ..."

He took another drag on the cigarette. The cherry glowed bright against the dark wet.

"She looked at me and dad ... Her eyes ... It was like she'd never seen us before. Like she was a wild animal that we'd caught in a trap. That's how she looked at us ... She got to her feet. Mike's blood was ..."

Another drag.

"Dripping from her lips. She still had some meat in her mouth. She was so pale. And those eyes ... She grabbed dad. He didn't do anything. He just said her name, like she would look up at him like she did as a little girl. But ... She didn't. And I knew she wouldn't. She pushed him into the hall. Some pictures fell down, I think. It was loud ... I had to step aside. At first, I didn't know what to do. I just ... Couldn't move ... I realized dad was calling my name. Yelling at me to help as he held her face. Her teeth were ... Chewing. Like she was so hungry."

I silently smoked my cigarette.

"I ... In my room was my bat ... I played baseball, man ... Back in high school. I grabbed it and shoved her off of dad. She fell to the floor, then got up and lunged at me. I shoved her back and just said 'Deb! Please! Stop this!'. But she didn't. She wouldn't stop ... I hit her. I had to. I hit her and she went down ... Tried to get back up ... I hit her again ... Again ... Aga ..."

William's voice broke and I heard him sob.

"I killed her, Nick. I killed my own sister ...."

He broke down into tears, slumping against the tree.

I didn't know what to do, how to console him. I had considered myself a compassionate person, back then. Now ... I didn't know how to react to this guy's raw display of humanity ... All we had left.

I said the first thing that came to my mind. All I could come up with.

You didn't kill her, William.

Thunder broke the clouds with a terrible roar. Lightning flashed, lighting up the tree, William, myself. But I didn't look at him. I just stared straight ahead, into the rain. And smoked that cigarette.

She was already dead.

Chapter 8

When we returned to the fire, all of the women but one had gone to bed. Christy? Crystal? Most of the men were still up, chatting.

I can't remember what about.

Douglas and Dan were still talking. They looked up when we came back. Doug had a pipe out and was loading it with tobacco.

"Howdy, boys. How's the storm?" Doug had one of those smiles that beamed outwards, shining on everything in its path.

Wet.

"Ha! It's good to have some humor these days! Have a seat."

William and I sat across the fire. The "radio" was now playing a song about how great Toby Keith thought America was. Was. Doug passed around a flask. Bourbon. I couldn't remember the last time I'd had a drink. It was good.

"Nick ..." Dan got my attention, but wouldn't look me in the eye. "Me and Alli ... Uh ..."

Doug took the cue.

"Dan and Alli are going to come with the group to Great Falls. We'll be safe if we travel together. The military will know what to do, and they'll come and clean this mess up soon." He puffed on the pipe, enveloping his face in smoke. "You're welcome to travel with us."

Thanks. I appreciate the offer. But I have to get to Butte.

"You won't make it alone, man. It's just a ... Pipe dream. Come with us." Dan's eyes pleaded louder than his voice.

"The cities are dead, Nick. What's in Butte? Why there?" Doug sat back.

Family. Friends. Familiarity. I just ... Have to go there.

"How do you know they're still there? How do you know they didn't go to Billings or Great Falls? How do you know they're still ..."

59

Alive?

"Yes."

I don't. But ... I had a dream that my brother wasn't in. So he has to be alive.

"Do you believe in God, Nick?"

I ... I don't think so. Not now.

"Do you have faith in anything?"

All I know is ... I just have to go. Just keep going. I think if we stop now- any of us ... We'll lose it forever. The darkness will set in and this nightmare will never end. Does that make any sense?

Doug puffed on his pipe. The rain had calmed.

"Yes. I think it does."

We all sat in silence for a while. Finally, Doug tapped his pipe out, dropping tiny embers onto the ground by his chair.

"Let's get some sleep. Nick, think it over tonight. We're headed up through Bonner in the morning."

I nodded at him. Pulled out another cigarette. Dan walked over and held out his hand.

"Come with us, Nick."

I stood and hugged him. I didn't say anything. I sat down and lit the smoke. The people around the fire slowly filtered off to bed. William sat on top of a horse trailer and took first watch. I sat and gazed into the low flames. The chaos of fire. The wood cracked and hissed. I smoked the cigarette, put it out, then lit another.

I sat for a long time, smoking and thinking. The rain stopped. The night was cold and damp. After a time, I heard snoring from the wall tent. I glanced over at William. I could barely see him through the dark, but could tell he was looking away. I got up, quietly. I went to the tent and pulled out my gear. I put on the pack, slung the rifle and hefted the crowbar. I turned to go.

"Leaving, then?"

I turned to see Doug standing halfway out of the tent opening.

60

Yeah. I am. I've never been the best at goodbyes.

He stepped forward and held out his hand. I shook it.

"I'll pray the Lord blesses you with a safe journey."

And I'll wish you good luck with yours. I hope you're right. I hope you find the military and they're already doing something about this. I hope everything can just ... Go back to how it was.

"That's what we're all praying for. Goodbye, Nick."

Goodbye, Doug.

I turned and walked away.

I walked along Deer Creek Road, headed north. Eventually, I came to a fork. Straight ahead, I knew, went into East Missoula. To my right ... A frontage road along the river. The trees were dark towers along the sides of the road. Bare light came through the low clouds. The road ran along a course of small hills. There wasn't much to be seen in the night, but I knew just across the river stretched that highway. My road home.

A cold wind blew up the valley. I put my hood up and kept walking. My headlamp played light through the trees, creating moving shadows. I felt jumpy. The road edged up to another hill and to my left, I heard something move through the brush. I swung my light over and grabbed at my revolver. I didn't see anything.

I walked along the road until my feet were tired and cold. My pack felt heavy. It must have been miles. The road paralleled the river, somewhere out there in the dark. I could hear it at spaces through the trees. The valley smelled damp. Musty. Like a swamp. The river slowed down and spread out here.

Maybe it was dead, too.

The road opened up onto the water, like a land bridge. The water looked black in the glow of my lamp. I kept walking. I didn't hear anything now, except the wind. In the distance ...

A light. Bobbing slowly up and down.

I shut off my lamp and crouched. My legs screamed in pain. I tried to convince myself my eyes were playing tricks on me. They weren't. There was a light, a little ways ahead. There was no reference point, so I couldn't tell how far. But it was there. I stayed low, turning my lamp onto its lowest setting and slowly made my way toward the distant glow.

A truck loomed out of the dull light of my lamp. It was upside-down in the river's braid, half submerged in water. A zombie was trapped underneath. It thrashed around when it saw me, but couldn't get at me. I watched it for a time. Its dead eyes, its fingers hooked like claws, reaching for me. Half of its neck was ripped out. Its head dangled to one side. All of its fingernails were torn off from clawing at the mud. The end of its fingers hung in tatters.

I kept walking. Toward the light.

A little ways on, a small stand of trees by the river opened up. I swung my light over there. The beam revealed the charred remains of a house, with a half-burned barn just past it. A short walk down the road, and I finally closed in on the light. I turned my lamp off and crept to the fenceline. I could make out the dark outlines of a house, a barn and some kind of machine shed. The light suddenly appeared from behind the house.

Bobbing slowly up and down.

It was a zombie. A middle-aged woman in a nightgown. Just ... Shuffling around in the barnyard. She gripped a flashlight that swung gently as it aimlessly wandered. Its soft moan and the cold wind was all I could hear. It didn't hear me. It lurched toward the barn and I slowly crept toward the house. When my light touched it, I could see a few of the windows were broken out and the front door stood wide open. I didn't dare go inside.

I stood and ran to the machine shed. When I reached it, I shut my light off and peeked around the corner. The zombie was standing in front of the open barn doors, its back to me. The garage door to the machine shed was closed. Next to it, the smaller, regular door was closed, too. I grabbed the handle, held my breath and turned it. The door clicked and swung inward with a low squeak. I stepped through, turned my light on and pulled my revolver from its holster. My first sweep didn't reveal any zombies, so I shut the door behind me

62

and listened. I didn't hear anything, not even the wind. That meant all the doors were closed. I scanned the garage again. A pickup truck with a snowplow on the front sat to the rear of the large, open space. There was an oil stain in the middle of the floor, but whatever was normally parked there was long gone now. An assortment of tools hung from the walls. An engine hoist cast strange shadows as my light swept past. There was a small set of stairs that ended at another door. I walked up and opened it. It was a small office. A desk, an old computer, stacks of paperwork ...

And a couch along the back wall. I put my pack down and sat heavily on the couch. I pulled my sleeping bag out from the bottom of my pack and removed my boots. My feet ached. All of my muscles did. I climbed into the sleeping bag, hoping I would be able to get to sleep ...

The next morning was cold and gray. Dim light shone in through a window at one end of the office. Streaks of icy rain ran down the glass, leaving dirty trails reaching up behind them. I didn't even remember falling asleep. It must have been fast. I climbed out of the sleeping bag and immediately regretted it. It was frigid. My muscles and feet were sore. I didn't relish the idea of stuffing those feet back into cold boots. I sat up. I glanced sleepily at the old, boxy computer monitor on the desk. A little amber light shone steadily by the power button ...

I shot to my feet. My legs screamed in rage. Power? Power! How ...?

I hobbled to the desk. I pushed the button on the CPU itself. A green light flashed and I could hear a fan moving inside. I sat down in the office chair and began laughing. I stopped when I noticed the thermostat on the wall.

What the hell ...

My own voice surprised me. It was rough, scratchy, like I'd smoked a thousand cigarettes the night before. I turned the dial ... And out in the shop heard the hiss of a propane heater light up. A moment later, warm air began blowing into the office. I felt like crying with joy. I sat for a time, letting the warmth wash over me. I closed my eyes.

I saw my mom and dad. I saw Dan and Alli. Katie. Professor Holden. Mark and the guys from pub trivia. I thought of skiing, kayaking. Lying on grass in the warm sun. Hiking through a living and vibrant world.

My bladder shook me from my reverie. I opened my eyes and wiped the tears that had gathered beneath my eyes.

Stop it, Nick. That world is gone and it's not coming back.

I went down into the shop. I found a light switch and the bay was immediately flooded in a harsh, fluorescent glow. Nothing here but me. All the doors were shut. The snowplow pickup still sat in the back. The garage smelled like oil. I pissed in a floor drain.

I walked around the shop after that. I found a crowbar that was a little longer than the one I carried. It had a double-hooked end. Perfect. I searched through all the cabinets. Band-aids that had been there for years. Dirty, the packaging ripped up. I left them. I found a sheaf of invoices for cattle medicine. Light, dry paper. I almost left them, but shoved the stack in my pocket as an afterthought. Underneath, I couldn't believe my luck. A full box of .30-06 shells. In a drawer, I found a box of waterproof matches.

I went to the truck. Inside, another half-box of rifle ammo. It was . 270. I found a small, plastic jerry can, full of gas. I grabbed it, too. On the wall, above a workbench, a picture. It was a large family, a few generations by the look of it. They all looked down on me, smiles frozen in time. Who knew where those smiles were now?

Beneath a pile of papers on the bench was a white box. It was a first-aid kit. I opened it, hoping at least the band-aids would be usable. When I flipped open the lid, I was surprised. Everything looked almost brand new. Bandages, gauze, a suture kit, peroxide, splints, painkillers. Even antibiotics. They were a few years expired, but it was better than nothing. I closed it and put it in a pile with the rest of my finds. I looked through the rest of the garage and found a few hand tools. Some screwdrivers and a wrench. There wasn't much else I could use.

Under a table was a mouse trap. The decomposed remains of a mouse still caught in its jaws.

I collected all the things I'd found and carried them upstairs. I put them down by my backpack and sat down on the couch, closed my eyes. My muscles were still sore, but I knew I had to get going again. Hiding in a garage wouldn't get me to Butte any faster. I opened my eyes and sat up and grabbed some food from my pack. The computer had booted up and was sitting idle on the desktop. I hadn't used a computer in months. I sat down at it. There was an internet window open on the taskbar. I clicked it and it popped up. The computer was no longer connected to an internet that probably didn't exist anymore, but this page was still up and loaded.

My heart skipped a beat.

There were 3 tabs open at the top … Each had a list of news stories. I scanned them, then clicked on each in turn:

Military Overrun in New York

(AP) New York City, New York

The United States Army has been overrun by what can only be described as "walking corpses". After an unsuccessful attempt to contain the outbreak in Manhattan, the bridges to the island were struck with missiles, rendering them impassable. A last-ditch effort was made to hold the- for the sake of the popular term- "zombies" south of Yonkers, but ended in disastrous defeat. The Henry Hudson Parkway and the bridge at West 220th Street have now been destroyed, effectively trapping any remaining survivors on the island. Army General Arthur Dowlin held a press conference shortly after the last explosions died down. "We're asking that any and all survivors get to the roof of the tallest building in your area. We're doing constant flybys with helicopters," he said.

When pressed with the fact that all power in the city was out and elevators wouldn't work, this reporter asked the general what to do about the elderly and crippled.

"Carry them. If you can't … Leave them …"

The story was dated over a month ago.

I tore my eyes away and looked at the next headline:

U.S. Government Abandons D.C.

(CNN) Washington, District of Columbia

The upper echelons of the U.S. government have fled the nation's capital, pulling back to undisclosed locations in the American West. Never in United States history has so much air traffic been spotted over D.C. The President wasn't available for comment, but a junior press secretary read a brief memo from the Vice President calling on the American people "not to panic" in this "time of crisis". Reassurances that the government was intact and still very much in control was met with a stony silence. This reporter felt bad for the young lady. Finally, a colleague asked how she felt to be left behind.

She burst into tears, right at the podium ...

This story ... Over 3 weeks ago ...

I looked at the next one:

Floods of American Refugees Flee SW, Cross Southern Border

(Reuters) Brownsville, Texas

In a city known more for drug cartel-induced gun violence and immigration directed north, the scene in Brownsville-Matamoros looks like something from the cinema. The United States-Mexican border is at a standstill with bumper-to-bumper traffic. But instead of holiday revelers destined for the white sand beaches of the Gulf, it is a flood of refugees hoping to escape the devastation of America's heartland. With urban centers such as Houston, Oklahoma City and Dallas hopelessly overrun with a phenomenon of walking, cannibalistic corpses, the living are vacating their homes as fast as travel will allow. Refugees from other places are headed north, hoping to cross into Canada.

Updated at 3:11 PM, September 19th

As the mass of refugees leaves the cities, a disturbing course has been observed by aircraft. The living are fleeing north and south in droves, and mass groups of the so-called "zombies" are following them, much like a predator will follow the migratory routes of its prey. More on this when more is known. Meanwhile, your government requests you travel quickly to the nearest aid station. If this is not possible, stay where you are and await ...

I tried clicking on the next page, but the familiar white screen with "Server Not Found" appeared.

I felt sick. I put the can of pears I'd been eating down. All of these stories, weeks old. An entire web of information ... Gone. There was no one around to run it. I was looking at pictures of ghosts. I imagined highways all over the country that looked just like the one a mile or so to the north. Derelict cars, still sitting where their owners had fled or died. Dead roads, stretching to the horizon.

I wished then I hadn't read those stories. Now ... I don't know, now ...

Then I thought about the refugees we'd seen. From California. Which meant there would be more. And that meant they would be followed by ... a lot of zombies. All headed north. Toward me.

I closed the internet browser. Out of habit, I guess. I lit a cigarette and smoked it slowly, bathed in the glow of the computer monitor. When I'd smoked it down to the filter, I dropped it to the floor and stepped on it. I don't think the owners of the machine shop would have cared at that point.

I stood and put my gear on. My pack was a little heavier now, but was nothing I couldn't handle. I slung my rifle, grabbed the crowbar and went back down to the shop. I took one last look around. My eyes fixed on the picture again. That big ranch family. So happy ...

I turned to go, and one of the women from the picture was staring through the window at me, that smile now locked in a savage snarl. Half of her ... Its face had been chewed away. It wasn't the one from the previous night,

67

either. This one must have been in the house or something. It raised its limp hand and smacked it on the metal screen that was bolted on the outside of the window. I walked toward the door, knowing that I could easily slip past the two zombies ...

On all sides of the garage, hands started slamming off the metal siding. Pounding. Trying desperately to get in. To get me. The noise was deafening, but that's when I heard the generator, faintly. It was out behind the garage, from what I could hear. It probably kicked on when I turned on the lights and heat. I cursed myself for being so careless. There must have been a few of them still in the house, and the generator had drawn them out. I went to the door I'd come in, but knew that would expose me if there was one right outside. There was a control switch on the side of the big garage door. I hit the "up" button and backed away. The door rumbled up. The doorway gave me a wide field of view. One zombie was right outside the door and fell into the garage when it opened. I ran, crowbar in one hand, the other resting on the butt of my revolver. It reached for me as I ran past. I took a left and hooked around the building, toward the river. On the side, there must have been 8 zombies. They all turned as I ran by, but I quickly outpaced them.

Ahead was an open cattle gate that led into a field ... And a zombie. A fat man in overalls. I ran at it and when I closed in, it reached out at me. I hit it in the side of the head with the full force of my arms and momentum. Its head caved in and the body fell to the grass with a wet thump. I ran through the gate and latched it behind me. I figured, if anything, that would at least slow them down. I kept moving along the fence row. The highway was about a half-mile ahead. I glanced back. The zombies were pushing up against the gate and fence. It was the family ... The whole family, from the picture. Shaking the gate and moaning, like they were angry at me for sleeping in the garage. But ... What did they feel now? Did they even have the capacity for anger anymore? They didn't seem to want to reason, or even have the ability to talk. People simply died, got back up and ... Went.

So did I.

I just ran. I ran until my legs threatened to give out and my lungs burned in the cool, morning air. I ran until I crossed the river. I ran through a section of fence that had been knocked down by an overturned police car. I ran until I reached the highway, and ducked down behind an abandoned station wagon. I did a quick look and didn't see any zombies. I slowly sank to the ground and leaned against the car. I breathed slowly and deliberately, trying to get my heartbeat under control. That had been too close. I couldn't afford to be that haphazard if I wanted to live to see another dawn. After a few minutes, I clambered back to my feet and started walking east along the dead highway. That's when the gunfire erupted, behind me, far down the valley. Back towards Missoula ...

Back towards Deer Creek.

Chapter 9

I stood on top of a semi-trailer that was lying on its side. At first I'd figured it was a stupid idea, but I had to know. As soon as I'd climbed onto the trailer, five zombies shuffled below me, towards the gunshots.

I looked west, back to where I'd come from. I had my small set of binoculars to my eyes and glassed the highway at Bonner. I could just make out the refugee convoy crossing the bridge over the river. Right up into Deer Creek. They must have figured an attempt at the frontage road would be faster. Or maybe they'd just seen the people from the camp coming right at them.

It didn't matter.

All I could do was sit there in silent rage as gunshots and screams echoed up the valley, and zombies shuffled slowly under my perch. I figured I was going to cry. But no tears came. I sat with clenched fists. Cold and angry. Angry at the zombies. Angry at the people. Angry at the cold wind that blew up the valley and whatever destiny would allow something as horrible as this world to exist. I bundled up and shuddered. The trees shuddered with me.

After a while, the gunfire stopped. I could make out distant yells and the rumbling of diesel engines. I thought about Dan and Alli. I had to will myself to move. I checked both sides of the trailer, then climbed down the tires. I walked east along the highway. Abandoned cars filled with people's belongings.

People long gone.

I looked into the cars. I saw books. Empty soda cans. Children's toys. I saw full desktop computers. Flatscreen TVs. In one van, I saw kitchen appliances. I kept wondering to myself, why would anyone bring stuff like that along? Were they afraid someone was going to rob their house before they got back? Did they think there would be a house to go back to? I thought again about those appliances. Those TVs. I began to think about the world that I'd left behind. Maybe that's why they'd brought their stuff with them. So they could still have that world. The world that we'd left behind. Or maybe it had left us behind. Maybe it didn't matter. Maybe this was just a bad dream I would wake up from soon. Maybe ...

Something grabbed my pack as I edged around a car. I spun, but slipped and fell. I looked up to look at a zombie still clutching at the air. It was strapped into a sedan, but the window was broken out. I backed away, sliding across the wet asphalt. My gloves slipped over glass. Bullet casings. A single shoe. I got to my feet. I swore at myself. Careless! Again! I gave the car a wide berth and made my way to the shoulder of the highway. As I walked, I started seeing more zombies, trapped in cars. Unable to get out. I figured they would stay in those cars until they finally rotted away. I kept walking.

I saw more belongings. Some cars were opened, like the owners had grabbed what they could and left in a hurry. There were things scattered all over the road. Lots of bullet casings. And bullet holes. And blood.

There was a lot of blood, all down that dead highway.

Occasionally, I'd see a zombie ahead. I would duck down behind a car until I heard it stagger past. Always moaning. Always moving. Like sharks, they would never stop. They would just keep going and keep eating until all the food was gone. And then what? Would they starve to death? Were we even food? Or was it something else?

Maybe they just hated us. Was that even possible?

I don't know why I was plagued with such thoughts. I would never know. I wasn't a scientist. I wasn't a psychologist. I was just a scared kid, slowly walking down a cold, quiet graveyard. A funeral that the dead themselves were attending.

A nightmare that came true. But there's no nightmare so deep you can't wake up, right?

Right?

I passed an RV and saw movement out of the corner of my eye. I looked up into the windshield as a family of corpses pounded against it. But they couldn't get to me, so I kept walking. I moved into a slight fog as the road dipped toward the river. The world turned into shadows. I came to the wreckage of a helicopter. As I got closer, I could make out "Montan-tional-Gu" in a twisted piece of dark green metal. I looked into the burned hulk as I passed it. I could see a few skeletons in it. One had its arms still wrapped around the remains of a machine gun. I looked forward just as I ran into a zombie. It was mostly turned away from me and stumbled as I bumped it. It turned and lunged at me. It was a man, had to have been close to my age. It wore a torn and bloody camouflage uniform. It still had a helmet on, strapped onto its head. Its last name was Orr. Private Orr.

I only had enough time to bring the dull edge of the crowbar up into its chin. I was able to get enough force that its jaw slammed shut and shattered most of its teeth. The helmet slid back and brought it off balance, but not enough. It regained its footing. I didn't have room to effectively swing the crowbar again. I jerked the revolver from my holster and blew half its head away. The shot crashed through the fog. My ears rang. I got down behind the bumper of a truck until I could hear again.

I stood and walked around the side of the truck.

Just ahead, half-obscured by fog, a figure leapt up. It wore a cowboy hat and its face was a skull. But, no. That wasn't right. It was a mask, for cold weather. A skull printed on it. I whirled and took cover behind the truck again. I pulled the gun again.

"Hey, man! It's cool! Come on over! I ain't got a gun! See?"

I peeked over the bed. He held his arms up.

"Come on, man! We got some food! You don't need that gun!"

I peeked again, around the side, this time. I could see him subtly move his fingers, as if to motion to someone behind him. I ducked back as my heart pounded. I could feel blood rushing to my head. My vision flashed with little popping bulbs of light. I took a deep breath, held it. Released it.

I jumped to my feet and shot him directly in the mask.

Then I turned and ran back the way I'd come ... I ran faster than I ever had. I didn't even feel my pack. I heard shouts behind me. I heard the thump of boots on wet asphalt as they came after me. I dashed around the wreckage of the helicopter and put it between myself and the ... Bandits, I guess. I heard a gun go off behind me. The shot went wide. Ahead, in the fog, I saw the RV, full of zombies. They were still gathered around the windshield. Right next to the door.

I don't know what the hell I was thinking. Not then, not now. I guess my brain just kicked into pure instinct ... I grabbed the door handle on the RV and ripped it open. A zombie tumbled out, almost on top of me. It hit the asphalt and I kept moving. I could hear them piling out the door, moaning. Following me. I ducked back into the frozen traffic, careful to stay away from open windows. Behind me, I heard shouts and gunshots. Ahead, I saw the overturned police car sticking through the fence. I ran over the undercarriage and dropped down into the ditch. I looked up the highway and saw a group of men shooting the zombies I'd released. One of them was down on his knees, zombies on either side of him, ripping chunks of flesh off. He was screaming.

I ran across the road. A bullet cracked the air in front of me and impacted in the dirt to my left. I dove into the ditch on the other side of the road and made for the bridge. I would be exposed, but I had to get across. Then I would be safe. The ditch dropped down to the river and I peeked my head up. The man aimed again. I took a shot with the .357 ... It hit the man in his hip. He spun and went down. A zombie emerged from behind a car and fell onto him, tearing the muscle off the back of his neck.

I took the opportunity and made a mad dash across the bridge. It must have been a hundred yards. No more shots came in my direction. I could hear the angry shouts behind me. I reached the end of the bridge and jumped back down into the ditch. It was half-filled with icy water. It soaked through my rain pants and got into my shoes. It didn't matter. I stayed low and moved as quickly as I could, following the curve of the road. As soon as there were enough trees to shield me from view of the highway, I climbed out of the ditch. I was cold and wet.

I stumbled along for another half-mile, shivering. I could already feel my feet rubbing against the wet socks. There were houses on my right side, spaced apart and separated by trees. I didn't see any movement. In the weeds, ahead. I caught a glimpse of red and black. When I got close, I saw what it was. An ATV, parked partially off the road. There was a plastic rifle case on the back. Open. Empty.

The keys were still in the ignition. It started up with a fuel-soaked cough. I'd only been on one once before, and was relieved to see it had an automatic transmission. I backed it onto the muddy frontage road and opened the throttle wide. It was faster than it looked, and the weight of my pack almost took me off the back. I gripped the handlebars tight and held on. The road curved right and headed straight toward the mountains south of the river. There were more houses here, on both sides. I'd occasionally see zombies wandering around houses and barns. One house was completely surrounded.

I wondered if there were still people inside.

I sped past side roads. A sign was bent down, obviously hit by a car. It said "Ocean View Drive". The absurdity of this struck something in me, and I began laughing uncontrollably. Wind in my face, hanging onto an ATV with all the strength I had left, speeding along a muddy road, surrounded by death. And I was laughing. Like some goddamned maniac.

The road suddenly hooked left around a blind corner. I hit the brakes and slid around it, nearly losing my hard-won balance. As soon as I gassed it again, I realized I'd made a mistake. A car was lying on its side, blocking most of the road. I twisted the handlebars, skidding around the car and immediately ran over a zombie. It must have been a middle-aged man. It went down with a sickening thud, and I punched the throttle switch. The wheel refused to grab for a moment, then spat mud and flesh out the back. The tires peeled out over the zombie's face and chest, tearing off skin and muscle. I looked back as the ATV picked up speed again.

The zombie's skull and ribcage were exposed. Even with most of its facial muscles torn to shreds, it still writhed and chomped at the air. A dirty

74

skull, silently crying out against the gray sky.

The gray world.

I leaned forward and gunned the engine. The road forked. The right fork went to the mountain, and I vaguely remembered hiking in the area in years past. I stayed on the main road, now headed east. After that, the road forked again ... In three paths. I couldn't remember which way to go, so I hung a right. Towards the mountains. The road began to climb and became heavily forested on the sides. Through the trees, I could see a house. There were several zombies out front, and they saw me, but didn't stand a chance of catching me ...

The ATV began to cough and jolt. I pressed the throttle switch all the way down, and it leapt forward for another hundred yards or so. Then it rolled to a stop, coughed once more and died.

Shit.

I climbed off the machine and walked swiftly along the road. I looked back down the road, towards the house. Some of the zombies had made the road now and were following me. On the ATV, I didn't realize how wet and cold I was. I did then. The wind began blowing up the valley again. I realized that if I didn't hunker down and build a fire, I would probably die of exposure. Especially when the sun set. I didn't know what time it was, but I guessed early afternoon. I still had some light left. I had to move. I couldn't stop with zombies following me. They wouldn't. I had to press on.

The road turned into a logging trail and ascended the mountainside. It switchbacked up multiple gullies. When I got high enough, I could see down to the highway. I saw no sign of the men who had chased me. At the next switchback, down through a glade, I could see 3 zombies, shuffling up the road. I don't know if they were still after me, or if they even knew they were still pursuing me. But they were definitely following the road now.

Shit.

I kept walking. My mind hit an almost ... Robotic state. Just putting one foot in front of the other and trying not to think about how I couldn't feel

75

my feet. Even the dull, throbbing pain that had come with each step was gone by the time I reached the top. The road had just kept switchbacking, so I'd finally hiked a ridgeline. When I reached the small peak, which wasn't the top at all, I was soaked in sweat. The instant I stopped, the wind began to freeze my clothes.

I built a fire to dry my clothes and warm myself. I sat for a long time, wrapped in my sleeping bag, smoking a cigarette. I thought about Dan and Alli. I'd just seen them ... Last night. It seemed longer than that. Days. Years. Now they were dead, most likely. I assumed the ranchers must have fought back, but they were outgunned. Now my friends were dead, and were going to be eaten.

And not even by zombies.

I shuddered at it. I began thinking about the world. My mind threatened to swim away at the extent of it. Was the whole world like this? I knew there had been outbreaks all over the planet. If us ... If the United States couldn't get it under control ... Could anyone? Our military had still been strong, even when the Second Depression worsened. Where were they now? It was like they'd just disappeared after the Collapse. Or maybe ...

Maybe they were like that kid down there ... Private Orr. Maybe they were back, wandering around, looking for ... What? Why was this happening? What lesson was there to take from it?

A fresh gust of wind blew over the hills and ... I'd never felt so alone in my life like I did at that time, in that place. My mind tried to grasp the idea that I was the last person in the world, surrounded by billions of the dead. I felt the blackness welling up and tried to breathe through it ...

I bolted upright and gasped. The fire was burned down to embers. I don't know what it was that woke me. I don't think I'd had a dream. I'd just ... Blacked out.

Then I heard it.

It followed the wind up the valley. That's what I'd thought it was at first. Just the wind, moaning up the valley. But it wasn't the wind that was moaning. It was just behind that. I couldn't tell how close they were. Still a ways off. But they were still coming. Just like they would always be.

I put my clothes on in a hurry. They were dry, but cold. I put the pack on and my muscles revolted. The pain brought me to my knees. I pushed myself up with the rifle and crowbar and started walking again. Up. Then further up. After thinking I'd reached the top two more times, I came to a network of logging roads. One looked to sweep around the mountain and head south, then east. I followed it.

It had to be late afternoon at this point and I knew I wouldn't have daylight much longer. I just had to put some distance between myself and the zombies. As soon as the road dropped down behind the hill, I realized how little light I had. The shadows were much deeper. I walked across a saddle between two peaks, then the road split. The left went up, the right down. I went left. The road cut alongside another mountain. The wind blew through the trees, causing them to shake. The whole forest moved around me, but something caught the corner of my eye. I looked across the small valley, to the ridgeline I'd come from. Just below it was the section of road I'd avoided. I squinted, not sure of what I saw. I pulled my little binoculars from the pouch on the pack strap and looked. There was a zombie ... Probably one of them that had followed me up from the river valley. An older man, wearing mechanic's coveralls. Stained dark ...

I watched it for a few minutes. It stumbled along the muddy logging road, never looking as though it knew where it was going, but never looking lost, either. It almost tripped a few times, but maintained its balance. I found myself wondering what was going on in its brain. If *anything* was going on in-

It stopped. Slowly, it turned. It looked right at me, through the binoculars. I remember thinking, *No, that's impossible*. And it *was* impossible! It had to be over a mile away, across a drainage valley. Hell, I could barely see it through the trees and I had binos! It stood for a moment, just swaying. Then it lurched forward, as though it was trying to walk through the binoculars to get at me. I just sat there, watching. There was no way it saw me. It got to the hill-side of the road ... The drop off. And it did. Tumbled right down the side like

77

a ... Shit, like a corpse. Made no move to stop itself. It bounced off a few trees before it finally wrapped itself around one, backwards. It was folded completely in half, its back snapped. An arm that had already been hanging in tatters had come off. Its low moan carried up quietly, on the wind. It struggled, slowly and in vain. It would stay there ...

Well, forever, I guess. Until it ... died.

At this point I didn't know whether I should laugh or scream in madness. I didn't do either. I put the binos away and started walking. The road climbed and curved over a small ridge. The trees thinned and I could see a taller mountain collecting the last bit of light. It didn't look that far off, but distances were deceiving in the haze. It looped over another saddle for a ways and I soon found myself standing at yet another fork in the road, at the bottom of the mountain covered in lines of trees. Literally, trees growing in perfect rows. Must have been some reclamation project by the Forest Service. I could see part of the road about halfway up, and I briefly considered just climbing for it. I started to, but knew my legs would give of if I tried. I didn't relish the thought of rolling down a wooded hill in the dark. The little sun that made it through the murky clouds had started to sink beyond the horizon. I pulled out my headlamp and ended up veering right along the road. I don't know why. I couldn't see which fork went up.

I guessed correctly. It was steeper than my legs would have liked, and by the time I reached the top ... The actual top, it was completely dark. The rain had stopped when I was still in the valley and the clouds didn't look like they wanted to drop any more. The only thing that dropped now was my pack, allowing my aching shoulders to rejoice. I gathered tinder and lit a small fire. I took my boots off, afraid to look at my feet again. They were blistered and raw. I wrapped up in my sleeping bag, not bothering with my tent. I sat by the fire, glowing and crackling in that dark night. I ate a can of beans, a can of tuna, and peaches for dessert. Canned peaches had never tasted so good.

The food settled heavily and I stared at the living coals until sleep took me.

78

I woke up in the cold darkness. The middle of the night, some time. I had to piss. Bad. The fire had burned nearly out, now just embers giving off faint light to each breath of wind. I slowly got out of my sleeping bag, pushed my feet into the cold boots and walked a few yards from camp. The night air was cold, but felt good, somehow. Maybe it was just soothing to my muscles. As I stood, gazing out into the darkness, the clouds above me opened.

There, on the raw, dark mountaintop, I saw the stars for the first time in almost 2 months. The haze parted and the heavens unfolded. With no light to detract, it was the most spectacular thing I'd ever witnessed. It suddenly didn't matter how cold I was, how tired and sore. It didn't matter that the world around me was broken. Nothing existed outside of me and that mountaintop. Not then, under those stars. I don't know how long I stood there. Just ... Awestruck. A shooting star cruised into the southwest sky, behind the Bitterroot Mountains.

It was followed by a flash on the horizon, then a low, rumbling boom.

I didn't know what it was. Not that night. I mean ... I *knew* what it was, but I didn't want to think about that. I didn't want to think that we would actually *do* that. Actually *have* to. I found out, later. And I was right. That night, when I saw it, I knew then. I played the story out in my head, feeling a sinking in my stomach ...

Los Angeles had been completely overrun. The military had tried to keep the hordes of dead contained in the city, but had been overwhelmed and suffered catastrophic losses. The surviving forces had been ordered back, and with the imminent reality of eventually facing down over 12 million zombies in southern California, the government made the choice. They nuked the city. A single, high-yield bomb.

That's what I saw that night. A shooting star, sent down from the universe to thrust me back into this horrifying new reality.

This nightmare.

I went back to the fire, started to build it back up. But I didn't want to see fire. Not after that. Not that night. I pulled my sleeping bag around me and stared to the southwest, until the real sunrise came and washed away the artificial one that had blossomed on the horizon.

Chapter 10

The haze moved back in slightly, but the sun was brighter than I'd seen in a long time. I sat for a while, just staring at the ashes of my fire. Brooding on the ashes of the world. Eventually, I packed up my belongings and went on my way again. I wasn't hungry. Just sore, tired. Dispirited. Was it really falling apart? They'd nuked a city. That's what it had to have been. Were the ... Dead going to win? The next evolutionary step ... Completely reversed from all laws of biology. How could Death become the next rank in Life? It made no sense to me.

I guess it didn't have to. This was happening, and no matter how hard I tried, I couldn't wake up.

I walked almost straight south, along the ridgeline. I knew this would eventually take me to Rock Creek. I could follow that to the next valley. All back roads until I got to Butte. The highway was far too dangerous. I squinted in the sunlight, cussing myself for not bringing a pair of sunglasses. I'd figured I wouldn't need them. I figured the haze would never break, leaving the world in perpetual gloom. The ridge eventually dropped to another logging road, this one barely discernible under the plants that had begun to reclaim it. I knew I'd barely walked a mile and already the miles from the previous days, the lack of sleep, the constant fear and sadness ... It was all catching up to me. I plodded along, my head down. Making sure each foot went in front of the other. Making sure my steps went where I placed them. I couldn't afford to trip and fall now. If I did, I knew I wouldn't get back up.

Within everyone's brain, there is a switch for survival mode. No matter how strenuous the task, or how enormous the odds are stacked against us ... At some point, everyone either gives up or flips that switch and keeps going. Most people, when asked later why they fought against such odds ... They can't really answer why. They just go. Because there's no question of not doing it. Even if certain death may be waiting at the end ... It's better to face it on our own terms than to lie down and wait for it to find us, I guess.

That day, after that first mile ... My switch flipped. It didn't immediately fill me with strength or give me a second wind. It was more subtle than that. Even if I got to Butte and it was full of zombies and everyone was dead ... I had to get there. I had to know. I realized, at that point, I would just keep on moving until my body physically shut down.

One foot. One step. Repeat. Just keep walking.

In years past, I would have gazed at the beauty around me, in awe of the Earth's power. But now ... Everything just seemed so gray. Dreary.

The haze moved back in.

I got hungry at some point and stopped for lunch. I lit a small fire and pulled the first can I felt from my pack. It was one of the cans from Safeway. No label. I opened it, spooned a little bit up, ate it.

It was dog food.

I put it in the coals of the fire until it steamed, then picked it up with a heavy leather glove. I sat on a rock, in a dismal forest, on some nameless mountaintop. And ate fucking canned dog food. I started laughing again. This time, though ... There was actual mirth behind it. It felt good to release all the built-up emotions with something besides tears. There had been too many tears. I figured there would be many more.

From my seat, I could see the tops of the Bitterroot Mountains in the distance. The tops capped with gray snow. When did the world become monotone? Was it dying, too? Were we all destined to fall, then get back up and wander the Earth? I dropped the empty can at my feet, wiped off my spoon and put it away. I walked a few yards uphill and pissed on a tree.

When I came back to my pack, I looked at my footprints in the muddy ground behind me. A little ways off, I saw something wrong with them. I went to investigate. Directly on top of my boot prints were animal tracks. Just a single set, as far as I could tell. Toes and pads. No claws.

A cat.

Shit.

Up until this point, I hadn't even thought about wildlife. I hadn't actually expected to see any. I didn't know if the zombies ate them. I'd never seen much wildlife, even on backpacking trips, so I figured they'd be hiding. Hiding like everything else. Now it struck me that if the zombies were eating animals, too, they would also have competition for food. I quickly gathered my belongings and set out, heading for another tall hill. The logging trails split here, going in wild directions. I went left and circled around the base of the mount. It dropped into a drainage and I consulted my map. It was the wrong one. The next one over would take me to Rock Creek. I climbed uphill at a pace that wouldn't completely exhaust me. I ascended the ridge. Below me was the other side of the wrong drainage. Across it was the mountain I'd need to go over to get to the correct one. A straight shot would have been ... I don't know. Just over a mile, maybe? But it was all rough timber with lots of up and down. To my right, the small mount became a ridge, leading directly to where I needed to go. Longer, but easier terrain. It was already mid-afternoon. I surmised I could reach the mountain and make a camp on the leeward side of the peak.

I picked my way along the old road and eventually pulled out my headlamp. I found a road that conveyed along the ridge. Darkness set in faster than I'd expected. The bright morning must have thrown me off. I figured I was getting close when I heard something behind me. I swung the light, hand on my revolver. Nothing.

I turned, tripped on a rock and went down face first. I caught myself, but tore a glove and abraded my hand. My right knee caught my lower body, but hit a rock. Hard.

Fuuuuuuuu ... .!

I growled in pain. Just what I needed! A hand to patch up *and* a bum knee! I was still more than 60 miles from Butte. Angry at my clumsiness, I quickened my pace up the road. A cold wind blew up the valley. I put my hood up to help shield my face. I shined my light uphill to see if the top was close. I saw a rocky knoll. I didn't know if it was the peak, but it would block the wind. I scrambled up the cold rock, favoring my knee and trying not to use my injured hand.

The wind wasn't nearly as bitter on the back side of the knob, and I swept my light over the area, looking for a good spot to camp. The wind gusted around the side of the knob, blanketing my ears with white noise. I don't know why I turned around. I had just come from that way, and hadn't intended to search for a camp behind me. Maybe it was just ... I don't know, some long-buried instinct.

A pair of eyes flashed in my light. A mountain lion was running at me full speed from about 30 yards away. It was fast and cleared the distance in a few bounds. I remember my hand sweeping the .357 from the holster at my hip. The barrel brushed my coat as I brought it up. The cat hit me in the chest with full force. It knocked the wind out of me. My head swam. I could feel myself going down backwards. The rocky ground rushing up to meet me. The revolver went off. Loud, in the night. The back of my head struck something hard and lights flashed all around my eyes. A dance of colors.

Then black.

I slowly opened my eyes. The sun shone hot white all over the sand. The clamor of the surf pounded my ears. The waves would retreat, playing music with the skittering of seashells. I sat up and gazed out at the vast expanse of deep blue ocean. The sunlight refracted off the water and exploded into millions of sparkling jewels. The sand burned my hands as I grasped handfuls of it. It was the beach in Florida I'd gone to as a kid. I looked up and down the beach. There was no one here. I turned and looked behind me.

Mom and dad were seated in beach chairs. They were both bleached skeletons. I didn't react to this, as though they'd always been skeletons. I stood and stretched. The sea breeze blew salty through my hair. I looked around for my brother. He wasn't there.

Mom, where's Andrew?

84

No reply. Her bones just sat there and grinned out at the crashing, glittering sea.

He went somewhere, huh? He went for a walk ... Should I go find him?

Sand swirled in the empty eye sockets.

Yeah, he and his boys went for a walk. I'll find them and then we can all go for a swim. How's that sound?

The skeletons sat in the chairs, still holding hands, bony fingers intertwined. They said nothing at all.

I examined the beach in both directions. Just sand and surf. I considered which direction to take when the surf behind me brought a different sound. I turned to the sea. Down by the water, lying among the seashells was a body. It was a man, older than me, dressed for work, still in his tie. He didn't look like he'd been dead for very long, but his face and neck were all torn away. A few yards up the beach, another body washed up. A woman in a jogging outfit, missing an arm. Beside her, another body washed up. Then another. Another and another ...

I stared out at the sparkling water. There were thousands of bodies floating in it. Stretching to the blue horizon. As far as I could see, bodies.

I opened my eyes and inhaled, then let out a yell. A mountain lion was staring me in the face, its jaws locked in a snarl. I didn't understand why it hadn't eaten me, why instead it had decided to sleep on top of me ... There was something wrong with it. One of its eyes was cocked at an odd angle. Its body was slightly warm. My right hand was trapped under its powerful, limp neck. I worked it free and saw it still clutched the revolver. Both were caked in dried blood. I pushed at the cat and rolled it off of me. The strain shot a fiery jolt through my ribs as the events of the night before flooded back to me.

There was no beach. Just a howling wind and a prowling cat. I looked down at the dead lion and saw I'd shot a large chunk out of the side of its neck. It must have bled out shortly after it had knocked me unconscious. I worked

85

my way out of my pack and sat up. I hoped my ribs were just bruised and not broken. I brushed the blood off the metal of my gun and holstered it. My left hand was still slashed and peppered with tiny bits of gravel. My knee still ached. I looked around.

The rocky knob was just above me, at the top of the hill. Below me was the drainage that would take me to Rock Creek. The sun was up, and I couldn't tell how high it was. I knew I had to get going, but I lay back against my pack and stared up at the hazy sky. It had been so blue in that dream. Such a beautiful blue. As blue as the ocean. My hand brushed the butt of my revolver and I briefly wondered if I could get back there.

Just ... Wake up.

I shook the thought away and stood. I checked to make sure my rifle was okay. The stock had been scuffed, but the sights were okay, and that's all that mattered. I worked on digging the larger pieces of gravel from my hand, then wrapped a bandage around it. I was hungry and wondered if I could eat the lion. I pulled out my knife, then realized I had absolutely no idea how to skin or dress an animal. I fished a can of Spaghetti-Os out of my pack and ate it cold. I contemplated the dead cat. Its frozen snarl and dead eyes. Another set to add to the ones all walking around out there.

Thunder rumbled across the sky as a heavy sadness settled over me. A gray, ashen rain began to fall. I pulled my collar up and readjusted the slashed rain cover on my pack, not that it would do much good now. I finished my food, ate some painkillers then got to my feet. At first I was afraid that my knee wouldn't support weight as I pulled the pack on. It threatened to give out, but I willed it to stand with as much energy as I could part with. I clipped the waistbelt of the pack, then the chest strap. I immediately unclipped it. I could barely breathe with it on.

I started down the mountain, into the drainage. The rain picked up and soon there were muddy little creeks rushing down the slope. I fought to keep my footing and took my rifle off to use it as a walking stick. I worked my way down to a washed out old logging road. The old roads spread in all directions, following hillsides and ridgelines. The wind whipped firm and cold, taking the rain sideways. I was afraid to put my hood up again.

I wanted to waste no time getting down, not bothering with the roads. I side-stepped and slid my way down the small valley and found the remains of another logging trail, now a gray and muddy creek. I stumbled blindly over rocks and fallen trees. The water soaked into my boots, but I didn't care. I just wanted to get down to Rock Creek and ... Then what? I had no idea, but I just wanted to get away from the mountaintop and the dead cat. The drainage valley met another and widened. There were small ponds here. Next to the largest one was an odd, horseshoe-shaped building. It looked empty. I kept walking ... Limping, I guess.

The light was beginning to fade in the western sky when I reached the mouth of the road. The braids of Rock Creek spread out below me. In better days, there would be anglers down there. Now, the only thing that moved was the bushes and water as the rain bombarded the deadened land. The road went left and paralleled the top of a bluff. Below me, through the trees, I could make out a cabin. There was smoke curling from the chimney. I figured this road would lead me to one of the only bridges to cross the creek. The dim light was already weakening. Darkness would fill the valley soon. The road passed over the cabin and switchbacked down to the creek. I stayed low as it approached the cabin and I tried to stay as low as possible. Something moved through the trees between the cabin and I, then howled.

I could just make out the form of a wolf as it bounded through the deepening shadows.

No ... Not now ...

I lazily reached for my holster, but suddenly my hand didn't want to move. It brushed the wood grip, but wouldn't close on it. Suddenly, I fell to my knees. My pack might as well have weighed a thousand pounds. I lay to one side, waiting for the wolf to finish the job. I closed my eyes, anticipating the hot clamp of teeth around my throat at any moment.

It didn't come.

I heard voices. A woman.

"Is it one of them? John?"

I opened my eyes. The world was wet and sideways. Through blurred vision, I could make out a pair of legs and boots walking toward me. A man. Holding a military rifle.

"I don't know, Lauren. Stay back. Call the dogs."

"Jackson! Avalon! Get back!"

I could see the closest wolf turn around and head towards the woman's voice. The man towered over me. I squinted up at him.

"No, he's alive! Boy ... You been bit?"

I ...

My voice was a hoarse rasp.

Walked ... Long ... Go to ... Butte ...

Blackness crept around my vision and consumed me.

Chapter 11

My ears came to first. I heard the distant crackling of fire. Then the smell of woodsmoke drifted into my nose. I opened my eyes into a squint. I could make out a wood roof supported by timber beams. It was a cabin ... It was the one my family had gone to the summer I was 10. I could smell coffee and knew it was early. My dad would be going fishing and would make me get up soon, too. I didn't open my eyes or he'd make me get up now. I wanted to sleep some more. I shut my eyes tight and listened to the crackling of the fire. I pulled my hands from beneath the pillow and grabbed at the blanket, rolling over ... My hands didn't move below my head. I couldn't reach the blanket.

I was tied to the bed. Nylon rope, like climbers use. Hands and feet.

I wasn't 10, it wasn't that cabin ... And my parents weren't here. I opened my eyes, turned my head. I looked at the two people seated at the table. He had a beard and brown and silver hair pulled back in a ponytail. She had dark hair peppered with gray tucked under a fleece hat. They looked at me. The man spoke first.

"You've been out for a while."

I was exhausted.

"You weren't bit."

No ... I fell.

"The claw marks?"

I ...

I could now feel the bandage on the left side of my neck.

I got attacked by a mountain lion. I killed it ... Barely.

The two traded a look, then both turned to me again.

"Where are you coming from?"

Missoula. I'm trying to get to Butte.

The woman's eyes darted over at the man when I said that.

"Sorry to tie you up ..." The man got up and walked over to the bed. He untied my wrists and my feet. My hands had been asleep and now burned with fiery needles as blood rushed back in. " ... But we couldn't be too careful. When you blacked out, we feared the worst. But you didn't take on a fever, and we couldn't see your blood."

My ... Blood?

"When a person gets infected, the blood at the wound turns black. You can see it as it works its way up the veins, toward the heart. It looks like something out of a horror movie ... It fades when they reanimate, but it's creepy as hell while they die."

I sat up.

You've dealt with someone who got bit?

He and his wife shared another look.

"My name is John Reid. This is my wife Lauren. That's Jackson and Ava." He pointed to the "wolves", a pair of Malamutes. "We're from Seeley Lake. We're headed to Butte, as well. We have family there and the last contact we had with them ... They said there was a small unit of soldiers that hadn't left when the government ordered the pull-back."

The government ordered the Army to leave? Why? Where did they go?

"It's bad out there ... Ummmm ..."

Oh, sorry .... I'm Nick ... Nick Jerritt.

"Nick, it's bad out there. We hunkered down at our place in Seeley Lake when everything went to shit, but even there, people started getting weird. People that had been our neighbors. One of our good friends, Sam ... He was shot by a neighbor named Arnold. They got into a fight over a tank of propane. Arnold pulled out a pistol and shot Sam ... We'd all lived next to each other for 15 years ... The Army pulled back when the towns started getting overrun and the highways plugged up with survivors. There was an aid station in Billings, but ... We're not sure. No one knows where they went. The whole Midwest, Nick ... The east coast ... It's all gone. All those people ..."

John stared off for a second. Lauren spoke up.

"You're the first person we've seen in over two weeks. We were so glad you haven't been bit. We have some breakfast here. Can I get you anything?"

Just some water, please. The military ... The government is ... Gone?

"So far as we know." Lauren handed me a glass of water.

"We saw some helicopters about a week ago and we heard a jet a couple days back." John sipped at his coffee.

We heard that ... Me and my friends, I mean.

"Friends? Where are they?"

They ... Stayed with a camp of people we'd come across at Deer Creek.

I pointed west.

They were headed for Great Falls. They ... I'm pretty sure they're dead. There are refugees beginning to filter up from the south. They were from California. They have guns, a bulldozer. They're eating people.

"Shit." John gave Lauren a look that everything but said aloud 'I told you so'.

There were also bandits on the highway. They almost got me a couple days back.

I had to stop and think if that was even right. How many days now? I didn't know anymore.

"We came across a few. That's why we came down Rock Creek." John had a look of finality when he said that. I could see two rifles- AR-15s- leaning on the table. He didn't elaborate. He didn't have to.

Can I get some of that coffee?

John poured some into a tin mug and handed it to me. It warmed me immediately.

"What's in Butte for you?"

Family. My brother. My parents lived there, but I think they're dead now.

The matter-of-fact way I said this took John and Lauren by surprise.

91

"How do you know?"

I've been having ... Dreams. My brother is still alive, though. I have to just get someplace familiar, with people I know ... Even if I die there.

John smirked and shared another look with Lauren.

"We've been thinking much the same thing."

The aroma of the food suddenly hit me as I drank the coffee. I smelled bacon. Hunger hit me in the stomach. Food was served and we ate in silence, just glad to be able to share a meal with other people. Scraps were tossed to the dogs and the world seemed like it was in order.

"I hope your family is okay, Nick." John stirred eggs around on his plate. "The infection ... We had a son ... About your age ..."

Lauren gave him an admonishing look.

We ate in silence. It started snowing outside. Huge, wet flakes. Soon, the road was covered, then the truck.

It snowed for five days. It just kept piling up. John would look worriedly out the window, then glance at Lauren. After a while, I was included in the looks, too. We hunkered down inside, only going out to answer the call of nature, and let the dogs do the same. We talked for those five days, getting to know each other well. They obviously needed human contact as much as I did.

John and Lauren had moved around overseas. They'd been to scores of countries, and every continent. As pragmatic as Lauren seemed, she'd still brought a photo album. She showed me pictures of them hiking in South America, and even standing in front of the South Pole in Antarctica. In lots of the photos, especially the mountaineering ones, there was the same young man throughout. I was too polite to ask who he was, but Lauren must have sensed that.

"That's our son Derek. He ... Was probably a few years older than you. We lost him when we fled Seeley Lake. There was a traffic jam, close to the highway. We stopped to see what was going on ... If anyone needed help.

92

Derek was always such a helpful kid. One of those things came from out of nowhere … From around a camper ... It grabbed onto Derek ...”

John sat beside her and put his hand on her shoulder. She lay her head against his shoulder and said no more.

“The infection ... Or whatever it is, seems to work pretty fast. It only took about seven hours. We stayed where we were, trying to sterilize the wound. He was feverish. His body was racked with pain and his veins ... They were black. He begged us not to leave him ... Of course we wouldn't. He died thirteen days ago.” John looked sadly out the window. From my seat, I could barely make out a marker sticking out of the snow. “After he died ... He came back. It didn't take very long. Just a few minutes ...There's nothing left of who they were. Just some ... Instinct. Some part of the brain. He attacked me ...” He sighed.

Do you think it's the end of the world?

They both looked at me, as if they hadn't been expecting that question.

“I ... Don't know, Nick ... We've talked about that possibility. We're not sure what to think. Not anymore. The world stopped making sense a few weeks ago. Lauren and I figured we would just drive ourselves crazy if we tried to speculate any reason behind all of this. So, we buried our son ... But we haven't buried ourselves.” The pained expressions on their faces cut into me. I nodded.

I guess that's all we can do ... We found some bodies, on the way out of Missoula. They'd ... Just given up. At the time, I remember thinking that maybe it wasn't a bad idea, you know? That maybe they had been right to opt out. But now I realize that you guys are right. The world right outside that door is ... Insane. On my way here, I just began to understand the true implication of what's happening. I mean, it was always a joke, right? My buddies and I would talk about it. Hell, it was all over popular culture. But now ... Now that it's actually happening ... I don't think anyone was actually ready for it. Where the hell is the military? Did this all happen so fast that there was nothing that could be done? I saw cars down on the road ... People had taken their shit with them. TVs, appliances ... Like they were just leaving

93

for the weekend ... But, they're all dead, aren't they?

I shut up then. I didn't know what I was talking about, what else to say.

"I suppose they are, Nick. But we're not."

When it stopped snowing, there was more than two feet of heavy snow. We weren't going anywhere.

We were, for all intents and purposes, trapped in that cabin for a month. Probably a few days over, even. I wasn't surprised to learn that John and Lauren were bowhunters. They'd each brought one, and John took me hunting after the first snowstorm. At first, I thought it was because they didn't trust me. That I'd try to steal the truck or something. As soon as I realized that was an absurd idea, I understood John's intention. He was teaching me skills I'd probably need to know. To hunt, to fish. To fight.

To survive. To keep living.

There were a few more, smaller storms, near the middle of the month. Sometimes we didn't see any animals at all. One morning, we stepped out the cabin door. The whole world seemed quiet, like the snow had blanketed all sound along with the land. Our breaths hung for a moment in the air, but faded quickly. It was warming up again.

"Winter will be here, soon. Should be, already ... Strange weather these days."

I nodded. We put on the snowshoes John and Lauren had brought and set out up the road I'd come down a few weeks before. John had taught me how to walk silently, even in snow. We slowly crept through the white forest, arrows set but not drawn. We trudged up the drainage I'd come down after my encounter with the lion. After a ways, we both heard a branch break. My heart started racing. I turned, hoping it wasn't a zombie.

It was an elk. A mid-sized female. I looked at John. He gave me a slight nod. I drew the bowstring back to my cheek. Until now, I'd only made

94

one shot at an animal. John had made every kill.

I released my breath, then the arrow. It thwapped off the string and sang through the air. It caught the elk just behind her front leg. She grunted, then fell. I began to walk up, but John held up and arm. We stood there, silent and motionless for a long time. The sun started to disappear behind the mountains. It was getting cold. Finally, John took a step forward. The snow crunched beneath him. I followed.

When we reached the elk, she was still breathing, but it was short and raspy. Her tongue was hanging out to one side. I knelt down and took out my knife. I looked into her eyes. It was so different than looking into those of a zombie. These eyes, though dying, were still vibrant. I could tell they belonged to a living, breathing creature. I saw her life begin to fade. I immediately felt bad about taking her life. I thought back to the man I'd shot, high up in that dorm room in Missoula. I wondered if I'd feel this same way, had I been able to look him in the eyes.

I plunged the knife into the elk's heart. The living eyes went dead. Just like a zombie's.

We dressed her out with minimal words, then each took a portion, strapped it to our packs and headed back toward the cabin. By the time we made it down, it was almost dark. We walked down the hill above the cabin when John stopped me. He was looking across the river, to the road along Rock Creek. There were dark shapes slowly lumbering north. At first, I didn't see what they were. I squinted, trying to get my eyes to adjust faster to the twilight.

They were grizzly bears. There must have been 11 or 12 of them. They didn't see us. They slowly marched through the silent woods until they vanished behind some trees.

They don't ... Normally travel together.

"No, they don't. Even the animals are doing what they can to survive. Life will find a way through anything. Even this."

We walked back to the cabin. After the animal was dressed, we ate heartily. Then, John stood and pulled his knife from his sheath. I did the same.

"Alright, Nick, like we were talking about last night, it's not easy to get a knife through a skull ..."

Chapter 12

The weather warmed, melting the majority of the snow rapidly. One week after the last, small storm and the road looked passable for the truck.

At least we hoped so.

I helped John and Lauren pack their things into their truck, an older Ford diesel. John pulled out a map and spread it out on the table. He traced Rock Creek south with his finger.

"It's about 50 miles until we reach the junction with Highway 38. Then up over the top at Georgetown Lake and through Anaconda. That will probably be the trickiest part. After that, depending on the condition of the highway, it's a straight shot to Butte."

For the first time since ... I couldn't even remember, but I felt a welling of excitement rise in my stomach. In just a few hours' drive, I'd be in Butte. I wouldn't have to walk after all. It was so close.

Ready when you are, John.

We did one last sweep to make sure nothing had been forgotten, then went out to the truck. A gentle, misty rain was falling. Lauren had already started it, the engine rumbling. The dogs were in the bed. I climbed into the backseat. My .30-06 lay across the backseat. The mud road went north, crossed the creek, then joined the main road. This section was paved. The truck roared along the wet asphalt. Lauren opened up the throttle, as most of the road was straight. Houses flashed by through trees, but I didn't see anything. No people. No animals. No zombies.

Fields opened on the sides. In one, to the right ... An entire herd of cattle. Dead. Their bloated bodies spread out through the grass. There was a ranch across the road. It looked abandoned. There were patches of dirty snow everywhere. Up ahead were more houses. I saw a few zombies wandering around. They turned at the sound of the truck, then disappeared behind trees.

"Hold on." Lauren hit the gas. Ahead, in the road, a zombie. A younger boy. The truck's brush guard hit it in the upper torso and its body disappeared underneath with a wet thud. His ... Its face, contorted in a sort of feral rage ... That will be burned into my mind forever. Snarling as it was crushed. Never giving up, even at the end. Even as its ribs were compressed, its head opened under the tires.

They would never give up.

I took a deep breath. John must have heard it.

"You okay back there, Nick?"

Yeah ... Yeah, I just ... I don't know if I'll ever get used to it, you know?

"No ... I don't imagine any of us will." He reached over and squeezed Lauren's shoulder. "But, it can't last forever. They have to stop at some point."

I hope so.

The road continued straight, past more fields. I saw the scorched tail of a plane, surrounded by wreckage. The Delta logo was still visible. I could hear Lauren swear under her breath.

The road became gravel as it entered a canyon. It took on a serpentine shape, which slowed us down. There was no sign of life here. Not so much as a squirrel. The road curved along the creek below as it rushed towards the sea. *At least the water could escape*, I thought, *at least it can get away from all of this ... Maybe even find a place that's still okay out there.*

I thought about the plane. Maybe they had run out of fuel. Maybe there had been an infected on board ... Who knows? Whatever happened, those people found their last destination in a small valley in western Montana. I thought of Missoula. I thought ahead, to Butte. I couldn't let my mind stray like this. If I did ... It would wander away, like a zombie. I knew it wouldn't come back.

The creek below was turbulent. Whitewater blasted over the top of sunken rocks. I watched it as the truck bounced down the road. I found solace in the water. It mirrored the upheaval in my mind. A restless, kindred spirit.

Ahead, a bridge had spanned the creek. It had been knocked down, most likely to keep intruders out. The sign said "Welcome Creek". It didn't feel welcoming at all. Further on, there were a few more houses. The whole canyon felt solitary. Like we were the only people there. I looked back at the dogs. They stood on the sides of the bed, ears blowing back, tongues dangling from their mouths. Not a care in the world. It must have been so nice.

After a while, the canyon began to open. The hills on either side got lower. There was no snow left on this side. We crossed a bridge over the creek and the canyon abruptly opened into a large valley. The fields were brown and gray, as though they'd never grown anything at all. The road curved right.

"Oh, fuck."

I looked out through the windshield. Just over a hundred yards ahead was a small bed and breakfast and out in the road ... About 20 zombies. There didn't seem to be any reason they were blocking the road until they turned and staggered at the truck. A cow carcass lay in the middle of the muddy way, torn apart by the small swarm. Its blood formed a puddle. Most of the zombies were covered, as though they'd bathed in it. One of them still clutched a hoofed leg.

"Nick, get those dogs in here!"

I unlatched the rear window and called the dogs. They looked at me, but didn't move. I was still a stranger to them.

"Jackson, Ava!" John let out a high-pitched whistle.

The dogs piled in through the rear window. I closed and latched it. Ava sat halfway on me and licked my face. I ran my fingers through her wet fur.

"We good? Okay, let's go." Lauren put the truck in gear and stepped on the gas. It launched forward and picked up speed. We neared the group of zombies and the closest one, a man in a torn, bloody shirt put a hand up, as though ordering us to stop. The truck plowed straight over the top of him. We pushed our way through the swarm. I could hear the slushy crunch as zombies were pulverized beneath the wheels. I held onto Ava. The zombies that didn't get run over pounded on the sides of the truck, their hands leaving bloody streaks down the windows. It seemed like it took us an hour to drive through the reanimated bodies, but in reality I knew it was only a few seconds. I looked back and saw the remaining zombies stumbling and falling in the gut pile that now stretched down the road. I felt sick. Ava licked my face.

I didn't even realize my eyes were clenched shut until I felt the truck slow, then turn. The familiar feel of asphalt under the gory tires. We'd reached Highway 38, which would take us by Georgetown Lake, then straight into Anaconda. My heart fluttered again. We'd be there in less than two hours ... On a normal drive.

There were a few cars, scattered and abandoned along the road. Nothing that blocked our progress. The landscape stretched out before us, a series of low hills stretching up into mountains. On the other side of those mountains ... Home. Lauren gunned the throttle for all it was worth and at the junction of Highways 38 and 1, pulled over.

"Just need to put some fuel in. Feel free to get out, stretch, piss, whatever you have to do."

The dogs ran free. It felt good to stretch. I walked around the side of the truck. In the middle of the highway, a Suburban had hit a police car. Both had burned. I could make out a number of skeletons in both cars. I walked over and looked into the Suburban. It looked like a whole family. The remains in the back were small ...

"Nick, are you ready to go?"

John's voice startled me and I jumped, then felt embarrassment warming my face.

Yeah. Let's go.

I turned and walked away from the wreck.

The road climbed up Flint Creek Pass and topped out at Georgetown's dam. As we crested the last portion of the hill ... A trailer blocked the road. It wasn't crashed ... It had deliberately been placed there. Lauren slammed on the brakes.

"What the hell?!"

As the truck screeched to a halt, a group of people, men and women, emerged from behind the trailer. They all wore what looked to be simple, plain-colored robes. Crosses hung around their necks. They all carried rifles. A tall man pointed his directly at the windshield. Another came to the driver's side window. Lauren rolled it down.

"Listen, we're just passing through. We don't mean you any-"

"We know." The man had a serene voice and calm demeanor. "We've been expecting you."

Shock registered on all of our faces.

"You've been ... Expecting us?" John sounded incredulous.

"Of course. He told us you were coming. He is never wrong."

"He? Who is he?"

"Why, our lord God who art in heaven. Follow us, please. You're just in time for afternoon worship."

The people on foot retreated and two ATVs zipped around from the side of the trailer. One of the drivers motioned for us to follow. Lauren sighed and put the truck in gear. I met John's eyes in the rearview mirror. He looked uneasy.

Shit.

Chapter 13

We sped down the highway, following the ATVs. The lake spread out to the right, matte gray reaching to the mountains on the other shore. The ATVs turned off the main road and headed north. A building here. It was a restaurant, once. Now it looked like a mess hall. There were pickup trucks and ATVs parked outside. We passed it, when the ATVs leading us stopped. One of them turned and waved us into the driveway of a small cabin. He pulled in behind us, then walked to the truck. I heard Jackson growl at him. He tried to ignore it.

"This is your home. Please, make yourselves comfortable here. Reverend Gaines will be down to talk to you shortly."

A dark SUV crept up the road behind us. The window rolled down. I could see a man with a beard, wearing a cowboy hat.

"Sheriff! Our flock has increased!" The man from the ATV waved to him. He merely nodded, almost imperceptibly, then drove off. "That's Sheriff McPherson. It's sad that we need a man to enforce Earthly laws until the will of the living God is received, but ... That's the way of this world. Washed in sin." He shot Lauren and John a conspiratorial smile. "Let one of the ushers know if you need anything. Worship is at 7:30, at the chapel." He pointed up the hill. "A bus will pick you up. We expect to see you there."

He crossed himself, then walked back to his ATV and drove away.

John turned to Lauren.

"Well ... Goddamn it." He chuckled slightly, then turned to me. "Lauren and I had discussed the possibility of something like this. We knew these kind of people were out there ... We heard stories of a cult on Flathead Lake, by Kalispell. I didn't expect it here, though. I guess we can unpack some stuff, then wait for the 'reverend'."

We got out, stretched, then called the dogs down. John started grabbing for the guns, but I stopped him. I don't know how I saw it ... A slight glint, just up the hill. I shook my head delicately. There was someone up there, watching us with binoculars.

Leave them for now. Hide them. We're probably going to need them later.

John followed my eyes up the hill, nodded just as slightly and covered the rifles with a blanket and odd items. I stealthily pulled the revolver off my belt and pushed it into my pack. We carried a few things in, then John and I stepped out on the porch. I pulled the pack of cigarettes from my pocket and offered him one.

"No, thanks. I quit years- Ah, hell, give me one. Cancer is probably the least of my worries anymore."

We lit the cigarettes and smoked them, gazing out at the lake. It had been so blue, in summers past.

I don't like this ... These kind of people. If they truly think it's the end and that their god willed it ... They can be dangerous. As dangerous as the dead.

"If they wanted to kill us, they could have just ambushed us. Maybe they're one of those creeped-out suicide cults. Remember those? Maybe they want us to journey with them in their spaceship or whatever."

I laughed at this. It felt good to be able to laugh with another living, breathing human.

You have a point. What do you suggest?

"See what they want. Get a feel for the place. The opportunity to leave will present itself."

I nodded and took a drag off my cigarette.

I suppose we don't have much of a choice.

We watched the last of the light disappear across the lake.

Inside, Lauren had lit a fire and warmed up some food. We ate and discussed different plans. We agreed to look around tomorrow, get our bearings and leave at the first sign of trouble. Soon, there was a knock at the door. John opened it. An older man with long white hair and a white beard stood there. He wore small glasses, black robes and a silver cross around his neck.

"Blessings. I am Reverend Joseph Gaines. May I come in?"

John motioned him in. He sat as we introduced ourselves.

"We at the Church of the Living God are so happy that you've come this day and devoted to our flock. When our lord returns to grant us ascension into his kingdom, his love will smile upon you."

"Actually ..." John hesitated slightly. "We're just passing through. The three of us are trying to get to Butte."

The reverend's face changed, almost unnoticeably, but it was there. His interest withdrew and his eyes glassed over.

"Butte? Why there? That's Satan's town. The lord's dead walk and the devil's followers kill the righteous!" Gaines' eyes flashed, but he immediately regained his composure. "Regardless, we invite you to savor God's hospitality. You may stay as long as you like, even until the day of judgment."

An engine clattered down the road and stopped. Gaines looked out the window.

"That's the bus that will take us to the Chapel for evening worship.. Please, follow me." He turned toward the door, but he stopped, his shoulders visibly tensed and he spun back around. "You good people do believe in God, don't you?"

John presented a garish smile.

"Yeah, of course we do."

"Good. The path of the righteous grows more arduous every day."

With that, Reverend Gaines stepped out the door and walked away, toward the bus. John, Lauren and I looked at one another, shrugged and followed him.

It was an old school bus, still painted a faded blue from its Job Corps days. Golden crosses had been painted on both sides, with flowing script proclaiming "Church of the Living God". We took our seats and the bus lumbered down the road, picking up several more people along the way. There were whole families with kids. They all wore robes. A few people were still

104

dressed in normal clothing. They looked as nervous as I felt. The bus climbed up a hill, trees and darkness on the side. Suddenly, through the trees up the mountain, I could make out lights. The bus turned into a parking lot filled with trucks and ATVs and I saw what the lights were from. Running along the path leading into the stone chapel were crosses. Six on the sides, one hanging over the entrance. Torches were set beneath them, casting an eerie glow on each cross. The bus stopped, the doors opened and we all shuffled off.

A line of people extended to the walkway under the crosses, entering the chapel. Over the low murmur of voices and crackling flames ahead, I heard a singing choir. We moved into the light from the torches when Lauren let out a sharp gasp. I looked at her, then followed her eyes up.

Nailed ... No, crucified on each cross was a zombie. They were still ... Alive ... Moving around, their jaws gnashing as we walked underneath. Their moans reached down to me, causing me to shudder. I could feel their dead, cloudy eyes watching me as we entered the chapel. Their arms and feet were held in with multiple nails and I saw why right away. The zombies were struggling against the nails and tearing their own limbs apart as they did so. One zombie's arm was torn in half from the ulna and radius all the way through its hand. It looked like a flipper, with bone and flesh hanging off. It had three nails holding its elbow up and even that was starting to come apart.

I heard John mutter under his breath. Inside, the pews had been arranged in a semi-circle around a pulpit. Another zombie was crucified behind it. Candles shed a ghostly light. Shadows danced. We took a seat near the back. Near the door.

A low murmur of voices filled the cavernous room. In the dim light, I could see some of the people in robes pointing at us and whispering to each other. I tried to brush aside the attention. I didn't like it. After a few minutes, Reverend Gaines took the pulpit. He now wore a dark red vestment over his robes. The chapel quieted down.

"Blessings from the Living God, brothers and sisters, children of the lion and the lamb."

The gathered people spoke in unison. It chilled me to the bone.

"Praise be unto you, son of Christ. Lord of the living, lord of the dead."

"We have been called to by God during these final days. Called to spread his word as his creation is judged by his own love."

All around us: "Yes, lord" and "Amen".

"The word of God is long written." Gaines' hand clutched a bible. "Revelations tells us this would happen." He opened the bible, adjusted his glasses and read: "'Then I saw a great white throne and him who was seated on it. The earth and the heavens fled from his presence, and there was no place for them. And I saw the dead, great and small, standing before the throne, and books were opened.'"

He looked out over the crowd.

"The dead have returned for the final judgment. And they seek to take us with them, as we all must be dead to be judged. The final plague. So it is written."

He read again.

"'Another book was opened, which is the book of life. The dead were judged according to what they had done as recorded in the books. The sea gave up the dead that were in it, and death and Hades gave up the dead that were in them, and each person was judged according to what they had done.'

"And what have we done, brothers and sisters? We have all sinned. Yea, we have sinned, but we didn't reap the wrath of God! Nay, it was those who lay with those of the same sex! It was those who lay with those of a different color! It was those who killed our babies and turned away from God's love, instead taking the devil's refuge in the form of drink and drugs!"

From around the chapel came affirmations. People had their hands in the air, as though trying to reach to their god.

"Our children have chosen television over the glory of God! The internet over salvation! Instead of reading the good book," He slammed his hand down on the bible, "They fill their heads with violent comic books! The non-believers have forsaken God's eternal love and spat in his face!

"The politicians worshiped money and left the rest to worship all matter of false idols! Well God heard, folks! He saw! And now he's here to reclaim the souls of his flock and all else will be damned! Judgment is among us!"

He cast his eyes at the bible again.

"'Then death and Hades were thrown into the lake of fire. The lake of fire is the second death. Anyone whose name was not found written in the book of life was thrown into the lake of fire.'"

The candles pulsed and outside, flames crackled.

"This is only the beginning, brothers and sisters! The dead have risen and soon, the lord will return for us. Let us pray for the souls of the sinners who brought this destruction upon us. Let us pray for God's forgiveness of our own weaknesses and pledge our loyalty to his fight against Satan's army."

Most of the people in the chapel bowed their heads. I pretended to, at first. When everyone began to pray in unison, I looked around. Some had fallen to their knees, obviously crying. I saw a woman clutching a bible closer than her own child. I saw ... A blonde girl, bowed halfway over, but looking directly at me. She couldn't have been older than 16. I gave her a small smile. She smiled back and I looked away. I swore under my breath. John gave me a knowing look.

"Praise be to the living God. Amen."

The crowd stirred, stood and headed back out of the chapel. We slipped out ahead of the main crowd. We headed for the bus, walking back underneath the zombies on their crosses. Most of them snapped their teeth at us, but one didn't. It just stared at me as I passed it. Most of its face was eaten away, giving it the illusion of a smile. We returned to the bus. Reverend Gaines wasn't far behind, speaking with a group of parishioners. The same group that had been talking about us. The young girl was with them. She stared at me. I got uncomfortable and stepped around the front of the bus. I pulled a cigarette out of the pack and reached for my lighter.

"We'll ask that you don't smoke on sacred ground."

It was the same man that had escorted us to the cabin that afternoon.

Oh, yeah. Sorry.

I put the pack away.

"Did you enjoy the service?"

I ... It was good. Very ... Fulfilling.

"Nothing is more fulfilling than being in the service of God."

He gave me a smile, then walked away. I shook my head in bewilderment. By now, I thought I wouldn't be surprised by anything, but I had been proven wrong. Vastly wrong. I went to join John and Lauren as the bus began to load ... The blonde girl, stood in front of me.

Shit.

"Hi!"

Hi.

"I'm Stacy. Sister Stacy." She held out her hand. I gave it a quick shake.

Nick.

I tried to let go, but her hand gripped mine. I twisted it out of her grip.

"Are you coming to dinner, Nick?"

No. We ate already.

A look of disappointment clouded her face.

"Oh ... Well, a group of us is going to go for a walk around the lake tomorrow. The youth leader is going to tell us some tales from the bible."

Yeah ...

"They want us to have chaperones when we do that ... Older chaperones." She bit at her lower lip.

I'll ... See what Reverend Gaines wants us to do.

"Of course. Good night, Nick." She smiled at me, then turned and joined who I assumed were her parents.

I hurried back to John and Lauren. They were talking with Gaines.

"I understand you're tired. Please, join us for breakfast. We start

108

serving at 7:00."

"We will. Thank you, reverend." John shook his hand. Gaines walked away. John turned to me, grinning.

"Your little girlfriend find you?"

Goddamn it.

"Whoa. Don't let the holy-rollers hear you say that. They might crucify you up there with the zombies."

I couldn't help but chuckle.

They'll have to get up pretty early in the morn-

I yawned, wide. I didn't realize how tired I was. John and Lauren looked beat, too. We got on the bus. I slipped between the waking and dreaming worlds on the ride down. I saw my parents. I saw zombies, crucified. Hordes of them taking their revenge on humanity. Our own past, eating us.

I jerked awake as John gently shook my shoulder.

"We're here."

I sleepily stumbled into the cabin and fell into one of the two beds.

"Well, Nick. Looks like we find ourselves in some crazy company."

Yeah ... they're certifiably insane. And ...

I yawned again.

...That makes them dangerous

"I know all too well. Good night, Nick."

Night John, Lauren.

I rolled over as they blew out the candles. The dogs snored gently on the floor, but I suddenly couldn't sleep.

I lay there, thinking of a man up on the hill, watching us through binoculars.

I thought of the crucified dead.

Chapter 14

Morning brought no rain, but it was cold. A freezing fog drifted off the lake, masking trees in gray frost. It was barely light out when John gently shook my shoulder. I hadn't noticed his tattoo before. An eagle, globe and anchor on his arm, the word "Recon" underneath.

"Nick, do you want to join us for breakfast?"

I considered sleeping some more, but suddenly remembered where we were.

Yeah, I'll get up.

I stood and stretched. My body was still sore, but not as bad as in days past.

I dressed. Lauren took the dogs out for a short run.

Your tattoo ... You were in the Marines?

John glanced at the ink and gave a humble smile. He'd mentioned military service back at the cabin at Rock Creek, but had never really gone into it.

"Yeah. The Corps. A while ago ..."

Did you ... See any action?

"I got around. Saw the world. Panama, Nigeria, Afghanistan. Some other places ..."

I could tell by his tone that he didn't want to talk about it.

Oh. Sorry.

He looked up and smiled wide this time.

"It's cool, Nick. Just a younger me, looking for adventure."

Looks like you get another one.

I smirked.

"Yeah, if I'd known, I would have waited a little while."

I was also meaning to ask you ... Why did you and Lauren trust me so fast? I mean, once you knew I wasn't bitten, you just let me travel with you. How did you know I wasn't some crazy like ...?

"Like these people?"

I laughed.

Yeah.

"I didn't. Honestly, Nick, Lauren and I discussed killing you while you were out. But you didn't seem dangerous and ... Hell, we were starving for any sort of human contact. After everything ... We just wanted someone to talk to. To remind us of how it used to be. Even with the two of us and the dogs ... It gets lonely on the road."

It does ... Thanks for helping me out. I don't think I would have made it even this far without you guys.

"No thanks needed. It's the living versus the dead now. We have to band together. In the Marines, they taught us to never give up, even if you know you're going to lose. 'Do not go gently into that good night'."

Dylan Thomas. Though wise men at their end know dark is right. Do you ... Do you think we'll wake up one of these mornings and find out this was all just a dream?

"Maybe. But, whether we do or not, you can't afford to start thinking like that. I knew guys that did, back then ... It never turns out good. The way I see it is, here we are. Best to just keep going until the end."

That's a good philosophy. I don't suppose the end is here, at Georgetown ...

John laughed softly.

"No. Definitely not."

We turned as Lauren let the dogs in and walked into the cabin.

"It appears the lunatics are starting to serve breakfast. Shall we stroll down?"

"Let's do it." John and I got to our feet. He abruptly stuck out his hand. I shook it. "Nick, it's good to have you on board. It looks like I'm building up a good platoon here."

Lauren rolled her eyes.

"So much testosterone."

We stepped off the porch and walked toward the "mess hall".

"Boys?"

We looked at Lauren.

"Don't drink the Kool-Aid."

She winked.

We walked into a large room, part of an obviously hastily-built extension onto the existing restaurant. It was made of plywood and I could see light through various cracks. Two large, propane heaters warmed the hall. We stepped into line behind a group of people about my age. One of the girls turned to us and smiled.

"May the blessings of the living God surround you this morning."

"And unto you, good sister." John caught the corner of my eye and winked. I had to bite my tongue to stifle a laugh. I don't know why I felt so good. A few days earlier, I didn't think I would ever laugh again. Maybe it was my new-found friends, maybe it was the proximity to Butte ... I don't know. There was just a feeling that the world would be okay. That the Army would come rolling up over the hill at any moment and turn things back to the way they were.

We received plates loaded with eggs, potatoes and bacon. There was even orange juice. We took seats by a wall. I could see John scanning the room. I did the same, and didn't see the couple from worship last night. The ones who wore regular clothes, like us. More survivors, I'd assumed. I wondered where they were when a quick movement caused me to look. It was that blonde girl, waving at me. Then she giggled and leaned in to her group of friends. John slapped me on my shoulder and gave a mock evil laugh.

I was about to eat a heaping forkful of eggs when a robed man stood up near the food line.

"Before we eat, let's pray to God, for showering us in his holy grace. Would you like to lead us in prayer?"

I was waiting for everyone to bow their heads so I could start eating when I realized he was looking directly at me.

Me? Pray?

"Yes. I think the lord would be pleased to hear from the newest members of our flock." His voice seemed sincere, but there was an underlying tone that I didn't like. It was like hearing a robot that was programmed to say that, but didn't really mean it.

Yeah ... Yeah, of course.

The people seated at all the tables joined hands. John, Lauren and I did the same.

Great ... Living god. We thank you for this bounty ... Spread before us. Thank you for ... Your love and the challenges we face to prove our ... Devotion. Please smite all the sinners and ... Send them to hell as we ascend into your ... Heavenly kingdom.

"Amen." The room, in unison.

"Thank you, Brother Nicholas."

I must have looked uncomfortable. It was mirrored in John and Lauren's faces.

"That was a ... Good prayer, Nick."

Jesus.

I ate my eggs.

We finished breakfast and carried our plates to a cart by the kitchen. The girl who had talked to us in line approached me.

"Sister Stacy says you offered to chaperone the bible walk this morning."

I ...

"We're meeting back here in half an hour. We would enjoy having you walk with us and the lord."

She smiled and walked off.

I don't suppose I have much of a choice.

"Doesn't look that way." John spoke in a hushed tone.

We walked back to the cabin. Once inside, I put on warmer clothes. John fished something out of his bag and handed it to me. It was a tiny pistol. A .380.

"Take this with you ... Just in case."

Thanks.

I tucked the gun into my coat pocket. I went back to the door, then turned.

If I'm not back by this afternoon ...

I'd meant it as a joke, but it didn't come out as one.

Just go.

John simply nodded. I walked out of the cabin and back down the road to the mess hall. A group of younger kids were gathered around along with a handful of people my age. I saw Stacy whispering to her friends. She looked at me, grinned, winked.

"Okay, everyone." It was the girl who had officially "invited" me. "We're going to walk along the lake until we reach the dam, where we're going to have our prayer session. Let's go out and bask in God's glory! Pray for sunshine, everyone!"

Outside was overcast, threatening rain. A damp wind blew across the lake. The group of us headed down to the lakeside, where a footpath ran alongside the highway. We headed west along the shore. The water looked cold, gray. It lapped gently on the rocky beach. Dead fish were scattered everywhere.

The youth group "leader", a boy of about 18, began bringing up verses from the bible. Revelations. End of days talk. I tuned him out and looked across the lake, towards the Pintler Mountains. They were capped with dingy snow, which was whipped off into smoky forms by a high storm. The rocks stood, cold and stark, towering over the deranged world below. I stopped for a moment as the group moved on. Suddenly, I felt a tug at my hand. It was Stacy.

"Come on, Nick. You'll get left behind."

I smirked at her.

114

Goddamn. Wouldn't want that, would we?

She squeezed my hand.

"Blasphemer. Come on."

She pulled me along by my hand. I twisted it out of her grip. She shot back with a flirty pout, then a grin. She ran and caught up with her friends. I muttered under my breath.

Shit.

I trudged along behind the group. The little .380 was heavy in my pocket. I began to wonder if I was losing my mind. I thought about pulling out the little pistol and pumping a round into the back of each head that hiked and laughed in front of me. Turn every one of those smiles into a bloody maw. I knew I was losing my mind when the only thing that stopped me was the fact that I had only 6 bullets and 26 heads.

I threw up, slightly. That watery bile in my mouth. I made it look like I just had to spit. It was sour. Acidic. Stacy smiled at me. I put on a disguise and smiled back.

It was less than two miles to the dam. We made it in an hour. It began to rain. More of a mist. The group of us stood on the dam. A guard on an ATV drove by. He waved. Everybody waved. Everybody smiled. The "leader" pulled out a bible and read a small sermon.

"'Jesus said to her, 'Your brother will rise again.' Martha said to him, 'I know that he will rise again in the resurrection on the last day.' Jesus said to her, 'I am the resurrection and the life. Whoever believes in me, though he die, yet shall he live, and everyone who lives and believes in me shall never die.'

"What that means, everyone, is all of our loved ones, who have come back ... They came back because the lord wanted them to. They came back to bask in the glory of his love. They haven't become abominations of the devil, as the heathens would have us believe. They're tools of God's love! And soon, he will come back for us and take us into his glorious kingdom for all eternity!"

A little girl raised her hand.

"Yes, Sister Alice?"

"So, we're not gonna die?"

"Yes, Sister Alice! We're all going to die! Only then will we be judged!"

This answer pleased the crowd. They all smiled and reached towards the sky. I already feared my mind's grip was starting to fall away. This only helped it along. The whole world had gone crazy and these people were enjoying it.

"Brother Nicholas, would you like to speak?"

Nick ... Nick is fine. Uhhh ...

I saw something, underwater, just in front of the dam. Everyone stood, staring at me. I don't know what they wanted from me. I tried to think back to half-forgotten childhood memories, from when my parents had forced me to go to church.

If this is the end of the world, aren't there supposed to be four horsemen? And a famine? There seems to be enough food here.

The "leader" rolled his eyes and scoffed.

"That's for the non-believers, *Nick*. We're God's chosen people. We're well taken care of, and will be judged favorably."

Then ... Weren't you all supposed to be raptured when this all started?

"Oh, look everyone. *Nick* knows the bible *so* well!"

The group laughed. I heard distant drumbeats. I thought either the zombies had learned to use drums, my ears were playing tricks on me, or the last of my sanity had just slipped into the abyss at the edge of the mad world. I took a step forward and grabbed the "leader" by the front of his robes.

Listen to me, you little asshole. Sneer at me like that again, and you'll be eating your fucking teeth for lunch!

The group let out a collective gasp. It was so cartoonish that I had to laugh. I let go of his robe and walked to the other side of the dam. There it was, down in the water. One of the female chaperones spoke behind me.

"Let's go, everyone. Don't let one bad apple spoil this lovely day!"

116

Another laugh, but this one had a nervous tension to it.

6 bullets, 26 heads.

Shit.

I felt someone come up behind me. The drumbeats were louder, now. Monotonous. Steady. Stacy put her hand on my shoulder.

"Nick, are you okay? That was ... weird ..."

I'm fine. You should catch up with the group. I think they're leaving.

"What about you?"

What about me? I ...

I fished a cigarette out of the pack.

...Am going to stand here and smoke this.

"Alrig-"

The drumbeats turned into a roar as a Blackhawk helicopter roared over the top of the damn. It was gray, but had a black skull and bones painted on the side and covering the 'U.S. Marines' stencil on the tail were the words 'Redick's Raiders'. A bearded man wearing a winter hat sat with his legs out the side door, manning a machine gun. He flipped me off as the helicopter sped past. I began to laugh. Its rotors thumped against the air, rippling the water underneath. It sailed over the lake, then disappeared up the valley on the other side. The youth group screamed.

"It's Satan's soldiers! We have to go back!"

The group took off at a trot.

Stacy had grabbed my arm and was holding on tight. At this point, I figured I'd gone completely insane. I smiled wide as I lit up the cigarette. I'd just been flipped off by the first person in *months* and here I was, laughing about it.

Stacy?

"Y-yeah?"

Go with them. I'll catch up. I just want to stand here and ... Pray.

"Alr-alright, Nick." She gave my arm one last squeeze and bounded down the road after the group. I watched as she disappeared behind the trees,

117

then began walking to the other side of the dam down to the shore. I looked one more time, just to make sure it wasn't just madness telling me I was seeing what I was seeing. It was real.

A red light, slowly flashing under the dark water.

I stripped down naked and took the last drag off my cigarette.

Fuck, this is going to be cold.

I dove in.

I'd been a fairly strong swimmer in the world past and had no problem swimming underwater, but when I opened my eyes, the murk took me by surprise. I got vertigo and couldn't decide which way was up. I kicked through and burst to the surface. My breath was smoky in the cold. I inhaled deeply and dove again. This time, I broke through the murky layer. Underneath was dim, but there was enough light to see.

The flashing light was coming from the rear blinker of a sedan, sitting on the lake bed. The pulse of the light was steadily dimming. Dying out. My eyes adjusted. Beyond the car was a pickup truck. Beyond that another car. And another. And another. There had to have been dozens of cars down there. Not crashed, but deliberately placed. Hidden ...

Other survivors like John, Lauren and I ...

I almost gasped, then kicked back to the surface. I broke through and took a breath of fresh, freezing air. I swam back to shore, shook dry as best I could, then started to get dressed. I heard gravel crunch behind me. I sat on my jacket, lacing up my boots. I turned.

Stacy stood there.

"You weren't supposed to see that, Nick."

I don't suppose I was.

"They're sinners. They had to satisfy God's commands."

And me?

"You will have to answer for your sins, too. We all will. I have to go find Reverend Gaines. I'm sorry, Nick. I really liked you, but now I realize it was Satan the whole time. Tricking me. You're just another of his faces."

I...

She turned and began walking up the beach. All of a sudden, it seemed like gravity was pulling at my brain. I felt like my eyeballs were about to sink into my skull. I took a breath as my hand swept over a smooth, softball-sized rock next to me. I picked it up. I stood. I caught up with little, blonde Stacy in just a few, quick strides. She spun.

"Back with you, sinn-!"

I hit her with the rock. All my force, straight into her temple. The side of her head gave way and I felt warmth spreading over my hand. Dripping down my wrist. Her body crumpled to the ground. She groaned. I got to my knees and hit her again. Her breath released. Her last one. I sat back. My head swam.

Shit Nick, what the fuck?!

The bloody rock fell to my side. It clattered on stones as it rolled down the slight incline to the water's edge. Behind me, a slow, regular blinking from a red light. Her red blood oozed out across the stones. My breath made ghosts in the air.

I dragged her body to the water and pushed her in. The shoreline fell off steeply in this area. Her blond hair, stained red, disappeared below the murky, black water. I slowly put on my jacket. The implications of what I'd just done hit me like I'd hit her. Poor little Sister Stacy.

I knew what had to be done. John, Lauren and I had to get into the truck immediately and get away from this place as fast as possible.

I started running back to the cabin.

I ran so hard, I didn't even notice the tears running hot down my face.

119

Chapter 15

I followed a dirt road up the hill on the other side of the highway. It led to a track underneath old powerlines. They no longer crackled with electricity. Below me, on the paved road, I heard several ATVs speed by, heading for the dam. I figured they were looking for Stacy.

And me.

I ran for all I was worth. I had to work my way across a marshy field to get back to the cabin. By the time I reached it, the front door was already opening. John stood there. He looked at my face, then my jacket. It wasn't until now that I realized I was spattered with blood. He waved me through the door and quickly shut it.

"What happened?"

I told him and Lauren what had happened. The sermon, the helicopter. The cars. Killing Stacy. They sat in stony silence, listening. I sat on my bed as I talked. My head felt heavy. When I finished, the two looked at one another, then back to me. John spoke.

"We have to leave as soon as we can. We should be able to sneak away tonight. They're going to be looking for the girl. Her body won't float for a few days. Clean your hands up and give me those clothes."

I obliged. After that, I lay back down on the bed. My head began to swim. I heard Lauren say something.

"What are we going to do, John? They have that lawman. He's going to be looking for Nick. We can't shoot our way out of here."

"Not now. Tonight. Nick? Nick!"

I sat up.

Yeah ... Yeah?

"You need to hide until we come get you. We'll tell them we haven't seen you. We have to withdraw tonight."

120

Wha ... Where?

"Two cabins down. It's empty. Sneak in there and lay low. Follow the treeline until you get there. We'll come get you tonight. Gaines stopped by and mentioned something about a "special prayer", outside. That'll make it easier to sneak away."

I nodded. John tossed me my coat.

"Go. Now. Fast."

We heard ATVs coming up the road. I ran out the back door, putting on my coat in the process. I stayed low and dashed through the underbrush, careful to keep any large trees between me and where I thought the man with binos was. I heard ATVs pull up to the cabin behind me. I cleared the short distance between the cabins quickly and ducked by the back door of the empty one. I reached up and turned the handle. It wasn't locked. There would be no reason for that. I slipped into the dim interior and quietly shut the door behind me.

Inside was a row of empty beds. There were blankets folded neatly at the foot of each. I sat on the nearest one and grabbed at the blanket.

I don't know if I blacked out ... I must've. I snapped awake. There was very little light coming in through the windows. It was almost dark. About time for service at the chapel, I figured. I got up, stretched, then went out the back door. The night was crisp and cold. I could vaguely make out a few stars above. I stuck my hands in my coat pockets and walked back down to the cabin. I didn't hear any ATVs. I didn't hear anything ... In the distance, though ... Shouts. Coming from far up the hill. I looked in the direction of the chapel and saw trees silhouetted against distant firelight. I jogged to the lower cabin. It was dark. I figured John and Lauren were up at the chapel. It seemed like everyone was up there tonight ...

Not everyone.

I came around the corner, toward the truck. There was a man standing there. It was the man from the first day, who'd led us to the cabin. He had a

121

rifle slung over his shoulder. Binoculars around his neck.

"Brother Nicholas. There you are. We'd like to ask you some questions." He motioned toward a waiting pickup. "Get on in. I'll take you up to the chapel."

You really think I'm going to go with you?

He lazily began pulling the gun off his shoulder.

"I know for a fact, boy, that you and your people's guns are in this truck. So put your fucking hands up and come with me or-"

I swiftly pulled the .380 out of my pocket and brought it up. We weren't standing far apart. Maybe 25 feet. His rifle was clutched loosely in one hand. I could see his grip tighten on it as his eyes grew wide.

I pulled the trigger.

The little pistol jerked in my hands. A pop resounded up the valley as the brow above his left eye caved in. A small cloud of blood and globs shot out the back of his head. His body crumpled to the ground. The ejected shell hit the gun with a small, metallic ping.

Shit.

I hoped nobody else heard the shot. I threw the door of the cabin open. A shadow growled at me and lunged.

Jackso-!

The dog hit me, knocking me over. The little gun flew from my hands. Jackson began licking my face. I pushed him off and grabbed the pistol. I ran to the truck and threw the door open.

Dogs! Load up!

The two Malamutes immediately jumped into the cab. John and Lauren had already loaded our things. I reached under the mat and found the spare set of keys. A moment later, the diesel roared to life. I raced up the road towards the chapel. The road curved around to a small checkpoint. A single man, ATV parked off the side. He held up his hand in a wave, then a halt, then terror as I ran him over.

Just below the chapel was a small field. I pulled the truck in and angled it back toward the road.

Dogs, guard the truck.

I grabbed my .30-06 and ran up the hill. I passed the chapel, lit up but obviously empty. The crucified zombies moaned at me. I sneaked around the side and scarcely believe what I saw.

It was ... An arena. Like the Romans would have watched the gladiators in. Lit by torches. Hanging in the center was the couple missing from breakfast. They had been dressed in sheepskins. The rope they were tied with held them just a foot or two off the ground. They struggled. The woman cried and screamed. The man yelled and shouted curses at Gaines, who stood on a pulpit overlooking the arena.

"Behold, brothers and sisters! Look upon God's wrath and revere our lord! Fear his fury when you cross him! Open your eyes and see how our loving God deals with those who trespass against him! 'But thank God! He gives us victory over sin and death through our Lord Jesus Christ!'. Repent now, sinners!" Gaines put his hand on a lever.

"Let us go, you fucking psycho! We didn't do anything!" The man pleaded. The woman cried.

"Nothing? Nothing, he says! You surrendered to the pleasures of the flesh, rather than the will of God! You allowed this honey-tongued harlot to take you into her bed! You created a child within her! An abomination of this earth!"

"She's my girlfriend! I love her!"

"And God loves you, sinner."

Gaines pulled the lever. I watched in horror as three gates opened. 7 zombies came stumbling through. They went directly for the hanging people.

Down in front, I could make out John and Lauren. Two men with rifles flanked them. Both held their guns, but not in a threatening manner.

Shit.

And so I was faced with ... Pardon the vernacular, the "devil's choice". Damned if I do ...

123

My grandfather had taught me to shoot when he'd given me the rifle. He'd taught me to shoot fast, but I hadn't taken it seriously at the time. I'd just enjoyed his stories of his war experience. I brought the rifle up. I lined up the sights.

Below me, a zombie had taken a bite out of the man's thigh. He screamed in pain and terror. Another zombie clamped onto the woman's leg. She tried to shake it off. She couldn't.

The crowd cheered. People were praying, arms to the sky.

I released my breath and fired. One of the men guarding John and Lauren went down, missing half of his head. I quickly cycled another round and shot the second through the neck.

The crowd screamed.

John! Lauren! RUN!

People began standing and running everywhere. A crowd turned toward me. They were packed in tight. I fired from my hip, striking a man in the stomach. He fell backwards, taking down a large group. John and Lauren dashed up toward me.

"Get them! Stop them! They shall be cast into hell along with-!"

I shot the Reverend Gaines in the right cheek. It evaporated in a spray of blood and bone. He screamed, tongue lolling out and fell forward, off the pulpit, right into the arena. As I turned to run, I saw two zombies fall on top of him. His shrieks echoed through the valley.

John and Lauren caught up with me. We headed for the truck. Behind us, I could hear shouts. John grabbed something from his pocket, stopped, whirled and threw it into the center of the crowd. I saw a glimpse of what looked to be a baseball, black against the torchlight.

"Frag out!"

What?!

Lauren tackled me to the ground as the hand grenade exploded. The boom made my ears ring, but I could still hear the shrapnel whizz and the screams of those hit. We got to our feet and ran through the trees. As we broke through, I could see the sheriff standing there, flanked by two men. I brought my rifle to bear, but Lauren beat me to it. She'd produced a small revolver and dropped the two "deputies". John hit the sheriff dead on, knocking the pistol from his hands. Before I knew it, John was holding a hunting knife. He plunged it into the sheriff's throat and pulled it across. He emitted a frothy gasp as his eyes rolled back into his head.

"Nick, get in the bed!"

He ripped the door open. We heard ATVs buzzing down the road. Lauren climbed in the driver's seat, tossing a canvas duffel to John as he jumped into the bed. The duffel and contained the two ARs, a supply of loaded magazines, and a smaller sack of assorted items. He tossed one of the rifles to me to me.

"Do you know how to use one of these?"

The truck jumped to life and lurched forward.

Yeah. My buddy had one-

"Good!"

Behind us, multiple pinpricks of headlights appeared. John raised his rifle and started shooting. I saw the first ATV veer off the road and roll over in the ditch. I aimed down the peep sight and began firing, too. It took a second to get used to it, but when I did, it was easy. The truck raced down the road. John opened the duffel and slid it between us. Then he pulled out some road flares and duct tape. He pulled one of the propane cylinders out from under a tarp, knelt and lit a flare. He taped it to the cylinder.

"Nick! Down!"

I threw myself to the bed of the truck as he threw the makeshift bomb and fired, dropping down as the explosion lit up the night. I looked back to see trees and two ATVs in flames. John and I got up and began firing again. The pops of the rifles were deafening. The world rang against my ears. The truck veered around a bend and I lost my balance. My shoulder hit the edge of the truck bed, knocking the wind out of me. I kicked out with my foot and caught the wheel-well so I didn't fly out.

"You okay?"

Yeah! I'm fine!

A pickup truck was gaining on us. There were a few ATVs and another truck behind it. We sped down toward the lake. Right by the mess hall was a gasoline tank on legs, sitting a few feet off the ground. John grabbed his tow chain, attached one hook to a connection point on the frame and tossed the other ...

It whipped through the dirt, then jumped up and caught one of the legs. The chain straightened and pulled the tank down. It zigzagged all over the road, shooting sparks. The truck pursuing us had to slow down to avoid hitting it. I knew what John was getting at. He pulled another flare from the bag and I shot a few holes in the tank. John threw the flare. A brilliant, pulsing, orange arc ... Then, in an instant, the road became a river of fire. The driver behind us must have panicked. The truck swerved, catching the fuel tank on its fender. I heard the screech of metal as they locked up. The chain jolted against the new weight, then the connection point snapped off. I could feel the air off of it as it whipped by my ear.

The truck flipped onto its side as the tank detonated, sending a huge fireball blossoming up into the night sky. The truck was engulfed in flames and lying across the road. The glow reflected off the dark waters of the lake. I sat back and took a deep breath, laughing ...

A few of the ATVs came around one side of the truck. I heard a crack and John yelled, then fell back.

John! John! Are you alright!

"I'm good ... Motherfuckers."

A bullet had grazed his arm, tearing a hole in his coat and ripping up the flesh. There was blood, but it wasn't serious. We both steadied our rifles on the tailgate and shot above the headlights. Two of the ATVs crashed and the third turned around. I took a potshot that must have hit the tire. It swerved right into the burning truck.

"Nice shot."

126

Nice shot, hell! Nice throw with that flare!

We looked back. There didn't seem to be any more pursuers. On the other end of the lake was another trailer, sideways in the road. There was no one around it. Everyone must have been watching the "sacrifice". I thought about that couple, getting torn to pieces by zombies.

I thought of Dan and Alli.

Bile washed up in my mouth. I spit over the side of the truck and grabbed for my pack of cigarettes. I only had a few left. I offered one to John. He took it. We sat, smoking in the back of the truck as the freezing night air washed over us. Looking into the darkness over the back of the tailgate. A few spent shells that hadn't made it out the back of the truck gently rolled around, clattering on one another. My hearing was starting to return.

John finished his smoke and packed up the duffel. He climbed in the back window and I handed the bag and the rifles in. I flicked my cigarette out into the night. It flipped around and landed on the road, showering the asphalt in embers.

A galaxy of tiny stars, flaring up and burning out.

I climbed in through the back window. The dogs flanked me as we cruised that lonesome highway down into the small town of Anaconda. There were cars here and there, but by the looks of it, someone had already pushed them to the side.

At one point, a herd of elk appeared like specters in the headlights. Lauren put on the brakes and slowed to a stop. They looked at us for a while, breath steaming in the air. Then they trotted off and disappeared into the night. The dogs whined as they went.

We dropped into the valley. No lights were visible from anywhere ahead. I supposed that could be a good thing ... Or a bad one.

Shit, what did I know anymore? I murdered a teenage girl with a rock on a beach.

Ahead, a road led off the highway to a small rock quarry. Lauren pulled the truck in, circling with the headlights. Nothing moved around the site

127

trailer or the derelict vehicles. She turned the truck off. Darkness flooded in.

"Well, boys, looks like we're here for the night. Too dangerous to go into town until morning."

We lay back, getting as comfortable as possible in the cramped cab.

I didn't close my eyes. I knew that if I did, I would see a pale, bloody face surrounded with blonde hair. Sinking into a black lake against the steady flashing of red light.

Chapter 16

We all awoke just before dawn, stretched, ate, ran the dogs and cleaned the guns. Lauren maneuvered the truck back onto the road into Anaconda just as the sun was cresting over the eastern mountains. The stretch of highway was long and straight. There weren't many cars on it. Just a few, abandoned. Some were dented and shoved off to the side. Some sat where they'd been left. In the middle of the road. People's belongings strewn all over. We passed a minivan as we neared town. Its doors were open, blood smeared on the doors. We ran over a doll in the road.

I hope it was a doll.

As the road curved slightly and entered town, I saw something wrong with the horizon.

Where's the Stack?

John and Lauren saw it, too. Anaconda was an old mining town. Up on a hill, just southeast, was a huge smelter that had closed down years ago. The giant smokestack was all that remained and now ... It was gone.

We passed a pile of sandbags. It looked like a military gun emplacement, but it faced east ... Toward town. I mentioned this to John.

"Yeah ..." His voice trailed off. The truck drove over thousands of bullet casings. They crunched against the asphalt.

In a field off to the right ... Burn piles. Dozens of them.

We came to a gas station. All the pump handles sat on the ground. A truck had hit the sign, breaking the pole. It had landed on the truck, crushing the cab. There was red and white plastic everywhere. The piece that remained read "NOCO" and flapped forlornly in the cold wind.

"Stop here." John pointed at the wrecked truck. "It's a diesel."

Lauren pulled in behind it, angling our own vehicle to drive away at a moment's notice. She shut the engine off and we all climbed out.

129

"Stay in the truck, dogs." Lauren put her hand up towards them.

Jackson and Ava whined slightly. John grabbed the two empty jerry cans and the siphon from the bed, then approached the truck. I followed, hand on the butt of my revolver. I heard a moaning hiss. John stepped back.

"We've got a ... Dead one. But ... Yeah, it's trapped. It's not going anywhere." He opened the gas tank and began siphoning fuel. It began flowing immediately. "We might have a full one, here."

I nodded, trying not to look into the cab. A gray arm stretched out toward me, fingernails broken off into ragged claws. I looked into its eyes ... Eye. Half of the zombie's head was smashed in. No airbags. Its gaping socket was brown with dried, infected blood. Its body was pinned under the sign pole and the remains of the windshield and roof. It reached at me, as if trying to shake my hand. Its moan chilled me. I turned away.

I walked toward the convenience store. The windows were all broken out, trash scattered everywhere. There was a paper box out front. It had Butte's local paper, the Montana Standard. It was dated over three months ago. The headline ...

"Military Plane Crashes in Anaconda".

Someone had smashed the change compartment open and stolen the quarters. For what, I can't even begin to imagine. I grabbed at the handle and it opened. I took a paper. It was slightly yellowed, but readable. I started reading the article.

Military Plane Crashes in Anaconda

By Gary Porter of the Montana Standard

The citizens of Anaconda got a surprise awakening early Thursday morning. At 2:43 AM, a loud explosion echoed off the hills just below Mount Haggin. The aircraft, a U.S. Army C-130 cargo plane was completely destroyed.

"I was sound asleep when I heard a big bang. Just a huge boom. It shook my house," said local resident Chuck Fleer, a retired miner, "I thought I was dreaming at first, but when I got up, I saw the flames."

First responders from the Anaconda Fire Department radioed reports of survivors stumbling around from the wreckage. One dispatcher swears she heard one of the firefighters say a man was walking around on fire.

"That's what [Ron] said on the radio. He said there were several people walking ... Stumbling around, and one was walking toward the truck, on fire." Doreen McCreary said in an interview over the phone, "Like the guy wasn't in pain or anything. Maybe he was in shock, though. Another bit Glen [Hirsham], the rookie. They took him down to the hospital, but I haven't heard anything since. The guys were going to put out the fire, but some helicopters showed up. The military ... They said they had it all under control."

With the stories about riots and attacks flooding the internet and various news agencies from around the world, it seems odd that the military would be able to show up so fast to get the situation "under control". The commander, Major Green said the plane was carrying an "undisclosed cargo to an undisclosed location" but didn't elaborate. Further attempts to reach him were unsuccessful.

It is curious that later in the morning, a line of military trucks rolled into Anaconda and cordoned off an area that residents say is over 2 square miles. Some people were even forced to leave their homes for the emergency shelter that was set up in the high school gym. Not many people got a good look at the trucks, but one man, Fred Gilbertson, swears he saw the crest for the U.S. Army Medical Research Institute of Infectious Diseases (USAMRIID) on them.

"I was in the service for 34 years. I was stationed at [Fort] Detrick. I'd recognize that shield anywhere. It's the doctors. The virus guys." He said in an interview.

The firefighters who initially responded were unavailable for comment, as they haven't returned to their homes. It is believed that the Army detained them for questioning, but no one knows for sure. Attempts to reach Glen Hirsham, the firefighter who was "bitten" by one of the survivors have not been possible. The military has locked down the hospital and set up checkpoints into and out of Anaconda ...

I stopped reading when I heard something crash. I looked up. In the store, a zombie had just fallen against a shelf. I folded the newspaper and put it in my back pocket. I retrieved the pack of cigarettes from my coat and slowly fished one out. The zombie was off balance and when it came around the shelf, I saw why. Its left leg was twisted completely sideways at the knee. It had just enough muscle left to prop it up, but it dragged the leg limply behind it. It was slow. I walked back to the truck and grabbed my crowbar. John looked up from the gas can.

"Nick? Everything okay?"

It's fine. There's a slow one about to come out of the store. I'll take care of it.

John nodded and went back to filling the cans. I walked toward the convenience store. The zombie was just shuffling out the door. It moaned and raised an arm, then stepped off the curb. It lost balance and fell face-forward onto the concrete. It began to push itself up. I raised the crowbar.

A middle-aged man. He ... It had a bald spot on the back of its head. It had bite marks all over its back. I could see ribs through one. I hit the bald spot with the crowbar. The hooked end caved its head in. The body went limp and the moans stopped ... From in front of me. Around the corner of the store, I heard another moan. Then another. I jogged over and peeked around. I could see 5, slowly making their way towards us. Another few appeared from behind houses a half-block away,

Shit.

I turned and ran to the truck.

Guys, we're going to have company.

I pointed. John and Lauren saw them. There were 11 now.

"I'm done here, anyways. Let's roll." John capped the second jerry can and secured them in the truck. We ushered the dogs into the cab and drove back out onto the road.

    We passed by houses that had messages spraypainted on them.

    "3 inside. 1 injured."

    "2 living."

    "Dead inside. Do not enter."

    One:

    "Families inside. Children. Please help us."

    The door was wide open and splattered with blood, a window shattered. All the way down the street, messages on siding, roofs, garages. Not a sign of life anywhere. Just zombies. Some were in yards. Some in the street. They would turn towards the truck as we passed. Always putting up an arm, as if trying to snatch us from the distance and pull us into those diseased jaws.

    As we passed through the center of town, our pace slowed. There were more cars on the streets. Some wrecked. Doors open. Abandoned in a hurry. There were more zombies, too. Everywhere we looked, there were some stumbling around alone. Sometimes they were in small groups.

    We approached the one stoplight in town. It was dark. There was a wreck at the intersection. Cars jammed into each other. The road was blocked. There must have been 20 zombies. They began walking at us.

    "Damn! Let's try a side street." Lauren swung the truck right. At the next intersection was a park. It had barbed wire and sandbags surrounding it. There were white tents set up in neat rows. The salvaged remains of a Blackhawk helicopter sat on one corner. There was a line of military trucks. On the doors, a black shield with a red DNA helix, a star and a petri dish. Underneath the letters "USAMRIID".

    Looks like the government knows something about all of this ...

    "Looks like they're just as unprepared for it, too." John snorted. "Maybe they're trying to find a 'cure'."

    "We've seen those things with limbs torn off. How can you cure *that*?" Lauren drove us slowly down one side of the park. There were dead soldiers, walking around, still wearing helmets and body armor.

"Stop here for a sec, babe."

Lauren looked at John quizzically, then slowed to a stop. There were no zombies close. John jumped out and ran to a small group of soldiers that appeared to have been shot. John leaned over them and grabbed items from their pockets. A zombie appeared a few yards from him, shuffling out from behind a military vehicle.

"John!"

He looked up and smiled, then ran back to the truck with his arms full. He had several loaded AR magazines and two more hand grenades. He pulled the door shut and we started moving forward again.

"These little babies come in handy sometimes." John grinned at me and tossed a grenade at me. I caught it. It weighed about as much as a full beer can. Its exterior was textured and cold. I couldn't believe so much power could come from so small a device. I handed it back to him. The road we were on was clear. A few cars and virtually no zombies. Lauren was able to drive faster now, and we neared the other end of town in no time.

Suddenly, as we passed a house with a jumble of bushes in the yard, a young woman ran at the truck, straight to Lauren's door. Lauren slapped the lock down. The dogs growled. She pounded on the window.

"Please! Please help me! Take me with you! PLEASE!"

"Shit." Lauren muttered under her breath. There was a wound on her forearm. A bite mark. Dark red. I could see trails of black shadowing her veins.

"Please! They… They got in! My brother ... He got bit ... Attacked me! Please ..." She was crying now. "Help me!"

Lauren looked at John and I, pursing her lips. No one said anything. There was nothing to say, I don't think. Lauren looked back at the road and pushed down the accelerator. The truck rolled away. She ran for a few steps, still pounding on the window.

"No! Don't leave me! I don't ... I don't want to die! You can't just leave me!"

The truck moved past her. She picked up a rock, threw it. Missed.

134

"Fuck you!"

I watched out the back window as she faded into the distance. Zombies emerged from yards behind her. Surrounding her.

"Goddamn! Stop, Lauren." John hopped out and loaded his AR. He raised it and shot. The woman dropped. The zombies kept coming. He got back in and sighed. "What else could I do?"

He put his head in his hands. Lauren gently rubbed his shoulder.

The road curved around and rejoined the state highway at a bowling alley. The Stack was still nowhere to be seen. There were cars scattered up and down the highway. Police cruisers. A few military vehicles. We drove past a large hill, jet black. An old slag pile from the mining days. I was beginning to wonder where the other military checkpoint was when we cleared the slag pile.

Ahead, the land was also black. Scorched black. There were bodies everywhere. Literally, everywhere. Thousands.

"Jesus." John stared out the windshield. "They did it. They actually did it ..."

People trying to escape the infected town, I'd guessed. Cars, on foot. Just trying to get away. They'd probably have overwhelmed the checkpoint. The government must have napalmed them. Just ... Burned up all those people. Nothing but charred bones, now. Off to the south, we finally saw it ... The fire had been so hot, it toppled the Stack. The giant chimney lay on its side, shattered.

We drove down the burned road in silence. Sections of the asphalt had buckled from the heat. The gentle grinding of bone under the tires rose through the cab. I shuddered. I watched the Stack as we passed it, as black and broken as the skeletons we drove over. I thought about people. All over. The whole world. We'd stood so proud and tall once, too, but now were burning out, buckling under the cold fear of this new reality. The world had abruptly changed and I don't think anyone- John, Lauren, the government, these people, myself- had been prepared for it. Maybe this was it ... Maybe this is where human civilization came to an end and we passed the world onto something

135

else.

The dead shall inherit the earth.

All we could do now was just keep moving forward. The living in a sea of death. Driving down that cold, dark highway, on the final stretch to Butte.

Chapter 17

The landscape took back on the gray and brown features that had become normal as we passed out of the napalmed area. The road was long and straight. There were no cars on this stretch. We passed the turnoff for a small community outside of Anaconda. Just beyond that was the old highway that went by a hot springs. Lauren pulled the truck onto the shoulder.

"What do you boys think?"

"We should probably stay away from the highway if we can. It's bound to be clogged with vehicles and the dead. And it's not them I'm worried about. There might be some scavengers out there. People are already desperate ..."

I nodded in agreement. Lauren turned right and we headed south to a chain of low mountains. Fields stretched to both sides. In one, another herd of cows, dead and bloated. There were ranch houses on both sides, spread out. They looked empty. The whole valley felt abandoned. I got the same feeling that had been coming on lately. A pinching in my chest, like I couldn't breathe. Nothing moved except for the long grass, blowing in the wind on the sides of the road.

I don't know why, but I suddenly remembered the soda from the store. I dug around in my bag until my fingers felt the plastic bottle. I pulled it out and examined it. The maroon label brought back memories of days gone by, a world faded and blown away like ash on the cold wind. A drizzling rain began to pelt the windshield.

I turned the cap and a muted hiss escaped. John heard it and turned around.

I found it in a store ... Back in Missoula. I figured we could all use something to forget ...

John smiled slightly.

"Or remember."

We passed the bottle of soda around in silence as the wet, gray road stretched out in front of us. There was a minivan that had crashed into a ditch on the side of the road as we rounded a long bend. Lauren slowed down as we rumbled by. Through the dingy windows, I could see dark shapes moving inside. A gray hand pressed against the glass.

I took another swallow of soda. Sweet on my tongue. I hadn't tasted anything sweet in ... A long time, I guess. I found myself surprised that my taste buds still recognized sweet in the bitter light.

In a field, far off to the right, I thought I saw two figures on horses. I grabbed my binoculars and looked out over the empty farms. A rotting haystack moved in between the field and my eyes. When it was past, I didn't see anything. Just that grass, blowing in the wind. Farther down the road was a farmhouse. Its windows were boarded up, and barricades had been fashioned from corral gates. Spray-painted on the front of the house:

'No Trespassing. Living or Dead.'

John grinned.

"I guess we're not going there."

I never understood how John could remain so optimistic in this world, but it was reassuring. It felt like it would be so easy to just lose it at this point ... Like my brain was trying desperately to wake up from a world that had to be a dream ...

There's no nightmare so deep ...

Lauren pulled the truck off to the side of the road.

"Well ..." She pointed straight ahead. "That way is the highway. To the right here is that hot springs hotel that we stayed at for New Year's a couple years ago." She squeezed John's hand and smiled.

The highway is still out of the question ...

"And we might find something useful at the hotel. Supplies, food, fuel ... Anything."

The three of us nodded in unspoken agreement. The breathing of the

138

dogs was the only thing that broke the silence as we finished the soda.

"Alright. Let's do it. Keep a lookout, boys." Lauren put the truck into gear, then turned right and headed south. There was an abandoned settlement at the intersection, but it had been empty years before the Collapse. In the past, it had seemed eerie and out of place. Now it just seemed ... Kind of normal.

Further down the road was a small trailer park. A dog ran between two of the houses.

The fields on the right side of the road were empty and overgrown. We passed a zombie that was trapped in a fence. Just twisted up in the barbed wire. One of its hands hung by just a tendon. It lunged at the truck. A coil of wire dug deeper into its neck.

The hot springs was now in view. Lauren said what I was thinking.

"There sure are a lot of cars there."

The parking lot was full. There were vehicles all over the place, in no orderly fashion. Just a jumble of cars. It looked like some trucks had deliberately been driven onto cars. As we drove closer, it looked exactly like an amateur demolition derby.

"Shit ..." John pointed out the windshield. A large, white banner was hanging above the pool. Painted in black letters was a skull and crossbones followed by the words: "End of the World Party". It was then that I realized I could see bodies slumped over steering wheels in most of the wrecked cars. Lauren gasped as we drove past the pool. It was filled with bodies, surrounded by bodies. There were bottles of liquor, cans of beer, pill containers, syringes. Most of the bodies in the pool were waterlogged and beginning to fall apart. The bodies around the pool were pale gray, but not badly decomposed. Though by the looks of it, birds had been eating them. It had to have happened fairly recently.

Lauren brought the truck to a stop at the entrance to the main parking lot. The cars in this one were intact, but still parked haphazardly. There were more bodies and evidence of a huge party.

"What do you think? Everyone seems to be dead. Do you think there are any zombies in there?"

"Could be. But if they all killed themselves, there'd be no reason for any to go in. If all these people were out here for a while, they may have brought supplies. They obviously won't be needing them. Nick?"

It could be worth a quick look. I used to come out here all the time. I know the layout.

"Alright. Just a quick look, Lauren."

She shot him a worried look.

"Guys, we have plenty of supplies to make it to Butte."

"We still have to consider the possibility that there's nothing left there."

"Okay ..." She sighed, then backed the truck a little ways into the parking lot.

"Hurry back. And if anything goes wrong ..."

"We'll get out. Honk if you see anything."

Lauren smiled, but still looked uneasy. John got out of the truck. I grabbed my headlamp and pistol. John opened the side opposite me and pulled out two guns I hadn't seen yet. 12 gauge shotguns. Not the duck hunting type, either. He loaded each with 8 shells and handed me one.

"Ever fire a shotgun before?"

Yeah. Just aim in the general direction and fire.

"Just like that." He donned a headlamp, then checked to make sure his pistol was loaded. "Let's go. Quick sweep. Don't grab more than you can carry. Be prepared to drop it if you have to."

I nodded. We jogged toward the hotel entrance. The automatic doors had been locked open. There were more bodies in the lobby. All these people ... All ages. They'd just ... Partied themselves to death. Decided this world was no longer for them and went out in grand fashion. It ...

It doesn't look like a bad way to go.

"No ... I suppose not."

The interior of the hotel was dark. We turned our lights on and kept them constantly moving, watching all directions at once. We stopped every few steps and listened. We heard nothing. Complete silence in the jovial tomb. We made our way down the hall, trying not to step on the dead revelers. They were beginning to stink. We walked past windows overlooking the pool. I thought again of their decision. They'd simply ... Gotten out. Woken up ...

"Nick? Stay close."

I caught up with John. I took the lead and made it to the kitchen. It looked nearly unused. The only two bodies looked to be a young couple who had decided to die in the throes of passion. We found multiple cans of food, along with bags of dry goods. We loaded the supplies into tablecloths and threw them over our shoulders. We headed back out.

Should we check to see if any trucks have fuel?

"If we have time. Only one can is empty at the moment." John bent down and picked up a cardboard box. An unopened case of beer. John gave me a sideways smile. "Hey ... It's the end of the world, right?"

I grinned, then picked up a bottle of whiskey. I pulled off the cap.

What the hell, huh?

I raised it to my lips and jerked it away. I handed it to John.

Smell that.

He put his nose to the top of the bottle.

"Poisoned." He threw the bottle behind him. It landed at the feet of a person walking toward us. It looked so much like a zombie, I raised my shotgun. John did, too. The figure was holding a large knife.

"We all have to go. Everybody else went. We're late, man. We have to get to the party." He raised the knife. It was a man, but I couldn't tell how old. His hair was disheveled and he looked like he hadn't slept in over a week.

You're ... At the party ...

"No, MAN! We have to get to the fucking party! Can you drive? You have to drive! Let's go!" He shook the knife at me.

"Calm down, kid. There is no party. Everybody here killed themselves. The world is ... Different now. Do you remember?" John lowered his shotgun.

"NO! Everyone is gone and we killed the kids. We have to go to the party or we'll be too late! I don't have TIME for this SHIT!" He lunged at John with the knife. John stepped aside and smashed him in the face with the butt of his shotgun. He then drew his pistol and shot the guy through the forehead. His limp body slumped over another partier.

"Kid fried his own brain out. Probably went to some other reality, but didn't take enough to die." He looked at me." This world ..."

I nodded, then picked up my sack of supplies.

The truck horn cut the silence. 3 long blares. John grabbed his bag and we ran for the entrance. I tripped on a body and nearly fell, but regained my balance. We ran out into the parking lot to see Lauren reversing the truck toward us. There were several zombies in front, and more were emerging from trees at the far end of the lot. Lauren slowed the truck and John and I jumped in the bed. Lauren backed under the elevated walkway that connected the wings of the hotel, then turned right and gunned it. The brush guard on the front of the truck crushed against a small car, pushing it out of the way and the truck jumped onto the golf course. We flew by a small duck pond. There were more reveler's bodies in there. The ducks must have gone to look for someplace safe.

I hope they found it.

The truck bounce wildly over a small, paved path, then skidded to the right. I almost flew out the back, but John grabbed my arm. We sped across the brown, dead golf course, almost running over an overturned golf cart. There were two bodies spilled out the side. The trees opened to the left, revealing more than 20 zombies.

Where the hell are they coming from?

I stood to look over the top of the truck when we hit a small ditch. My feet went out from under me and I flew over one side of the bed. I hit the ground and lights flashed behind my eyes. The truck kept going with John banging wildly on top. I'd landed on my shoulder, and it felt numb. I saw the brake lights go on. I got up, ran and jumped back in. I was favoring my shoulder.

"You alright? Anything broken?"

Some of the zombies had seen the truck and slowly made their way toward it. I moved my shoulder in the socket. It hurt, but my full range of motion was there.

It feels okay. I think my pride hurts worse than anything.

"Never stand up in the back of a moving truck. I learned that the hard way, too, when I was a boy."

There was a road ahead, and on the other side of it ... An RV park. Full of trailers, tents, campers. We skidded onto the road, headed back to the highway. Most of the camper doors were wide open. The tents were shredded. A row of cabins stood by the road. There was a zombie on the porch, just standing and swaying, like it was out enjoying the view. It raised an arm as we passed, as though it was waving to us. I suppressed the urge to wave back.

We turned back onto the main road and had to swerve immediately to avoid an RV lying on its side. The road was long and straight. As soon as we got a safe distance from the hotel, Lauren stopped the truck. John and I climbed into the cab.

"Nick, are you okay? You landed pretty hard."

I gave Lauren a half-smile.

Yeah, my shoulder took the brunt of it. It's fine, though.

"Good. Let's get the hell out of here."

John and I simultaneously nodded in agreement.

There was no sign of life along the rest of the road. Just cold, gray skies and dingy landscapes. We went up a small hill and the highway came into view. It looked just like it had outside of Missoula. All 4 lanes were jammed with vehicles of all shapes, sizes and condition. There was even an ancient-looking tractor abandoned beside a semi-truck. This traffic, though ... All of the traffic leaving Missoula, all lanes had been headed east. All of these cars were facing west.

I guess I hadn't realized how much panic had set in, how quickly it all

143

must have happened. I tried to think back to Missoula, when Dan, Alli and I had been hiding in our house. I tried to remember when outside noise had gone away, when the sirens and gunfire had stopped. When I could no longer hear car horns and human screams. And I couldn't. We'd barricaded ourselves in that house with canned vegetables and bottled water and the outside world had just ... Gone away. There had been thousands of people, running for their lives and I had just concealed it behind the walls of an apartment. I hadn't allowed myself to really think, in depth, about the events of the world I had been thrust into that sunny day at the store. I don't think I'd really been prepared for it, even when I'd run from the bandits and the zombies outside of Bonner.

It was at that point ... That's when I really began to believe that we would find nothing in Butte but the dead. The sinking feeling in my stomach hadn't gone away since I'd killed that girl, and now it rushed up, threatening to swallow me, to push me right over the edge. I tried to imagine what to do, where to go, if Butte really was gone.

Nowhere.

I knew that now. The whole world was probably like this, *in a matter of months*, and if the U.S. military couldn't handle it, who could?

All of the traffic below was headed west and would have met the traffic coming out of Missoula. Complete chaos, no one knowing what to do. A choke point for the humans, a banquet for the zombies.

I looked down and saw a baby stroller, tipped over on the shoulder of the highway. I thought again of those people back at the hot springs. They'd gone out the way they saw fit, not being ripped apart, then eventually getting back up to wander the Earth. Maybe that's all there was left to do ...

I heard the familiar cracking hiss of a beer. John turned around and handed it to me.

"You're pretty quiet back there, Nick. Here's a distraction. Can't go too far into those kinds of thoughts, you know what I mean? They go to a dark place, and it's hard to get back." He opened a beer of his own. He offered one to Lauren.

144

"Not this time. It's been a while. I'll wait 'til we're off the road. Wouldn't want to get pulled over." She grinned, but it quickly disappeared.

We passed a Highway Patrol car that had been halfway run over by a pickup truck. I could see movement behind intact, dirty, gray windows.

John took it in, then turned back around.

"Lauren and I discussed that, too, early on. Just going up into the woods and killing ourselves. But we didn't ... We didn't because we're still alive. Maybe we ... All of us, I mean, Maybe we aren't supposed to be. Maybe this is the end for everyone and we're just the hangers-on. But that's fine with me. Nick, if Death is going to take over this world, no sense in giving him any advantages, right?" He took a drink. "Something to think about. It's not over yet, Nick ..." He turned back to the windshield. "It's not over ..."

We passed over the silent tomb of highway. I didn't see anything. No survivors, no zombies. Nothing. Just trash and people's belongings blowing in the wind. The road split. A frontage road along the highway and one that wound up and hugged the foothills. Lauren took the second. I watched as we passed by empty farms and empty fields. I drank a beer and tried to understand my place in this world.

The dirt road we were on eventually connected back to the frontage road, and we were forced to go along the highway for a couple of miles. I saw a few random zombies, but not the cluster I'd been expecting. We came to another highway overpass, at a small town just before the junction of interstates I-90 and I-15.

"Lauren, pull over on that bridge real quick. I want to have a look ahead."

Lauren backed the truck onto the overpass. John grabbed his binoculars and got out. I followed. In the distance was the East Ridge- the wall of the Continental Divide that Butte sat at the foot of. We scanned the horizon to the east. There were a few zombies interspersed with the cars, but I didn't see any sign of people. Neither did John. He put his binos down.

"It looks pretty clear. We'll stop again when we get closer. We can probably go in through-" He stopped and squinted to the southeast, then raised his binoculars again. "Shit."

I looked in the same direction. It was hard to see at first, but when I did, it was obvious. Smoke, belching toward the sky. Black smoke, most likely from a diesel. Headed north. We got back into the truck and John unfurled the map.

"There's movement to the south. Probably more refugees. We'll have to go in to the north."

That takes us right into the middle of town.

"I know. But I'd rather take my chances with the dead than with some psychopaths with guns."

I thought of Georgetown and shuddered. Lauren hit the gas. We took numerous dirt roads, one that was little more than a wet pair of tire tracks across a field. The road forked. One end went south, straight to the highway junction. We headed north. The road wound over low sagebrush hills. We passed a gated driveway and through the barricades I could make out men on horses, holding rifles. They watched us drive by.

It began to rain again.

The road finally came to a T-shaped junction. The left went into the small mountains to the west. The right went right by Butte's county dump, then down a gulch that would take us right into the Uptown- Butte's business district. We went right.

The road crested a small hill and we entered a bank of low clouds. The world grew foggy. We couldn't see 20 feet in front of the truck. Lauren slowed down to a crawl. We started down the other side of the hill and the fog thinned slightly. The dump spread out before us ...

It was full of bodies. Wrapped in sheets, gunshot wounds to the head. Thousands ... Just thousands. They looked like blood-soaked mummies, stacked into dreadful pyramids. The dump was filled with them.

"Oh ..." Lauren whispered and let out a breath.

We sat in silence as we followed a short paved section, then turned up

146

the gulch into Butte.

Chapter 18

Oro Fino.

That's Spanish for "fine gold". That's the name of the narrow road we found ourselves on, winding its way over low hills to Butte. There were several houses, strung out along the road. Most of them had barricades up. Windows boarded. I figured they weren't empty. People hiding from this world, just like I had.

But it would find them, eventually. It found me.

The landscape here was covered in mine tailings, adding hues of ocher, red and yellow to the gray light. There had been miners here, a century ago. Coming from the world over, looking for opportunity, a new life. A life for the living.

Nothing but ghosts now.

The tightness in my stomach didn't relent as we closed in on Butte, but instead got worse as we crested the last rise. We were behind the "Big Butte" now, a cooled lava dome that had given the town its name. On the other side, I knew, was a big, white "M", built by college students long ago. Below us, in a gully, was the old town shooting range. I remembered target practicing there in the summer, with my brother and friends ...

There were bodies down there. I grabbed my binoculars. They had been zombies. People torn apart. Their hands were tied behind their backs, bullet holes in the head. It looked like it was a target range at the very end, too. We came over the last hill, and Butte spread out below us.

Home. At last, I was home. Down in the valley below, I could see a lot of houses and buildings that had burned. Slight wisps of smoke still reached for the sky as the larger ones still smoldered. Black smudges all over the land below.

We passed an old water tank. I'd joked, long ago with my brother, calling it a "zombie factory". I felt bad about it, at that point. I don't know why. Just ... Foolish.

The road abruptly opened into neighborhoods. More houses, just like Anaconda. Spray-painted with messages, warnings, pleas for help. If the dump was any indication, it looked like that help had never arrived. We turned above one of the stark, black steel headframes from the mining days and drove by an old open pit. There was no sign of life anywhere.

We passed over an empty hill, the grass wet and brown. There were low storm clouds over the mountains in the distance. The rain picked up and started to turn to snow. Lauren stopped at the next intersection.

"No matter which way we go, we'll have to skirt the business section. Nick, where do your parents live?"

They lived on the Flats.

The beer had made me light-headed.

"They might still be alive."

They're not.

I looked out the window. There was a zombie in one of the houses next to us. It began clawing at the window and curtains, then plunged its head through the glass, shearing most of its scalp off. Lauren put the truck in gear and continued on.

Where do your aunt and uncle live?

"Just down a few blocks down. We'll go there first."

We drove down through the neighborhoods, seeing the occasional zombie. No people, but some houses were boarded up. I think what struck me the most was the lack of cars. There were a few, parked here and there, but not the amount I'd expected. I guessed most of them had taken to the highways.

"Doesn't look like a whole lot of dead. Do you think maybe the military cleaned the town up, John?"

"If they did ... Where are they now?"

The storm began dropping bigger flakes. They were wet, but accumulating. We drove down a hilly street. Ahead, in the storm, we saw 4

149

ATVs speed past on a cross street. We heard a few gunshots shortly after that.

"Looks like someone is still hanging on here." John clutched his rifle.

We passed by the courthouse, a stark shadow through the snow. We were on one edge of the Uptown District. I looked down the streets as we went by. Some cars, an overturned bus. Just a few zombies. Maybe they were down in the valley? We turned and parked in front of an older, Victorian-style house. Lauren left the truck on.

"Nick, will you guard the truck? John and I will wave if everything is alright. I just ... Need to know ..."

Yeah, no problem.

John and Lauren each grabbed a pistol and got out. They walked up the stairs. The door seemed to be locked, but it looked like Lauren put a key in the lock. I stepped out of the truck, motioning for the dogs to stay. I lit a cigarette and heard the front door of the house close quietly. I looked down the street to see a man in slacks, shirt and tie slowly shuffling toward me. The snow made everything seem like it was happening in a mute, slow way. The clouds had made a dim world darker, and I barely heard it moan. I picked up my crowbar from the back seat and walked toward it. It grew frantic as we drew near one another. That same feral excitement. Like a dog gets when you have a bone for it. It tried to speed up, but an ankle was dragging at an odd angle. Most of its lips were missing, revealing a stained snarl. I looked into its eyes. I don't know what I was looking for ... Nothing, really. That's all I saw. I supposed if they hated us, it would make it easier. Assign emotions to give the enemy a weakness. Help us bury our own ...

But there was nothing in those eyes ...

Nothing.

I swung the crowbar into the side of its head. Its eye socket caved in sideways and its body slumped to the ground. I had a momentary panic when the crowbar got stuck in its head and almost pulled it out of my hands. I ripped it out. I'd been using the hooked end, but was now rethinking it. There was another zombie, two blocks down. It had seen me kill the one at my feet, and

150

was headed towards me. At the rate it was moving, I had a few minutes. The house door opened behind me. I turned. John and Lauren emerged. Lauren was crying ... And there was a zombie, in the front yard, just a few feet from them.

Shit.

I ran around the hood of the truck and up the steps into the yard. John had started grabbing his pistol but stopped when he saw me. I hit the zombie with the blunt end, sending it sprawling. I hit it again, cracking its skull.

Sorry, guys. It must have come around the side of the house. I got another one on the other side of the truck.

"No harm, Nick. Good job."

Lauren had made a beeline for the truck as soon as I'd hit the zombie the first time. John got into the driver's seat and I got in the back again.

"I don't blame them for doing that ... I don't blame them at all ... What other choice did they have?"

John reached over and gently rubbed Lauren's shoulder. I looked out the back window. The zombie was still a block away. John put the truck in gear drove to the next block.

"Alright, Nick, where am I going?"

I gave him directions back up to where we'd been. More gunshots echoed through the city.

We can use back roads to get around the Uptown.

We found ourselves across the street from the courthouse.

"Is there a police station near that?"

Yeah. Just up around the corner.

"What do you think? I haven't seen many of the dead, and we can always use more ammo."

If they're this sparse everywhere, we should be fine.

Lauren had stopped crying. She turned and nodded, then went back to staring out the window. John throttled the truck forward. The tipped over bus was right by the courthouse, surrounded by a clutter of other vehicles. We drove around it, onto the sidewalk and partway into a parking lot. John gunned the truck around the side of the bus, then a truck ...

The street was filled with zombies. They were just ... Everywhere. Down the entire block and up the street by the police station. There was a jumble of police cars and hastily constructed barricades. One of the cruisers had burned. I saw quite a few zombies wearing uniforms.

"Ah, shit!" John cranked hard on the steering wheel and accelerated the truck forward into the crowd. We'd just gone through a maze of cars. There was no way to back out. John drove up on the sidewalk, avoiding more cars and, luckily, most of the zombies. He turned hard down a side street. It ended and John went to make a left, until we saw more zombies filtering up from another block. Trapping us in.

"Hold on!" We sped down the connecting street. The next intersection was also full of zombies. Everywhere. All of them turning their dead eyes onto the truck. John overcorrected on the wheel and we lurched over a sidewalk then took down a small tree and some metal railing. The diesel engine sputtered, lurched and died. John tried the ignition once, but the truck didn't start. The zombies were closing in, less than 50 feet away.

"Fuck! Get out! Move! MOVE!"

John, Lauren, the dogs and I jumped out of the truck right into a mob of zombies. The nearest swarm was barely an arm's reach from the tailgate ... I had my pistol and coat, but my rifle got stuck on a blanket. I gave it one final tug when I felt a hand on my shoulder.

"Leave it! Let's go!"

I turned, expecting John, even though his voice had come from the other side of the truck. I found myself staring at a zombie as its bloody, jagged mouth opened. Its breath made me gag.

Shit!

I brought the crowbar up under its chin, breaking more of its teeth. It stumbled back, but didn't lose its balance. I began to raise the crowbar again when a shot rang out. The bullet from Lauren's pistol split its head temple to temple.

152

"Come on!"

John had managed to grab only one AR. We turned and ran from the onslaught. The dogs took off through an opening up a small alley.

"Jack! Ava!" Lauren called to them and changed direction to go after them. John grabbed her by the arm and pulled her along.

"They'll be fine! Come on!"

We ran, knocking down zombies with the crowbar and rifle, then turned down an alley. There was a parking lot at the end ... Along with about a thousand zombies. Suddenly, a man appeared at the mouth of a connecting alley. John raised his rifle, then realized he was alive. The man motioned.

"This way! Follow me! We've got a place!"

There was no time to think. The moans and howls of the swarm grew louder. We ran after the guy ... kid. As we got closer, I could see he looked younger than me. He ducked down and we thought we'd lost him.

"Hey!" He motioned from a low door into a building. We ducked inside. The kid closed the door, enveloping us in black darkness.

Chapter 19

A flashlight split the dark and made us all squint.

"Sorry. Sorry." The kid aimed the light at a wall. Our faces were illuminated in reflected light. "My ... My name is Paul. Well, they all call me Little Paul, because the boss is Big Paul, but everybody calls him BP, so ..." He suddenly looked self-conscious and quieted down.

"I'm John. This is my wife Lauren, and our friend, Nick." We gave nods all around. The boy smiled tightly. "There are others here?"

"Yeah. Big Paul and the guys are upstairs. They sent me out to get you. We saw your truck crashing through all the Shuffles. They want to meet you. They're ... Upstairs ... I already said that. Sorry." He turned to a set of stairs. In the alley, we heard a zombie moan past. We followed Little Paul up the stairs.

"How old are you, Paul?" Lauren asked when we were up the stairs a ways.

"I'm 15." Paul puffed out his chest a little, then shrank and smiled back sheepishly. "Well ... Almost 15. In a month, I think. It's hard to tell time now days."

At the top of the stairs, Paul knocked three times. I heard some kind of locking mechanism move and a huge bearded man stood there, holding a shotgun.

"We thought maybe the Shuffles got you, kid. You get the people?" He looked past Paul at us, answering his own question. I was already beginning to feel uneasy. The big man stepped aside. We entered the room.

There were several men inside, 7 or 8. Most of them held shotguns. A few had scoped rifles. One guy, at the end of the room, held an AK-47. He also held a skinny, mousy-looking girl by the neck. He shook her, then pushed her. I felt my blood get hot. He turned to us. He wore a loose hooded sweatshirt. His

154

hair was cut short and his face boasted an overgrown goatee. He carried himself with an arrogance, like one of those people who pretend to be your friend, but will sell you out at a moment's notice.

"Hey. Hey! Welcome to BP's House of Pleasure!" He chuckled at his own joke. Various chuckles came from some of the men in the room. The girl turned away and leaned on a wall. "And who might you fine folks be?"

We made our introductions. Everyone around the room nodded in greeting, but Big Paul introduced everyone for them. The big one was Mike. The others ... Their names ... Hell, I can't remember. It didn't matter.

"And this ..." BP put his arm around Paul's neck and rubbed his knuckle over his head. "Is Little Paul. He's like my brother, you dig? He's our go-to man. Can outrun Shuffles like no one!"

"I wondered about that." Lauren looked BP in the eye. "You have a room full of men with guns, and you sent a kid out into a horde of those things? Any reasoning behind that?"

BP's demeanor changed instantly. I could almost feel the chill in the room.

"You ..." He wagged his finger. "We've gotta guard the fort, darlin'. Someone has to watch for all the others." He paused prior to saying "for". "Besides, Little Pauly here is fast. Those things will never catch him!"

There are others?

"Hell yeah! We got families of all sorts! We're a regular commune here!" More forced chuckles.

And her?

I motioned to the girl.

"Her? Don't worry about her, Nicky. She'll be alright."

Does she have a name?

BP's eyes narrowed, slightly.

"Yeah, but it don't matter. Her name is Flower Girl, right boys?"

"Yeah! Flower Girl!" Men hollered from around the room.

BP walked over to her and put his arm around her waist, pulling her

155

close to him.

"She's real sweet, Flower Girl is. Real sweet on everyone." Flower Girl tried to pull away. Everyone quieted down. "So what the fuck were you all doin', drivin' straight through the Uptown? Place is lousy with the damn Shuffles!"

"We were looking for anyone we knew. Any survivors."

Big Paul gave us a smile I didn't like.

"Shit, guys. There ain't no survivors! It's just us! Even Billings is gone!"

This was the first we'd heard of any recent news from the outside world. It was sobering.

"I see ...Well, can we stay for a night? I don't think our truck is wrecked, and once it's not surrounded, we'll most likely get back on the road. There has to be someplace."

"Nah, man, there ain't no place. Nothin' left out there. Come on in and meet the others. We're gonna rebuild, yeah! Start a new world, right here!" BP winked and walked toward another door, then suddenly stopped and turned, bringing up his AK. I didn't like what I saw in his eyes. "But, since we don't know you good enough just yet ... Lets have them guns."

Out of the corner of my eye, I could see John's face harden. His eyes flicked toward mine, issuing a silent warning. Without a word, he handed over his rifle, and Lauren's and his pistols. I handed over my revolver.

"The knives, too. Don't fuck with me."

The knives, too.

BP opened the door and we found ourselves on the third floor of the old power company building. The office looked immaculate, like the employees would be coming back into work tomorrow. There were more people in here, standing and sitting in various groups around the room. Some eyes lit up as we entered.

An older man and woman stood and confidently walked over to us. I heard the door shut behind us. Big Paul and his gang hadn't come in. Little

Paul walked across the office and looked down at the street from the giant windows. We were on the 4th floor. The man held out his hand.

"I'm George Dressler. This is my wife Linda."

She gripped our hands with both of hers in turn.

"We're so happy to see more living people. We ... Weren't sure if there was anyone left."

"Which direction did you come from?" George had a very calm demeanor.

"Lauren and I came down from Seeley Lake, through Rock Creek. That's where we met Nick."

I came from Missoula.

"What's there? How is it?" Linda had big, moist eyes. Kind of despairing, in a quiet way.

It's ... A lot like here ...

George and Linda shrank a little when I said that. I wanted to add something else, some kind of encouragement. I couldn't come up with anything.

"Nick?"

I turned. It was David Colvin, a guy who had been a good friend in high school. I hadn't seen him in 2 years. I grabbed him and hugged him.

David ... Holy shit!

I turned and introduced him to John and Lauren.

Where have you been, man? Last I talked to you, you were going to school in Baltimore. What are you doing back here?

"I was visiting my family. My brother was sick, so I came home. I got stranded here when it all started. Which is probably a good thing ... I talked to some of my friends back at school, before communications went down. It's ... Not good in the cities."

"What about the government? The military?" John sounded concerned. "They didn't just abandon all those people ..."

The look on David's face gave us the answer before his voice.

157

"They did, though ... I talked to Malia ... My girlfriend .... She was in Norfolk. She said everything was chaos there ... The Navy was loading people onto ships and going to sea. I could hear yelling and gunshots in the background. The line went dead after that ... I don't know what happened to her. She said the military was pulling out of cities, into the heartland. The government ... Shit, no one knows where they went. They disappeared."

"Come on, David, goddamn it! I thought you were going to stop talking about that. You're scaring the women!" A younger man sitting in a chair by a pregnant woman shouted over to David. She didn't look at us. She was staring at another woman who was holding a newborn baby. David spun.

"Just pretending it isn't happening won't make it go away, Lee! I appreciate you trying to remain optimistic, but I'm just being pragmatic!"

"Guys, let's just-" John stepped in, but the door behind us slammed open. BP came in, pushing Flower Girl.

"What the fuck is goin' on in here?! Why are you all bein' so fuckin' loud?!"

The gunmen filtered in behind him.

"David was just talking about the east coast and the government ... Again." Lee looked at the floor and grabbed the pregnant woman's hand. I realized that everyone here, not just Flower Girl, was afraid of BP. Even David looked away.

"The government? Shit! There is no more government! I'm the government now, and when those things rot away, we'll all start a new world here! Yeah?!" He walked toward the windows, brushing the hair of the woman with the baby as he passed. She jerked her head away and rolled her eyes. "So, David ... Shut the fuck up about it."

"Yeah. Sorry." David looked down. I almost said something, but decided not to rock the boat. Not while Big Paul and his gang held our guns. Instead, I walked slowly to the windows, on the other side of the office. I looked down into the street.

The block was littered with vehicles, debris, bullet casings and bodies.

Ones that hadn't gotten up, or had been put back down. The entire block, though, street to street, was filled with zombies. It looked like one of the big festivals that the town had hosted in better days. Except then the crowds had stumbled because they were drunk, and they hadn't been covered in blood and gore. I had no idea how we were going to get back to the truck and get out of the masses of dead below. Hell, I didn't even know if the truck still ran ...

"They thin out at night. I don't know where they go. That's when we move around. Night. Really bad idea go out in the day."

Yeah. We found that out.

The man had startled me, causing me to jump a little. He was sitting halfway under a desk, his legs to his chest. He held each side of his head in his hands.

I'm Nick.

"I had to kill my wife and little girls. They attacked me when I came home one day. Our youngest, Heather ... Got bit when she was on her way home from school. We ... We hid her, because they were rounding up the sick then ... She was always ... Telling stories ... Really creative ... She fell sick, then they attacked me ... I ... Had to ..." He stopped. After a moment, it was clear he was done.

We've all had to do some pretty terrible things to get here ...

"But what's the point?" I turned. It was the woman with the baby. "My husband died protecting Fynn and I and now I don't even know if I want to be here without him. I have my boy, but ... What's happening? Why did we live this far into it ... I ..." She looked down at the baby in her arms, still sleeping even through the commotion. "Sorry, Nick. I'm Sally, and this is my son Fynn. That's Phil. Those are the most words he's said in two days. He ... Doesn't talk much."

I'm surprised any of us do.

"You're from the outside. Missoula? Do you know anything? How this happened? Is the government doing anything about it?"

I don't know. I may have been the last one out of Missoula, for all I

159

know. We saw some military vehicles in Anaconda. Scientists. They must be doing something.

"The Army was here-"

The man with the pregnant girl cut her off.

"Did you say Anaconda? You guys came through Anaconda? Is there anyone there? We're from there-" He motioned to the girl with him. Her eyes were still fixated on Sally's baby. "Did you see anyone?"

I opened my mouth to answer him, but John cut me off.

"No, we didn't see anyone."

"Oh ..."

"Well, it's nice to see that social hour is off to a great fucking start." BP stretched in mock exaggeration. "We'll leave you ladies to your gossip. Come on, boys. You, too, Little Paul."

The gunmen filtered out. Little Paul looked scared, but didn't say anything. He just followed them. Flower Girl disappeared into a cubicle. I could hear gentle sobbing after a while.

The man from Anaconda was Lee and his pregnant girlfriend was Amy. The group of us spoke of our experiences in the past few months. All of them had been hiding various places in Butte. They had no idea what was happening in the outside world. Eventually, the conversation turned to talk of where the dead had come from, what caused them to rise.

"Maybe it's a virus or something. That's why the military was in Anaconda, right? You said scientists, right?" Lee looked at me. I nodded.

"Guys, there's no sense in speculating where this thing came from. It could be space aliens, it could be spores, it could be the devil. Who knows? We may never know. What we have to start thinking about is how to get out of here." George had a very rational way of handling things.

I figure we can go north, up into the campgrounds. I met some people outside of Missoula who were headed for Great Falls. They said there was an aid center at the Air Force base there.

George turned to me.

160

"I meant get out of here. Out of this building. Away from that psychopath Paul and his merry band of thugs."

John, Lauren and I faced him.

"What are you talking about, George?"

"Oh, I guess he wouldn't come right out and tell you." George pointed at my holster. "They took your guns?"

We nodded.

"He won't let you leave. He hasn't let any of us leave. We're not here by choice."

I saw a look cross John's face. It was similar to the one I'd seen back at Georgetown.

"Oh, we're leaving. We haven't been killed by the dead, and I'll be damned if some son of a bitch that's still alive-" Lauren put her hand on his shoulder.

"Why is he keeping us here? What could he possibly hope to accomplish?"

Everyone in the room looked to one another, as if deciding how to say it. Finally, George did.

"We're the bait, Lauren. At least the men are. There was more of us, a week or two ago. He sent ... Forced some to go out for supplies that might not have even been there. None of them came back. Since then, we've moved from building to building at night. Paul ... He makes a few of us run up alleys and streets. Draw the dead out and lead them away from his group. He and his boys never do it, mind you. They're too concerned with rebuilding a new "society". They're a bunch of goddamned cowards-"

The door opened behind us. Little Paul walked in, followed by BP and his gunmen.

"How's the ice cream social, ladies?" Again, the thugs laughed at BP's lame joke. "As you all can see, it's gettin' dark. The Shuffles are startin' to thin out."

I looked into the street and saw he was right. Light was fading fast and

161

the block was nearly empty now. I could just see a handful wandering around.

BP stood like a triumphant general.

"You all know what that means?"

An icy silence greeted him. The wind whistled by the window.

"It means, a group of us is goin' out to get some supplies. There's a grocery store a block from here. We're gonna go see if there's anything left."

Lee glared at him in aggravation.

"We went out last night, man! There was nothing in that fucking restaurant except some of those things! What makes you think-"

"Aw. Looks like Lee can't go because he has a busted face."

I saw Lee's eyes widen just as BP smashed him with the butt of his rifle. He fell back in his chair, blood running from his nose and mouth. Amy jumped up and swiped at BP, but Mike caught her and held her.

"You asshole! I'll kill you!"

BP looked at her and smirked arrogantly.

"Do you want some too, bitch?" He feigned another rifle strike and she flinched. "Shut the fuck up." He turned to the rest of us. "Let's see ... Tonight, I want David and ... How about you two. The newbies."

He pointed at John and I. John stood.

"Alright. Give me my pistol and rifle." He held out his hand. BP laughed cruelly.

"So you can shoot me in the back with it? Not fuckin' likely!" He motioned to Mike, who released Amy and handed over our knives.

I held the sheathed knife up.

Are you kidding me?

"NO! I'm not fuckin' kiddin' you! Want to know why? Because I have the fuckin' gun! ME! Paul fuckin' Larson!" He brandished the AK threateningly. On the other side of Mike, I could see John delicately shake his head.

Right. You're right. Sorry. Let's go, then.

"See, boys? I told you the newbs could be reasonable. Let's go, then!"

162

We set forth down the stairs. Amidst the boisterous talk of the gang, John leaned in close.

"Just hold off, Nick. I don't like this guy, either, but we have to wait until the time is right."

Just like Georgetown.

"Just like Georgetown."

We reached the bottom of the stairs. Flashlights clicked on. We all faced the large, metal door that led into the alley. The talk and jokes from the gang had stopped.

"Well ..." Mike, the big man, looked scared.

"Open it, fucker!" BP was still trying to play tough, but I could see the fear written all over his face.

Mike grabbed the two latch bolts, pulled them and pushed. The door swung out with a sluggish groaning and in rushed the cold night air that carried the heavy stench of death.

Chapter 20

The seven of us stood cautiously outside the door. BP and his gang just stood there, looking at one another. John's head snapped toward them.

"You guys want to shut those fucking lights off?"

It wasn't so much a request as an order. To my surprise, the flashlights immediately clicked off. There wasn't much wind, just a cold breeze blowing up the alley. What sounded like automatic weapon fire thumped over the wind from somewhere to the west. As our eyes adjusted, I realized I could see in the gloomy light of a moon trying desperately to shine through the hazy sky. Nobody moved. John looked at me and quietly walked to the mouth of the alley. I clutched my knife tightly and followed him. We looked up and down the connecting street. I could barely make out two zombies at the next intersection. Moans carried across the wind, but they sounded like they were a ways off. I heard footsteps behind us.

"The store is the next block up. Let's go." BP didn't sound confident. Again, he waited for John and I to move first.

We crept up the street. The bootsteps from BP's men sounded loud across the asphalt. They hadn't spotted the zombies, apparently, as one of the guys gasped and brought his shot gun up.

"Don't!" John hissed and leapt forward. The nearest zombie, just below the intersection, lunged at him. John's knife was fast, plunging directly into its temple. It dropped. The other one moaned and turned. I jogged up behind it and stabbed at it, but my blade slipped off of its skull and I ended up slapping it on the side of the head.

Shit.

It turned, slightly growling, as though I'd pissed it off. It raised an arm, then hit the ground as John's knife sank into the top of its head.

Sorry ... Damn ...

"Don't worry about it. Remember what I told you. It takes some practice to get a knife into a skull."

"Good! Let's fucking go!" BP clapped John on the shoulder.

"Keep your fucking voice-" A moan cut John off. Down the street, towards the heart of town, we saw a few zombies. Then a few more appeared. A few more, after that. There looked to be 20 or so, slowly coming at us. John ran across the street, taking cover behind an overflowing garbage can, scouting ahead. I knelt beside him, partially concealed behind a light pole. I sensed David duck down behind me.

"Jesus, Nick! You got close to that thing!"

I know. They're pretty slow. You'd better get used to it. Keep your voice down.

"Right ... Right! I-"

I shot him a look and he shut up. There didn't seem to be anything ahead. I looked at John. He nodded. We both stood and jogged up the street, ducking down behind a car. A tall, brick building loomed over us. David wasn't far behind. A moment later, BP and his three men came running up.

"What the fuck? I thought you were gonna wave when it was all clear!"

"What made you think I was going to do that?" John wore an expression of baffled mirth.

"Because you're ... You're fuckin' military or somethin'. Not just some useless old man!"

John's voice remained even and low.

"I'm going to tell you one last time, Paul. Keep your voice down or I'll cut the tongue out of your head."

BP's eyes flashed and he swung out with his rifle. John smoothly batted it aside, grabbed BP by his collar and swung him around against the car. The knife was instantly at his throat. The other two pointed shotguns at John.

"If you idiots want to make it to that store and back, you'll have to listen to me. Keep quiet, keep low, keep fast. Don't use your guns ..." John

165

turned and looked at the two gunmen. "Especially if you're pointing shotguns at the guy you're trying to protect."

"Put those down ..." BP's eyes were wide with terror. His voice was quiet. They lowered the guns. John let him go.

"You're fuckin' dead, man ... When we get back, you're d-"

John looked at him with calm, cold eyes.

"We're all going to die of something, at some point. In the meantime, let's make sure we get back. And I'm not 'waving when it's all clear'. Keep up or stay here."

A moan drifted up the alley behind us. John and I jogged up to the next corner. We didn't see any more zombies between ourselves and the grocery store. At least none that the low light revealed. There were several cars parked randomly down the block, doors and trunks open. We crept along, doubled-over, from car to car. Most of the gloveboxes in the cars were open. They'd been looted ... Who knows what the thieves were even looking for? I sure as hell didn't. Someone tripped behind us, kicking something metal across the ground. John spun, glaring in the direction of the noise.

"Crap. Sorry." The guy was standing, looking around at his feet to see what it was. John made a lowering motion with his hand. The guy didn't seem to get it at first, then his eyes widened in realization. He squatted.

"If you assholes insist on getting us killed, Nick and I are just going to get my wife and leave. We didn't come here to die." John looked BP in the eye.

"You fuckers aren't goin' anywhere. You're pretty good at this game. We can use people like you. Everyone else is scared to go near those things, even with a gun to the head, ya know?" BP grinned smugly at what he'd just said.

"Then stay quiet and watch where the fuck you step. If we get surrounded, I guarantee you'll be the first to die, Larson."

"Don't forget, I've got a fuckin' gun-"

"I've taken guns from better men than you." John turned back and looked ahead. I gazed with him, into the gloom. I could make out a shadow, a

166

few cars ahead. It was slow, small. I figured it was a kid ... A kid zombie, I mean. We went around opposite sides of the car. My foot kicked something heavy and soft. I could make out a shape. It looked like a baby, missing parts ... I'm still trying to forget that.

I don't think I ever will.

We worked our way to the car next to the small zombie.

"Nick, like I said before, it takes practice to effectively get a blade through a skull. Power and precision take time to combine effectively. This will be an easy one. Go for it."

I felt the blood drain from my face.

Me? Uhhh ... Are you sure that's a good idea ...?

"I'm sure. You'll probably need to know this sooner or later. Better sooner. Remember- power, precision. Don't second guess yourself halfway to the kill."

I nodded, took a deep breath. I slowly made my way around the car. The grocery store was ahead and to my right. The giant windows facing the street were strangely intact. The zombie was a small boy. Maybe 10 years old. He ... It stood with its back to me, staring at the building across the street and swaying. I could hear its teeth gnashing. Constantly gnashing. I stalked up behind it and raised the blade.

I don't know how it knew I was there. Maybe I made more noise than I'd thought. Hell, maybe it *smelled* me. It spun so quickly ... I didn't know they could move that fast. One of its hands grabbed my left wrist. Its touch was so cold, and much stronger than I'd expected. I tried twisting my arm out of its grip, but it held fast. I slammed the knife down into the top of its head. The skull gave way easier than I thought. Its hand slipped limply off my arm and its body fell to the ground. John came around the car. I was shaking, slightly.

"Good job, Nick. You have to let the fear fall away and just go for it, sometimes."

Easy for you to say.

"No. It isn't. Everyone here is afraid. Use it to your advantage."

167

I nodded. I was beginning to understand what he was saying. We slowly crept to the front doors of the grocery store. It was dark inside. I couldn't see anything. John and I were on opposite sides of the glass double-doors. John reached out and grabbed at the handle, pulling at it. It wasn't locked. It swung out towards John ...

I saw the gray hand come up to slap against the window before we all heard it. The door swung open and a zombie came stumbling out. John and I jumped back, raising our knives. Another zombie followed it out the door, then another, then another. And another. Another.

Shit!

John and I backed off in opposite directions. Flashlights clicked on, illuminating the large glass windows running along the storefront. Zombies were lined up inside, pounding on the windows. The grocery store was full of them. It's still hazy what happened then. One of BP's men raised his shotgun and John yelled at him to stop. He fired anyway, and the others joined in. A multitude of gunshots rang off the buildings as the windows exploded. Zombies just came pouring out, filling the street.

We retreated back down the street as more zombies exited out the windows. John was on the other side of the swarm. Some turned and went after him. The larger group turned and came after us. David, Mike and I backed against the remaining windows. Zombies inside slapped at them, trying to get to us. We were soon cut off from BP and his other two men. I saw John disappear down the block, running from the swarm.

David, Mike and I came to the mouth of an alley. We jogged down it as a mass of dead stumbled down after us. Mike turned and fired a shotgun blast from the hip. It caught the nearest zombie in the center of its torso and pushed it backwards. A group of zombies fell like dominoes. I didn't think I would laugh at the absurdity of it, but I must have. Mike shot me a look. I turned to run down the alley, just in time to see a zombie emerge from behind a dumpster and sink its diseased jaws into the side of David's neck. His scream echoed up the alley.

168

David! Fuck!

I ran down to him and stabbed the zombie in the side of its head. It released him and dropped. David fell to the ground. I knelt by him. I could hear the zombies moaning as they shuffled down the alley. The blood around the wound was already turning black. Dark tendrils were climbing out from around the bite mark.

"Oh ... Oh shit ... Nick ... Oh ...No-no-no ..." David put his hand up to the wound. Blood squirted through his fingers. "Shit ... Nick ... Don't ... Don't let me be- become ... One of th-them ... Please!"

I turned to see Mike shoot a zombie that was faster than most. It didn't quite run, but its shuffle was more of a lope. It fell back. A few zombies tripped over it, tripping more in turn. They immediately began climbing to their feet.

"Kid, we gotta go!" Mike ran down to me. His eyes were wide with fear. I stood. He bent down over David. Tears were streaming down David's cheeks. His breath was coming in ragged gasps. The black veins had reached his face. Spiderwebs of death. "Jesus. This kid looks like-"

Power. Precision.

I plunged the knife into the back of Mike's head. I expected his body to fall as quickly as the zombie's had. His hand shot up and grabbed my wrist, pulling me towards him. I couldn't let go of the handle. He looked up at me. Blood ran from his mouth.

"Son ... of a ... Bitch!" The light faded from his eyes. His grip loosened and his body hit the ground. The knife slid out of his skull, dripping dark red. I quickly grabbed his shotgun and scooped a few shells from his vest. The zombies were about 30 feet away. Another faster one pushed through the crowd and charged at me. I raised the shotgun and shot it. The shot must have been a little off. I blew one of its shoulders away and its arm fell off. Its head lolled to one side as it spun and fell. It started to clumsily climb to its feet, but was having trouble with one arm.

I racked another shell into the chamber and pointed it at David.

Please tell my mom and dad I love them.

169

I don't know why I said it. I didn't believe in any sort of afterlife. No heaven or even hell. But maybe there was something. A crossroads, where you'd meet everyone you'd ever met. Something. I don't know.

I pointed a shotgun at one of my best friends from my school days. A kid I'd gotten into my first fight with, who I'd smoked my first joint with. A guy who I hadn't seen since our buddy's wedding, summers past. In a brighter world, more colorful when seen through the lens of memory.

I pulled the trigger.

Gunshots are a lot louder at night.

I ran deeper into the alley. It split a few yards down. I took a left, back toward the street, fumbling to feed shells into the magazine as I went. I'd only handled a shotgun a few times before. I dropped a shell and cursed. I looked up as another zombie appeared feet in front of me. I hit it with the butt of the shotgun, then blew the top of its head off. I turned right when I reached the end of the alley ...

The street below was filled with zombies. They were turned away from me, as though they were chasing something else down the street. And they probably were. BP and his remaining two guys would have run for their lives. I would've. One of the zombies had turned, probably due to the gunshot. They came after me. I had 7 shells, about 40 zombies, and a city block between where I was and where I needed to be.

Shit.

I darted across the street and into the next alley. It narrowed, then emptied into a parking lot across from a tall, old hotel. I ran down and crossed at the connecting street. The main crowd of zombies was still headed downhill, but a smaller group was now headed up to where I had been. I looked in all ways at the next intersection. I couldn't see anything. I ran down. I came up to a small, hatchback car. Its doors were closed. At that moment, the remaining moonlight drifted behind a dark cloud. The world turned pitch black.

Great.

I turned and banged my knee on the car. I swore silently and lifted the

170

shotgun, then grabbed the car door and ripped it open. The dome light illuminated the interior. It was empty. I quickly climbed in, then closed and locked the doors. I found a blanket in the back. I leaned the seat down and covered myself up, hoping they couldn't smell through cars. I kept an eye peeked out, hoping the clouds would part and give me some more moonlight. Then I could get back to the door and ...

But, no, I couldn't do that. There was a swarm of zombies that would now be gathered around the door in the alley. I didn't know how long they would be there. Until they lost interest, and that could take all night. I leaned back and cradled the shotgun. The seat was hard and uncomfortable. I lay there, thinking about what had happened and what would happen next. It was too much and I felt myself getting dizzy. I closed my eyes and tried to make the world still. I felt myself tipping over a black void, then falling in.

Chapter 21

I opened my eyes to a dingy light beginning to reveal the world around me. I took the blanket away from my eyes in time to see a zombie come up on the car. It stumbled past, scraping alongside the car as I quickly hid again, peering out through a tiny fold. It stopped, looked into the car for a chilling moment, then shuffled on. I could hear it moan through its cracked and bloody remains of lips and teeth. I pulled the blanket down. Something hard dug into my hip. I reached for it.

It was the shotgun.

I'd wondered if last night was some twisted nightmare. But it had happened. I lifted the shotgun. It was a short barrel, "tactical-model" pump-action. I reloaded a few shells into the magazine and sat up, looking up and down the street. I saw a few zombies, but none were looking in my direction. The one that had passed by the car was disappearing down the street that I had to follow. I slowly, quietly opened the car door and swung my legs out ...

I kicked a zombie right in the head. It was crawling on the ground. Both of its legs were bloody tatters just below the knee, trailing bloody muscle and bone. I fell back into the car, bringing my legs up, but it grabbed one of my boots. It was stronger than it looked, and tried to pull itself up into the car. I kicked it again with force and it fell back, sprawling on the pavement, moaning and hissing. I grabbed the knife off my belt and planted it in the top of the thing's head. It went silent and limp. I took a deep breath, turned.

The one that had passed the car must have heard the crawler moan. It was standing on the street corner. It stared at me for a moment, then charged forward. It looked like a fresher corpse. It was faster, like some of them last night. Not running, but ... Fast enough I didn't trust myself to kill it with the knife. All it took was a bite ...

As it closed the distance, I brought up the small shotgun. The barrel

172

was short, so I didn't know what distance it would be effective to. When the zombie was about 15 feet out, I took a deep breath, then thought better of it and exhaled. I tried to hold the gun steady, pulling it tight to my shoulder and pulled the trigger. It bucked hard in my arms, tweaking my right shoulder back. I lost my grip on the small forend, nearly hitting myself in the face. The buckshot tore off the top of the zombie's head and half of its face. It jerked backwards and went down. The shot echoed off the buildings around me. I turned to see if the zombies the next block up noticed.

They did. Of course they did.

There had been 7 or so, up the street. They all headed down toward me as more came from around both corners. Within less than a minute, there were now upwards of 25, all stumbling down towards me. I turned and ran. I stuck to the middle of the street, so I would have a better view as I came around the corner. Just when I did, a figure came running down the street a block over. It was Little Paul. Behind him was the main mass of zombies from last night. More zombies had joined in the swarm behind me. I ran down the center of the block below me, through a small park with concrete picnic tables and around the back of a small restaurant. I hooked over to intercept Little Paul as he came down the street. I stepped out and he raised a small hatchet, then realized I wasn't a zombie. He lowered the weapon, but didn't stop running. He called out as he passed.

"Nick! You're alive! Follow me, we've gotta go!"

I ran after him.

Where are the others?

"They're coming! We have to meet them a few blocks from here!"

We dodged down an alley and stopped to catch our breaths. We were both panting. I loaded a shell into the empty chamber on the gun and peeked around to see if the zombies were still coming.

They were. Of course they were.

I turned to ask Paul where the others were going, when I saw movement of the street beyond the alley, a few blocks down. It was our group, running as fast as they could. BP must have sent Paul out to bait the zombies away from the door. I looked down at the kid, impressed by his bravery. He looked up, nodded. I nodded back. We turned and ran again, back down the street. The front wave of zombies had gained some ground. I let Paul have a slight lead and he ran straight down toward the high school. I could see our group already next to a set of double doors. I heard a shotgun blast, and they entered the building. In an alley behind a big, blue building to our right, a few zombies wandered aimlessly through an old, dirt lot. They turned as they heard the now merging swarms coming down the street and gave chase.

We entered the parking lot of the school. I stopped and turned to see if I could shut the chain-link gates, but both had been crushed and bent. One was hanging off its hinges. The car that had run through it was on its side on a patch of grass. It had hit the curb too sharply.

The first wave of zombies were less than 100 feet away, some coming at a near-jog. I swore and ran after Little Paul, who hadn't stopped and was now almost to the doors that hung wide open, the lock shattered. I passed a large banner with a purple dog, stained with blood. It said "Let's Go, Bulldogs!"

I ran through the double doors and pulled them shut behind me, closing myself into darkness. As my eyes adjusted to the little light filtering in tiny windows, I looked for something to block them with. The zombies were now streaming into the parking lot. I fumbled around and felt something long and somewhat solid. I picked it up.

It was a human arm, hand still attached. It was decomposing, giving off a sour odor. It was small ... A teen or young adult.

Fuck ...

I jammed it into the two handles, sealing the door. The rotting arm wouldn't hold for long. I saw a flashlight waving at me from down a hall.

"Nick! Over here!"

I pulled out my headlamp and ran down to Little Paul and we headed through the broken hallway. It was littered with books, backpacks and coats.

Some of the lights hung down from the exposed ceiling, many of the panels broken on the floor. Lockers hung open. Pictures of smiling kids on bright, sunny days. I ran into Paul, tripping us both. We fell among the abandoned symbols of a civilization that seemed so far away now.

Sorry, Paul.

I helped him to his feet. His cheeks glistened in my light. He sniffed and turned away.

You okay, man?

He pointed at the nearest open locker. A picture of a pretty brunette girl.

"My ... My sister ..." He bent down and grabbed his flashlight and hatchet. "Let's go ..."

Behind us, the double doors slammed inwards, sending a booming echo down the hall. We took off, rounded a corner and saw George wave out a door to us. We slipped in and he shut it quickly, sticking a metal bar between the handle and the wall. The room smelled like oil and burned metal. The school's auto shop. There was a truck in the bay, engine in various pieces. Flashlights around the room revealed everyone except John, Mike and David. I turned to Lauren.

John didn't-?

BP shoved me from the side. I almost fell, but caught myself and wheeled on him.

"What the fuck happened last night?!"

I should ask you the same thing! Who the hell shot that goddamned window out! None of this would have happened if-!

BP brought up his AK and pointed it at me. In his waistband, my revolver stuck out above his waist.

"You'd better shut the fuck up, man, or I'll kill you."

I brought up the shotgun and jammed the barrel into his chest.

We all may be dead because of you or one of these idiots. Better this way.

175

The remaining men all pointed their guns at me. BP's eyes widened.

"Mike's ... Where the hell did you get that?! Drop it now or you're dead!"

They may get me, but I'll sure as shit get you, too.

My finger tightened on the trigger. BP looked around and made a downward motion with his hand.

"Stop ... Stop!" He put on a false smile. "Hey! Come on, now d- dude. Go ahead and hold on to it. We could use someone like you."

I reached down and grabbed my .357 from his belt, placing it into mine.

I'll take this, too. We could really use someone like John, but I don't know where he is ...

Lauren shot up.

"He's ... Not dead?"

I don't know ... I don't think so. Last I saw. He was running from the dead. I didn't see where he went.

Lauren looked slightly relieved.

"And Mike? How'd you get his gun?" A big guy looked at me.

"This here is Mike's brother. Better have a good story for him ...N ..."

Nick. My name is Nick.

"Right ... Nick ...

I looked at the big guy. He looked a lot like Mike had.

Mike got caught up by a group of those things. They tore him apart.

"Then how'd you get his gun?" The big guy took a step forward.

He dropped it. I grabbed it.

"So you only have one shell in there? I heard a bunch of shots while we were running down here. Seven, to be exact." He eyed me suspiciously.

Hell, I don't know. What does that have to do with-?

"Show me."

What?

"Show me how many shells you have in that fucking gun, or I'll blow

176

your head-!"

A loud boom resounded down the hallway outside the shop door. We heard moans filtering down the hall to us.

They're in! They're in! Shut up!

I saw the big guy's eyes flash as I extinguished my light. I motioned for everyone else to do the same.

"I'm not done with you, boy."

I didn't respond, but felt my way over to where I'd seen Lauren. I leaned in close.

We have to go, or we're going to get killed. There's a door to a different part of the school in the office behind us. See if you can quietly spread the word to the rest. I'll try to distract BP and his guys ...

Lauren nodded in the low light that made it in the minimal windows. She moved toward George, Linda and Phil. Flower Girl was sitting by the large bay door, knees hugged to her chest. Lee, Amy, Sally and Fynn were seated near the office door. They looked terrified. Outside the door, we could hear dozens of zombies filtering past, constantly moaning and chewing.

I walked toward BP when Fynn began to cry. The wail of a tired, scared baby. It was loud. The zombie's moans changed pitch and the door began to shudder as hands pounded on it. BP ran over to Sally and pulled out a pistol.

"Shut the fucking kid up, or I will!"

All the color drained from Sally's face and she cradled Fynn tight, cupping a hand over his mouth and nose.

"No ... Shhhh, baby ... Shhh ... Mommy's here ... Shhh ..."

As the door shook, the metal bar that held the door began to shake loose.

Hold the door!

I ran and shoved against it, trying to set the bar back in it. As I'd hoped, three of BP's men ran over and pushed with me. The pounding began to cease and I slowly backed off the door. The baby was silent and the zombies

177

were quickly losing interest ... I hoped so, at least. Suddenly, Sally let out a scream.

"NOOO!!! FYNN! NO!!! MY *BABY!!! NOOOOOOOO!!!*"

The fists started pounding again with renewed ferocity. I spun to see Sally holding the limp body of her child. She must have ... Suffocated it by accident. She dropped to her knees, shrieking as BP ran over and grabbed her by the hair.

"Shut up, you stupid-!"

She laid Fynn's body down and lunged at him.

"I'll kill you, you bastard! Son of a bitch!" She clawed at his face. He slapped at her, dropping his rifle. I dove and slid across the oil-stained floor, grabbing it. I tripped Sally and BP in the process. They fell on top of me, but I rolled out. I jumped to my feet.

The bar!

I pointed just as the bar started to slip out of the door handle. One of BP's men grabbed at it, but inadvertently pulled it free. The door slammed inward with a wave of zombies that fell onto BP's three guys. They screamed as they started getting torn into. One of them tried to crawl out, but a zombie latched onto his leg, tearing his calf muscle out. His scream was louder than Sally's.

Lauren, everyone, we have to go!

I ran to the big garage door and jumped off a stack of tires, grabbing onto the rope that led up to the opener. I slammed down into the ground, burning my hands on it, but the door rolled up into the ceiling. I didn't see any zombies. I ran out backward, making sure everyone got out alright. Lauren, George, Linda, Phil and Little Paul appeared in the daylight. Lee was helping Amy run when a zombie grabbed onto her. Lee spun and punched it in the face, causing it to fall backward. They ran out the door. Lauren shouted in.

"Sally! Flower! Come on!"

Sally and BP were still struggling on the floor when the wave of zombies reached them. They realized it too late as they were pulled into the snarling mass of dead. BP's last two guys came running out the door towards us, Mike's brother one of them. I raised the AK and aimed at him, pulling the trigger. Nothing happened. Lauren reached over and slapped the safety switch down.

"Do it!"

I fired, catching the big man square in the chest. He went down. I fired again, striking him in the throat as Lauren unclipped the small shotgun from around my chest. She shot the other man in the chest, caving in his ribs. Mike's brother's eyes were wide in surprise, fear and rage. The zombies fell onto him. That's when I saw Flower Girl. She was walking straight into the mass as they charged her.

Wait! Don't ... !

She looked back and smiled sadly. Then she turned and ran straight into the crowd. She went down as they fell upon her, ripping chunks from her flesh.

She didn't make a sound as she was torn to pieces.

Shit.

We turned and ran as zombies began to swarm around the side of the school. We made it to a gate, but this one was secured with a chain and padlock.

"Nick! Do you have more shells? I'm empty!"

I nodded, and Lauren brought the shotgun up, when we all heard a low rumble. The truck, John at the wheel, flew down the street turned, skidded, then crashed through the gate, snapping the chain. Jackson and Ava hung out the passenger side window. They whined when they saw Lauren.

"Ride's here! Let's go!" John beamed. I suddenly felt elated. I turned and began shooting into the zombies. I'd never fired an AK before and wasn't very accurate, but the rounds were powerful enough to knock them down when they were hit. Lauren climbed into the cab and I jumped into the back when everyone else was loaded. John hit the gas and we reversed out of the small lot and shot down the street. The road split, and we took the left fork. Behind us, zombies poured out into the street.

This section of town had nearly empty streets, so the trip was fast. We drove through a small neighborhood, dodging a few cars. I saw some zombies in houses and yards, but not in the numbers that we'd seen even just a few blocks up. We turned onto a road that eventually met the highway and the mountains to the south. I looked back. George said what I was thinking

"Oh, dear god ..."

On the hill behind us, it looked like we'd stirred up a nest of dead. The streets were bustling with what looked like thousands of zombies. All coming south. Slowly making their way after us.

Lauren leaned halfway out the back window.

"How's that rifle on ammo?"

I figured out how to remove the magazine and looked into it.

Maybe ... 10, 11 rounds?

She handed me the remaining AR and a bag of loaded mags. I passed the AK in. I looked behind us, then looked around at everyone. The fear was beginning to fade off of their faces ... All except Lee. He looked terrible. Pale, sweaty ...

His right hand was bloody, but it had already started to coagulate. The veins in his hand and on his forearm were black tendrils.

You punched that thing?

"Yeah ... It attacked ... My wife and ... And child."

In the mouth?

"That's how ... We did it back in Ana ...Anaconda. Break ... The fucker's ... J ...Jaw ..."

Shit.

"What? What is it?" Amy grabbed his non-injured hand.

He's infected. He's going to die, then come back as one of them ...

Tears welled up in Amy's eyes.

"No ... No, that's not true ... He'll be fine ..." She put on a weak smile and patted his hand, looking at him. "He'll be just fine."

I shared a look with George, then crawled forward and stuck my head in the cab. Jackson licked my face.

Guys ...

"Nick? Everything okay back there?"

No ... Lee punched one in the mouth ... He cut his hand on its teeth. He's infected.

"Damn! We can't stop yet. Lots of neighborhoods coming up. Is he still breathing?"

Yeah. He's still cognitive, talking. We'll have to deal with him ...

"I know ... Shit! Keep an eye on him for now?"

You've got it. John ...

"Yeah?"

It's good to have you back. Thanks for bailing us out back there.

"You don't ever have to thank me for that, Nick. We're all in this together."

I smiled, nodded and climbed back into the back of the truck bed. George gave me a knowing look. I gently shook my head. Lee reached out with his uninjured hand and grabbed my shoulder.

"You ... You're going to have to k ... Kill me, right?"

I don't ...

His eyes burned into mine, silently pleading.

Pleading for an answer I didn't want to believe.

Yes. You're going to die regardless, then come back. You'll be a threat to all of us.

Lee's face took on an alarmed look and he quickly glanced at Amy, then back to me.

All of us.

"No! That's a lie! Lee would never hurt me!" Amy cradled his head.

"It ... It burns, Nick ... I can feel ... I ... It-it's in my brain ... It burns so bad ..."

Just ... Hang on, Lee. We'll be there soon.

181

We sped down the street. I looked into neighborhoods on the side. Zombies emerged from houses as we passed. Behind us, I knew ... We'd awoken a whole dead town. I pulled up my collar and stared out the back. No one talked. We couldn't have heard each other, anyway. Not with the cold wind whipping in our ears. A freezing rain started falling. It was sour to the taste.

We came back to the highway. One of those giant mine trucks, from the open-pit ... Someone must have stolen one. It was tipped over on the on-ramp. Too wide for it, I guess. People's belongings had spilled out into the wet, brown grass. There were a few bodies. The highway beyond was crammed with cars, all headed east, towards Billings. I thought of Billings, imagining the highway there was cluttered by vehicles headed this way.

I wondered if there was anything left ... Any place we could go to.

Suddenly we heard a clanging crunch, followed by a metallic bang. The truck jumped slightly and skidded to a halt. It threw all of us forward. I landed on Phil. As we all scrambled to our feet, I saw John clambering out of the truck. He had a bloody knot on his forehead and Ava had a slightly bloody mouth. Lauren looked dazed. They both began grabbing weapons and supplies from the truck and handing them out.

What ...?

"We just blew a piston. Goddamned tree did more damage than I thought. We've gotta start walking."

To where?

"South. We've gotta hit those mountains. Maybe cross over into the Jefferson Valley. There's nothing left here. I found a radio. But we have to go. Now."

I looked over my shoulder. There was a small, rural neighborhood a little less than a mile away. A spread out line of dead had begun to stumble out from it. They were a ways off, but there was easily 30 or more. And we had an infected man and a pregnant woman to consider.

We all started walking south as fast as we could. We immediately started leaving Lee and Amy behind.

182

What are we going to do about them?

"I don't know." John stopped. "I've been trying to figure that out. Maybe one of the vehicles ahead still works-"

A low buzz interrupted him. The zombies were a lot closer now, filtering through gates into the fields between us and them. Suddenly, a small helicopter shot overhead and stopped to hover above the field. It was dark green and had a red skull and crossbones painted on it. "TELUM" was painted in the same red on the underside. It had two stubby wings that carried what looked like rocket pods and guns ...

The guns lit up. They whirred to a start, then made a *crack-buzz* sound. The first wave of zombies dropped instantly. Behind us, a heavier thumping filled the air. John had already turned. I imagine he knew the sound.

Two Blackhawk helicopters swooped in and landed on either side of us, blocking the road. They were also painted with skull-crossbones and 'Redick's Raiders'. Men in camo vests but civilian clothes jumped off, ARs drawn. They jogged at us in a staggered formation, covering each one of us. I raised my own rifle, but saw John was already putting up his hands.

"They're trained, Nick ..."

"Drop your weapons and get to your knees!" The lead man yelled from behind his rifle. We all complied. Someone came up behind me, threw a hood over my head and zip-tied my hands behind my back. As they tightened the hood, I heard someone yell.

"Infected!"

A single gunshot.

I was picked up and thrown onto one of the helicopters. The small one lit up its guns again. It sounded like a giant zipper. I don't know why I thought that. I guess my whole world had turned completely insane in a matter of months. Things that were never supposed to happen were now happening. How could any concept of reality still exist?

So this was real, now. I had to take it for what it was. I'd already prepared for death a long time ago, I think ... Probably that day when I saw the

183

first zombie in the parking lot. Reality had changed and now this was it.

I heard shouting over the heavy thump of the blade. Wind blew through the open doors as we lifted up into the sky.

Chapter 22

I'd never been on a helicopter before. I felt like we didn't climb very high in elevation, and we started swooping from side to side, as though we were flying through a valley. Air whistled around the hood over my head and the heavy thump of the rotors bounced in my ears. I started feeling nauseous. I shut my eyes tight and bit my lower lip, trying to take deep breaths, trying not to vomit.

I had no idea who these people were. It had to be the same ones from the helicopter over Georgetown. But who were they? Military? Bandits? Why hadn't they just killed us or left us to the swarm of zombies?

Questions swam though my head, making me all the more nauseous. I felt some watery bile come up in my mouth and I forced myself to swallow it again. Bitter and acidic. I figured they would probably kill and eat the men when we got there and keep the women like those refugees ...

We must have been going a lot faster than I thought, because in a matter of minutes, I heard the pitch of the rotors change as we started to descend. We came to a hover, then thumped down softly. I was violently dragged to my feet, then walked a few yards up a small hill and pushed back down to my knees. I don't know if my other senses were compensating for my lack of sight, but I sensed a few guys standing behind us with guns. I understood why John had surrendered so fast. He knew this kind, and these weren't thugs like BP and his gang. These were dangerous professionals with the gear to back it up. They patted me down, taking the headlamp, cigarettes and tiny .22 pistol I'd stupidly forgotten until now.

The hood was roughly pulled from my head. Standing in front of me was a man of average height. He looked about a decade older than me, short hair, wearing civilian clothes, a heavy, metal-studded, crude leather jacket ... But shiny, hardened-looking leather. Like a medieval tunic. Over it was a military vest. Two bars, side by side, adorned the collars of his coat. Beside him was a woman of about the same age, shorter, but tough looking. She also wore a heavy, leather coat. They both held military rifles and wore pistols on their legs. Civilian clothes or not, they carried themselves as military. The man looked at each of us in turn.

"I'm Captain Ian Redick. These are my Marine Raiders."

I heard more of the men coming up from the helicopters. Redick opened his mouth to speak again, when someone cut him off.

"Nick ...?"

I looked to my left. Standing beside Phil was a familiar face. One of the most familiar in my life. It was Marine Sergeant Andrew Jerritt. My brother.

I could see his eyes moisten. Mine did, too. He ran over, knelt and hugged me. My hands were still bound behind my back.

"Jesus ... Nick, shit, Nick ... I thought you were dead!" He leaned back, then pulled a pair of snips from his vest. He reached over me and cut my hands free. He pulled me to my feet.

I ... Thought I was, too ...

"Jerritt?"

"This is my brother, Redick. My kid brother. Are these your people, Nick?"

Yeah, yeah! They're all good people.

Andrew nodded at Redick. Redick nodded back, then made a hand signal to the other ... Soldiers, I guess. They cut everyone loose.

"What about her, Redick?" One of the men pointed to a figure still aboard one of the helicopters. It was the bound, hooded , pregnant figure of Amy. She was writhing around screaming something unintelligible. A man stood over her, an open med kit by him. Redick called up to him

"Give her something to calm her, Doc. Just a little though ... She's pregnant."

The man turned, smiled, nodded.

186

"This ain't my first rodeo, Cap!" He turned back and started rummaging through his med kit.

The casual manner they all shared had me somewhat confused. They were military ... They *had* to be. They were organized. They had automatic weapons. They had *Blackhawks*. And my brother ...

I turned back to Andrew. He grabbed me by my shoulders.

"I can't fucking believe you're here. What happened to you? How did you get here?"

I told him about Missoula, how Dan, Alli and I had hid from the worst of it. I told him about the refugees, the cat, meeting John and Lauren. Georgetown, Anaconda ... Butte. It felt good to get it out, to tell my brother about it, glad that he was ...

Where are the boys? Where are Anthony and Andrew?

Andrew looked away momentarily, then back. His eyes were holding back sadness.

Andrew led me around the corner of a tent. His oldest son, Anthony, sat on a bench just outside a bunk tent. His hands were clenched by his sides, but he looked at the ground, staring off into space. I put my hand on his shoulder.

Hey, Anthony. How are you, buddy?

His body was tense. He didn't look at me. He didn't move, didn't make a sound. I could barely feel him breathing. Andrew patted my shoulder and we walked back out onto the main route.

"He's been that way since I found him."

I hadn't even taken into consideration that Andrew's estranged wife and the kids lived in Butte. He'd happened by here after Billings ...

"When I got here ... To Butte, I mean. We set up shop at the airport, first. It wasn't secure ... But a few of us went in, looking for family, friends ... I got to Amanda's house, the door was locked, so I figured, that's a good thing, right?"

We walked through the tents, by others. More survivors. They looked

187

at me like I was a ghost. Sometimes, I felt like one.

"Me and Lilton went in. Our families lived in the same neighborhood ... I called for everyone, didn't hear anything. I went upstairs ...."

Andrew looked at me. His eyes were moist, but hard.

"I found Anthony curled up, in a closet. His mother and Andrew were ... Well, their bodies were on the floor. There was a cast iron skillet ... He's just kept saying 'Mommy was so sick, then she got up and got really mad at us. She hurt Andy, then tried to hurt me. I just wanted her to stop. I'm sorry, daddy ... I'm sorry ...' He said that a few times, until he fell asleep on the helo. More of a coma, I guess. He just woke up a about a week ago. He hasn't spoken since. Fuck, Nick. He's only eight. What kind of world is he going to grow up in?"

I don't even know what kind of world we're in now. What's happening, Andrew? Do you know? Does anybody know?

Andrew shook his head.

"There were rumors ... Always rumors. Shit, the enlisted ranks are a gossip mill. Some of the guys said we made the initial virus. Used it on North Korea as a means of clandestine retaliation, after their surface nuke test. I don't imagine it was supposed to ... Do this. But, you know, it's the 'my buddy's-brother's-friend's-dad's CO at Detrick' telephone game. All I know- it's worldwide, brother. It's everywhere. I don't even know if there's anyone left to care ..."

We walked through the camp, surrounded by actual, living people. Neither of us spoke, for a time.

Have you heard from mom and dad?

"I talked to them, right before we got deployed. They said they were headed to Billings ..."

I thought so ... I've been having these weird dreams ...

"About a beach?"

I stopped and looked at him.

Yeah.

"Me too ..."

I knew you were alive ... From the dreams ... And I knew mom and dad were dead ...

"Yeah ..."

Is everybody in Billings dead? What happened there?

"You'll find out soon enough, little brother."

Ahead, I saw Redick and the female Marine walking. The rest of my group was with them. Isn't that funny? People I hardly know, but they're my family now. Really, all we have left ... Is what's left.

We passed by an assortment of people doing tasks throughout a city made of tents, RVs, and trailers of all shapes and sizes. I figured it had the feel of a shantytown, from the gold camp days. Most people seemed friendly enough. Some nodded, some even smiled. Some looked sad. They just kind of stared off, beyond whatever they were working on. I saw people cleaning guns, filling magazines and links with ammo, tanning leather hides, mending assorted pieces of equipment, making more of the same leather coats ... They even had a little saloon in one tent we passed. Just past it was the cooking area. Andrew looked at it, then turned to Redick.

"Cap?"

"Yo?" Redick was already headed to a tent.

"Chow time?"

"What the hell do you think we're doing?" It didn't come out as an admonition, but as a jibe. "Make it happen, Jerritt!"

I was looking over the camp. We were nestled right up against the Tobacco Root Mountains that jutted up out of the Jefferson River Valley. Below us, farmland spread out below us ... I paused.

The fields ...

Green farmland, slowly turning brown. Land that had been taken care of. The fields were dotted with cows, all the way to the river. A ways off north and south, I could make out tall fences and barricades.

"Welcome to the Last Ranch On Earth and Boomtown, little bro. Let's eat."

I suddenly realized I hadn't eaten in ... I couldn't even remember. We'd been given a few candy bars the previous night by BP. I turned and looked at the others. The promise of food made many of their faces shine.

Covered in a huge canopy and connected to two huge tents, it was an actual kitchen. At one end, I saw a man chopping up what looked to be a freshly butchered cow. After seeing several torn apart, I wasn't sure if I'd ever want beef again. As soon as the steaks were thrown on the flames, I knew I'd been wrong. Andrew led us to a seating area. He pointed out water, toilets and other services we might need. Down an alley between tents and sheds, I saw Amy, on a stretcher, going into a building with a big, red cross painted on it.

"Is that a good idea? Having the smoke and the smell?" George looked worried like only an older guy could.

One of the Marines turned and smirked.

"We were out on a CRP when we found you. There's nothing within 10 miles of the Ranch. We're good."

I saw George mouth the words 'CRP'. John leaned over.

"Combat reconnaissance patrol. Military lingo."

George nodded thoughtfully. Redick, the woman who was with him- introduced to us as Sergeant Jen Rourke- and the rest of the men from the helicopters joined us. Introductions were made. Andrew turned to me.

"What happened, Nick? You were still in Missoula when this all started? How did you get out ... When?"

Everyone listened in silence as I shared my story, starting with leaving Missoula and ending with John, Lauren and I entering Butte. Others told of their survival, as well. I realized then that I only knew John and Lauren's story.

George and Linda had been on vacation, coming up from Tuscon to see Glacier Park with another couple. When everything happened, they hadn't been able to make it back. Their friends had disappeared when they were forced to flee Great Falls. This was the first I'd heard of this.

"We had a parrot in Arizona. An African Gray. He was so smart, he

190

could say his own name. He even knew some colors." Linda smiled wistfully, but it faded. "He's probably dead, now. No one there to feed him."

I whispered to Andrew.

Great Falls is gone?

He nodded grimly.

This was only a couple weeks ago, George told us. They'd fled the government aid station at Malmstrom Air Force Base when the fence had been breached.

"So many of those things." George's eyes glazed over. "Just … Thousands of them …"

They'd reached Butte, they'd hid for a few days, then had been found by BP and his thugs.

"Who's BP?" Redick spoke up.

John answered for us.

"Punk kid and a group of idiots. Big men with guns. They almost got all of us killed. They did get some …"

"Where is he? Can we expect resistance when we step up incursions?"

He's dead. Got ripped up by those …

"Zees?"

Zees? Zees … Yeah.

I liked their term. Simple and fast to say. I grinned.

BP called them Shuffles.

"Shuffles? Sounds like a fucking clown. And clowns, they are not …"

"Incursions? You're going back in?" John had the stone-faced look I'd seen before.

"We've been going back in. Fortifying the airport. That's where all those Zees that were headed at you came from. Drawn by the sound of the birds."

I was confused for an instant, then realized "birds" meant helicopters.

"What's at the airport? Fuel?"

"Not anymore. We took the fuel. That's what we've been doing since we set up base here. Flying to regional airports and getting as much fuel as possible." He pointed to a row of tanks down by the "airfield" and an old barn I assumed was a hangar of sorts.

"Not with those Blackhawks?"

"Hell no. We've got a Chinook getting some repairs done in the shed. She's our heavy lifter."

I was so confused at this point, I had to speak up. My question was directed more at Andrew than anyone.

Who are you guys? What happened?

"Brother, a bunch of these guys were in my Marine unit. Some were National Guard ... Sent to Billings. We were sent to help them out when things got bad. Phones were down then, so I had no way to contact you. Us grunts and the pilots and some of the mechanics ... I guess you could say we defected when the military pulled back ... Things got really ugly, Nick."

"So you're ... deserters, then?" George raised an eyebrow.

"I prefer 'semi-conscientious survivalist'." Redick deadpanned.

"'Pulled back'?" Phil spoke up for the first time since Butte. "To where?"

Andrew looked at him.

"None of us knows for sure. We picked up some radio chatter out of Denver. We think some of the higher ranks went to Cheyenne Mountain in Colorado. The suits in DC all got on ships and headed to sea. No one has had any contact with them since. As far as I'm concerned," Redick met all of our eyes in turn, " it's just us."

"But you guys came here. Why? Why not go with the rest of the Army? Fight back against these things?"

"Because ..." Redick shook his head. "I'll tell you after we eat."

Plates of steak and fresh and cooked vegetables were handed out. I couldn't remember when I'd last had a meal like this. I also couldn't believe how hungry I was.

I ripped the flesh apart with my teeth, trying desperately to put aside the thought of the Zees doing the same to Sally and BP.

Chapter 23

Over lunch, Redick and some of the others took turns explaining the Ranch. Everyone who was able worked at anything they showed prowess in. Everyone nodded in agreement. I don't think anyone could even consider arguing. For the first time in months ... I can speak for myself, at least- I felt safe. Actually, genuinely safe. Though I still wasn't sure about what Redick and his people were going to try to do, here was someone doing *something*. It was comforting, in a way I thought I'd left in Missoula.

George was a curious kind of man, and immediately changed the subject back to the earlier discussion.

"You said you all came from Billings. That's where one of the largest aid stations is ... Was, right?"

The mood instantly turned somber. Redick looked at him.

"Yeah. We were there."

"What happened? Why did the military leave? Is anybody doing anything about this? Or know how it started?"

"Well ... We're doing something. Trying to carve out an existence here. As for the origin ... You probably know as much as I do, from what the news said a while back. China, maybe? That's where some people say the first Zee was spotted. But there was Brazil, too. And the Gulf States, here ... Hell, no one knows."

We saw USAMRIID trucks in Anaconda.

"We saw them, too. Unfortunately, not everyone in uniform was kept up to date on what the germ spooks were doing."

"Were they in Billings?"

"No. Just a whole bunch of scared grunts, civilians, and a whole lot of bullets ... There was the aid station, there. Western part of town. Farmland." Redick took a pack of cigarettes from his pocket, lit one, then threw the rest to

194

me. It was the pack I'd found. "The Guard was charged with keeping everyone under control. Bunch of panicky, poorly-trained kids. They were herding people into these massive ... Corrals, really. Quarantine them. The infection. It doesn't take long. Maybe 10 hours. Sometimes only 4 ... If your metabolism is fast, we think. That's why we shot that kid who was with you ..." Redick stared off, smoking.

Rourke, the Marine Sergeant, spoke up.

"My platoon was ordered in with the NGs at the main 'quarantine zone'. Even sounds like something the Army would set up. Like something out of a damned movie. People were ... Shit, they were tired, hungry, cranky, frightened. People were starting to get mean. Some were injured. We couldn't tell if they were bit, or ... I just didn't know. Some people started shoving, and an NG got knocked down. Some stupid-ass kid. He jumped up and hit one of the guys. This other one ... Jumped on the kid, grabbed at his rifle. It went off and blew some lady's head away. That's when the riot started. We were ordered back ... almost couldn't hear our LT over all the shouting. That NG kid ... Disappeared into this mob. People just turned terrible ... Climbing over each other, biting, clawing ..."

She took a breath.

"We were ordered to close the gates. Big, heavy gates ... But the fucking fences were chain-link. Go figure, huh? We pushed against them. Some in the crowd saw what we were doing ... Pushed back. Our LT, fucking 'Rambo', jumped in a Humvee and ran it into the gates. Nearly got me. The gates slammed shut on a few people ... That's when LT jumped up onto the .50 cal on top and shot over the crowd. There were shrieks and they started to back away ... And that's when the moaning began, right in the center of that crowd. See, if you're already infected, and you die ... It only takes about a minute to reanimate. This whole shitshow had been going on for two hours, and the riot had been about ... Shit, maybe 20 minutes. At this point, there must have been over a hundred Zees in there with them. More were getting up as we watched. Everyone had been so busy fighting ..."

She motioned at me with two of her fingers. I looked at her in confusion and John fished a cigarette from my pack and tossed it to her. She nodded in thanks, lighting it.

"Those in the crowd closest to these Zees, they started pushing. Shoving everyone in front of them, who shoved everyone ... You know ... People started screaming, getting attacked. Those closest to the fence ... They were banging on it, getting pushed up against it. There was this little kid ... He got pushed through ... Through the fence ..." She shook her head, as if trying to make the memory go away. "That's when LT opened fire again, and yelled for us to do the same. Into the crowd this time. People getting thrown backwards, chopped to bits. I guess they'd rather have faced bullets than Zees. Another push from the crowd and the fences began to buckle and come apart. They pushed through. A few of the rest of us had opened fire when LT had ordered us to... I didn't ... But this mob rushing towards us ... It was full of people, Zees, I couldn't tell which was which. Everyone was stumbling, covered in blood. We all started shooting, falling back. LT's Humvee was overrun. He disappeared into the sea of violence, too. I started running, then. Marines don't fall back ... But we also know when to use discretion. If I hadn't, I be with the rest of my platoon. Dead ..."

She breathed in another drag, saying nothing more. Redick filled in the silence.

"She ran up to me as we were pulling back from one of the other corrals. Same deal, there. Infected mixed into a riot. We pulled back to the Humvees, then back further, still, as everything was overrun. We got to the helos and we got the order to pull back to "Line Red" as they called it. Just outside the city. There was a colonel there, telling us to rendezvous at Malmstrom. We flew over the line ... There was that big refinery, at Laurel, just outside of Billings. They had all kinds of construction equipment down there, digging trenches. Filling them up with fuel. They'd been at it a while ... They'd planned for this. They knew what would happen, and they did it anyway ... Who knows what the hell their motives were? Less Zees to deal with, I

196

suppose. Same goddamn deal with L.A., too ..."

Redick looked around at his troops, then back to us.

"We couldn't stay. Not after that. The higher-ups were even more ignorant about the reality of the situation on the ground than anyone. We heard some radio chatter from other places ... Same situation. Herding people into corrals ... They filled those trenches up and didn't even wait for the guys in the equipment or the rest of the troops to retreat. The fast movers came in and just lit up the whole place. Billings and its refinery just burning up. Laurel burning up. Hell, even the river was on fire. Those trenches put up a wall of fire ... Nothing ... No one was getting through. They told us to report to Great Falls immediately. I told him to fuck himself, then offered sanctuary to anyone who came with me. My company ... What's left of it ..." Faces were somber around the group. " Everyone was on board. The other birds came with. We headed south, into the steep valleys in the Beartooth Mountains, then over into the Madisons. I grew up down here. Raised on my grandpa's farm." Redick motioned around us. "I figure it's as good a place as any to ride out the end of the world."

Little Paul was silent throughout the whole story, but his face changed as it was told. George looked at him. So did I. I'd never seen that look on his face, even running from the Zees in Butte.

"Are you alright, Paul?"

He shook his head and put his plate down.

"The fire. I remember the fire. It was so hot ... We were all there. Me, my dad, mom, my brothers ... I had two ... And my sister. We came up from Cody when everything went crazy. The radio said to go to Billings. The highway was just packed with cars. Almost bumper to bumper. We barely moved. People were yelling at each other. There were helicopters everywhere ... Military, some news. We heard the screams from Billings. We were far out, but I could hear them ... I saw all the military helicopters pass over. Then screams started coming down the highway. I jumped up onto the roof of our car and could see them, coming down along the backed up cars ...

Attacking people who couldn't get out of the way fast enough. I looked at my dad ... I think he was starting to panic. He yelled at us to run. He picked up my little sister and we all started running. I could hear my mom crying behind me. People around us started to run. I got pushed around by people. Everyone was panicking. I lost view of my family ... They were somewhere behind me, I think. I couldn't stop. I couldn't turn around." He stopped and took a deep breath. George patted him on the shoulder.

"That's when I heard the jets. That fast whooshing, like you hear at the air show. Then it faded and then ... I was thrown forward with a bunch of other people. I remember a thump of hot air in my ears, then ringing ... Just ringing. The smell of burning fuel and metal. I fell and hit my face against a car. I went out for a while ... I stood and ... Behind me ... Everything was burning up. When the ringing began to subside, I could hear the roar of the flames ... My family ... I think they were somewhere behind me ..." He breathed in. It came in short gasps. He looked down at the ground, most likely to hide the tears on his face.

"A few miles on, I met BP and his guys ... They had a school bus ... They said they were going to Great Falls, but we took the interstate all the way to Butte ..."

Linda sat down next to him and put her arms around him as he began to sob.

"So no one has any idea as to what's going on? Why this is happening or if anyone is trying to stop this?" George looked pale.

"I hate to break it to you, ladies and gents, but it's just us. We have to consider the possibility that we're some of the last people alive." Redick motioned to those seated and Boomtown in general.

"The scientists had a term for this ... ELE ... Extinction level event ..."

George looked like he was going to be sick. He set his plate down and excused himself.

"You mentioned incursions to Butte. Why go back there if you already have the supplies you need?"

Redick looked at John and smiled a smile that scared me.

"We're taking it back. If the Zees can swell their ranks, so can we. We've been amassing a whole lot of ordnance ... That's why we call this place 'Boomtown'."

Lauren raised an eyebrow.

"You're ... Taking it back? Why?"

"We're going to rebuild. A lot of people are giving up, running away. We refuse. We're going to fight back, prove that it can be done."

"*Can* it be done?"

"There can only be a finite number of Zees there. We'll kill every last one of them."

John looked impressed. George looked skeptical. I looked at Andrew and he at me. We nodded.

"We'll regroup for a few days. There's a stormfront coming through, so the birds are down. We'll get you familiarized with the Ranch, then begin your ... Trial by fire. Rest up, everyone."

What's the first thing on the agenda when we get to Butte? Work on the airport?

Redick sat back, lit a cigarette and squinted through the smoke.

"No. We'll have to get the Zees away from the fence. There were quite a few following you guys down the hill. No ...There was an Army outpost in a park there. The germ guys. There's a Blackhawk there."

"Are we going to take it or just part it out?" John sat back and folded his arms. I could see he was back on familiar ground.

"Just parts. We have a gunship that needs some engine work. It'll be a quick in, quick out."

That doesn't sound too bad.

Redick looked at me and smirked. Andrew wore a strange expression.

What ...?

"The park is at the hospital."

Chapter 24

The horse, aptly named Lefty, bobbed slowly beneath me. The gray and red roan had been attacked by a pack of coyotes when he was a colt, so his left, front leg was shorter than the rest. The ride was shakier than the other horses, but he listened well and was forgiving to a new rider like me. Ahead of me, John was riding beside a tall, weathered cowboy. Art Roland owned a ranch to the south of Boomtown. After the Raiders had arrived, when the refugees started showing up, he'd moved his family, livestock and equipment up to the ranch at Boomtown. It had been abandoned for a few years but had now been fixed up. The barn had been turned into fortified sleeping quarters. We rode past it as we headed to the north fence.

Art had been a horse-mounted border agent in Glacier National Park for years before retiring to his ranch in the Jefferson Valley. His border patrol experience showed, and everyone even called he and his men 'Boomtown Border Patrol'. The ranch had a few ATVs, but to combat noise and additional fuel consumption, but they'd decided to use the original off-road vehicle.

Lefty whinnied underneath me and shook from head to tail. I reached down and patted him. The weather had cleared, after 3 days of gray sleet, but a heavy fog still cloaked most of the valley. The formerly green fields lay buried underneath. Above us, patches of blue tried to show through wispy, wet clouds.

John and Art stopped. Both produced binoculars and surveyed the land ahead. John lowered his binos and turned to look at me and the two horsemen a few yards back.

"Looks like we've got one wrapped up in the fence. It's moving."

I nodded and spurred Lefty forward. We trotted across a field, then crossed a small stream. Droplets of icy water splashed onto my face. It didn't take us long to reach the north fence, just beyond the last of the cultivated fields. The river came close to the foothills here. An existing barbed wire fence had been strengthened with boards, steel bars and military razor wire. As we approached the barrier, I heard a moaning hiss. There was a gap in the fence, guarded only by razor wire- a gate of sorts.

Wrapped in the wire was a Zee. It must have been there for some time. Most of its flesh had been peeled away by the fence, hanging off of it in tatters like dirty rags. Its neck was wide open, and a section of its facial bones were exposed. One side of its jaw hung to one side, but it still bit the air. Most of its muscles had been severed, but it still struggled, vainly trying to reach us. Its one good arm shot through the wire, then it, too, got wrapped up. I could hear the razors sawing into its flesh and muscle. There was a loud snapping sound and the arm that had been thrust towards us suddenly bent down at the elbow.

Art slowly got off his horse. He motioned for us to do the same, then poured himself a cup of coffee from a thermos. He procured several tin mugs from his saddle bags and poured coffee all around. I must have had a strange look on my face.

"Hell. It's not going anywhere. We may as well enjoy the view of those mountains." He turned and looked up at the mountains that reached skyward behind us. I gazed up at the snowcapped peaks. Thin clouds passed over them. The wind moaned in time with the peeled Zee. The coffee was hot and good.

Since it had all started, I hadn't really taken the time to just stand and enjoy anything beautiful. The world had turned so ugly, and I had accepted that the ugliness was everywhere. But here, above us, was something that we still had. Something the dead hadn't been able to take from us. They'd taken so much. Or maybe we'd handed it over ...

An upwelling of anger blossomed in my core and heated my face. I gulped the rest of the coffee and hung the cup on the saddle. I grabbed my crowbar from a leather pouch and walked up to the Zee. I could feel everyone watching me. I raised the crowbar. The Zee bared its upper teeth at me. Probably the only muscles it had left.

Fuck you.

I brought the bar crashing down into its skull. The bone crumbled and dark, tainted brain matter spilled out. It stopped moving and slumped down into the razor wire. I turned back to the rest of the patrollers.

"I wish they could feel that." Art took another pull off his coffee. In the distance, we heard the whine of a helicopter engine starting up. The whine quickly turned into a heavy thump.

"Sounds like they're getting everything ready." Art put the thermos away and mounted his horse. "You two head on back. We'll finish checking the north fence."

I climbed back on the horse. I'd been in the saddle for a little over an hour and my legs were aching. I was looking forward to not being on Lefty for the rest of the day ... But I wasn't looking forward to the task ahead. Not the helicopter ride, and definitely not flying to the hospital.

I nudged Lefty forward when he suddenly took off at a gallop. I wasn't expecting it and his front leg unbalanced me. I hadn't even gotten my feet into the stirrups. We hit a small dip and I went right off the back of him. I landed flat on my back, knocking the wind from me. John trotted his horse up.

"You alright, Nick?"

I slowly sat up. My body hurt, but nothing was broken.

Yeah, I'm okay. Damn, first the truck and now this. Maybe I should stay away from moving things.

John jumped down from his horse and chuckled as he helped me to my feet. Lefty had stopped a dozen yards away. I slowly limped over.

Great. Just as we're about to head back into Butte.

"If nothing's broken, just stretch it out. They have some painkillers at the infirmary."

We rode back towards Boomtown.

The heavy thump of the helicopter blades threatened to push me to the ground. I braced against the downdraft, legs still burning from the ride, ribs aching from the fall. I'd popped a few ibuprofen. There was harder medicine, but Redick didn't want me to take any before a mission.

He'd said: "Jerritt, when we get back, you can have all the vicodin you can handle and wash it down with beer. But I need you level-headed for this mission." I'd agreed.

Now, trotting to the helo with a small field pack, heavy leather coat and M4 carbine slung over a shoulder, I was wishing for those vicodin. I knew I hadn't cracked my ribs, but I'd definitely bruised a few. I climbed into the Blackhawk, fumbling with the harness. I'd practiced several times over the last few days, but with wind whipping in my ears and adrenaline pumping through my body, my fingers didn't seem to want to operate the clip. One of the Marines reached over and buckled it for me. He flashed an amused smile, then hung his legs out the open door and leaned on the machine gun mounted there. The Blackhawk lifted into the sky with a sickening lurch, and for a moment I was afraid I'd left my stomach somewhere on the ground. I closed my eyes, but that just made it worse. When I opened them, the helo banked sharply. I panicked slightly, grabbing at a crossbar above me. John was seated next to the Marine at the door. He pulled on my harness, reminding me it was there. I released the bar and sat back, trying to relax.

Next to me was a pile of body armor. I hoped we wouldn't need it.

I sat back and closed my eyes, which turned out to be a bad idea. My head began to spin as fast as the helicopter engines and a sharp pain shot up through my ribs. I leaned out the door of the Blackhawk and vomited, barely missing the boots of the door gunner. He didn't even look up. The cold wind rushed over my head and neck, lessening the nausea.

So much for the painkillers.

I looked at John, but realized he couldn't hear me. I wiped my mouth and sat against the armor vests.

The small helo- the Cayuse, as the military called it- buzzed past us. Its complement of rockets and ammo had been replenished. Behind us and down to the right was the giant, double-rotored Chinook- nicknamed '*Dolores*'- carrying the "bait cows", as the Raiders called them.

Redick had explained the concept over dinner- steak- the previous night. With the weather changing and the ash falling, a lot of cows were falling ill. There was a herd at the Ranch that was well kept, but other, sicklier cows had been raided from abandoned ranches throughout the area. These were the bait cows. They were loaded into a suspended cage and delivered a little ways from the drop zone, preferably downhill. Their legs would be cut. The smell of blood and the sound of the cows crying out would attract most of the Zees in the vicinity. As soon as they were distracted, the team would be inserted between the objective and the swarm of dead. This had worked well several times in various towns and cities.

George had, of course, frowned at the "inhumane" aspect of the bait cows. His argument was:

"If we randomly kill and sacrifice any living creature, how does that make us different from ... from those things?"

Redick's reply was simple.

"Because they're dead and we're not."

The conversation ended there.

Our Blackhawk, the other one and *Telum* stayed south, hugging the low hills that turned into snowcapped peaks. The Chinook banked north and flew directly over the center of town. I could see the cage, with its terrified cargo, hanging from the bottom. I could hear the big helicopter beat through the air even above the roar of our own engines. It flew over the airport, about 3 miles to the north. I could see most of the massive swarm of Zees that had followed us down the hill. From the air, the view was chilling. I hadn't realized how many there were. Thousands of them ... Scattered around the airport. As the Chinook flew over, they began moving in a mass, following a few in the front ...

Like cows, really ...

We followed the hills, then headed north. In the distance, I could see the Chinook dropping the bait cows just south of the hospital. The target park was one block northwest. We flew over the cows to make sure the cage had opened properly. It had. The emaciated cows stumbled out, not sure of their legs after the flight. A pair of Marines rode atop the cage. They quickly roped down and pulled out long knives ... The Blackhawk banked sharply and I lost sight of the Chinook. Below us, from the hospital, a swarm of Zees had begun to filter down towards the noise. There must have been over 500 here. More and more emerged from inside the hospital.

Shit.

We passed over, then swung back to the north, then west. The landing area Redick and his sergeants had chosen was the football field at the college on a hill overlooking Butte. The field sat in a depression, and Redick figured the hills would mask the noise of the rotors enough to not draw more Zees than we could readily handle. The Blackhawks landed in the field with a thud. The little helo would stay aloft and provide air cover if we needed it. Rourke started grabbing the body armor from the back and handing them out. She threw one to me. I misjudged the weight, almost dropped it, but caught it clumsily. It weighed close to 30 pounds. The helos lifted off and vanished over the hill, their rotor noise fast disappearing.

"Sorry, everyone, but we haven't been this far into the city, yet. John and Nick said there are still live ones here, so better to be safe. If we get into a situation with the Zees, don't be shy about dropping it. We have plenty."

Everyone nodded, then loaded magazines into their rifles and chambered rounds.

"Remember, ladies and gents, melee tools only. Don't go weapons hot unless I say so, or unless there is no other choice. We want to keep quiet and do this fast. In and out and back to base in time for evening chow. Oo-rah?"

"Oo-rah!" The rest of the Marines chanted. Even the few Army soldiers did.

I suddenly felt a boost of confidence. I was surrounded by

205

professionals. I had a military rifle in my hands and knew how to use it. The body armor was heavy and I was still scared and sore, but I was ready. I was pretty sure I was, at least.

"Alright, people, let's move out!"

The collection of Marines, soldiers and civilians slung weapons and we grasped our motley assortment of bars and blades, then headed down into the lower parking lot. We began jogging east towards the hospital and a swarm of Zees.

Chapter 25

After two helicopter flights, I was far from used to it. My legs wobbled as the "platoon" began jogging toward the hospital. I forced them to move, trying to keep up. The Marines were fast and began pulling away from the National Guard troops. Most of the soldiers were young and grasped their rifles nervously.

My ankle hit a small divot in the brown football field. My leg gave way and I fell to my knees. I caught myself with my hands, but my elbows jammed the armor plate into my tender ribs. I vomited again.

Goddamn it!

John was suddenly there. He helped me to my feet.

"How are those ribs, Nick?"

Sore. I tried to smile, but figured it must have looked like a grimace.

"You sure you're good to do this?"

Yeah, I'm good. Too late anyway, if I wasn't.

John gave a slight chuckle.

"I suppose so."

We took off at a jog, now bringing up the rear. There was parking lot behind the field, which dropped down to a walking trail. There were a few cars still parked in the lot, doors shut and probably locked. The windows were all covered with a dirty, gray grime. The clouds over the sun thinned and the world suddenly brightened. In the neighborhood stretched out below us, nothing moved.

A little ways to the east, a series of gunshots cracked the air. I saw a few of the soldiers flinch. We kept going. The lot dropped onto a section of a walking trail, and that opened onto a street lined with houses and dead trees. A lot of the houses looked empty. Most had broken windows. Some were boarded up. Spray-painted messages from long-dead hands threatened trespassers, warned against Zees and cried for help. A lot of it was red. A lot of it looked like blood.

A Zee stumbled out of a garage ahead. It wore stained coveralls, as though it had just been working on its motorcycle. The nearest Marine turned and sauntered over to it, drawing a machete from a sheath on his vest. He brought the blade crashing down through the top of its head, splitting bone and rotting flesh all the way to the nose. The Marine raised a leg and kicked the corpse in the chest, drawing the blade back out. The body hit the pavement with a muffled thump. The Marine wiped the blade on the Zee's clothing, then turned and jogged to catch back up. He didn't look back.

Up ahead, Redick raised his hand, then dropped it. The troops stopped and took a knee, weapons ready. John was already down and I joined him. Just beyond Redick, where the road went slightly downhill, a small group of people was running at us. There looked to be a young couple with two kids, an older, heavier couple, and a pair of dark-haired girls who looked so much alike, I immediately assumed they were sisters. The younger man held an automatic pistol. The older man cradled a hunting rifle. When they saw the weapons trained on them, they held up their hands. The older man hollered out to us.

"Don't shoot! We're alive!"

Redick's eyes flashed and he put his finger to his lips in the universal sign for 'shut up!'. He then waved us forward. The Marines moved first, weapons still aimed at the newcomers. As the soldiers moved in, most of the Marines branched off and surrounded the small group in a defensive position. The soldiers mimicked them. The civilians were on their knees when John and I trotted up.

"Please, help us." The young mother had pleading eyes. She and the younger men held the children and each other tight.

The older, fat man looked defiant, but scared.

"We've been hiding out for weeks. We're running out of food. Are you the Army? What the hell is going on? Why are these people attacking us? Has everyone gone craz-?"

208

Redick cut him off.

"We don't have time for a goddamn interview. The Zees will be finished with those cows soon. We have to keep moving."

"Zees? Cows? Wha-?"

"Grab your weapon, shut the fuck up and follow us. You'll have answers later. We have to get to the hospital-"

"The fucking hospital?! We can't go there! Those cannibals are every-"

Redick smashed the man in the side of the face with the butt of his rifle.

"Shut your mouth and follow us or stay here and make all the noise you want. I don't give a shit either way."

The older woman gave him an admonishing look. He wiped a slight stream of blood from the corner of his mouth. He looked pissed, but said nothing. He grabbed his rifle.

The younger man got to his feet.

"Thank you so-"

"Marines! Move out!"

Redick and his Raiders began jogging east again. I gave the family a slight smile in an attempt to instill confidence. I don't know if it worked. Behind me, a hissing moan escaped from behind a dead hedge. Wet leaves sloshed as it came through an open gate. The children gave out a whimper and the young mother screamed. I pulled my crowbar from my belt and stepped toward the Zee. Out of the corner of my eye, I saw the young father raise his pistol.

Don't-!

He fired. I was in line with the barrel, and the gunshot cracked in my left ear, leaving behind a high-pitched ringing. The bullet hit the Zee in the right side of its chest. The Zee was a reanimated teenage boy, and the bullet was a small one. It lurched back, but didn't go down. It focused its attention on the family, now quaking in fear. The man raised the pistol for another shot, but

209

his hand was shaking like a leaf.

I was faster. I stepped forward and swung. The Zee noticed me at the last second, but was too slow to do anything about it. I hit it in the back of the skull and the crowbar split the bones. Black-red, viscous blood and brain matter spilled out. The Zee crumpled to the sidewalk. I turned. The man was still aiming the pistol, but held it limply. His eyes were wide.

"You ... You get close to them? What if one bites you?"

Hasn't happened yet. Keep that pistol quiet. If you can't, at least hit the damn target. I raised the stained crowbar. *Or I'll plant this in your fucking head next.*

I turned and joined the platoon. My voice had said that, but it wasn't me ... Or, it hadn't been. It was now, I guess. Redick looked over his shoulder and gave me an approving glance. I breathed through the pain in my ribs and kept moving. At least my legs weren't shaky, now. I wasn't looking forward to the ride home.

The street cut through the center of a quiet, empty neighborhood. When we got within a few blocks, we could hear the moans ahead. It flowed across the wind like a melancholy sea. We could see a few, down where the streets opened up at the hospital. The hospital loomed in the gloomy light. Six stories of dark brick and broken windows. The north wing had burned. Who knew how many Zees were in there ...

The swarm was headed south, towards the bait cows. They didn't notice us. We moved closer and took a knee. The civilians huddled in the center of the platoon. Redick and his troops scanned the area ahead. There were a small number of Zees scattered around the objective site, which was one block ahead, in a small park. Nothing we couldn't-

Gunshots crashed across the park ahead of us. Bullets whizzed over our heads and impacted on the pavement around us.

"Goddamn it! COVER!"

The Marines and troops scattered, pulling and pushing the newcomers behind cars, trees and the concrete walls of raised yards. I darted towards a parked truck as a Zee emerged from around it. I skidded to a halt and grabbed for my crowbar out of habit. A split-second of indecision later and I felt as if I got punched in the upper chest, right by my already bruised ribs. White-hot, searing pain exploded through my chest as I jolted and fell onto my back. The Zee shuffled forward, then its head blew up as a gun went off behind me. A strong arm grabbed the back of my vest and pulled me behind a truck across the street. Theissan , the Marine who had pulled me to safety, patted my chest. Even through the vest, each touch made lights flash in my eyes. I felt like I did when I broke my arm skiing a few years back ... Like I was going to pass out.

"Is he alive?!" I heard Redick yell as the Marines and soldiers opened fire on the building across the park.

"Yes, sir! Hit his vest! Cracked the plate, but he'll be okay!" The Marine looked down at me. I nodded, forced a slight smile. I sat up and coughed, wracking my body with more pain. I hacked and spit. It was pink with blood. I climbed to my knees and shouldered the M4, flipping off the safety. The pain seemed to help my eyes focus. I aimed the rifle at the squat, rectangular building. I saw a flash behind a broken window, followed by a sharp crack and a whizzing sound.

That fucker shot me! He fucking shot me*!*

I pulled the trigger. The bullet screamed out the barrel as the buffer spring buzzed under my cheek. I hit the remaining pane of glass, shattering it. I ducked back behind the truck. Theissan slapped me on the helmet.

"Get some, Jerritt!"

A SAW gunner opened up, peppering the building with bullets. I heard those closest to the connecting street swear, and as I aimed around the truck again, I saw why. The Zees that had been following the rest of the swarm had now turned to the gunfire. More were still filtering from the hospital, also coming at us. Someone gasped behind me. I turned. It was one of the raven-haired girls. Behind us ...

The street was filling with Zees from houses and backyards.

Shit.

More bullets whizzed by, coming from the building.

"Redick! We've gotta get the fuck out of here!" The Marine behind me saw the steadily filling street behind us. He and I were the closest and turned, concentrating fire on the Zees.

"Cooke! Get that rocket and light up those sons of bitches!" Redick motioned to the building. He then turned to the Marine with the radio. "Get the birds on the horn! Tell Clifford and his boys to ditch the cage and put the full harness on *Dolores*! We're just going to take the whole goddamn bird! Have *Telum* sweep the park to the south of the objective. We'll pop smoke!"

The Marines immediately went into motion. The National Guard soldiers moved back to where the big Marine and I were shooting the Zees shuffling up the street. A Marine behind me pulled a large, dark green cylinder off his back and fiddled with some switches, then rested it on his shoulder and knelt behind a tree. He flipped a trigger and a whooshing smoke trail leapt out towards the building. The rocket hit in through a window. It was followed by a silver-gold flash and an explosion blew the rest of the windows from the building, along with an exterior wall. The gunfire ceased.

"MOVE MOVE MOVE!!!"

The group of us got up and ran. The young couple picked up their kids and followed. The older, large couple were pushed along by Marines. We came around the last house and the objective appeared. It was a small military encampment, surrounded by razor wire and USAMRIID trucks. There was a Blackhawk in the center with a red cross painted on the side and two small wings carrying external fuel tanks. Inside the sharp perimeter, I could see several Zees. Some were already hung up in the wire. The Marines raised rifles and fired mid-stride, taking Zees down with each trigger pull. A canister flew from the group of Marines. It hissed and purple smoke drifted towards the dingy sky.

"Purple smoke! Confirm purple smoke!"

The radio crackled. A tinny voice confirmed purple smoke. Above us, the small helicopter buzzed over, then stopped in a hover. The downdraft

212

thumped against us. The extra weight on my ribs made the painful lights dance again, but I breathed through it and kept running. The guns above us lit up. The first wave of Zees coming across the park dropped. Some of them were cut across the midsection. They tried to crawl with splintered bone. Still coming ...

Always coming.

We entered the perimeter of razor wire. There were bodies everywhere. Most had been shot through the head. There was a Zee laying under a table, a woman in a stained lab coat. She'd been torn apart. With only one arm, a torso and a head left, she still tried to crawl towards us. I yanked the pistol from the holster on my hip and dropped her.

Always coming.

One team swept through the maze of tents and vehicles to check for more Zees, another began to take the blades off the Blackhawk, as the rest of us lined up against the fence and began firing at the Zees. The radio crackled.

"This is *Raider Three*, we've got another group of Zees inbound from the north ..."

A Blackhawk passed over.

" ... Numbering one-fifty or more. Half a click. *Dolores* is incoming."

Shit.

Glances were exchanged, but we kept firing. The SAW gunners extended bipods and kneeled over sandbags. We all stood on bodies of soldiers. Each one was shot through the head. The SAW gunners had what they called the "head zone". They sprayed bullets into a 5° zone where most human heads, no matter how tall the person, would be. More Zees appeared from over the hill behind the hospital. It looked like one of those protests I'd seen back on campus. A sea of people.

But, no ...

Not people.

The gunshots must have been more tempting than the bait cows. It seemed like there would be two more Zees for each one that we shot. Down the line, men began running out of ammo.

213

"Mag!" Someone would yell, and get passed a fresh. But there was only a finite amount for all of us. The older guy with the hunting rifle was a fair shot, but only had a handful of ammo.

The Zees had closed into less than 200 feet when heavy thumping filled the air. *Dolores* blasted the air overhead, draping long cables. The engineers roped down and immediately went to work building a sling around the salvage helicopter. The rest of the helos hovered above us, opening fire into the Zees with machine guns. There wasn't enough room inside the razor wire perimeter to allow for landing. We had to run out to the south portion of the field.

Straight towards the Zees.

There were so many of them. Shoulder to shoulder, almost scrambling over one another to get to us ...

The SAW gunners covered us as we ran. The Blackhawks touched down in a line between us and the swarm, corralling us in. I climbed into an open door and immediately buckled my harness. The older lady got in across from me, and the older man jammed in next to me. The harness wouldn't go around his girth, and he was still fumbling with it when we leapt into the air. The Blackhawk swooped sideways to give *Dolores* room to get the salvage out. I heard a grunt as the old guy slid out the door. He grabbed my wrist and stretched me against my harness. My ribs screamed in protest as lights flashed in my eyes. I gasped against the tears and darkness overtook my vision. The pain brought me back to reality just in time to see the man lose his grip and fall 30 feet to the ground, on his back. I could tell he was shouting, but couldn't hear him over the rotor wash. Then his wife was leaping for the door. A Marine grabbed her and restrained her. She was screaming.

I looked back down. The Zees had closed in on the man and had begun to rip into his flesh. The door gunner swung his weapon down and sprayed the man and the Zees with bullets. Half of the man's head and most of his torso exploded in a shower of red. The attacking Zees were ripped apart. The Blackhawk thumped towards the sky. Below us, the land looked alive, like it was covered in ants. Even with all the Zees we'd shot, there were still so many of them ...

We banked southeast. *Dolores* lumbered behind us, carrying the salvage helicopter. Below us, the city looked vibrant, teeming with life.

But we all knew it was dead.

Chapter 26

"You have three broken ribs, Mr. Jerritt."

The white-haired doctor jotted notes down on a sheet of paper and tucked it into a folder. I leaned back in the chair and breathed deeply, through the pain.

That would explain the blood.

"Nothing to worry about. It's from bruising, not a puncture. Rest easy for the next week. Light duty only. I'll let you know when you're combat ready again."

Light duty ...?

"No helicopters, no horses. No heavy lifting. If you absolutely have to get somewhere, an ATV will be fine, but take it easy on the throttle."

Everyone else will be carrying my share, then.

"You're alive, Mr. Jerritt. You've already done more than most people out there. Rest up. It's just a week. If you find yourself bored, perhaps you could write your memoir." The doctor gave me a wry smile, stood, patted me on the shoulder and walked into the next tent to check on a different patient. I stood slowly. It hurt to breathe. I put my shirt back on, the pain almost buckling my knees. I walked out of the tent. George was coming down the narrow thoroughfare.

"Nick! How are you feeling?"

Like I got shot.

I chuckled. The vibrations shot pain through my ribs. It must have shown on my face.

"The water heater is all warmed up. Go grab a shower. The cook said dinner will be ready soon, and Captain Redick gave the go ahead to crack a few bottles of wine tomorrow. They're just going to strip down that new helicopter. They said the fuel tanks were full."

216

That's good news. Has anyone heard from any other survivors? The government? Any radio chatter?

"No ... The radio has been silent. They finished tweaking the new antenna up on the mountain. Hopefully we'll hear from someone ..."

There has to be more people left. If a group this size can make it here ... I don't think the Zees do well in mountains.

"I think humanity is just reeling and dazed. We'll be back. This isn't the end. It just wouldn't be right ... Go clean up and lie down. I'll come get you when dinner is ready."

I watched George walk away. He held his head up, but I could see the sadness in the way he walked. We all talked like that now.

"The government is doing everything they can to control this."

"It's not the end of the world."

"We'll fight back and build a new civilization."

"Everything will be okay."

But, deep down, we all knew it wasn't. It was bullshit. Scared people telling each other hope-filled lies. No one knew why this was happening. No one knew where the government had gone. No one knew what was going on outside of our section of the dying world. All anyone did know was that most of the people we ever cared about had died, but had gotten back up and were walking around out there.

I stood for a while, these thoughts running through my head. I finally shook them away and walked to the shower facility. The shower water was piped directly from the river, filtered for particulates and heated. I hung my towel by the sign that said: Water Not Potable. Do NOT Drink. I let the hot water wash over me. It hurt my ribs, but washed away the fear of the day.

A huge, purple-black bruise was spreading across the left side of my chest. I stayed in that shower for a long time. I thought, maybe ... I don't know ... That I would emerge back to my house in Missoula. That this had all been a dream and I'd woken up. That I would get on my bike and go to class and never think about Zees ever again.

217

But that, too, was bullshit. This world was very real. Very cold. Very dead. It was a nightmare and there was no waking up. I left the shower feeling even worse than when I'd gone in. I shuffled back to my tent and sat on my cot. The weight of everything seemed to press down on me then. I lay back, breathing through the pain in my ribs. I closed my eyes, but ...

All I could see was a sea of dead, walking corpses. Stretched out across an empty, brown plain. Dark clouds boiled overhead. Lifeless eyes all stared at me. Lips turned up into feral sneers, as though ridiculing me for still being alive. Gray, bony hands clawed at the fence between them and myself. The fence stretched out both ways to the horizon, as far as I could see. On one side, the dead. On the other, her and I. There was a woman standing next to me. Dirty-blonde hair. I'd never seen her before. Her mouth moved, but no sound came out.

Help me, her lips said.

How? We're trapped here.

We have to go. Up the mountain. Please, help me.

The dead pounded on the fence. It clanged and shook all the way down to the dark horizon.

What mountain? There's no mountain.

There is. Over there.

She pointed.

Beyond the fence, beyond the swarm, I could suddenly see a tall, rocky peak, reaching high into the black sky.

We can't get there. There are too many of them.

We have to. Help.

No. It's impossible-

The fence broke and the dead came pouring through. They grabbed onto the woman and tore her flesh. Her face contorted into a scream, but no sound followed. She grabbed my arm. Her grip was like iron. I couldn't get away. A Zee grabbed my other arm and pulled me back into that sea of

218

chomping jaws ...

Gah!

I jerked awake and sat up. My ribs burned. George took his hand off my arm.

"Nick, I'm sorry. You were dreaming. It didn't look good. I didn't mean to startle you ..."

It's okay. My dream, it ... Thanks for waking me.

"That's not all you're going to thank me for."

He extended a glass of red wine. I took it gratefully and took a drink. It was dark, dry, good. I took another sip and swallowed wrong, coughing slightly. I winced.

"Dinner is ready. They roasted a pig."

I took another sip of wine.

You know, George, I've eaten better here than I ever have before.

He laughed.

"Me, too." He extended his hand and helped me up. I put on a coat and we headed toward the chow hall. The smell of cooking pork filled the air. The sun had sunk below the western mountains. The haze had thinned enough to allow the orange and purple sunset to show through.

We ate and drank and told stories. Stories that didn't have to do with Zees or this new world. We all laughed as Redick told of a time he'd been arrested in Germany for getting drunk and pissing on a police car. George and Linda told of the time they'd traveled to Kenya to build houses. Andrew and I jibed each other over past girlfriends and reminisced about our annual trips to Glacier Park. For a couple of hours over dinner, everything was right with the world. We stuffed ourselves with roasted meat and fresh vegetables. I drank wine until my head felt heavy.

It helped ease the pain in my chest and the visions in my head.

As the chow area was cleaned up, we wandered our separate ways, back to our bunks. I noticed one of the dark-haired girls we'd picked up in

Butte looking at me. Her name was Alicia, a year younger than me who I remembered from the bakery she'd worked at. I smiled and kept going. I turned the final corner and grabbed my tent flap. There was a small woodstove, and the night was chilly. I felt a hand on my arm. It was Alicia.

"Hi, Nick. Thanks again for ... rescuing us." She smiled in the faint light. "Can I come in?"

Yeah ... Yeah, of course.

She sat on the cot as I built a small fire. When I turned around, she kissed me.

"I'm sorry for being so forward, Nick ... But ... It's the end of the world ..." She turned bright red. "Wait, I didn't mean it like ... You're a guy I'd want to ... Because we're going to die ..."

I chuckled.

I understood what you meant.

"Good."

We fell asleep in each other's arms.

I awoke when I heard a commotion outside. I sat up. I heard shouts. My heart raced.

"What is it? Is this it?" Alicia grabbed onto me.

I don't know. Stay here.

I quickly dressed and grabbed my M4. I ran outside, ducking through the shadows of the tents as I made my way to the edge of camp. I saw floodlights ahead. There was a large crowd of Marines, a few soldiers. My brother was with the Marines. George and some of the other civilians stood back.

Two soldiers, younger guys, were on their knees in the center of the Marines. They'd been beat up pretty bad. Redick stood at the center, holding an empty wine bottle.

"My God ..." George was wide-eyed with fear.

What? What's happened?

"They just beat the shit out of those poor kids ..."

What? Why?

Someone stepped up behind me. It was Alicia. Redick answered the question for all of us. He faced the gathered crowd. One of the National Guard soldiers held his rifle at the ready.

"Sorry to wake you, ladies and gents. It's probably best that you all see this. This." Redick held the bottle aloft. "Caught these two passed out drunk on sentry duty."

"S-sorry ... We're-"

"Shut the fuck up." One of the Marines kicked him in the side of the head.

Redick faced the gathered National Guard troops.

"I know you're all poorly trained and undisciplined. I've let some shit fly. But I think what you don't grasp," He turned to us, "And this goes for *all* of you. We're at war. We're in a combat zone, fighting for our lives. The entire world is hot. Don't believe for one second that just because we built a fucking wall around this place that it's impregnable. It's not. Better men than us have made that mistake throughout history. We will only be safe ..." Redick turned back to the two bloodied soldiers. " ... If we maintain *constant* vigilance. There is no complacency in war. Is that understood?"

"Understood!" Various shouts. The same soldier who held his rifle simply stood there, saying nothing, looking insubordinate.

Redick stared him down.

"You have something on your mind, there, Corporal?"

"No ... Sir."

"Sure as shit sounds like you do." Redick stepped up and put his face inches from the young soldier's. He didn't back up, but his mask started to crack in fear.

"Would you like to join your friends there?"

"No, sir."

"We're not in a fucking library. Do you?"

"NO, SIR!"

Redick turned and walked back to the gathered Marines. He wheeled again and pointed at the obstinate soldier and the three others standing behind him. They were hanging their heads.

"Why don't you take your fire team and go watch the section of fence these idiots were supposed to."

A few of the soldiers shuffled their feet.

"That wasn't a fucking suggestion! Fly!"

The soldiers jogged off to the stable. Redick looked over at Roland.

"Mr. Roland, will you set those boys up, make sure everything is secure? Tell those Marines I posted to report back."

"You got it, Redick." He left.

"Captain Redick." George stepped forward. "They're just kids. They made a mistake. No harm came from it. Let's say we just ..."

"Let them go?" Redick's eyes narrowed. "George, I understand you're the kind, old, liberal type. The professor. But this affects all of us. No, nothing happened, not this time. But all it takes is once. Believe me. I've seen it happen before, but not under my command. Nor will it. They broke a military rule of combat *and* a law of the constitution of Boomtown. This can't go unpunished."

"What are you going to do? Put them in the stocks?" George looked concerned. "You can't just kill them. They're just kids, for God's sake ..."

Redick gave George one more glance, then turned.

"Marines, on me!"

The Marines, Andrew included, lined up between us and the soldiers.

"Private McMillan, Private Ramirez, you two are guilty of sleeping while in the position of a sentry, considered desertion in wartime."

"Redick, what about a trial?!" George stepped forward, but thought better of it.

"This is the trial." Redick pulled his pistol and pulled back the slide, loading a round. The other Marines, Andrew included, did the same. "Aim!"

The pistols went up, pointed at the two beaten, cowering soldiers.

222

They looked so scared. So pathetic.

"Fire!"

The pistols went off almost in unison. The soldiers took multiple shots to the chest. Both were dead before their bodies slumped to the ground.

"Jesus ... Sickening." George muttered and stormed off. More soldiers appeared from their tents.

"Just in time to dig a hole, sergeant!"

The National Guard master sergeant- the highest ranking soldier there- stepped forward.

"Yes, sir." He saluted and ordered the rest to follow him. The Marines holstered their weapons and walked back into Boomtown. Andrew looked at me with eyes I'd never seen before. He didn't say anything. Neither did I.

Alicia and I walked back to my tent. I didn't rekindle the fire.

We held each other and wept until sleep took us.

Chapter 27

No one mentioned the incident for the next few days. In fact, the Marines acted as though nothing had happened. I still didn't know what to think, so I kept quiet. I wanted to speak to Andrew about it, but didn't get a chance to talk with him in private. I figured Redick knew what he was doing, but it was still a shocking event. I'd never thought about this new world as being in a war. War. It had always been such a foreign word to me. Something to bitch about with my friends in college. It wasn't something I'd ever expected to participate in. Especially not in my own backyard.

Especially not against people who had already died.

We sat at breakfast one morning as the sun was beginning to lighten the haze. George walked in- the first we'd seen of him since that night. He looked troubled, but said nothing as he loaded up his plate. He took a seat away from everyone and began eating, but his gaze was fixed on Redick.

"Can I help you with something, Mr. Dressler?" Redick's eyes burned into George's.

"I think what happened the other night was wrong. Those boys made a mistake. They didn't deserve that ..."

"How long did you serve, Dressler?"

"Pardon?"

"How many years were you in the military? How many combat tours did you have? Surely you're old enough to have gone to Vietnam."

"I ... I was a conscientious objector ..." George set down his fork and dropped his gaze.

"That doesn't surprise me. You don't seem to have the stomach to do what needs done, no matter how distasteful in may seem. I've been in the Marine Corps for eight years. I was sent to the sandbox and the jungle on six separate occasions. I know a thing or two about war."

"I never implied that you didn't. But war? Do you think those things know what they're doing? Are they maliciously trying to wipe us out? I think *war* may be a little ..."

Redick narrowed his eyes, his face taking on a stone-like quality.

"It doesn't matter if they're doing it on purpose or if they're mindless animals operating solely on instinct. Hell, I don't even think we're an actual food source for them. I've seen those things eat until they burst, then just keep on eating. The hard fact is, they will keep eating their way across this planet until there is nothing left for them to eat. They will never stop doing what they're doing, or they would have by now. Bleeding-heart sensibilities aside, this is war, Dressler. A war the likes of which we've never seen, nor did we prepare for. Why do you think things fell apart so ...?" Redick stared off, his eyes slightly glazed over. He then shook his head and snapped back. "Because we're at war, I expect everyone to do their part to make sure everyone else comes out alive. I understand you didn't sign up for the Corps, but I sure as shit didn't sign up to have my family devoured by the dead. If I allow laziness in any capacity, the cohesion is lost and the machine breaks down. Every part has to do its job. Does that make sense?"

Redick looked around. The question was directed at everyone. There were nods all around.

"If we allow it to break down, we may as well just give up, throw open those gates and march out to join the Zees ..."

John cleared his throat.

"My platoon was guarding an ammo dump just outside of Da Nang in '69. Hill 191. Overlooked a little, green valley. We called it 'Slanted Ireland'. One night ... Early spring, I remember. Our sentries fell asleep and got their throats cut. A few of us were up, playing cards. Didn't know anything was wrong until the mortars started to drop. We ran outside, trying to reach our trench. That's when they opened up with machine guns. Five of my best friends ... I completely agree with what you did, Redick. Not an easy decision for any commander, but it had to be done."

225

He turned to look at George.

"We *are* at war, George. There is no reasoning with this enemy. Whether intentionally or not, they mean to kill every last one of us."

George swallowed hard, saying nothing.

Redick nodded at John, then set his eyes on George again.

"If you don't agree with my command, you're not a prisoner. You're free to leave anytime. You can go and have a fucking pow-wow with the Zees. Hell, I'll even give you a lift personally. But ..."

His eyes looked like steel.

"I wouldn't recommend it."

George nodded and looked back to his plate.

"You're right ... I apologize, Captain Redick. I won't criticize any more of your decisions."

Redick turned to leave.

"Jerritt?"

I was intently watching the terrified expression taking over George's face.

"Jerritt?!"

My head snapped up. I realized Andrew wasn't here.

Yeah ... Captain?

"Finish up. Browne is sick. You're training to be a door gunner today."

The sun broke through the clouds, giving us a rare, sunny day. "Sunny" in a sense of the word. The sky was a dingy blue between banks of clouds, and pale shadows stretched across the land. Dark clouds piled over one another to the west, reaching far up into the sky. The little bit of snow that had fallen the day before was already melted. Streams of dirty water flowed down hillsides. The Blackhawk I was on, *Raider Four*, swooped low over the dying forest. Most of the pines were red or gray. A few green ones remained.

The rotor was muffled by the headset I was wearing. The speakers crackled.

226

"Okay, Jerritt, remember. Kung Fu Grip, then shut the cover, then pull the bolt back. You have to push this one back forward."

The Marine, Corporal James Ortega, was teaching me the basics of the M240 machine gun. I pushed the first belted round into the receiver, shut the cover and operated the bolt. I pushed it shut.

"Nice, Jerritt. Just right." Ortega looked below us. "Fucking sweet. Hey, Chief, bring it back around!"

"I see 'em." The pilot's voice came through the headset.

The helo banked hard, moving my stomach into my throat. I knew it would take a few more rides before I got used to helicopters. I looked down and saw five Zees shuffling down a stretch of road. They were all headed for a small stand of trees.

"Looks like you get some real-life target practice today, Jerritt." Ortega slapped me on my shoulder.

I leaned into the stock and lined up the sight. I squeezed the trigger and flinched. Nothing happened. The trigger didn't even move.

"Safety, Jerritt."

Oh. Duh.

I pushed the switch and aimed again. I squeezed and the end of the gun erupted with fire. Empty shells leapt out the side of the gun. It jumped wildly. I missed the Zees by about four feet.

"It takes some practice. Start low and climb your fire into them."

Raider Four stopped to a hover. Aim low. Squeeze. I could see tracers reaching out for the Zees. The trailing two had stopped and turned towards us. A middle-aged man and a younger, naked man. The naked one got both of its legs blown off. It hit the ground face-first. Two rounds caught the older one in the chest, tearing massive chunks out of its torso. It fell backwards, then slowly tried to get back up. The naked one was crawling toward the helicopter. It reached up as though it wanted to pluck me from out of the door. I sent another volley, opening the heads of all of them.

This is a weapon I could grow to love.

227

"That's what I'm saying, man!" Ortega smiled. He pointed to a large pine tree. "There's a few more."

Ahead, across a road and up a slight hill, I saw a group of Zees gathered around a tree. They were clawing at the trunk, now stripped and covered in abraded flesh. I trained the weapon on them.

"They must have treed some animal. Take 'em down, Jerritt!"

I aimed through the peep sight, but something gave me pause. Movement, in the tree. A flash of dull color. Blue and orange. I flipped the safety.

There's someone in the tree. It's a person.

"You sure?" Ortega grabbed his binoculars. "Shit, you're right. Chief, we've got a live one in that tree. Can you put us down on the road?"

"Affirmative. Got plenty of room."

Raider Four descended to the road. The landing gear thumped down and we piled through the door. There were only four of us, as this was only supposed to have been a training flight, but there were only seven Zees and we had rifles. We marched toward the tree and one of the Marines gave a shrill whistle. Even with the thump of the rotor behind us, I could hear weapons being loaded and safeties being flipped off. Five of the seven Zees turned and shambled towards us, moaning and chewing. The other two were intent on whoever was in the tree.

"Marines!"

The Marines dropped to a knee and took careful aim. We didn't want any stray rounds going up into the tree.

"Steady!"

The Zees ... A fair-haired man, a brunette woman. The rest were brown-haired kids. A family. An entire family of death. The man's right hand still loosely clutched a pistol. It dangled uselessly.

"Fire ..."

Semi-automatic weapon fire shouts down the valley. One shot ... one kill. The family fell in a group. We cautiously stepped forward, around the pile

228

of bodies. A family's last hug.

The pistol, still clutched in the gray hand. The slide was halfway back. Jammed.

The other two Zees finally noticed us, but seemed almost reluctant to leave the tree. As though they understood they had an easy meal up there. We wouldn't be so easy. Ortega motioned for us to hold as he moved to the tree, dropping the last two. He looked up into the tree. Through the branches, I could see a young boy's face. I couldn't tell, but it looked like he was cradling something. Ortega slung his rifle.

"Hey, little man. You're safe, now. Is that your sis-"

"No! Not yet! Watch out!"

It was too late. Not seven Zees. There were eight. A tiny one, what could only have been a little girl appeared from behind the tree and latched onto Ortega's leg. Her teeth sank in just above his knee. He screamed and ripped her off. A chunk of bloody flesh came off with her mouth. It lunged again, but another Marine shot it through the side of its head. Ortega fell backwards, eyes wide at the oozing wound on his leg.

"No ... Shit, shit, shit ... No ...."

The Marines charged forward. I followed. The radio at Sgt. Theissan's side crackled.

"This is *Raider Four.* What happened, boys?"

The sergeant snatched up the radio, keyed the mic.

"We took out the Zees, but there was a small one we didn't see ... A kid. Ortega's been bit."

We were answered by silence, filled in by the low hiss of static until the pilot spoke.

"Roger that. I'll notify the Ranch. Grab the survivor. Take care of Ortega and get your asses back on this bird. Out."

The Marines exchanged glances. Ortega's face dropped.

"Guys, it ain't that bad ... Really ..."

Sgt. Theissan stooped and tore Ortega's pants up and down the leg.

229

The wound flowed with thick, red blood. It was already turning black around the teeth marks. Dark tendrils were climbing up the leg, under the skin.

"He's going to become a monster, isn't he? Just like my mom and dad ... My brothers and sisters ... My ..."

Our heads all shot upwards in unison. We'd almost forgotten the child in the tree. He looked barely older than Anthony, but it was hard to tell. His hair was matted and his face was emaciated and dirty. He wore a stained, oversized Denver Broncos jacket. He held an object in a bloody towel.

"You're safe now. Will you come down? We can take you out of here." Sgt. Theissan's voice stayed flat and non-threatening.

"Are you the Army?"

I saw a few of the Marines smirk.

"Yeah. We're the Army. Come on down."

The boy slowly climbed down. He refused to give up the towel. We ushered him towards *Raider Four*, away from Ortega and the bodies of his family.

"Is your friend going to be okay?" The boy looked at me.

He ... He won't be in any pain.

We jogged towards the helo. Behind me, Theissan was knelt in front of Ortega. He had his helmet against the wounded Marine's, and was talking with him. The noise from the rotors washed out all other sounds as we approached. Just a heavy thump in our ears and chest. Even so, I still heard the gunshot behind us. I looked over my shoulder to see Sgt. Theissan and another Marine loping after us, carrying Ortega's body. We stopped at the helicopter door. I could barely hear the boy over the engines.

"Is my sister going to be okay? She's just a baby." He unfolded a portion of the towel.

Wrapped in it was a tiny, baby girl. Black tendrils reached into what was left of her face. She'd been shot through the head.

Chapter 28

Missing a man or not. End of the world or not. There was always a mission. We had a mission and still had to fulfill our objectives. We rode on the Blackhawk in silence, a somber mood filling the cabin. The boy, whose name I still didn't know, sat staring at the towel, his sister's tiny, ruined face covered once again in the bloody cloth. After a while, I took off my headset and let the whooshing of the air and the thumping of the helicopter wash over me. I wanted the wind to blow away all the ugly memories and horrible experiences, but I knew it wouldn't. I closed my eyes, trying to forget ...

Raider Four banked sharply, snapping me back to reality. I fumbled with the headset, getting it back in place just in time to hear one of the Marines.

"-f a bitch."

I looked down, over the door gun to where he was pointing. Below us was Butte's airport. Most of the Zees had cleared out from the perimeter, likely wandering off to find new victims. The fence had been fortified, but regardless, there were a few Zees wandering around on the airport grounds.

How in the hell did they-?

Then I saw it. On the western side of the fence- A large hole. A wrecked pickup truck sat a few yards away. Further in, towards the terminal itself, were a number of trucks, cars, and a pair of green National Guard Humvees. SSgt. Theissan switched channels and keyed his mic.

"Cap, we have some Zees and some possible intruders at the Field."

A moment of static.

"You've got that kid with you still?"

"Yes, sir."

"He still holding that corpse?"

"Yes, Cap."

231

Another moment. I could almost hear Redick swearing.

"Do you want us to return to base, sir?" The pilot joins in.

Static.

"No. Circle over the city. Make sure the crowd isn't interested in the airport. Put down and fix that goddam hole. Take care of the Zees inside."

"What about the intruders, Cap?"

"If they're stupid enough to break through a barricade like that, they either expected to drive into a fight, or they've seen us and know who we are. Put down and I'll send *Telum*. I'll follow with Raiders *One*, *Three* and *Six*."

SSgt. Theissan looked at the Marines. At me.

"Yes, sir. If the intruders prove to be hostile, we'll fall back to rendezvous point Sierra."

"Roger that, staff sergeant. Give 'em hell."

The pilot turned north, giving me a clear view of the ground below. We climbed up over the dark city. I could still see a large amount of Zees, but not as many as I remembered. Were they setting a trap for us? I was glad my mic was off. I started chuckling at such an absurd thought. We skirted the East Ridge and came in low over the airport. I sat behind the M240 and pulled it tight, but my heart was still pounding in my throat. We flew so low over the Zees inside the fence that I instinctively lifted my legs, hoping they wouldn't be able to snatch me from the helo.

Foolish thoughts.

We landed by the hole in the barricade. We leapt from the helicopter. The engine cut down to a whine as the rotors slowed. There was a line of hangars ahead. A few Zees loitered outside the fence, but they were too far away to reach us before we could block the hole. There were two Zees coming around the side of the hangars. I raised my rifle, but thought better of it. As squeamish as any of us might have been about getting in close after what happened with Ortega, there was no sense in taking the chance of drawing in hundreds more.

The door to the truck was open. There was no sign of any violence.

Just a spot of blood on the steering wheel. They must have underestimated the strength of the barricade. One of the tires was flat and the front end was smashed in, but the group of us pushed it across the gap in a few minutes. A Marine popped the remaining tires. It wasn't the perfect obstacle, but it would suffice until something more permanent could go up. We jogged in to deal with the Zees inside the perimeter. The two had approached close now, but the big Marine with us, Corporal Durant charged them. He pulled his machete and buried it in the nearest Zee's head. It momentarily got stuck and his eyes grew wide, but he quickly kicked the Zee in the chest, pulled it free and dropped the second one.

He turned to us and grinned, but I could see the fear veiled behind it.

"Marines! From here on out, we don't go solo hand-to-hand with the Zees. Buddy up!"

I teamed up with the copilot. The pilot stayed with the boy at the helicopter, ready to lift off at the first sign of trouble. SSgt. Theissan and Cpl. Durant stayed a few paces ahead and to the left. We slowly made our way across a brown, grassy field. Ahead was a square of tarmac, abutted against the hangars. There were several small planes still sitting, props covered and wheels chocked, on the asphalt. I could see movement behind one. I motioned to the pilot, Chief Warrant Officer 3rd Class Kuyper. He nodded. Theissan and Durant saw it, too. They moved around the side of the aircraft as Kuyper and I approached from the front. I was nearest, and pulled the crowbar from my belt. The pocked, stained metal felt good in my hands. Shadows from the low clouds flowed lazily across the valley and hills. I rounded a wing of the plane, weapon at the ready.

I stopped. The Zee turned towards me and moaned. It still wore its glasses and its mustache was caked with dried blood, though the lower right side of its face had been eaten away. It still wore a nametag.

"Everything alright, Jerritt?"

I chuckled dryly.

Yeah. This guy ... Zee ... I worked for him. His name is ... Was Joe

233

Jensen. He owned a couple fast food places in town.

"You gonna be good putting him down?"

I grinned as Jensen's body approached. Its left arm shot out at me. The other arm dangled uselessly, hanging by a scrap of bone and torn muscle. I could still see holes from a shotgun blast.

Oh, yeah. He was a fucking asshole when he was alive.

"Go get him, Jerritt."

I stepped forward. The Zee's moan turned into a growl. I raised the crowbar and sank it deep into the top of Jensen's head. His ... Its glasses broke in half as its forehead caved in. I gave the crowbar a twist and pulled it free. The top of its skull crunched and snapped. I stood over the broken body for a moment.

It's a different world now, Chief. Should I have enjoyed that as much as I did?

"All I can say, Jerritt, is enjoy what you can. As long as we can feel *something*, we're still alive."

I nodded, stepping over the body. Another plane sat on the taxiway ahead. Apparently someone had tried to get away. The left door was wide open, the cockpit covered in dried blood. A woman was still strapped into the passenger seat. It looked like she'd been stabbed repeatedly in the neck. Her skin was gray, and-

She turned and gazed at us with milky eyes. Her cracked, black lips pulled back into a sneer. I could clearly see the bloody bandage on her shoulder.

Almost made it.

"What?"

I hadn't realized I'd spoken out loud.

Nothing. We'd better leave it, for now. It'll be hard to kill in such a confined space without a gun. We'll wait until reinforcements arrive, but we'll have to take care of her ... It, eventually.

CW3 Kuyper nodded agreement.

"They'll be here soon. Let's clear out the remaining Zees on the tarmac and find out who left us the gap."

We took a few more steps when the wind kicked up. Hard. It blew dirt everywhere. Grittiness in my teeth, stinging my eyes. Thunder rumbled. We turned and looked west. Dark clouds were moving quickly over the mountains. Lightning flashed.

Shit.

The minute sunlight faded, casting a dreary darkness over the land. Already, tiny drops of rain were beginning to fall. A few yards to the left, Durant dropped another Zee. Theissan was using a parked plane as a windblock, his radio pulled in tight against his ear. His expression was grave. We jogged over to him. The rest of the Zees inside the fence were still a little ways off. Most of them were shuffling to the airport terminal itself. Theissan turned, opened his mouth to speak, but a loud crack of thunder, followed by a trident of lightning bolts, cut him off. Durant eyed the storm nervously.

"That was Redick. They have eyes on the storm. It won't allow any flight operations. Not until it passes. That includes us."

His words took a moment to sink in, but when they did, the gravity of them hit me, tying a knot in my stomach.

"What about *Telum*? They should be here any minute."

"No dice. The wind up the valley forced them to turn back before they even cleared Zone One."

"How long until the storm passes?" Kuyper now looked concerned.

"They don't know. It's a big one. The civilian weather guy said at least nine hours. Maybe thirteen. We're stuck here until then. Redick's orders. No birds in the air."

More lightning cut across the sky, illuminating the Zees in the distance. Thunder crashed, shaking the sheet-metal hangars.

Should we take refuge in one of these hangars?

"We may as well. No sense in chancing a firefight while we're at the disadvantage."

235

The rain picked up in force as another peal of thunder- no, not thunder. It was a gunshot. The Zee nearest the terminal dropped to its knees, then its face. The sky growled. Cloaking the hills to the west was a sheet of gray. Lightning flashed through it. The rain turned to snow. It was laden with ash. Heavy. Wet. Ugly. Gray. Theissan keyed his mic.

"Chief, how's the storm looking? Can you grab the kid or do we need to lock the bird down?"

Our mics crackled.

"We need to lock it down. We can't let this shit get into the engines."

"Roger that. Marines, double time!"

We jogged back toward *Raider Four* in the face of a howling wind. Ahead we could see the pilot struggling with the intake covers and blade guylines. The boy had put down his dead sister and was helping him.

Strong kid.

We grabbed portions of heavy canvas and attached them to various parts of the Blackhawk. The wind howled as the storm worsened. The snow was heavy and we had to keep moving to stop it from building up on us. It felt like wet cement. Lightning slashed overhead, illuminating the land. We couldn't see the Zees ahead of us, but behind the fence, I could see several pounding vainly at the chainlinks. Sgt. Theissan's voice came out of the gloom. We could barely hear him over the wind.

"Let's get to the hangar, Marines!"

We jogged sightlessly through the blowing, gritty snow. Out of the gloom, the hangar loomed. A larger jet stuck halfway out of a wall. The whole side was open to the storm.

"Shit! No good! We have to head to the terminal!"

"What if the survivors there are hostile?!"

"If they are, we'll deal with them! Can't be any more hostile than this storm!"

The sky was dark now, hiding the sun and plunging us into an early dusk. The terminal was somewhere south east of our position, but we couldn't

236

see anything.

"Marines, form up! Clearing formation!"

The Marines formed a line, hand on the shoulder of the man ahead, weapons held ready. I pushed the boy into line and emulated. The point man, Durant, flipped his weapon light on. It reflected off the dingy blizzard, momentarily blinding us. It clicked off.

"Shit, sorry!"

We pressed forward into the storm, stumbling blindly like a heavily-armed conga line. Lightning arced through the snow, bathing the world in a brilliant, blue light. I could see the dark forms of two Zees ahead in the gloom. Durant double-tapped, dropping both. Every time my eyes adjusted, more lightning would blind me again. More Zees, stumbling out of the snow.

A nightmarish shooting gallery.

The boy's hands clutched Kuyper's pants tightly, as though if he let go in the slightest, he'd be whisked away in the storm. Another blue glow. Something caught my eye to my right. I turned.

A Zee lunged out from behind the gray-blue wall.

Shit!

I barely had time to react. I drew my pistol from its holster and swung it upwards, catching the Zee in the chin. I heard a crack and several of its teeth shattered out its mouth. Pistol-whipped, like some goddamned gangster movie.

It fell backwards, but didn't go down. The lightning faded and I was blind again.

Shit!

I fired into the gloom. The muzzle flash lit my target. I hit it in the upper chest, just under a shoulder. It spun the Zee around, sending it to the ground. I fired again, striking it in the back. One more shot blew half of its head away.

A lucky shot. Win the prize.

I turned and my heart dropped. The Marines, the boy. They were all gone.

Oh ... Fuck ...

In the darkness, just beyond where I'd shot the Zee, I heard the moaning that carried over the wind. I froze. It was like the storm ripped right through my clothes, my skin. Right down to my blood. Lightning flashed.

A Zee. Not three feet away.

Its diseased claws reached out, clutching my gear vest. The pistol dangled limply in my hand. Its mouth opened. Bits of flesh still hung from its mouth.

Its head exploded in time to a crack of thunder. Hands grabbed me from behind, spinning me around.

"You coming, Jerritt?! Jesus, man!" Theissan ran back into the storm. I followed him. The others were just a few paces away. We regained our conga-line and within a handful of Zee-free minutes, the terminal loomed out of the snow. More lightning and Durant hit the ground. At first I wondered if there'd been a shot I hadn't heard, but ... Everyone dropped. I dropped. A shot rang out, whizzing over us.

"Motherfucker!" Theissan returned fire. I heard glass break ahead.

Then, scarcely heard over the wind, a voice.

"Stop! Don't shoot! We didn't know if you were them! I won't shoot again!"

A red flare blazed up in a darkened window. A young soldier in fatigues held it aloft, waving it. Theissan waved us forward. We ran and jumped over the slight sill. Theissan grabbed the flare and stabbed it into the snow that was piling up outside. It hissed and the world went dark again.

"Who are you, soldier?"

"F-first Lieutenant Mitch Amos, s-sir!" The young man, more of a kid really, clumsily saluted.

"Keep your voice down, LT."

"Yes, sir."

"I'm a staff sergeant. Don't call me sir. Are there more of you?"

"Yes, sir ... Sergeant. More upstairs."

238

"Are you in charge?"

"They ... Seem to think so, sir. I'm just an ROTC cadet." Even in the dark, he looked sheepish. Apologetic. Scared.

"The upstairs blocked off?"

"Yes, sergeant. I came down here to keep watch and keep those things-"

"Don't bother. This storm will keep them at bay, same as us. You'll only draw attention if you keep firing out into the dark like that. Take us to the others."

The young officer seemed relieved to have someone who obviously had confidence in what he was doing. His eyes swept the insignia on Theissan's vest.

"You're Marines? The government ... Came for us?" Amos' face lit up.

"Just lead the way upstairs, lieutenant."

"Yes, sir!" He saluted again.

"And knock that shit off."

Once we were away from the windows, we turned on our flashlights. We left a waiting room that was still full of abandoned luggage. A lot of people had left in a hurry. Our beams danced across the walls, making shadows move.

"Did you clear and secure the building?"

"Yes ... Sergeant. We checked all the doors that were unlocked and barricaded every entrance as best we could. We can lock the upstairs, as well."

We jogged up the stairs and went through a doorway. Amos closed the door, locked it and a middle-age man helped push a desk in front of it. The door opened outward.

"Are you the military?" The older man had the same hopeful look the young lieutenant had downstairs.

"We ... Were. We set up shop over by Whitehall after Billings fell."

"Where's the government? What are they doing about this?"

"Sir, I don't know where the government is. Maybe Denver, maybe Hawaii. And I'm not sure they even know what this is."

Theissan's words seemed to deflate the man. He turned to a woman. He took her hand.

"I told you, honey. I told you these were the end times. No one is coming for us ..."

"We came." Durant stepped forward. "We may not be in touch with the powers-that-be, but we're still Marines. All we have to do is ride out the storm and our reinforcements will be here after it blows over. We can get you all-"

Lanterns slowly flickered to life around the room. Faces. Faces. Lots of faces. Whole families. Old people. The watery eyes of children. There must have been at least 70 people jammed into that airport office. More lightning flashed outside. The runway was littered with Zees, slowly making their way towards the terminal. Way more than there had been.

Shit.

"Put those lights out. Everyone keep quiet. Marines, refresh your magazines. Nothing comes through that door. This is a bunker until reinforcements, oorah?"

"Oorah, staff sergeant."

"We can keep the Zees at bay. You folks try to grab some sleep. We may have to do a bit of jogging tomorrow."

"You don't have enough helicopters to evacuate us in one trip, sir-sarge?" Amos sounded frightened. More than he had.

"It'll be a tight fit, but we may be able to cram everyone on the big bird. For now, we have more than enough firepower and equipment to take down the Zees out there."

"It's not the- Zees?- I'm worried about. It's the refugees."

"We know about them. Recon flights estimated a small group moving up from the south days ago, and Jerritt said there's another group coming in from the west. Just small bands of-"

"Not small, sir. The ones from the south ... They arrived just west of town, on the highway yesterday. That's why we came here. To find you, so you could get us out of here and warn the government."

"We can handle them."

"A lot of them looked like ex-military, too. Military equipment."

"How many?"

"Before they chased us off ..."

Eyes around the room dropped at the mention of that.

" ... I got a good look at their camp. I'd estimate ... at least 500 of them
..."

Chapter 29

None of us slept that night. The Marines didn't. I didn't. I don't know if any of the refugees did. It stopped snowing after a couple of hours. Enough had piled up on the ground to slow the Zees that were on the airfield. It didn't stop them, though.

By now, I was beginning to believe nothing would.

A handful of Zees had half-scrambled, half-fallen in through the broken window downstairs. We could hear them shuffling, knocking things over and moaning in the building below. One of the civilians grabbed Theissan's shoulder, trying to spin him around. His reaction was automatic. The Marine knocked the man's hand off, spinning, hand grabbing for his knife. He stopped when his fingers touched the hilt. In the darkness, I couldn't see the man's face, but knew by his voice it was the football coach from my high school.

"Aren't you going to go out there and kill those things?"

"No. Gunshots will only bring more of them and I'm not risking my Marines by sending them into a dark building for hand-to-hand combat. If any approach the door, we'll take care of it. If we stay quiet, they won't even know we're up here. They don't seem to have any cognitive thought or spatial reasoning."

"They're going to come up here and eat my family! If you want to be a pussy and hide up here, fine! I'll deal with them myself!" The coach patted a pistol at his side.

"No one is going in or out of that door, sir. Just sit tight until morning and we'll get out of here as soon as the birds come. And keep your voice down."

"I'm not one of your soldiers, bud! I don't have to take orders from you! We still live in America, where we have freedo-!"

242

Theissan was lightning fast. His hand shot up to the coach's throat, shoving him backwards into a wall. The Marine leaned in close.

"I don't know where the fuck we live anymore. If America was a place where the dead returned to life to eat the living, I sure as hell don't remember it. What I'm going to do is keep everyone in here safe and alive. That means not opening that door. If you want to remain alive, you will keep quiet and follow every last one of my orders. If you don't, I will shut you up forever. Clear?"

The coach's voice was strained and hoarse.

"Yes."

"Good." Theissan released him. He turned to the darkened faces. "That goes for all of you. If we want to make it out of here alive, you have to do exactly as I say. This is a new world, and it's not a pretty one. If any of you opts out ..." Theissan's voice suddenly got distant. " ... I'd understand ..." He turned and went over to one of the windows overlooking the airfield.

No one spoke aloud after that, not for the rest of the night. There were hushed conversations. Some people pretended to sleep. Maybe they even tried. I didn't.

I approached Theissan.

Staff Sergeant, should we check these people for bites?

"No ..." He trailed off, his eyes distant. Suddenly, he shook his head and looked at me. "No. No sense in stirring up this nest anymore. We can do that ..." He gazed out the window again. "Tomorrow."

I took a step back and began to turn.

"I tried to pull that trigger. Tried as hard as I could."

I don't know why, but I quickly looked to each side. Maybe to make sure he was talking to me.

Trigger?

Theissan didn't look at me. He continued to stare out the dark window.

"I was stationed in California. Pendleton. I'd never even been to Montana before this. We ... My wife and kids ... Things got bad there fast.

243

Faster than here. It seemed like one day we were watching news reports from China, Russia. The next the Zees were roaming through the streets. There were massive riots in Los Angeles. The military tried to lock down San Diego, but it was too late. We were ordered to pull back, into the desert. I rushed home to grab my family, to get them to safety. When I got there ... The kids, two girls and a newborn boy, they were dressed in their Sunday finest. They were sitting on the couch. My wife was in the chair by the lamp ... She was still holding the gun. The note said 'If you love us, then take this gun and meet us in Heaven'. I tried, Jerritt. I sat down in the other chair and stuck the pistol in my mouth. I pulled on the trigger, but it was like my hand was locked. I ... Just couldn't. So I grabbed my gear and got onto the helicopter ...”

I stood in silence. I didn't know how to reply. I suppose he didn't even want me to. He just needed to tell someone. We all needed to talk. To make sure this world was real and not just some twisted nightmare that wouldn't end.

Lightning flashed outside, illuminating the dark shapes slowly making their way to the terminal. Illuminating a nightmare that wouldn't even end when the sun came up.

Sunrise was dingy. The wet snow had stopped in the early hours, replaced with a steady drizzle of ashy rain. Dirty streams ran through the snow, creating gray islands spread across the land. The Zees that had stumbled across the tarmac now crawled, their clothes heavy with the ash. We could still hear the ones in the terminal crashing around below us. Theissan keyed the radio.

“*Last Ranch*, this is *Raider Four*. How's the weather?”

For a few moments, we listened to the low hiss of static. I could see panic begin appear on several faces. Then the radio crackled. Over the air, we could hear the thump of helicopter engines.

“*Raider Four*, this is *Last Ranch*. Weather is cooperating and flight missions are go. *Telum* is already inbound. The rest will follow.”

“We're going to need *Dolores*.”

A pause.

244

"*Dolores*? Jesus, how many do you have there?"

Theissan did a quick count.

"Seven-five."

"*Raider Four*, please repeat. Seven-five?"

"Confirm, *Last Ranch*. Seven-five civilians for evac."

"Hold on." Another pause. "Affirmative, *Dolores* will take off after pre-flight. If you have any Zees to take care of, now is the time."

"Roger that." Theissan put the radio away. "Alright, Marines, we're going out the windows, fast repel to the ground and shoot anything that moves."

Nods from the team. I nodded, though I'd only done a single repel at the Ranch. My heart sped up. Theissan faced the civilians.

"Do not open that door until you get the all clear from us. Even if the shooting stops. Clear?"

Nods from the civilians. The Coach rolled his eyes, anxiously tapping the butt of his pistol.

The Marines went to work, quickly setting up three repel lines. We each clipped on and the front three smashed the windows out with their rifles. There was a tap on my shoulder, then the rope jerked. I stepped backwards, hesitating. I slipped and slammed my knee off the windowsill as I descended. I braked at the last moment and hit harder than I'd meant to. The Marines around me were already taking aim. I swung my rifle up, aiming through the optic. We flipped on the lights mounted on the barrels, illuminating a crowd of Zees slowly turning towards us. A few already were, and the closest ones stumbled and fell against the windowsill. *Telum* circled the airfield perimeter.

We opened fire, one shot at a time. Headshots only. Two Marines quickly dispatched the ones that were close behind us. From up the stairs, we heard a scream. A man's voice. It was followed by two gunshots.

We dropped the Zees that wandered in from other areas. Two Marines went for a sweep as the rest of us ran to the stairs. The Coach was at the bottom, his wife cradling him in her lap. A dead Zee was laying in front of them. A large, bloody chunk was taken from his neck. The blood oozed thick, quickly turning black. His breath came in short, ragged gasps. With each inhale, more blood flowed from his neck.

"Ma'am, you have to step away from him. Now." Theissan raised his weapon.

"NO! I won't let you take him from me! You can't-!"

"Lady!" Durant's voice boomed. "Get the fuck away from him! Now!"

The Coach's breathing was slowing down. His skin looked waxy and grey. The black lines were already fading.

"I won't! I won't! He'll be okay!"

His breathing stopped. He was dead.

"Ma'am, listen. Whatever caused this is fas-"

"I'LL DIE HERE WITH-!"

His eyes snapped open, but there was nothing behind them. No sense of recognition or relief. No humanity. His head jerked sideways and he bit all the fingers off her left hand.

"GOD! NOOO!!!"

Theissan double tapped, shooting husband and wife through the head. Up the stairs, a group of the survivors watched. The boy we'd rescued from the tree was in front.

"Move! Now! Our ride will be here in a few minutes!"

We ran out through the broken window, taking defensive positions and shooting the Zees that appeared from around the side of a hangar. In the distance, we could hear the low thump of a helicopter. Theissan gestured forward to the civilians, towards an area devoid of Zees.

"Out into the field. We'll hold them off until-!"

Something was wrong. The sound of the helo grew louder, deeper. It reverberated through my chest.

"Shit! DOWN!"

The Marines dropped. I went down with them, but kept an eye turned up to the sky. A few of the survivors got down, but most looked around, dumbfounded. A helicopter swooped over the terminal. It was an older one, like they used in Vietnam. A red spade with an 'A' inside was painted on it. Its stubby wings carried guns ...

It passed overhead and the guns opened fire, sounding like giant zippers. It strafed the larger group. Bodies exploded into red mist. Empty bullet casings rained down onto the slaughter. The group of civilians scattered in all directions, diving for cover. The Zees that we hadn't killed had now closed in. Some of the people even tripped over them while trying to escape the bullets that lanced down toward us. I could see people grabbing onto each other, and had no idea if they were survivors helping one another, or Zees attacking.

Durant leapt to his knees and began firing at it with his rifle. It didn't seem to have any effect, but the helo flew out over the perimeter, then turned around for another pass. It was now headed straight at the Marines. The world slowed down. The helo fired again. I could see the tracers walking their way toward me, blasting spouts of muddy water into the air. Empty casings rained down.

The helicopter exploded.

Telum blasted by and swung around. The burning hulk of the helo dropped to the ground. Ammunition popped in the flames. People ducked as pieces of the blade whizzed by. The now familiar sound of Blackhawks echoed down the valley. *Telum* circled around and fired down at the road that paralleled the airport. In the hazy distance, I could see a pair of pickup trucks stop and turn. *Telum* caught them before they got a quarter mile. Two blossoms of flame lit the gray air.

The Marines were surveying the wounded. Seven had been killed outright by the ambush, and another nine were wounded, three critically. Four Blackhawks touched down in the field behind us. *Dolores* was cruising in low over the hills. *Telum* picked up CW3 Kuyper and his co-pilot and returned them to *Raider Four.*

"Get the lightly wounded up and into those Blackhawks! The able

247

bodies can help us litter the bad ones onto *Dolores*!"

"You got it, staff sergeant!" Durant and I helped people load the birds. As I helped up an older woman who had been shot through the ankle, I saw something out of the corner of my eye. At first I thought I was imagining it. Something moved. I pulled the pistol from my holster. One of the dead, a young man whose chest had been blown open, suddenly sat up and opened his eyes. He hissed, trying to stand. I shot him back down.

"Jerritt?"

"He must have been bitten, staff sergeant."

Theissan nodded. With the wounded, we wouldn't be able to tell who had been shot and who may have been bitten.

As soon as *Dolores* was loaded, Theissan ordered us onto it. We stood in the front of the cabin with the pilots behind us. As we took off, I saw Theissan casually but deliberately raise his rifle into a ready position. I followed suit. I knew what we had to do. If any of the wounded died and came back ...

We lifted into the sky and above the dingy layer of clouds. The cabin grew a little brighter. Most of the survivors, the ones who weren't tending to the wounded, were looking at us. Some with hope on their faces, others with desperation. A couple of looks could have easily been mistaken for restrained hostility.

No one died on the flight home. When we landed, Redick had all the survivors line up under a group of canopies. Everyone was inspected for bites and triaged on the seriousness of their wounds. We'd checked almost everyone's wounds when one of the corpsmen came to a young couple. The mother was cradling a little girl. She pulled back when the corpsman reached for her.

"I'm not going to hurt her. But I have to make sure she's okay." He pulled back the blanket. It was soaked with dried blood. The mother started sobbing. The young father was pale.

"Sh-sh-she ... It just barely got her. It barely broke the skin! W-we killed it! Please don't ..."

"Ma'am, we have to take care of this-"

"She's not some ... Piece of trash to be dealt with! Sh-she's my little baby ..."

The father put his arms around his wife.

"Baby, we have to-"

"No! If they shoot her, they're going to have to shoot me, too!"

The father swallowed hard.

"They'll have to shoot all of us, baby."

Everyone seemed to be looking at Redick. I imagine the newcomers thought he would back down. His face remained impassive.

"Very well." He walked towards them and swiftly ushered them back across the landing pad and behind one of the Blackhawks.

I turned and walked away. I knew what was going to happen next. In a sick way, this was becoming the norm. Part of the daily routine in this twisted, nightmare world. Judging by their faces, I don't think many of the newcomers understood the new order yet. They would. They had to.

We all had to.

Three gunshots rang out through the leaden sky.

Chapter 30

The storms came back later that day. They were getting more violent as the winter moved in. The air grew noticeably colder, and I knew it wasn't going to warm up for a long time. Redick canceled all flight operations. *Telum* had been going to take a look at the refugees from the south, but turned back due to the wind.

The Ranch and Boomtown were locked down for four days as another blizzard awash with lightning swept over the mountains and down into the valleys. Alicia and I took shelter in my tent. The wind ripped across the land and thunder cracked overhead. We played cards and discussed different theories and philosophies about what was happening in the world. We tried to imagine people like us sitting in Germany. Or Yemen. Australia. China. Bolivia. What was happening outside of those walls? Beyond our valleys and mountains and blinding, brilliant storms? Was there someplace safe on the planet? An area unaffected by this horror? A place where mankind would be able to thrive ... To wait out the storm.

Or maybe we were it. All that was left.

That's what I thought. I didn't tell Alicia.

After four days of eating MREs, pissing in a bucket and playing the handful of card games we knew, the fifth morning arrived cold, still ... And clear. A rare morning where the clouds swept low and thick over the mountains and the sky above was a vivid, frosty blue. I put on the cold-weather gear I'd been issued and peeled back the frozen layer of canvas. A two-foot wall of snow blocked the entrance.

"Yo, Jerritt!" Cpl. Durant threw a snow shovel to me. "Help us dig a path to the head!"

We worked for a couple hours on the narrower alleys of Boomtown as the ATVs and trucks plowed out the streets. We didn't care about noise. No

Zees were coming today. We cut for breakfast and hot coffee. As the sun cut over the top of the mountains, I could see them capped with not the dingy, gray snow that blanketed the valley, but pure, dazzling white. The camp began to bustle around us. The Marines only ate with the other military members and the border patrol. The National Guard soldiers had the option of not joining us, and due to the incident a week back, only the NCOs and officers did.

Redick began discussing resumed flight operations. The flight zone at the airport was next priority for clearing. We also needed a look at our newest neighbors. They were down a helo, and we were hoping it was the only one.

"Though, if it's another piece of shit bird like that dinosaur we took out, we'll have no problem with it." Redick added with a smirk.

"Still, it goes to show they're military trained and equipped." Major Hudson, an Army officer and the highest-ranking officer added. He was an older man, close to retirement, with a large handle-bar mustache. He'd handed over full command to Redick ceremoniously, though it was obvious he wanted nothing to do with leadership anymore. "The markings on it … That was a Nevada National Guard bird."

"They're still no match for us."

"And if they have anti-aircraft capabilities?"

"We'll be careful. I'm having *Telum* do a flyover this afternoon. As soon as we get an idea of who and what we're against, we'll form a plan. We'll do some ground recon, if it comes to it. Provided this goddamned snow melts."

As though the weather had listened to Redick, the day warmed considerably by the afternoon. The snow began to melt, turning the streets of Boomtown to dirty rivers and tiny ponds. The tents were mounted on pallets, and the water streamed underneath. The two civil engineers and some of the soldiers were already trying to expand the trenches on either side, but the snow was melting faster than they could dig. Finally, they began laying down gravel in an attempt to make most of the streets passable. Over the noise of their backhoes, I heard helicopter engines starting up. I grabbed my gear and sloshed through the runoff down to the landing area. Redick approached me.

251

"We're only sending *Telum* right now, Jerritt. The Blackhawks aren't going up today."

What if there's trouble?

"We're keeping our distance. Just a look and some photos today. Unless they have some heavy artillery, they won't touch the little bird. However, I do want you and Jerritt to escort our tech gurus up to the radio array. They're putting on the final components and it should be up and running after that. We'll be able to broadcast all the way out to the West Coast. It'll be a hike, but, you boys are from here. You love that shit, don't you?"

Yes, sir. I do.

"Good. Go stow that gear. You won't need half of it."

I nodded and headed back to my tent. I grabbed my smaller pack and found Andrew.

"Brother! Ready for a stroll?"

Yep. When was the last time we hiked?

"July. Before ... Travel was suspended."

Yeah ...

"Well, we're on again. Let's do this!"

I'd never understood how my brother could remain so cheerful in even the worst situations. I guess that's why he was a Marine and I wasn't.

We checked out snowshoes from the quartermaster and headed for the meeting point for the soldiers and radiomen.

"Little Bro, isn't that dude that came with you ... Phil? Wasn't he a radio guy? Maybe we could use his help."

I hadn't seen Phil since before I'd returned from the airport. He and I had talked in passing, and I knew he'd been given a job in the welding shop, but he'd withdrawn in the last few weeks. He'd taken his meals in his tent, started sleeping late. Others had tried approaching him, and each had been given the same "fuck you". He'd been left largely alone at that point.

His tent was still shut, with a large pile of slush melting away in front of the door. I slapped the canvas.

Phil? It's Nick. How did you ride out the storm?

"Phil? It's Sergeant Jerritt, Nick's brother. We could use your help today, if you feel-"

I'd parted the tent flap slightly. He was lying on the bed. He hadn't moved in some time.

"Jesus ..."

I stepped in. Phil cradled a picture of a pretty brunette woman and two beaming little girls. He'd stabbed himself in the neck with a steak knife. An empty bottle of bourbon lay at his feet. A drying pool of blood spread out around him.

He finally went with his family.

I stepped forward and shut Phil's eyes. It wasn't out of any sort of religious belief or anything. It wasn't even out of compassion. I shut his eyes, because I didn't want them, even truly dead, looking at me. I turned around and stepped toward the door.

Don't let Theissan see this.

Andrew nodded slightly and we stepped out of the tent.

We alerted the medical staff and asked them to remove Phil's body as quietly as possible. Then we headed to the mountain. We found the soldiers and radiomen stowing gear onto ATVs. An Army sergeant turned to us.

"Staff sergeant, we're going to take the ATVs as high as we can, then snowshoe in from there."

We each put our gear onto the nearest vehicle. Andrew looked at me.

"Do you still remember how to drive one- oh, yeah. You mowed a Zee down with one, didn't you?"

I both shuddered and smiled at the memory.

I sure did.

"Pretty badass, brother."

Let's hope no one does today.

I meant for it to be a joke, but I saw the timid smiles on two of the younger soldier's faces float back into fear.

We took off up an old logging road. The sun was beginning to illuminate the valley below. The sky stayed blue, and though it kept a haze over it, it was one of the most beautiful sights I'd seen since ... I don't know. A long time.

We splashed through mud and slush, slowly switchbacking our way up the side of the mountain. After a while, dark, rocky peaks came into view through the trees. The snow began to get deeper, melting less. Just short of the top, we were forced to park our ATVs and put on the snowshoes.

Why didn't we bring snowmobiles?

"We don't have any yet. We had no use for them until snow began to fall, and gathering fuel and fortifying the airport took priority. We have a dealership scouted out in Whitehall, but wanted to wait until all the Zees had cleared out. We were afraid we might lead some of them back here. We barricaded most of the bridges ... There were a lot of them."

A lot? Whitehall wasn't that big on its best day, Andrew.

"True. A lot of people fled. But there were still some 400 infected in the chaos of the escape. On top of that, the highway ... Shit, Nick, you should have seen it. All those cars, all those people. Trying to get somewhere. But there was nowhere to go, no place left to hide. A lot of people headed into the wilderness. Lots of them are still out there, I imagine. But those people on the roads, with the kids and the dogs and the TVs and appliances. They were all city people. People used to turning on a light switch or a faucet. People who expected the garbage to get picked up every week and expected the police to protect them. But after Billings, when it all fell apart ... There was no protection. They were out on that highway, trapped. Before we knew it, there were hundreds more. They didn't know enough to leave the valley. They just milled around, eating every living thing they could catch. We knew we had to clear them out. We baited them ... That's when we first tested the cows. We led them east, towards Bozeman and Billings. After that, Redick declared airspace over Whitehall a no-fly zone. Couldn't risk leading them here. We blocked the bridges and left it alone. Until now. We're planning a mission to comb

Whitehall for supplies. Snowmobiles, fuel, weapons, food. Whatever's left. That's why I've been scarce the past week. We pulled some recon missions. There are some Zees left, but not nearly as many as there was. We're going to do it in a day. In and out, then blow the bridges if we have to. Keep them as far from the Ranch as possible."

That's crazy. Incursions into Butte before Whitehall?

"Before the military fled, the National Guard cleared out quite a bit of Butte. That's where these guys were." The soldiers nodded grimly. "There's also some amount of resistance left in Butte. People that have been taking down and distracting the Zees. Whitehall ... Whitehall is dead, so far as we know. Everyone either fled ... Or stayed."

We hiked up the hill into the chill, cool air. The sun had crested the peaks, blowing up into thousands of glittering scintillations above. The snow was cleaner here. We'd left the gray dinginess with the ATVs. Here, the snow dazzled our eyes and crunched smoothly under our snowshoes. Andrew and I hung back, talking about old times. Our hikes as teenagers in these very mountains. Days now gone forever. After a while of that, we both got quiet.

It made me sad, more and more as time passed, to think about the old world. A world we all knew would never return. Not how it was. I figured Andrew felt the same way. The strain, the terror and uncertainty, was beginning to show on everyone's face. Dark bags under restless eyes. Gaunt cheeks. Mouths that forgot how to smile.

We kept walking, the snow underfoot the only thing to break the heavy silence.

We finally reached the ridgetop. Just up the hill, about 200 yards, was the radio array, a motley collection of antennas and scavenged electronic equipment. We removed tarps and the radiomen went to work. We stood guard, but knew there was nothing up here to guard against.

"Hey, Nick?"

Yeah?

"When it's all said and done ... Let's make a backpack trip up to our

255

favorite lake here. A brother's hike, like we used to, alright?"

I smiled slightly.

Alright, Andrew.

It didn't take long before we heard one of the radiomen behind us.

"That should do it." He knelt in front of a control panel and flipped a few switches. Lights turned from red to green. A slight hum began emitting from the array. "Gentlemen, we have communications." He connected a headset and began flipping through channels. By the look on his face, I could tell there wasn't much he was receiving. There probably wasn't much *to* receive.

Suddenly, his expression turned grave. He tore the headphone off. "We have to get back. Now."

We didn't ask for an explanation. We would find out when we got back. We half ran, half stumbled back down to the ATVs and roared back to Boomtown. There, we found Redick. The radioman approached him.

"Sir, the array is on and transmitting, but-"

Redick held up a hand to silence him. In the distance, we could hear the familiar buzz of *Telum*. But something was off about it. It didn't have the monotonous consistency that we had become acquainted with. It sounded ... Lopsided, I guess.

Out over the river valley, we could see the speck grow in size. We knew immediately why it sounded so odd. Smoke poured off one side of the little helicopter.

"The last transmission we had from them said they were taking fire. I didn't think they were going to make it back. I almost deployed a CSAR team." Redick watched the small helo come in. We all ran down to the landing area. *Telum* swept over and landed harder than I'd ever seen it come down. The engine immediately shut down and the crew climbed out. The pilot, an Army captain, approached.

"There's a lot of them, sir. Shit, their camp is almost as big as Boomtown ..."

"Air support?"

"Yes, sir. There were at least six more birds, and ... They have tanks. At least seven. They also have anti-aircraft capabilities. No missiles, at least what we saw. But whatever they hit us with was big. .50 cal, probably a rifle. If they have marksmen with anti-material weapons, they could pose one hell of a threat. They also seem to have pens set up. Most contained people, but a few had Zees in them."

I could see the gears turning behind Redick's eyes.

"Are they going to stay, or push in to Butte?"

"They look to be digging in for the winter, sir. Semi-permanent buildings are going up. They're here to stay."

"All in that valley ..." Redick seemed to be talking to himself. "Get the boys working on *Telum* immediately. I want it back in the air by the end of the week, if not sooner." He turned to us. "Start gathering up armor, weapons, ammo. Looks like we're going to war." Redick turned to go, then stopped short. He spun on the radioman. "There was something you wanted to tell me."

"Yes, captain. We got the transmitter up and going. It works fine. Good, strong signal."

"And?"

"And ..." The radioman leaned in, taking on a low, almost secretive tone. "There was interference. On our bandwidth. Someone else is transmitting."

"I thought we gathered all the survivors in the valley. Who could be talking, and why aren't they talking to us?"

"I think it's coming from inside the camp."

"Who would they be talking-" One of the soldiers began, but we all realized at once. We looked west as a group. All except Redick. "Oh ..."

Shit.

Redick was looking back up the hill, towards Boomtown.

"Belay my last order. I want you to round up every one of those motherfuckers from the airport. I'm taking care of this mole problem. Right now."

Chapter 31

"Is that it? Are they all here?"

"Yes, Cap."

All the survivors we'd picked up in Butte, except the kids, were gathered inside one of the mess tents. Some looked nervous, most looked confused.

"What's the meaning of this, Captain Redick? You can't just detain us-" An older man spoke up but quieted when Redick cast a cold stare at him.

"Yes. We can. As many of you know, there's been some amount of activity today. One of my helos got shot up and ..." He paused, looking across the gathering. "We got a newer, more powerful radio transmitter working." Again, he looked at everyone.

I stood behind and to the right of him. I looked at all the faces, searching for a sign of recognition, of fear. I saw a lot more confusion.

The older man spoke again.

"What does that have to do with us?"

"One of you has a radio. You were transmitting early this afternoon."

A low murmur went up through the crowd. They began looking at each other. I followed eyes, trying to pick out an accusing glare or any knowing looks. Small arguments began.

Hey!

The room froze and looked at me. I glanced at Redick. He nodded almost imperceptibly.

How many of you are from Butte?

Hands went up.

Get to that side of the room.

I pointed. The crowd shifted. It left seventeen people on the other side of the room. I looked at them.

"Newcomers, all?" Redick stepped forward. They nodded. A variety of couples, young and old. A few singles. All manner of races.

My eyes picked over them, but kept stopping at one guy.

You? What's your name?

The blonde man regarded me dispassionately. The quiet, young, brunette woman with him suddenly looked shell-shocked.

"Ken Bowman."

Where are you from, Ken?

He smiled. Well-worn lines around blue eyes. Deeply tanned skin.

"Dillon. Just south of here."

Bullshit.

His eyes narrowed.

"Yeah?" He started to stand up, taking on an aggressive posture.

"It's him! It's his radio!" The young woman started screaming. "They ... They said they'd kill my husband if I didn't go along with this!"

"Bitch! I'll *kill you*!" Bowman lunged at her, a knife suddenly in his hand. I saw it slip into her side. Blood gushed out. I tried to raise my rifle, but it suddenly felt heavy. My movements felt sluggish and the world seemed to slow down, as if it were all playing out underwater. I could see Marines raise theirs out of the corner of my eye. The man pulled the knife out and went in for another thrust.

I didn't even know John had been there. He must have been standing in the entryway to the tent. He moved fast and silently. It was like seeing a man's caricature of a cat. He slipped in behind Bowman before he even got a chance to turn. John's knife sliced along the inside of the spy's arm. Dark red blood spilled out. I could hear and see the tendon recoil as it was sliced through.

Bowman screamed and let go of his knife. He fell back into a table, holding his limp, now useless left arm. John grabbed it and tightened a zip tie above the wound. The bleeding slowed considerably.

"Fu-fuck you. I'll lose my arm."

"I hope so." John hit him across the face, knocking him out. The Marines surrounded him. A corpsman was checking on the young woman. The wound was deep, but hadn't hit anything vital.

"Holy shit, Reid. I haven't seen anyone move like that since I worked with Delta in Africa."

John smiled hesitantly.

"It's been a while."

Redick glared down at Bowman's slack body.

"Ken-fucking-Bowman, huh? Get this piece of shit to the trailer. Have Doc fix up his arm. Then wake him up. I want to have a few words."

A half-hour later, we stood outside a large truck trailer that had been converted into a brig. Bowman had been taken inside. Redick looked at John and I.

"Do you boys want to come in and see what this asshole has to tell us?"

"No, thanks, Redick. I've seen enough of that to last lifetimes." John turned to go.

"We could use your help with this new threat, Reid. Zees aside, this is where the real danger is. Will you reconsider going into the field?"

"I'll think about it." John disappeared into the fading sunlight.

"Jerritt. You coming?"

Yeah. I am.

We walked up the steps into the trailer. LCpl. Durant shut the doors. It was dim. Bars had been welded from ceiling to floor a third of the way into the trailer. Inside was a cot and a plastic bucket. Directly in front of me, a chair sat under a single light. On the chair sat Ken Bowman. Still unconscious and stripped completely naked.

Redick cracked a cylinder under his nose. He inhaled and his eyes snapped open. He blinked, regaining awareness.

"Rise and shine, princess. I want to answers. You're going to provide

261

them."

Bowman blinked. He smirked.

"Fuck you. Just kill me. Those people, out west of here ... They're the scary ones, man. You're just some fucking grunt, trying to piece together the remains of the government."

Redick smiled.

"No, I'm not. We were Marines. Now we're just survivors. Like you."

The smirk began to fade from Bowman's face.

"I see you have a Ranger tattoo. You were a Ranger, huh?" Redick slapped his bicep.

"That's right. We were sent to California. Things went to shit, they vaporized L.A. I barely made it out of there. The General ... He's picking up survivors, helping us out. He said the mountains in the north was a promised land."

Redick's eyes narrowed.

"The General? Who's that?"

"General- You know what? Fuck you, *captain*. I don't give a fuck. Just kill me. You Marines act all bad, but you don't have the stones-"

Redick reached down and broke three fingers on his right hand.

"FUUUUUUUUUUUUUCK!!! SHIT, shit, shitshit ... General ..."
Bowman swallowed hard. "General Theodore Martinez ... He was the-"

"I know who he is. Commandant of Pendleton. He's raising an army?"

"He ... Thinks the government abandoned us to die in L.A ... They fucking did! You weren't there ... It was bad ... We scavenged as much military equipment as we could find along the ... Way. Most of it was just ... Abandoned. We even found some Blackhawks, like yours. But no one could ... Could fly them."

"What's he going to do? Set up a kingdom in the wild west?"

"Y ... Yeah. Pretty much."

"Why did your people fire on mine at the airport?"

"Who knows? They ... They must have thought you were Zees!"

262

Bowman smirked again.

"Hand me the master key, lance corporal."

Durant handed him a pair of bolt cutters.

"Bowman. I have no time for bullshit. Tell me exactly what your people know about mine and what's going on in the next valley. Do it now, before I start cutting pieces off of you."

"F-fuck, man! The General ... He thinks you're still part of the government ... He's seceding and doesn't want any interference."

"He was mistaken, and now he has it. My pilot said he saw giant pens before your people started shooting. What are they? Are you keeping Zees?"

"No ... Well, yeah, but that's not it ... Those are ... Safety fences. For the families, man." Bowman attempted a smile. Redick shook his head. He cut off the big toe on Bowman's left foot. He screamed. Durant cauterized the wound with a blowtorch. I shuddered. I realized this probably wasn't the first time they'd done this. Watching the man's tendon get severed was one thing, but I hadn't been expecting the crunching sound that accompanied his toe being lopped off. Bile threatened rise in my throat, but it was replaced by spit. I swallowed it.

We didn't hear the door open and close and didn't realize anyone was there until Bowman broke down into choking sobs.

"It's a breeding camp. They're trying to repopulate the 'promised land'."

We all turned. The woman who'd been with Bowman stood in the outer circle of light. Sgt. Rourke stood at the door.

"They're forcing women to have babies?"

"And girls. Anyone old enough. Anyone that puts up a fight is killed and eaten. They're all barbarians."

"Fucking ... *bitch*! Your husband will be a dead man!"

"He already is, you fucking pig! I saw him running after the truck! I saw him get beaten. I've accepted the fact that he's gone!"

"It's ... It's all part of the plan. Embrace it. We're going to save the human race! Everyone ... Thought these were the end times! But ... But they're not. Can't you see? We survived the mass slaughter. We've all lived this long. We're the Chosen Ones! That ... That's what the General said! Don't you see? Come on! Don't you ...? " Bowman's face didn't mask the pain he obviously felt, and his eyes betrayed the desperate madness behind them.

Redick said nothing. He merely kept his cold gaze fixed on the pathetic figure in the chair.

"T ... Tell you what? F ... Fly me back to them. Bring your people! Join us, captain. We could use people like you. Help ... Help us save humanity!"

"That's what passes for humanity now, huh? Rape and cannibalism? Don't insult me, Bowman." Redick cut two more toes off his foot. His shrieks bounced off the wall of the trailer. When he finally got quiet, Redick turned to the woman.

"Ma'am?"

"Leigha. My name is Leigha."

"Leigha, do you remember the layout of the camp?"

Her face was devoid of emotion. There wasn't any light behind her eyes.

"Too well."

"Will you draw us a map?"

"Only if you promise to kill every one of them."

"That's what we do, Leigha." Redick nodded to Rourke, who ushered her out.

"Are ... Are you going to kill me now?"

"Oh, no. We're not going to kill you. Not while we can still use you. We're going fishing for savages, and you're our bait. Throw his ass in the cell." He turned and walked out. I followed. The sound of Bowman being tossed violently against a metal wall echoed in my mind as I stepped back into the world. The sun was almost down now. The generators had kicked on, running the low lighting that illuminated the main streets in Boomtown.

I slowly made my way back to my tent. I wanted to find Alicia and crawl into her arms. I wanted to hide there until I could wake up and this nightmare was over. But I knew it wasn't going to be that easy.

I turned away from my tent and instead walked down to the flight line. The helos were silhouetted against the fading sky. I lit a cigarette and listened to the still night. I hadn't heard crickets in months. I wondered if I ever would again.

I heard footsteps approaching. I moved around to the other side of *Dolores*. I didn't feel like talking to anyone. I heard the voices from around the helo. It was Redick and Rourke.

"What do you want to do about these intruders, Ian?"

"Shit ... Jen, we can't feed that many mouths."

I extinguished my cigarette and peeked through one of the windows. Redick looked strained. I'd never seen anything on his face except cold calculation. Seeing raw emotion from him unnerved me.

"I know ... What do you propose to do? We can't just shoot them all."

Redick sighed and looked west.

"We still have the packages from Billings. It doesn't work on Zees, but it sure as shit will work on humans. Fuck ..."

Rourke put her arm around his shoulders.

"It's not an easy decision, baby. But you have to do what's right for the people here. They put their trust in you."

"I know. I've already decided. It's just hard. I'll tell everyone in the morning. I want the pilots okay with it. They'll be carrying the goddamned things. I'll pull the trigger myself. That needs to be on me."

"It ... It won't hurt them, Ian."

"I know."

Neither of them seemed to believe it.

They walked away together, back into Boomtown. I stood by *Dolores* for a while more, then made my way to my tent. Alicia was reading. I looked at her, she at me. I shut off the lantern and lay down next to her. I drew her into

265

my arms.

Neither of us said anything.

I gripped her tight, pulling her down with me into the darkness.

Chapter 32

I awoke to the sound of waves lapping gently on the shore. I sat up, expecting to see the vast expanse of ocean. But it wasn't the ocean, it was a lake. A mountain lake I'd never seen before. The sky above was blue, but there was no sun. No shadows. Just a blue sky reflecting on deep, dark green water. I stood and looked up and down the shore. No breeze moved the trees. No sun, no wind. Just the constant lapping as waves rolled in, then back out. I picked a direction and started walking. I never saw the sun or felt the breeze.

I found a dirt road and followed it through a dead forest. Even the pine trees here were stripped of their needles. My boots crunched softly on the gravel path. I came over a small rise.

A campsite, situated along the small stream coming out of the lake.

I walked down to it. It was empty, but looked like it had just been set up. A fire burned silently in the ring of stones, but there were no people, no bodies. The table was set, waiting for a family. Resting against an empty glass was a small box. On it, written in the neat handwriting of my mother:

'Nick.'

I pulled off the brown, paper wrapping and opened it. On the top was a small note.

'Hello, son! We're very proud of all you've accomplished. We know you were feeling confused on which way to go with your life, so your father and I got you this. We hope it helps. We'll see you soon. Love, Mom and Dad'

Under the note was a compass. It was filled with liquid, but had no needle in it. I put it into my pocket. I turned.

She was standing there, silently. Watching me. The girl I'd killed at Georgetown. She was decomposed from the water. Her dead eyes burned into mine.

I'm sorry I killed you.

267

She said nothing.

I ... I had to. We all ... Have to.

Silence. No wind. No sun. Just a blue sky, a gray forest. A little, blonde girl, blood still caked around a head wound, standing. Watching me.

This world ... It isn't a place for you anymore. I don't think it's a place for anyone.

I didn't know what else to say. She wasn't going to respond.

I'm sorry. It was ... For the best. You're probably in a better world than me now, anyway.

I started to turn away. I didn't believe it. Here I was, lying to a dead girl. Lying to myself.

She reached out and grabbed my arm. Her fingernails cut into my skin. Pain shot up the side of my body. She spun me back and lunged, hissing. I fell, grabbing for the pistol at my side.

There was no pistol at my side.

Her jagged, rotting teeth sank into my arm. Blood oozed hot as I felt the tendons ripping ...

I jerked awake, nearly falling off my bed.

Shit!

I fumbled in the dark, finally finding the switch for my lamp. I flipped it and a dim glow lit my tent. The bed was empty. Alicia must have gotten up to go to work at the infirmary. I was glad. I didn't want her to see me like this. I checked the time. 0417. Without knowing why, my hand reached down to my side. Not for a pistol, but for ... My pants were on the floor. I tried stopping myself, but I reached out and grabbed them, jamming my hand deep into the pockets.

There was no compass. Of course there was no compass.

Feeling stupid, I pulled them on, got dressed, put on my heavy coat and gear. Redick had ordered all military personnel to the briefing tent at 0430. I hadn't meant to sleep in, so I stepped outside and lit a cigarette for the walk.

The air was chilly. The haze that had begun moving in the night before now obscured the stars. Another dark day. In the distance, I heard the whine of a helicopter engine starting. I began quickly walking to the briefing tent. The landing area was lit up. I saw a flurry of activity around every bird but *Dolores*. As I passed by the armory, I could see several Marines inside. Durant nodded to me. He was wearing night-vision goggles on a helmet and was twisting a sound suppressor onto a rifle. Andrew was inside and looked up when Durant slapped his shoulder and pointed at me. He came out of the tent, the night-vision looking like insect antennae.

"Hey, brother, what's up?"

Are you coming to the briefing? It starts in a few minutes.

"No, we've already been briefed."

What's Redick have you guys doing?

"He wants us to drop in with the spy and take out as many of the snipers as we can."

Why is Bowman going?

"He ... I'm sure Redick will tell you at the briefing. The spy won't be coming back here." Andrew turned to go back into the tent, then looked back at me. He started to say something, but seemed to think better of it. "Just, be careful out there today, okay, Nick?"

You do the same, Andrew.

I jogged down, slipped quietly into the briefing tent and took a seat in the back. Redick had a map of our region hanging at the front of the room. At 0430, the front of the tent was closed off. Cups of coffee were handed out.

"Well, ladies and gents, I'm sure it's made it through the grapevine by now that we have a pretty major problem just west of Butte." He went over the map.

Nods of affirmation from around the room.

"We took in the people we found at the airport. A pretty charitable act, seeing as how we're already strained on several resources. However, we were able to, and we won't leave anyone behind. Oorah?"

"Oorah, captain!"

"The refugees ... Well, they pose an entirely new set of problems. First and foremost- and this is *not* open for discussion- is there are probably 200-300 civilians being held in that camp. We *cannot* absorb numbers that high. We don't have the housing, the food, the clothing or medical facilities. Which brings me to the next problem. Not only are the hostage takers mostly ex-military, they're also savages. They're running breeding camps in an effort to repopulate the country, and they're eating everyone else. Were we to even consider taking in the prisoner population from the camp, we would be dealing with deep psychological problems and trauma. And we already had a spy come onto the Ranch." Redick's eyes swept the room. "Which is why we're not going to rescue anyone from that camp."

Silence settled over the crowd like the wet, ashy snow that had fallen.

"I won't accept any dissent. That's why I'm not telling the civilians about this operation. If any of you opt out from under my direct command, you may do so after this mission is completed. Not before. You will not breathe a word about what happens today, to anyone. Understood?"

"Oorah, captain!"

A few of the small number of higher-ranking National Guard soldiers who sat off to one side shifted uncomfortably.

"What are you going to do, Captain Redick? Shoot them all?" Capt. Lynn Murray, one of the doctors glared at him.

"No. We're going to gas them."

I could almost see the short, blonde officer's draw drop to the floor. She jumped to her feet.

"You're *what*?! Are you *insane*?!"

"Please keep your voice down, *captain*. I just explained my reasons for not bringing them here. Do you have a better idea? Would you rather I just let them all get raped and eaten?"

"I ... I ..." Capt. Murray's jaw quivered and she sat down, staring at her boots.

"I don't expect this to be a popular idea. I don't like it, but as far as I can see, this is the safest and most humane course of action. And the only choice we have. I'm going to pull the trigger. I carry that burden. The people on the ground ... We have a large dose. It won't be that painful."

Capt. Murray's voice was quiet. I barely heard her.

"Isn't this why we left after Billings? For this very same thing?"

Redick cast his cold gaze down at her, but I could see something behind it. I could see the heavy burden he was holding. He was in command of a small group of living, in a world largely dead. His voice came out, hushed and hoarse.

"We have no other choice."

Redick nodded to Durant, who stood in the corner. He began handing out gas masks to everyone involved in flight operations. As soon as I held the thick rubber in my hands, the gravity of what Redick proposed settled on me.

"Let's move."

Those gathered began moving about. A lot of the personnel looked shocked over the plan. I don't know how I felt. Across the way, I could see Redick give a slight nod to Murray. She looked mournful, but nodded back and walked out.

"Jerritt! Young one!" I turned to see Theissan. "You're with me on Raider Four. Let's go!"

I followed him down to the landing area. *Telum* and all five working Blackhawks were fired up. When I reached the helo, Durant threw me a helmet and armor. I quickly put it on. Behind me, I heard a scuffle. I turned to see a hooded figure, wearing bandages, get thrown onto *Raider Two*. As I watched, I noticed *Raider Five* next to us. It was the long-range bird, with stubby wings that normally held fuel tanks. They now held two racks, each carrying two missiles. They were gray, but painted with bright yellow stripes. A yellow circle with a black 'G' inside was painted above:

'WARNING! Activated warheads will disperse "VX" - *O-ethyl S-[2-(diisopropylamino)ethyl] methylphosphonothioate* ! Gas is colored **orange** for

271

ID! Check safeties! If activated STAND CLEAR!'

My blood turned to ice as I read the words. A hand patted me on the shoulder. It was Redick. He had his familiar, cold face on, but he looked older than when I'd first met him.

"You disapprove?"

It's not up to me. And if it was my decision to make, well ... We really have no other choice. That's the reality of this world now, isn't it?

Redick nodded. In his eyes, behind the cold facade, I could almost sense a deeper, sadder wisdom. When I was young, my grandfather had told me that the necessary thing was seldom the easy thing. I hadn't understood it then.

"Time to roll, Jerritt." He stepped into the co-pilot's seat of *Raider Five*. I turned and leapt onto *Four*, buckling in.

The thump took on a heavier quality as the helo rose into the early-morning dark. As we approached the mountains between the Ranch and Butte, we switched our running lights off. All the other helos stopped blinking and I saw faint, red lights click on in the cabin of *Raider Two* and the cockpits of all the birds. We passed through an almost pitch black sky. I couldn't see anything below us. Far, faint to the east, I could see first light. I squinted that direction, trying to make out the shapes of distant mountains when we abruptly dropped and swooped low.

Shit.

I don't know if I said it or thought it. I racked a round into the M240. Below us, *Raider Two* stopped in a hover. In the red light, I could see ropes drop out the sides and figures moved down, accompanied by equipment and Bowman. I clutched the machine gun tight. We swept by, descending to a low circling pattern. The sun began to brighten the landscape through the haze. I could see Butte off to the northeast. To the north and just slightly west, at the end of the long ridge we were circling, a large encampment had been set up. I could see lights and smoke from cookfires. I could almost hear the shouts as the sounds of the blades from our helos reached them. On the outskirts, something moved. I fumbled for a moment with my binoculars, then got them to focus. It was a tank. My heart leapt into my throat.

Telum flashed under us, just clearing the treetops. As it got closer, a trail of smoke and fire lanced out, whooshing down onto the target. The anti-tank missile hit the vehicle on top, blowing the turret off. *Telum* veered off. The tank burned. I almost started laughing when I realized the tanks really didn't pose a threat to the helos. I aimed down the gunsite, wearing a slight smile.

Telum circled back around, hitting two more tanks, then aimed at a row of fuel trucks. Tracers reached out, but the little helo deftly evaded the anti-aircraft fire. Its own tracers cut down from the sky and the three closest tankers burst into flame, then exploded. Tremendous orange and black fireballs shot into the hazy sky. Two more of the trucks exploded shortly after.

Four helicopters began lifting off from an area just beyond the huge pens of captive refugees. *Telum* swooped back down and shot down two of them, but more anti-aircraft fire forced it to abandon the others. They split, one headed north, one south. *Telum* began to give chase, but was called back.

That's when I saw *Raider Five* going in. It passed down the ridge slowly. Deliberately. I saw tracers reach out for it, but *Five* dropped low and they passed harmlessly overhead. It flew down the ridge until it disappeared into the series of low hills just west of Butte.

The anti-aircraft fire began to slack off. The Raiders on the ground, my brother among them, were opening a pathway for *Raider Five*.

A voice crackled over the radio. Redick.

"All birds stay clear. Zone is hot in three, two ..."

" ...One."

The Blackhawk turned and more spears of fire and smoke reached out. Eight in all. They impacted in the middle of and on the western end of the camp. I saw more tracers come up. *Five* turned. As the initial explosions ballooned off, the smoke began to rise. Orange. It crept along the ground, moving eastward with the wind. It quickly swept over the pens. Below, over the headset and the engines, I imagined I could hear the terrified screams drifting up on the tendrils of orange gas.

Maybe it was just the wind.

Four circled again. Back towards Butte, I could see what a portion of the ground team had been doing. Most likely using Bowman as bait, I could see a few hundred Zees slowly working their way towards the refugee camp. From there, a group of terrified defenders was headed east, right towards them.

"Holy shit ..." Theissan breathed over the com. "He really did it ..."

The entire camp was covered in orange gas by now. It was beginning to dissipate where the warheads had landed. I turned away, suddenly feeling sick. We passed back up the ridge and over the hills just to the south. The forest below still had some green spots. I tried to focus on them. I tried to get my mind as far from possible from that orange cloud and all the people who had just been killed.

But then ... They were already dead, weren't they?

We all were ...

A loud metallic clang snapped me back to reality. It was followed by a thudding, screeching sound and the helo dropped twenty feet.

"What the hell was that?!" Theissan was looking out the other side of *Four.* I scanned the ground, but couldn't see anything below. Just trees and rocks whizzing by. Kuyper's voice crackled into my ears.

"We're hit! We're losing oil pressure!"

Another clang, and the screech became a shriek. An alarm began buzzing in my ear.

"Hang on, Jerritt! Try to spread your surface area!"

I didn't understand what they meant, or even who said it. I grabbed onto the webbing that lined the rear bulkhead and spread my arms. I closed my eyes. I could hear the blades still spinning as CW3 Kuyper tried to bring the crippled bird down.

"Fuck!"

I heard the blades lock up.

Raider Four dropped from the sky.

274

Chapter 33

The world outside was a blur of brown, green, gray. The alarm kept buzzing through my headset. It seemed like it took the Blackhawk a long time to crash, but I knew it couldn't have been more than a couple seconds. I saw Butte to the north, then trees, then ...

The sound of twisting, crunching metal filled my head as the alarm abruptly cut out. Trees rushed up. A branch smacked me across the face. I tasted blood. The helo hit another tree and partially bounced off, snapping the trunk and breaking the locked-up blades. I lifted my legs to avoid impact with the ground, knowing even then it was a stupid idea. I was going to die and there was nothing ...

Raider Four slammed down onto a rock outcropping. Jagged pieces of stone and metal shot up through the center. I felt myself get pitched forward ... Then out of the helo. Something must have cut my harness. My inner thigh smashed into the M240 and I was launched over the top of it. Trees rushed into my vision. Behind me, I could hear more metallic sounds as the Blackhawk skidded down the wooded hill. I closed my eyes, waiting to break my neck on a tree ...

I struck a pine sapling, then careened down the hill a little ways, sliding over gravel and a heavy, wet mat of pine needles. I flopped onto my back and threw out my arms to catch myself, like I'd learned skiing. My shoulder glanced off a rock and I landed in a knee-deep puddle of cold, dirty water. The world spun around me. My left shoulder was on fire with pain, and I knew I'd broken it. Even in the frigid water, I started to pass out.

I couldn't let that happen.

I forced my eyes open and sat up. Pain exploded in my shoulder. I tried moving it. I barely could. I crawled to my feet, gritting my teeth, and looked downhill. *Raider Four*'s tail had broken off, and had started a fire, but the fuselage looked remarkably intact. I tried jogging, but had knocked one of my knees a good one, too. It wasn't broken, but all I could manage was a fast limp. As I approached the twisted, burning hulk of *Four*, one thought kept running through my mind.

Holy shit ... I just survived a fucking helicopter crash.

I had to slide down a slope that was now a mixture of hydraulic fluid, pine needle, rock and broken glass to reach the helo. My M240 was still hanging on its mount. I used it to pull myself into the helo. Kuyper and Renner- the co-pilot- were slumped over the controls. Both were dead. I surveyed the other Marines that had been on board with me. None of them were moving. Corporal Pesaturo had smashed his face off the back of Kuyper's seat. I couldn't even recognize him. His rifle was snapped in half. I could see the flames moving around the door of the helo, and I looked quickly for anything useful. Theissan's M4 was still slung over his vest. His body had protected it from impacting the airframe. I grabbed it and began pulling it free when Theissan grunted.

Jeez-!

I shook him and his eyes fluttered open. His voice was hoarse.

"Jerritt ... You're alive ..." He tried to lift himself up on his arms, but his face contorted with pain.

So are you. The bird's on fire. Let's get you out of here.

I produced my knife and cut through his harness. I pulled at him. He tried crawling along with his arms, then stopped.

"Jerritt ... I can't ... I can't feel my legs."

Shit.

I grabbed onto his vest with my right arm and pulled with all my might. He slid across the floor of the helo, but when we got to the other door, his vest caught on a piece of metal. I lost my grip and fell backwards, directly onto my broken shoulder. I hissed at the pain and tore Theissan out of the wreckage. We both tumbled to the ground. I got back to my feet and began pulling him away from *Four*. The fire had now moved into the fuselage.

Fuck! A radio!

But it was too late. The fire had moved fast. The interior was now engulfed in flame. I pulled Theissan to a flat section on the hill and collapsed next to him.

We have to get word to Redick. They'll be looking for us. Do you have a flare gun, or ...

Even over the crackling flames and distant gunfire, I could hear the moans. Even over the acrid burning of metal, I could smell the stench of rotting flesh. Around the front of Four, through the heat mirages that made the air dance, I could see them. A group of Zees was headed for us. I grabbed onto Theissan's vest with both hands and, ignoring the pain that ripped into my shoulder, began dragging him across the hill, trying to keep the wreckage between us and the Zees. A Blackhawk- I couldn't tell which one- flew over. I could barely see it through the trees. I realized then that the Marines in the air probably thought we were all dead. Of course they did. No one survives a helicopter crash. Not one like that.

I moved us around a tree, lost my footing and fell backwards. The fall winded me, and the pain in my shoulder threatened to knock me out again. I sat up and saw the Zees coming around the wreckage. But there wasn't just a few. There were dozens. I pulled on Theissan's vest again, but he grabbed my arm with one hand and unslung his rifle with the other.

"Leave me, Jerritt. They won't be able to catch you, but you have to go now. I'll hold them off."

I can't just leave you, Theissan. Come on, we're getting out of-

He looked up at me, his eyes cold and lucid.

"Leave me here, Jerritt. I'm going to join my family. Go. Now." As he said this, he began working a hand grenade free from his vest.

I ...Goodbye, Theissan.

"See you in the next life, Jerritt." Theissan smiled one last time.

I turned and stumbled as fast as I could. Behind me, I could hear the popping of the Marine's rifle. The gunfire faded as I worked my way downhill,

277

then it stopped.

It was followed by an explosion.

I kept going until I reached a dirt road. I stumbled down it, casting glances over my shoulder. The Zees were still up the hill, obscured by shadow. I didn't know if they saw me. I didn't care. I kept going down the road. Not far ahead, I could make out a house with a large outbuilding. A garage of some sort. Parked in front was an 18-wheeler. I stumbled down toward the house. As I approached it, I could see the windows had been barricaded. I quickened my pace, scanning the sky. I didn't see any helicopters.

When I reached the road in front of the house, I saw movement through one of the windows. I dropped to the ground as the gun went off and the bullet cracked over me. I tried yelling. My mouth was dry.

Stop! I'm alive!

A door opened and a number of figures stepped out. One of them yelled something and they began to jog in my direction. They were all armed.

Shit.

I reached for my pistol, but it suddenly felt like my fingers were made of sand. My head swam. My left shoulder screamed in silent pain. They ran up to me. Three men. Two young, one older.

"Have you been bit?" One of the younger.

The older man stepped forward.

"His blood would show it. Let's get him inside."

"Are you military? Were you on that helicopter that went down?"

I ...

Darkness flooded into the corners of my vision. I tried to hold on to reality, but it seemed too hard. I let my head flop back as I blacked out.

Through a grayish haze, I heard voices all around me.

"Is he alive?"

"Who is he? Military?"

"Is he bit? He's not bit, right?" I heard the sound of a cocking

278

shotgun.

"He led all those things this way. We should put him out there with them."

I tried to open my eyes. They fluttered, but wouldn't. I was laying down.

"He hasn't been bit, he's just injured. I can't believe he's alive. I've sedated him. All of you, go back to your posts. Stand watch. I think most of them will just pass us by. They have before."

"They haven't followed someone here before, either."

"And you think putting this man outside to get ripped apart will make them go away?"

"Well ... At least distract them so we can escape."

"Son, I'm not having this conversation. Go to the garage and see if Ray has finished replacing that fuel filter. This forces our hand, but we need to leave, anyways. We can't stay cooped up here. If these guys are the military ... Hell, even if they're not, they're our only hope."

"I'm taking this, then." I felt a hand grab at the pistol in my holster. My own reached out automatically and seized his hand. I still couldn't open my eyes.

"Let him have it. We're going to need him when he wakes up. Go to the garage. Now. I won't tell you again."

A sigh.

"Okay, Dad."

Footsteps disappeared out the door.

"Katie, dear? Hold his shoulder just like this. I'm going to try and set it before I wrap it."

I felt my shoulder wrenched. Pain lanced through my body, an almost electric feeling. I gasped as lights flashed in my eyes. Then I passed out again.

When I awoke, early morning gloom filled the room I was in. The spikes in my shoulder had turned into a dull, throbbing ache, matched only by the pain in my head. I slowly sat up, willing away a headrush, determined not to black out again. I was lying in a bed, on top of fresh sheets. My shirt, coat and vest were hanging on a chair next to the bed. My boots were off, but my pants and belt were still with me. The pistol was still in its holster. I stretched a little, favoring my shoulder, then pulled myself over the side of the bed. I felt like I was a hundred years old.

I was lacing up my boots when I heard the door open. I looked up to see a younger woman standing there. She had a water bottle in her hand.

"You're up. Dad said you'd be coming around about now. How do you feel?"

Like I was in a helicopter crash.

I gave a slight smile. She returned it, seemingly distracted. She looked pale.

"You ... You're probably thirsty." She handed me the bottle.

Thanks. How long was I out?

I drank deeply.

"Only two hours." She looked down at her feet. "Well ... We're eating upstairs now. I think we're going to try and leave today ... If you feel up to it. That's what Dad said."

I feel okay to travel. Thank you again. Where are we going?

"We ... There's a bathroom through that door. Once you freshen up, come have some breakfast." She shot another awkward smile and gave a weak curtsy. She then blushed and disappeared back through the door. I finished the water and went into the bathroom. After using the toilet and washing, I looked at myself in the mirror. It seemed like both yesterday and ten years ago I was looking into a mirror, shaving, going over in my head what homework I still had to do. What papers I had to write. Who I was going to drink with on the weekend.

Now the tired face of an old man stared back.

I would have given anything then just to have more papers than I could finish. A pretty girl turn me down for a date. The back window of that

280

Honda just to be a fucking movie screen ...

I splashed cold water on my face from a bucket on the counter, then dried off with a crisp, clean towel. Everything felt surreal, like it was just a dream I would wake up from. I tried to justify it as the sedatives wearing off. The pounding in my head matched the pounding on the sides of the house ...

I pulled the curtains aside and looked down into the yard. The house was surrounded by Zees. Some milled about the yard, as though they were looking for something to do. Most beat hands and fists against the side of the house.

Shit.

Across the yard and a small parking area, the 18-wheeler sat by the garage. I could see now the flatbed trailer attached to it had metal shields welded onto it, and protruding from the front bumper was a basket that looked like a cow-catcher on old trains. Between the house and the truck, there must have been 40 or more Zees.

I left the bathroom, stepped out into the hall and followed voices to a room at the other end of the house. I stepped through the door and a group of nine people looked at me. They were various ages and genders, and from the hair and facial features, I could tell seven of them were related. The oldest one, a man at the head of the table stood up. Before he could say anything, a younger man- the other voice I'd heard- glared at me.

"Good job, dickhead. You've killed all of us. We should've just thrown you-"

"Lawrence! That is no way to talk to a fellow survivor, much less a guest. Leave this table at once."

The young man cast his glare on the old man, but got up and stomped from the room.

"Sorry for that ... Marine, is it?"

I am now, I guess.

I sat down as introductions were made. The old man was a local doctor named Mark Leary. Most of the people in the house were his family, but some were neighbors. They'd been hiding in the house for over a month. Supplies had run low, so they'd been making forays into Butte. They'd seen our helicopters and had once shot a flare to signal it. No helicopter had come, but a group of Zees had. Four of their people had died that day. Since then, they had laid low, hoping that the military would come back in greater numbers. When they were done telling me their story, the questions started.

"You have reinforcements?"

"Is there a safe place anywhere?"

"What happened over the hill?"

I looked from face to face. Most of them looked at me like I was there to rescue them. I took a sip of coffee and proceeded to tell them everything I knew about the world outside. I didn't tell them anything before I hooked up with my brother and Redick. They didn't need to know any of that.

"And your people ... This Redick. He gassed them? All those people over the hill?"

Yeah. He did. He didn't see any other choice. I don't think there was one. This world ...

I didn't know what else to say.

No one spoke for a second. Some of the faces around the table wore frowns. Finally, Dr. Leary put his fork down.

"No. I suppose there wasn't. Winter will be here soon, and I believe it's going to be a bad one. We have a group that went into the Uptown looking for supplies and weapons. We're going to take the truck and get them this morning."

What were you going to do after that?

"Go to the airport and speak with ... This man, Redick. We thought you were the military, but even so, we need your help. There are fifteen of us, total. Can your camp support that many?"

Yeah, it can. We can use another doctor, too.

A shy voice spoke up from the other end of the table. A young boy.

"Is the military going to come? Have you guys talked to them?"

We haven't. Last anyone knew, they were pulling back to Colorado.

A woman glared at me.

"So that's it, then? We're on our own?"

A man put his arm around her shoulder.

"Keep calm, baby. We saw all the military trucks, all the doctors. What if this whole thing is their fault, somehow? Can we really trust them to just swoop in and fix things?"

She dropped her eyes to the floor.

I don't know what's going on outside of this area. Maybe they're doing something. Maybe we're all that's left. Redick may not seem like the ideal leader, but he has a plan and the resolve to keep us alive. It's up to us now.

"And he'll take us in?"

I'll see to it.

That seemed to relax everyone, and eating resumed, though the tone of conversation was somewhat hushed. When we were finished, the young boy and one of the women began collecting the dishes. Leary wore a look that was both amused and melancholy.

"Just leave them. We aren't coming back here."

The woman looked to him, then back to the table. She left the dishes.

An hour later, all supplies were ready and staged at the top of the stairs. The Zees still pounded relentlessly on the house and the boards over the windows and doors. Their moaning and stench filled the air. The people in the house had planned for this. They'd set up a zipline that led down to a pair of dirt bikes they'd stashed in some trees. The riders would lead the swarm away from the house, and the rest of us would make a break for the truck. It was a solid plan, but when I looked at the two young men putting on the harnesses, all I could think of were the bait cows.

We grabbed the supplies as they zipped over the Zees. Some of them reached up and immediately turned around, trying to reach the two guys. A few of them stumbled and brought down a large swath of the swarm. We heard the

283

bikes buzz to life and begin driving up the road. The guys called out to the Zees.

"Hey, zombie! Hyaah!"

"Soup's on! Come and get it!"

The pounding on the house grew weaker and weaker, then stopped altogether. From the second floor windows, we could see the main portion of the swarm begin following the riders up the road. There were now only a handful still moving around by the truck.

"Everyone ready?" Leary held a machete. Others held an assortment of axes, bats and pipes. I was pleased to see they'd realized not to use guns when they didn't have to. Everybody nodded. "Okay. In 3 ... 2 ... 1 ..."

Leary and another, older man popped the boards off the door and threw it open wide. We rushed out into the gloomy day. The buzz of the dirt bikes echoed in the hills to the west. I didn't hear any helicopters. We jogged across the yard. My shoulder ached, but I gritted my teeth and ran with all I had.

Behind us, a blood-curdling scream split the air.

"MOMMY! HELP!"

I spun in time to see a Zee that hadn't joined the others had come from around the side of the house and grabbed the young boy. The mother tried to pull him away, but it was too late. The Zee sank its teeth into the side of the kid's head, biting off his ear and most of one cheek. Stringy, red flesh and muscle tore away. He screamed again, the scream of a wounded animal.

"DAKOTA!!! NO!!!" The lady lunged at the Zee.

Stop her! Grab her!

A man caught her around the waist and pulled her back. She swung, slapping his head and shoulders.

"Get the fuck off me! You bastard, let me go!"

It's too late!

It was almost automatic, now. I pulled the pistol from my holster, aimed and shot the boy, then the Zee.

I turned and ran back to the truck. I assumed some of the Zees on the hill above had heard the shots and would come back this way.

We have to go! Let's go!

"My baby! My baby ..." The woman had fallen to her knees, but the man picked her up and carried her.

I climbed into the trailer and helped others in with my good arm. A few people jumped into the cab of the truck, and a middle-aged man with a long beard got behind the wheel of a front end loader. Diesel engines growled to life and the truck lurched forward. High on the hill, we could see the dirt bikes taking a different road. Half of the Zees in the swarm had turned back around and were coming around the sides of the house. The woman shot me a look filled with hate. Her face had a familiar look to it ...

"I'll fucking kill you."

I cast a cold gaze back.

Better you than them.

The loader and the truck turned onto the dirt road and we headed back into the heart of the city.

Chapter 34

The truck rumbled past empty houses and yards full of Zees. We passed a park, the equipment stark against the gray sky. The swings moved slightly in the breeze. The haze allowed no shadows, but everywhere shadows moved.

The woman stared venomously at me throughout the ride.

As we got into the commercial areas of Butte, we began taking detours. Roads were blocked with cars, Zees and barricades. Every so often, a gunshot would protest the deadly silence. On a few streets, we pushed through small swarms of Zees. Some were crushed under the wheels of the big truck. The rest pounded on the sides of the trailer. Most of the survivors huddled down and shut their eyes. I stood and looked over the side. Zees of all gender and size stood there, reaching for us like kids at a parade begging for candy.

One of the Leary boys stood up next to me, looking down at the sea of dead faces.

"Do you think they have any memories? Do you think any of them would recognize us?"

I thought back to Missoula, when I'd smashed in Katie's head. Her eyes ...

No.

"Yeah ..." He suddenly raised the double-barreled shotgun he was holding and shot a teenaged male Zee in the face. Most of its head disintegrated in a dark red mist.

"Travis?! What the hell are you doing?!" One of the older boys jumped up and snatched the shotgun from his hands.

"I ... It was Sean. He was my best friend at school. He ... I didn't want him to end up like that. Like one of those things." His eyes were wet.

The older boy suddenly looked ashamed.

"Well ... Save your ammo. We may need it ..." He handed the shotgun back.

Travis and I stood in silence for a while, watching as more and more Zees came from inside buildings and houses, drawn by the gunshot and the rumble from the truck. There were hundreds of them, mindlessly drawn to us, like moths to a burning candle.

"It's easy to hate them, isn't it?"

Yeah. It is.

"Will the world ever go back to the way it was? Will the sun shine anymore?"

I didn't answer him. I looked over the Zees to the darkened city looming on the hill ahead.

We slowly picked our way through the city streets. The driver tried to gauge which ones had the least amount of cars and barricades. The more we zigzagged, the more Zees shuffled towards us. The stench of death was overwhelming, and everywhere I looked, all I could see were the feral snarls, the blank stares. I began to think that getting on this truck was a bad idea.

The woman's smoldering stare burned into the side of my head. It was getting harder to ignore.

Dr. Leary was on the radio, getting the position of his people in the city. He said something to one of the men next to him, then spoke into the radio again. We turned down a side street to avoid another jam of cars. The big truck pushed more out of the way. In the distance, I could hear the thumping of a helicopter.

Dr. Leary tapped me on the shoulder.

"Are those your men?"

Probably.

"Do you have the radio frequency?"

We run on military channels, but constantly monitor civilian transmissions.

He handed me the radio. I flipped to a new station, lifted it to my

287

mouth, keyed the mic.

I could feel everyone in the trailer go silent, watching me.

This is Stray Dog *to* Last Ranch.

I used the handle that I'd been taught if anyone ever got separated.

Come in Last Ranch. *Do you copy?*

The muted hiss of static.

Last Ranch, *I'm in the Uptown area of the city. I have a dozen survivors with me. Do you copy?*

Still no answer. The eyes around me began to plead. Behind us, a crowd of walking corpses followed us slowly through the streets. At that moment, I wondered if my mind had finally snapped. I was going to wake up tomorrow in some kind of psychiatric hospital, and-

The radio crackled.

"I have you, *Stray Dog*. Jerritt, is that you?!"

One of the teenage boys let loose a cheer, but was cut off from an admonishing look by the man sitting by him.

Affirmative.

"Holy shit! We have birds in the air! Let me patch you through to Redick."

Another moment of silence.

"This is *Raider Three*. Glad to have you back from the dead, *Stray Dog*. Anyone with you?"

I never thought I would be so glad to hear Redick's cool, flat voice.

I have 13 survivors here.

"Any of our men?"

No ... It's just me.

"That's what I was afraid of. I can't fucking believe you survived, Jerritt. Where are you?"

We're on South Dakota Street, two blocks south of-

The truck suddenly jolted and bucked sideways. On the street below us, a large puddle had formed. A water main must have blown. The road gave way into a shallow sinkhole, but it was still enough to pull the trailer down to street level on one side. Everyone tumbled out into the frigid water. I rolled on my bad arm and the white light shot through my eyes again. I took a deep breath and threw my legs out to help myself up. My foot impacted with something that gave way slightly. I opened my eyes to see a Zee reaching down at me.

Shit!

I kicked at its knee, but not hard enough to make it go down. It tripped on something under the water and fell forward. My hand reached for my pistol, but wouldn't clear the holster in time. I grabbed for my knife when the Zees face exploded. I pushed the falling body aside. The boy I'd spoke with on the ride up stood beside me, the shotgun barrel still smoking.

That was close. Thanks.

"We're all in this together, man." He smirked.

I climbed to my feet in time to see the other survivors scattering into the blocks north. Below us, the swarm completely blocked off the streets and alleys. I got up and ran, wondering what I was doing back in the city. The next block had Zees dispensed about, but not in enough number to be a threat. I pulled my pistol and shot the ones that got too close. I didn't care about the noise at this point. Ahead, more of the survivors cut off into alleys. They all seemed to be heading northeast.

I ran across the next main avenue. This street was packed with cars and Zees. I dodged around the side of a wrecked truck and slipped on fresh blood, landing hard. Two Zees were eating one of the young women from the group. They were intent on their meal, and only one looked up before I blew their heads off. I turned to leave when I heard a gasp. She was still alive. Her midsection was completely torn open and her blood was everywhere, but she looked at me with hysterical fear in her eyes. Her mouth moved, but she couldn't speak through all the blood.

She was mouthing the word "please".

I shot her and kept running.

289

I'd lost sight of most of the others now. I ran north some more. Overhead, I could hear a helicopter. I checked the magazine in my pistol. 3 rounds left. I slapped at my lower abdomen, where my extras were ... The pouch was empty.

Shit.

I was near the top of the next block when I saw a Zee come into view on the left. Then another. And another. Then it looked like a faucet had been turned on and corpses poured around the corner. I yelled out loud and turned. 50 meters away, the other swarm had blocked off the road south. To my right was an alley I knew would take me out two different ways. I dashed down it. There were two Zees pounding on a car window. As I ran up, one turned and I shattered it's skull with a bullet. I shot the other through the back of its head. I turned to go when I heard the car door open. I aimed, but it was the women whose child I'd shot. I lowered the gun and she ran towards me.

"Please, help me!"

Let's go!

I grabbed her arm and pulled her down the alley. Up ahead, I could barely make it out, and my brain told me it must be a trick of the eyes. But as we got into the deeper shadow and our sight adjusted, I could see a welded, iron barricade, topped with jagged metal, blocking the end of the alley. We'd run right into a trap. I turned back around, but the swarm of Zees that had been coming up from the south had now entered the alley. Their moans echoed off the ancient brick.

I stopped, my mind and heart racing. There was one intact fire escape we could reach, but it was halfway down the alley, back towards the swarm.

Shit.

I grabbed the woman's arm and ran down to it. I looked up. We could reach it if I helped her up. I ripped the sling off my arm and took a deep breath, preparing myself for the pain that was about to follow.

Alright, just-

Pain exploded across the side of my head. The vision in my left eye

290

went blurry and my ear began to ring. I could feel a few of my teeth loosen. Warm blood began to ooze down my face. I turned and with my good eye, saw the woman holding a bloody brick.

What the fuck?!

"You son of a bitch! You took my baby from me!"

I-

"You stole him away!" She raised the brick to hit me again. I lazily aimed my gun and shot her through the elbow. She screamed and dropped it, clutching her now useless arm.

Your kid was already dead! There's nothing you or I could have done!

"Except that." She began sobbing as she slid to her knees.

Except that. I'm sorry for it, but it had to be done.

"Yeah ..." Down the alley, the Zees had almost reached us. The smell of the swarm was unbearable, mixed with the dizziness in my aching head. I spit blood onto the gray pavement.

Could we discuss this later. When we're not about to get eaten alive?

She stood as I turned back to the fire escape. It was closer than I'd thought. I could even jump for it if she couldn't haul me up. I just hoped my arm would cooperate.

Come on. We have to go. Now-

Two things happened in the next instant. The woman's ear-splitting shriek rang off the alley walls and a hand with hooked claws grabbed onto my neck, digging into the flesh. I panicked, spinning out of the grip. It was the woman's hand. Two Zees had come up behind her. One had bitten the flesh off the side of her head. The other was eating her right hand. I raised the pistol, but the slide was locked back.

It was empty.

Shit.

She batted my hand away and grabbed the front of my vest.

"You're not going anywhere, asshole." She hissed through the frothy blood that spilled from her lips. Another Zee reached over her and grabbed my

291

arm. Her grip was like iron. And that's when I recognized her.

It was the dirty-blonde woman from my dream. I felt a wave of panic begin to rise in my chest.

Let go!

More hands grabbed at me from all sides, ripping at the weathered leather and nylon. I dropped the gun. I tried to shove away, but more gnarled, gray and green hands reached out. Caked blood underneath broken fingernails. The stench of rotten meat.

I had never imagined this is how I was going to die. I'd always pictured a nice, warm bed somewhere, surrounded by loved ones.

But they were all gone, too.

I pulled once more against the woman's grip, trying to force myself loose. The Zees lunged forward again. Something, in the back of my brain, cut through the pain, fear and confusion. I felt the weight in one of my vest pockets. I ripped my arm from the grip of the woman and the Zees. I pulled out the tiny .22 pistol I'd been carrying for months. Such a small piece of metal. It now wielded such immense power.

One round left.

The last one.

The Zees loomed behind the woman, grabbing again at her shoulders and hair. I could see the burning madness in her eyes.

I aimed and shot her in the stomach.

She crumpled with a grunt, and the Zees were on her like dogs on a piece of meat. I almost stood and watched. I don't know why. It had nothing to do with hatred for her. It wasn't even morbid curiosity. I'd seen enough to sate that for a thousand lifetimes.

I think my brain was debating within itself whether it should just give up.

One of the Zees got halfway up and, still crouching, lunged. It stumbled, going low. My body reacted automatically. I kicked it in the face, crushing it's nose and knocking out some of its remaining teeth. It dropped flat on its face, then started crawling towards me. I turned and jumped for the low-hanging iron ladder. I gripped it with both hands, but my broken shoulder wouldn't hold. I could feel the fractured bone scraping against itself inside. The white lights flashed on and off, but my right hand closed on the cold metal. I thrust my left arm above my head and started to pull myself up. A hand grabbed at my boot from below and almost pulled me off the ladder. I fought it with everything I had, crying out through the pain. I kicked out of its grip and got my feet onto the ladder. I looked down at the Zees crowded around the bottom of the fire escape. They thrashed at the air and howled.

I climbed.

A little over halfway up, the ladder began to shake. First slightly, then noticeably. I could see dust pouring out of the bolt holes in the brick. I could hear the faint scraping of metal on rock, and the groaning of the rusted ladder. I neared the top when the ladder suddenly gave way. It bucked, almost pitching me back down into the alley, but I held with all my strength. It fell back. I took the only option open to me. I jumped onto the rusted, metal pipe running up the wall parallel to the ladder framework. My left arm caught on a jagged piece of metal and it dug in deep. Blood began pouring from the wound. I pulled it off with an angry scream. Some of the rivets holding the pipe in popped out of the wall, raining down in to the alley, but the pipe held. I climbed it as fast as I could, but my left arm was almost unusable at this point.

Finally, I made it up to the roof, an expanse of white rubber. I crawled over the ledge of brick and lay down on it. I felt like passing out, but stopped myself. I opened my vest and jacket, ripped a part of my shirt off and used it to bandage my bleeding arm. When I was satisfied with it, I passed out.

I don't know how long it was. I snapped awake to heavy wind on my face. I opened one eye- the other was shut with dried blood. The sun had come out from behind the haze, and the silhouette of a spider was dropping down from a giant, hovering dragonfly.

But, no. That wasn't right.

293

Cpl. Durant grinned.

"Holy shit, Jerritt, is it good to see you. You look like shit."

I feel like shit.

I was surprised at how croaky my own voice sounded.

"Are you broken?"

Just my shoulder.

"Okay."

Durant slipped a harness on me and we ascended to the Blackhawk. Two gunners, Redick and Rourke were inside. A headset was slipped over my ears and Rourke began wiping the blood off my face with alcohol pads. Redick almost wore a grin, but it vanished when he saw me clutching my wound.

"What happened to your arm, Jerritt?"

I fell off a fucking fire escape and caught it on a broken pipe. It's deep, but I think I have the bleeding under control. I'm going to need a tetanus shot.

Redick's face took on an amused expression.

"Jerritt, you have the worst goddamned luck of anyone I've ever met. Let's get you home."

We sailed away from Butte, over the city and through the valley.

The others that were with me. Did you find them?

"We only got 3." Durant frowned.

Shit ... Where's Andrew?

"He's on *Raider Two*. It and *Telum* are doing a sweep of the refugee camp, checking for survivors and any supplies that can be decontaminated. He wants to see you."

In minutes Boomtown was in sight. We swept into the landing area. Durant leapt off and tried to help me. I gave him a pained smile, but shook my head. I jumped off and walked towards the tent city. Redick called out.

"Jerritt! Report to the infirmary. They're expecting you. They'll give you your shot, check your wound and set your shoulder. Then, clean up for chow and a debrief!"

294

You got it, Captain.

The weariness was beginning to set in, now. I just wanted to go lay down in my tent and sleep. But, I couldn't do that.

I walked up the hill, skirting the infirmary, the chow area and my tent. I approached the quartermaster's tent. He looked at me as I walked in and he smiled.

"Little Jerritt. Back from the dead ... I guess that's a horrible joke to make nowadays, isn't it?"

I gave him a tight grin.

"You look like ass, kid. What are you doing not at the infirmary?"

Redick sent me up. He needs to talk to you about ... Well, it's Redick. I don't really know.

"Sounds about right." He stepped towards the tent flap. "Get down to the doc, man. Get fixed up. It's good to have you back." He disappeared into the daylight.

I grabbed a pair of snowshoes and walked outside. I knew the same trick would never work for the armory, so I just started walking. East. Towards the back of Boomtown and the mountains. I looked around when I reached the fence, but this border was rarely guarded. There was no need for it. I started up the hill, then looked back one more time. So many faces down there. I wished I could have talked with Andrew.

Suddenly, from around a tent, John appeared.

"Hey, Nick. Good to see you."

Good to see you, John. It's been some tempest.

"It has. It really has." He took a deep breath and looked over me, at the mountains. "Lauren and I are leaving this place. We're going to try and find the dogs and ... Hell, I don't know. Up to the hills, I guess. Let the chips fall ..."

I nodded. I didn't know what to say. I could feel the hot sting of tears threatening to shut my eyes. I blinked them back, but one escaped. John looked me up and down.

"It looks like you've seen better days, Nick." He sighed. "It looks like we all have ... It was great meeting you, Nick. You really stepped up when everyone needed you. I wish we could have met under different circumstances ... In a different world. If I could have had two sons ..."

He looked out across the camp, then back at me, nodding slightly.

"You have to go, too."

I couldn't tell if it was a question or a statement.

I didn't ask.

"Goodbye, Nick."

Goodbye, John.

We shook hands, then embraced. We released, looked at each other once more, then John turned and walked away, vanishing into the late-afternoon light. I wondered if I had met him at all, if he was real.

If any of this was.

I turned, too, and began walking again, ignoring the pain with each step. I pulled back my left sleeve and checked the edges of my makeshift bandage. Blood oozed out, but underneath ...

The veins were turning black.

Chapter 35

I'm walking up the mountain now. I've reached the snow. I fumbled for a few moments with the snowshoes, but I got them on.

I rip the makeshift bandage from my arm, exposing the monstrous wound to the world. No more hiding. Not now. When she grabbed me ... That woman, when she wouldn't let me go, one of my sleeves peeled back. A Zee that had lost its place ripping into her neck had found my arm ...

Even though the air is cold, the fever is burning me up. It's like a fire deep inside my body. I can feel the infected blood coursing through the veins, up my arm. Towards my heart. Sweat pours down my face and temples, steaming off. More ghosts to add to this haunted world.

I wish I could have said goodbye. To Andrew. To my parents. To Alicia. To David. To the blonde girl whose head I crushed.

I think of them, then. Andrew. John and Lauren. Redick and Rourke. George and Linda. All the faces down in that camp. And all those who didn't make it. Those of us who have finally been written onto the fading tapestry of humanity.

Now it's my time to take my place on that tapestry. I wonder now if anyone will be around to behold it. To experience and realize the potential we all had. I think again to the faces in the camp, far below.

The Last Ranch on Earth, containing some of the last people on Earth. A valiant few to survive, to march on in the face of hordes of our past that's ultimately come to gather us. I understand, now, at the end. It doesn't matter what we did in the past, before all of this. The people we were, the things we did ... It all changed over the course of the past year. Black or white. Rich or poor. Gay, straight, man, woman, elderly, young ...

None of those labels mean anything anymore. Now, it's just *alive*.

Now, I understand.

297

It's more than one person can do alone. The living, those left carrying the torch of humanity now have to band together, no matter the cost. Because the other cost, that of failure, is far greater. I think of the beach, the water washing in and taking the sand and stones away with each wave. Grinding down. Eating away. Reclaiming.

It's a new world that I walked away from in the valley.

A new origin for Mankind. A time to start over, to live for something greater than the next car or TV show or paycheck.

Out with the old world.

And in with the new.

Generation Z.

Still, I walk upwards. I can see the radio array ahead. Down in the camp, I can hear shouts, the whine of a helicopter. They must know I'm missing. I wish I could have said goodbye. But it's too late for any of that now. Still, I walk.

Ahead, in the sunlight dazzling off the snow, my eyes play tricks. I see the figure of a young boy. A flash of blonde hair as a girl runs away. I can see my parents, smiling and waving me forward.

The radio mast hums with energy. I can sense it in my teeth, my blood, my bones.

I can feel the infection spreading into my neck and chest.

I'm almost there. I can see it ahead. The path is lined with ghosts. Those I killed. Those I couldn't save. The figures on the fringe of the old tapestry.

I trudge through the snow. It crunches gently under my feet. I get warm, so I shed my vest and coat. I don't need them anymore. I walk for what feels like a minute. A year. A lifetime. Up the ridge I walk. I should be exhausted, but the infection has me so delirious at this point that I just keep going. I have to keep going. One foot in front of the other, straight up towards the golden sun. I come around the side of a rock and spook out a swarm of butterflies. Their wings glow black and orange in the sunlight as they dance through the air around me.

I can't tell if they're real or hallucinations.

Up ahead ...

Not much longer to go now. I ascend the final ridge. The mountain drops off on both sides. A vast expanse of snow and rock. I always loved the mountains. I felt that I always had a place in the mountains.

I stop and look to the west. Towards my old home. That place where I died. Valleys and mountains extend as far as I can see.

Suddenly, I feel at peace. Weight drops from my heart. I keep going up the ridge. I reach a snowy shale field and begin to climb. I step carefully, pulling myself up with both arms. My left screams in agony, but I have to ignore it. I have to go.

I skirt a small rock face. One of my feet slips and I tumble down a few feet, landing with my back in the crevice of two rocks. I feel bone in my left shoulder crumble. Tears of pain stream down my face, and I almost lay down and give up. But I can't. I have to keep going. I won't ...

I crawl back up the snow and rock. The cold surface burns on my infected skin.

I keep climbing, two feet, one arm.

Finally, I'm standing on top of the mountain. Montana stretches out around me. The world below, brown and gray. As sick as I feel.

But this can't be the end. Not for it, not for them.

I look back down at the camp. I can see people moving around.

Goodbye.

I slide down a small slope and finally, I'm here. Standing on a knob I'd seen long ago, as a child on a camping trip. I'd always looked up on it in awe. It held a power over me I could never explain.

I step to the edge. Look down. A drop to a snowy rock field, far below.

Bitter cold wind whips at my torn shirt, my broken body. I push it away and focus on the past. Of warm, sunny days. I think of all the things I want to hold onto. I turn around.

299

I think of lemonade and flowers and rivers glowing in the sun ...

I step backwards into space and watch the clouds fall up, away from

me.

Have you ever had one of those dreams where you're falling?

Falling.

There's no nightmare so deep you can't wake up.

Caleb Hill is an engineering student who has been a baker, a driver, a soldier, an archaeologist, a cowboy, a skier, a kayaker, a carpenter, and- of course- a writer. He lives in the frozen northlands of Butte, Montana with his wonderful wife Jen and the two hungriest Cocker Spaniels on the planet, Beans and Ryan.

They're all prepared for the zombie apocalypse.

Join more Survivors on the web at

www.nonightmaresodeep.webs.com

and

'Generation Z' on Facebook